MW01282734

DEADLY
STORMS

\\\\\\\\\\\\\\\\\\\\\\\\\\\\\\\\\\\\

THE CARPATHIAN NOVELS

DARK HOPE	DARK WOLF	DARK MELODY
DARK MEMORY	DARK LYCAN	DARK SYMPHONY
DARK WHISPER	DARK STORM	DARK GUARDIAN
DARK TAROT	DARK PREDATOR	DARK LEGEND
DARK SONG	DARK PERIL	DARK FIRE
DARK ILLUSION	DARK SLAYER	DARK CHALLENGE
DARK SENTINEL	DARK CURSE	DARK MAGIC
DARK LEGACY	DARK POSSESSION	DARK GOLD
DARK CAROUSEL	DARK CELEBRATION	DARK DESIRE
DARK PROMISES	DARK DEMON	DARK PRINCE
DARK GHOST	DARK SECRET	
DARK BLOOD	DARK DESTINY	

ANTHOLOGIES

EDGE OF DARKNESS
(with Maggie Shayne and Lori Herter)
DARKEST AT DAWN
(includes Dark Hunger *and* Dark Secret*)*
SEA STORM
(includes Magic in the Wind *and* Oceans of Fire*)*
FEVER
(includes The Awakening *and* Wild Rain*)*
FANTASY
(with Emma Holly, Sabrina Jeffries, and Elda Minger)
LOVER BEWARE
(with Fiona Brand, Katherine Sutcliffe, and Eileen Wilks)
HOT BLOODED
(with Maggie Shayne, Emma Holly, and Angela Knight)

SPECIALS

DARK CRIME
THE AWAKENING
DARK HUNGER
MAGIC IN THE WIND

MURDER AT SUNRISE LAKE
RED ON THE RIVER
DEADLY STORMS

DEADLY STORMS

CHRISTINE FEEHAN

BERKLEY
New York

BERKLEY
An imprint of Penguin Random House LLC
1745 Broadway, New York, NY 10019
penguinrandomhouse.com

Library of Congress Cataloging-in-Publication Data

Names: Feehan, Christine, author.
Title: Deadly storms / Christine Feehan.
Description: New York: Berkley, 2025.
Identifiers: LCCN 2025000673 (print) | LCCN 2025000674 (ebook) |
ISBN 9780593638804 (hardcover) | ISBN 9780593638811 (ebook)
Subjects: LCGFT: Thrillers (Fiction) | Romance fiction. | Novels.
Classification: LCC PS3606.E36 D447 2025 (print) |
LCC PS3606.E36 (ebook) | DDC 813/.6—dc23/eng/20250108
LC record available at https://lccn.loc.gov/2025000673
LC ebook record available at https://lccn.loc.gov/2025000674

First Edition: September 2025

Printed in the United States of America
1st Printing

The authorized representative in the EU for product safety and compliance
is Penguin Random House Ireland, Morrison Chambers, 32 Nassau
Street, Dublin D02 YH68, Ireland, https://eu-contact.penguin.ie.

Jayne Ann Krentz,

Thank you for being such an inspiration to me.

FOR MY READERS

Be sure to go to http://www.christinefeehan.com/members/ to sign up for my private book announcement list and download the *free* ebook of *Dark Desserts*. Join my community and get firsthand news, enter the book discussions, ask your questions and chat with me. Please feel free to email me at Christine@christinefeehan.com. I would love to hear from you.

Dear Reader,

Writing *Deadly Storms* was truly a labor of love. The Eastern Sierra is beautiful, one of the many treasures of our country. Anytime I'm able to bring my readers there, it makes me happy.

I particularly love these powerful women. They embody sisterhood. I've met so many wonderful women throughout my journey of writing. In doing so, I've learned that women together can be a force to be reckoned with.

Post-traumatic stress disorder is very difficult to live with. Not only does the person suffering from it live with the illness but friends and family do as well. Many people believe only soldiers suffer from PTSD, but the truth is crimes, sexual violence, childhood abuse, physical assault, accidents and a multitude of other traumas can cause PTSD.

Repeated, prolonged exposure to trauma where there is little chance of escape can lead to complex post-traumatic stress disorder, complicating it even more. This disorder affects more women than men. The disorder often can be identified by changes in the brain itself.

I consulted counselors and worked with three different primary sources, two women and one man, suffering from this disorder, to better understand it and provide realistic consequences and ways to help. They were gracious enough to share the horrific details of what they endured when something triggered them. The information regarding how to help a friend or partner through a very real crisis is as close to reality as possible, given every case is different.

I am certain my readers are aware I love research. I get caught up in the beauty and culture of other lands. This story allowed me to indulge my love of learning. Again, I must give credit to Anaruz Elhabib, a translator who was absolutely wonderful to me. He went out of his way to assist me each time I asked him questions. A second translator, Alaa As., was gracious enough to verify the translations for us.

While writing *Deadly Storms*, I wanted it to be as authentic as any work of fiction can be. I worked with two primary sources regarding Arabic translations. What we discovered is that if you use an online translator, such as Googe Translate, only the actual Arabic spelling translates correctly. If you use English letters instead, though that makes the flow of reading easier, the translator is incorrect.

لا تمنحي هذا الرجل متعة رؤية دموعك. اذهبي إلى المطبخ. سأتعامل مع الأمر is *la tamnahi li hada arrajol motaata roayati domoik, idhabi li almatbakh baynama aatani bi hada,* which translates to "Do not give this man the satisfaction of seeing your tears. Go into the kitchen. I will handle this." Rainier says this to Shabina. If you were to take the Arabic words and put them into Google Translate, you would find the line is correct.

The tattoo artist, Yassine Boussetta, who drew the art for *Deadly Storms*, was amazing to work with. It didn't seem to matter that we had a bit of a language barrier. He got the concept I was looking for and drew three incredible tattoos for *Deadly Storms* and then repeated the entire process when I went back to him and asked for Shabina's tattoos—Eye of the Storm. Again, he drew three different exclusive designs. I loved the six tattoos he sent to me.

I appreciate so much that they were willing to work with me, fulfilling each request in a timely manner so I could meet the deadline for this book.

If you're looking for beautiful artwork or you need translations done, I highly recommend both of these men. You can find Anaruz Elhabib at https://www.fiverr.com/lhoubi, and Yassine Boussetta at https://www.fiverr.com/customtattooart.

I hope you enjoy the men, women, dogs and amazing beauty of the Sierra in this story.

Best,
Christine Feehan

ACKNOWLEDGMENTS

Thank you to Diane Trudeau. I would never have been able to have gotten this book written under such circumstances. Sheila English, for working with translations and artists. Brian Feehan, for making certain you were here every day to set up the pages I needed to write in order to hit the deadline. Denise, for handling all the details of every aspect of my life that was so crazy. And to my amazing, invaluable researcher Karen Brownfield Houton, you are a miracle to me! Thank you to Cindy Hwang for the suggestions to fix problem areas. Your wisdom was invaluable. Most of all, thank you to Yassine Boussetta for your amazing artwork for Rainier and Shabina. I think it is truly beautiful. I would like to thank Anaruz Elhabib and Alaa As. for working with me on translations and culture issues. Also, a huge thank-you to Anaruz Elhabib for translations and checking to make sure I was using everything correctly. Both men are easy to work with and so kind.

Thank all of you so very much!!!

DEADLY
STORMS

CHAPTER ONE

Shabina Foster sighed as she shut down the Zoom meeting with her therapist and closed the lid of her laptop. For one brief moment she rested her head on the top of the lid. It was always more of the same. She knew exactly what Talia Warren, her therapist, was going to say to her, the same thing she said all the time. She had PTSD. She should expect to have setbacks. To have bad days. To have nightmares. Work through them. Use the tools she'd been given over the years to cope.

Shabina turned her head to look at the three Doberman pinschers crowding around her. Malik, Sharif and Morza were her constant companions and always knew when she was distressed. "Great advice. Like I haven't tried all those so-called tools. Am I paranoid? Most likely the answer is yes. Sometimes I think I really am going crazy."

Malik pushed up tight against her leg. Automatically she scratched the fur between his ears. She didn't know what she'd do without the dogs for comfort—or protection. They were trained guard dogs. She worked with them every day to keep them sharp. She needed to know she could stop them if they attacked, or if there were a threat, she could send them to attack.

She glanced out the window at the gathering darkness. A shiver went down her spine in spite of her determination to be positive. The ominous feeling she had was nothing but lack of sleep and paranoia. It wasn't real. No one was out there watching her. If someone were in her gardens, the dogs would have alerted.

Squaring her shoulders, she forced a cheery voice. "Tonight's our night for entertaining, boys. If we're going to have everything ready for our guests, I'd better stop feeling sorry for myself and get moving. I suppose you boys want your dinner. Who knew you liked to eat?" She was in the habit of talking aloud to them and was convinced they understood everything she said. Affectionately she patted each of them.

Shabina was an avid bird-watcher. Not only that, but she documented and recorded their migrations. She noted rare birds and located nesting sites. She was acknowledged as one of the leading experts in the state. The data she sent in was documented and kept for the records. She had special permission to take her dogs on the trails with her when dogs weren't allowed to go just anywhere in Yosemite. She hiked alone in the early morning hours on little-known trails to find the birds, and the dogs were her protection unit. They knew better than to chase anything off the trail.

The dogs were tuned to her every mood and realized she was still distressed as she got up to get them their food. Two of the large Dobermans followed her closely. Morza padded over to the bank of windows in the great room and peered out and then began to pace around the room, stopping every few feet to look outside. She stood watching him, hand to her throat as he patrolled.

It was impossible to see into the house, yet they had an excellent view of the surrounding gardens. Cameras were placed in strategic places throughout the area. She should have felt safe. There was a high wall surrounding the house and immediate gardens, but for the last few days, she'd had this terrible darkness invading her mind. She found herself looking over her shoulder everywhere she went. She looked at everyone with suspicion, not a good thing when she owned a café. Sometimes she could barely breathe. She tried to convince herself it was paranoia, that there was no one out there, but she didn't believe it.

"I'm actually quite happy it's our turn to have girls' night here." She forced herself to sound cheerful. Sometimes she thought she might be going insane. She'd been afraid to go to sleep for the last couple of nights. Her therapist told her she had to sleep, and she had lied and said that wasn't a problem yet. It was a good thing her friends were coming over. She could check in with them. Find out if they thought she was being totally paranoid.

Once every six weeks, Shabina's five best friends did their best to get together. As a rule, she loved spending time with them and always looked forward to the one night they worked at setting their busy schedules aside so they could come together.

Shabina had a very large four-bedroom home that she'd done her best to make warm and welcoming for her friends. She had an indoor pool that was very popular with them, and her kitchen was spectacular. She *loved* her kitchen. She'd already done all the baking and set food in warmers. She'd made dog treats because her friends were always welcome to bring their dogs with them and she believed in giving them good healthy treats as well. The house often smelled of the various baked goods she whipped up. She liked to try new recipes at home before she used them in her café.

Shabina owned the Sunrise Café. It was her pride and joy. She had worked hard to get the café off the ground, designing every aspect of it from the building to the dishes to the daily menus. She served breakfast and lunch only. The specials changed depending on her mood. It had always been her dream to open her own little café. She hadn't wanted a big restaurant. She wanted a small boutique diner where she created the menu and could interact with her customers. In the beginning, her business had mostly been a deli, with take-out sandwiches and a few special orders, but it had quickly grown and now was a full restaurant with seating outside on the patio and inside the large newly renovated building.

Her parents had paid for her education, but she had worked hard to earn the money for her business. She did have a silent partner. It had been impossible to swing the amount of money she needed on her own, and she didn't want to take any more from her parents. Their loan would have come with conditions she didn't want to meet. Thankfully, her silent partner remained very silent and gave her no input whatsoever. Just start-up money.

It was Stella Harrison, the glue that held all the women together, who had truly been the miracle worker to make the Sunrise Café such a success. "I have to remember she's Stella Harrison-Rossi now, boys," Shabina murmured aloud. "She's married to Sam. I keep forgetting that little detail. It seems like Sam's always been around and nothing has changed, so it's hard to remember they actually got married."

Shabina, like most of the other business owners in the town of Knightly, attributed her success to Stella's brilliant business plan. Stella had turned two failing resorts into an extremely successful multimillion-dollar business. She'd done it by including the smaller, faltering businesses of Knightly.

Knightly was a small town made famous for the boulders that climbers came from all over the world to ascend. Stella had gone to many of the smaller places in town, such as the Brewery, a small pub owned by Bruce Akins, a great bear of a man who brewed fantastic beer. She'd talked him into giving tours of his brewery to the high-end clientele at her resort. They'd marketed his beer as being extremely rare and difficult to get. Consequently, he'd been able to secure lucrative contracts with private clubs in Los Angeles, making his beer even more sought after.

Stella had approached Alek Donovan, owner of the local Grill, a floundering restaurant at the time, and talked him into including music at night and changing his entire menu. Shabina had helped with the menu, and Alek had added recipes from his mother's side of the family. Raine had created brochures, and overnight the Grill had become a local hot spot and success with tourists and resort people.

Most important, Stella had made the Sunrise Café a huge destination for anyone coming to visit in Knightly. She'd practically campaigned to put the café on the map. Shabina was grateful for her friendship as well as the fact that Stella had so generously aided her in making the café such a success from the very start.

The dogs ate their food with relish. She gave them hearty meals, making certain what they ate was nutritious. Shabina showed love with food. Each of her friends had their own dog— or in Vienna Mortenson's case, a Persian cat very aptly named Princess. The cat ruled Vienna's household. Vienna was head of Search and Rescue, a brilliant surgical nurse, gorgeous and practical, but she was a complete pushover for her cat. Despite the ominous feeling she couldn't shake, just the thought of Vienna and her cat made Shabina smile.

Vienna had been certain her cat would become friends with the dogs. None of the dogs were opposed to the friendship. They didn't chase cats. They didn't look at them with great disdain, but Princess not only snubbed dogs, she attacked viciously if they came anywhere near her, using teeth and claws in a feral manner. The dogs could have torn her to pieces, but instead they ran away and refused to go anywhere near the cat.

Sharif lifted his head and gave a short bark. The alarm went off, and then the green light on her watch signaled the gate code had been put in. Shabina's heart accelerated. She forced herself to breathe normally. She was expecting company, and only her friends knew the gate code. Her friends and Rainier—her savior and the bane of her life.

She looked up at the security screen and recognized Harlow Frye and her beagle, Misha. Harlow was the daughter of a senator. She worked as a nurse at the hospital, but her true calling was art. Her landscape photos were gaining fame and many hung in galleries all over the world. She'd made quite a name for herself. She also did pottery, but it wasn't her first love, although Shabina thought her work was amazing. Harlow had grown up in political circles and was graceful, knowing exactly how to respond to any situation. She was one of the strongest climbers but did prefer trad climbing to bouldering.

She threw her arms around Shabina the moment the door was opened. "I feel as if I haven't seen you in ages."

"You work too much," Shabina pointed out.

"Thank you for sending food three days in a row," Harlow said, reaching down to remove the leash from Misha. The beagle instantly rushed over to say hello to the giant Doberman pinschers. "When I'm working so many hours like that, I forget to eat."

"Zahra called me from the hospital and told me both you and Vienna were called in three days in a row with trauma patients. She said you slept there one night and had asked Raine to take Misha for you."

"I really felt bad asking her, but Misha couldn't be in the house alone that entire time."

"And you and Vienna can't go without decent meals. You should call me when you're in that situation," Shabina said. "I don't mind fixing food. You know it's my thing, and I always have leftovers from the café. It isn't extra trouble."

"You didn't send leftovers," Harlow pointed out.

She hadn't. But the food was for two of her best friends, and they were saving lives. She wanted them to have fresh, nutritious meals, ones she knew they both liked. She gave Harlow a little smile. "Maybe not. I had to send your favorites so I knew you'd eat. Sometimes, when you're really tired, you forget all about eating."

Harlow followed her across the great room and through the large archway separating the dining room into the kitchen. Shabina had an open floor plan, so she could talk to her guests and see them while she was cooking. She had dog beds placed along the walls for her dogs as well as her guests' dogs. They were frequent visitors, and each pet had its own bed.

"Sharif seems a little on edge tonight," Harlow observed. She turned to watch as the big Doberman paced along the window, staring out. He paused every few feet to listen. "Does he want out?"

Every muscle in Shabina's body tensed. Two of the dogs were supposed to patrol outside the house while one stayed inside with her. But there was no way she was allowing her dogs outside her house without her. She needed them close to her. If she went out, she was armed at all times, and she'd protect the dogs. She could never say that to anyone, because somehow, she knew it would get back to Rainier Ashcroft. He seemed to have eyes and ears everywhere. He seemed to think he was responsible for her security.

Rainier. She just couldn't allow herself to think about him. He was her biggest weakness. The moment she let him into her mind, her entire being believed she needed him. That she couldn't survive without him. That she didn't even want to. Not when she was in crisis. She was on a downward spiral, and she had to learn to cope on her own.

"No, he needs to stay in tonight. They have a routine, and they don't like to deviate, but I think it's good for them to occasionally do different things." Another lie to a friend. She detested lying to any of the women who'd been so good to her. They'd let her into their lives and supported her dream of owning the café. They'd helped to make it a success.

Harlow carried a tray with two food warmers on it to the long sideboard in the dining room. It would be easy access for the women from most of the rooms. Shabina had already put out the silverware, napkins, plates and glasses.

"I love coming to your house, Shabina. It always smells so welcoming."

That was the nicest thing Harlow could have said to her. She needed to hear that her home was everything she wanted it to be for her friends. Before she could reply, the alarm went off again. This time it was Vienna Mortenson, accompanied by Zahra Metcalf. With Vienna being so tall and blonde and Zahra being extremely short with her large dark eyes and dark hair, they were striking together. Zahra carried a little bundle of fluff in her arms.

She had loved her half-mix, rough-coated, twenty-pound Pyrenean shepherd, a joyful, energetic dog she'd had for years. When she lost him, she refused to even entertain the idea of another dog. She wanted the same mix, which would be impossible to find. Somehow, just recently, the local vet, Dr. Amelia Sanderson, through her numerous connections, had found a little Pyrenean shepherd in a rescue shelter who had just given birth. The girls had hastily gotten together and, with Dr. Sanderson's help, managed to secure a little female for Zahra as a surprise. Zahra and the puppy were inseparable.

Originally from Azerbaijan, she had come to the United States with the help of Harlow, whom she had met in college. Now a US citizen, she worked as the local hospital administrator. She was very gifted in securing grants and organizing fundraisers. Between the money Vienna often donated from her gambling wins and what Zahra managed to raise, their trauma and surgical units were considered the best in the vicinity. They were able to attract good doctors and nurses with the pay they could offer.

Zahra was a man magnet. No matter the age, men flocked to her. She was flirty and fun, but she didn't date. For a long while everyone thought she would eventually end up with Bruce Akins, owner of the Brewery, but he never actually got up the courage to ask her out, so the relationship never got off the ground. Shabina thought it was probably a good thing. Privately, she thought Bruce would never have been able to handle Zahra. He wouldn't understand her.

Zahra was all smiles as she entered, greeting the dogs and showing them her puppy, letting them take their time sniffing her thoroughly. Misha came rushing up to be introduced as well. Shabina found herself laughing with Vienna and Harlow because Zahra didn't seem to notice there were humans in the room. She was too busy explaining to the dogs who her new baby was and how they were all going to be such great friends.

Already, Shabina was feeling so much better. Just having her friends around her with their different personalities and their caring made her world seem brighter. She handed Vienna and Harlow the other two trays of food warmers and took baskets of freshly baked bread wrapped in warm linen to the sideboard.

"It's a good thing you have a swimming pool," Vienna said. "This much food is crazy, but you know we're going to eat it all. Especially that one"—she nodded toward Zahra—"and Raine. The two of them can put away food and never gain an ounce."

"That one?" Zahra, sitting tailor-fashion in the middle of the floor, surrounded by dogs, looked over her shoulder with one eyebrow raised, proving she was listening. She managed to look adorable as only Zahra could look. "I do have a name."

"You do?" Vienna shot back. "I can think of several, but you've objected to every single one. Are you going to help?"

"I'm introducing Misty to her friends right now," Zahra said. "And the names you come up with for me are ghastly. I don't flirt, and I don't complain, and I don't eat too much chocolate. Every name you choose for me has something to do with one of those subjects." She gave a haughty sniff and turned her attention back to her puppy.

Shabina, Vienna and Harlow burst into laughter. It was the first genuine laughter Shabina had experienced in days.

"Zahra Metcalf, lightning is going to come right through the roof and strike you dead for that whopper you just told," Harlow predicted. "I would venture to say that at this very minute you have chocolate candy in your backpack. You'll tell us everything in there is needed for Misty, but we all know dogs can't have chocolate. And you've got it."

Zahra gave them the haughty eyebrow. She'd perfected that particular look. "The chocolate is for emergencies."

Another round of laughter went up, and Shabina could see that even Zahra smiled, although she pretended to be annoyed.

"Of course it is," Shabina soothed. "I haven't met Misty yet. She doesn't look in the least bit timid."

Zahra flashed her grin, the one that could melt men at fifty feet. "She's so brave. She's had all her vaccinations, so she should be safe on the ground. I do take her running, but I'll admit I'm still a little afraid of putting her down where other dogs I don't know have been."

Shabina couldn't imagine losing one of her Dobermans, especially to parvo. Her dogs were her constant companions. Her heart went out to Zahra. "I don't blame you. I'd be the same way. I did make treats for all the dogs. And I have a brand-new bed for Misty. You don't have to use it today, but when you're ready, you can start teaching her that it's her special spot if she gets tired of the other dogs. When she's there, the other dogs know to leave her alone."

The alarm sounded again, announcing the arrival of Stella Harrison-Rossi. Raine O'Mallory was with her, leaning heavily on a cane. She was still recovering from several surgeries on her leg. She'd been shot, the bone shattered, and she'd been fortunate that a top orthopedic team had been able to save the leg. Raine never failed to surprise Shabina with the way she was so quiet, usually the least talkative person in the room though she was scary intelligent.

She appeared to be an independent contractor, working mainly for the US government, she claimed as an analyst, but helicopters came for her at all hours and took her and her dog, Daisy, away. She'd be gone for days. When she was injured, she was guarded day and night by the military as if she were a national treasure. To say the least, Raine was a mystery woman.

Bailey, Stella's Airedale, and Daisy, Raine's mischievous Jack Russell terrier, ran eagerly to Shabina to greet her.

Stella laughed. "They know who gives them all the treats. Blatant kissing up right there." She stepped back to ensure Raine made it safely into Shabina's house.

Shabina could see it wasn't easy for Raine to walk, even with her cane. Her progression was slow. There was no expression on her face, but without a doubt each step caused pain. Raine had always been an adventurer. A bit of a thrill seeker. She'd hiked the entire John Muir Trail alone, nearly three hundred miles of wilderness. She'd summited Mount Whitney several times and been up Half Dome numerous times. She'd hiked the Alps, been in a dormant volcano in Iceland, gone to the ice caves in Romania and hiked all over that country. She'd hiked the backcountry of Thailand and gone down the Amazon River as well as traveled to many other countries. She parasailed and bouldered, and she loved anything involving problem-solving, which made her good on aerial silks and rope. It was difficult to see her struggling to walk.

Shabina crouched down to pet and scratch both dogs, greeting them enthusiastically. She loved them both. Once they had their fill of her attention, they raced to meet the new puppy. Shabina carefully washed her hands as Stella put Raine's backpack on the end table in the great room. Raine never went anywhere without her backpack. It was waterproof and contained her laptop.

"I made us late, Shabina," Raine said. "I'm so sorry. The General." She rolled her eyes. "You have to remember him; he insisted I find information for him."

"What?" Vienna whirled around, pressing her back to the sideboard. "You're on sick leave. You aren't supposed to be doing *any* work at all."

"Well, he believes I shouldn't be working, but that rule doesn't apply to him. I told him there were others he could use, but he was insistent it had to be me. He also pointed out there was nothing wrong with my brain since I was too stubborn to use painkillers, and all I had to do was sit on my ass and figure it out."

"He said *what*?" Zahra was outraged.

"Yep. Actually, he said *skinny* ass." Raine sounded amused.

No one with the exception of Raine knew if the General was

really a general. Raine always called him that, but when anyone inquired, she made a joke of it and insisted he simply liked to be called that. Shabina believed he was a general. For some reason, Raine seemed to think most things he said to her were humorous. Even his insults.

"If Rush knew," Stella said, "he'd take your cell, and if that didn't work, he'd take away your laptop again. Doctor's orders take precedence over a boss who doesn't respect your leave."

Raine made her way to one of Shabina's very comfortable chairs in the great room. She lowered her body slowly into it, stretching her leg out in front of her. It wasn't difficult to see that the journey had been painful. There were little beads of sweat on Raine's forehead, but she appeared triumphant.

"I would go crazy if I sat around doing nothing. And technically, I don't have a boss. I'm a private contractor and I prefer it that way. The General can puff up as much as he wants but he knows he can only push me so far. In the end, I'm going to get my way."

"Don't let him say you have a skinny ass," Zahra said with a little sniff of disdain. "That's so insulting. He has no right to make personal comments. There should be someone you can make complaints to." She stood up, puppy still in her arms, and went to the little crate Vienna had placed in the corner of the room. "While I eat, I'll put Misty in her crate until I train her to stay on her bed like the other dogs. I don't want her to bother everyone."

"It isn't like he's older and we can make allowances for a different generation," Harlow added. "He's being a jerk."

Shabina indicated the food. "I'll fix your plate, Raine. I made your favorites." She gave the command to her three Doberman pinschers to go to their dog beds.

The other women followed suit.

"He was goading me. He doesn't think my ass is skinny," Raine explained with a little sigh. "He asks me out all the time."

Zahra lifted her eyebrow. "That's his way of flirting?"

Raine laughed. "Yep. He thinks he's very clever."

Zahra made a face. Vienna and Harlow exchanged a long, confused look. Stella and Shabina laughed.

"He's a geek, isn't he?" Stella asked.

"Totally," Raine said.

"Just how many men do you have asking you out?" Harlow asked. She began lifting the lids from the food warmers. "Shabina, you've outdone yourself."

"It all looks delicious," Stella agreed. "You'll have to roll me into the swimming pool."

"There should be plenty left over to take home to Sam," Shabina said as she got into line to fix Raine her food.

"Don't think you can stay silent over there, Raine," Harlow persisted. "We saw you in that hospital room with all those male visitors. What the heck, girl? You're keeping secrets. And they aren't national ones. Those are girlfriend secrets."

Raine flushed a soft shade of pink. "Seriously? There's such a thing as girlfriend secrets?"

"Yes, and you have to confess to your besties," Stella added. "You're so used to keeping your high-clearance bullshit secrets that we don't want anything to do with anyway, that you just don't talk about the important things." She settled on the low cushions close to Raine's chair rather than taking a seat.

Harlow followed her. Shabina handed Raine a tray with her plate and placed a fresh glass of water with fruit in it on the end table beside her, grateful Raine was in the hot seat and not her. She would have no idea what to say if her friends asked her about men. She didn't date. She didn't look at men as a rule. When someone asked her out, she considered the invitation carefully because she was always trying to be normal, but in the end, she always found herself giving a reason as gently as possible as to why she couldn't go.

They settled comfortably in her large great room to eat, rather than the dining room. They were used to eating there. Vienna lifted Raine's bad leg onto an ottoman to prop it up to add to her comfort. The laughter and camaraderie were exactly what Shabina needed. The dark, ominous feeling inside didn't go away completely, but it lifted so she felt she could breathe again. She could think more clearly.

"In all honesty," Raine replied after thinking the question of men over, "I don't have time to entertain the idea of dating. I hurt too much. Dr. Briac Brannan—you remember him from when he came to Vegas and helped us out with Rainier's wound? He came to see me several times when I was in the hospital. He'd wanted to go hiking in Yosemite with me as his guide and I'd agreed to that, but . . ." She shrugged and nodded at her leg. "He said he was still coming. He took the vacation time and wants to see me. He'll be coming up this week. I told him to stay in one of your cabins, Stella. Sunrise Lake is the halfway point between Yosemite and Knightly. He'll have easy access to both places."

Harlow groaned. "That doesn't say a thing about the way you feel about him, Raine."

"I love talking to him. He's intelligent and doesn't make me cringe when he opens his mouth. He doesn't pretend to know everything and spout off about how superior he is." She sighed. "Physically? I'm not all that attracted. I wish I were, and I'd hoped if we went hiking and I saw him in that setting, I'd feel something, but so far, nothing."

"Anyone else? What about that Lucio Vitale?" Zahra asked. "Sam's father's bodyguard. He seemed very interested in you."

Raine shook her head. "Not a chance. I knew him a long time ago. He was a self-centered jerk then, using everyone he could to make his way up the ladder. I would never trust him. He's doing his best to act like a lamb, but he isn't."

"Sometimes there's great chemistry with enemies," Vienna said.

"Nope, no chemistry with him." Raine took a drink of the fruit-infused water. "Shabina, if you get any better at cooking, I'm moving in with you."

Shabina sent her another smile. "That's so lovely of you to say." Cooking was one of her favorite things to do. Knowing others enjoyed what she made for them gave her huge satisfaction.

"What about Rush?" Vienna asked. "Do you have chemistry with him?"

Raine scowled at her. "Rush is a doctor. He likes to be very bossy. That isn't the same thing as someone who is trying to date me, which he isn't. He isn't like your Zale, Vienna. I thought the two of you were getting married immediately. What happened to those plans?"

Shabina thought it very clever the way Raine managed to turn the tables on Vienna. All eyes had instantly turned to Vienna.

"That's right," Stella said. "Zale put that ring on your finger and insisted the two of you were getting married without waiting for anything."

Vienna lifted her chin. "I know. And I agreed. I did." She flashed a quick grin at Raine. "We have amazing chemistry. But he's still under contract with my dear old estranged father, Elliot Blom, head of the Special Activities Division, who has no intention of claiming me. I think he hopes Zale will forget all about me if he keeps him busy enough."

"I don't even have words to describe your father," Stella said. "I'm so grateful I met Sam after he was out of that business."

"But you do intend to marry Zale?" Harlow asked. She gathered dishes and took them to the kitchen while Stella carried empty breadbaskets and butter dishes in.

Vienna rubbed her temples as if she might have the beginnings of a headache. "I'm such a coward when it comes to trusting men. All that brainwashing my birth mother did on me, but when Zale is with me, I don't have any doubts."

She helped put the food away, leaving only the trays of desserts. They usually ate their dessert after swimming.

Raine opted not to swim. She'd done her physical therapy in a pool, and she admitted it was difficult to get in and out of a swimsuit. She was tired enough that she just wanted to relax. She'd stay with the dogs and give them their treats while the others swam. Shabina stayed with her, finishing up the work in the kitchen and making take-home packages for each household with the leftovers while her friends swam. Just the sound of their laughter was comforting. The murmur of Raine's voice as she talked to the dogs kept the uneasiness at bay. For the first time in three days, she felt so much lighter. It was good to have friends.

When the others had showered, changed and were back in the great room, Shabina indicated the desserts and drinks. Zahra immediately removed Misty from her crate and took her out to do her business with the other dogs, and then everyone settled with their favorite dessert.

Stella dipped a chocolate-covered strawberry into the whipped cream on her plate. "Do you remember that terrible tragedy last year? There was a little family found dead up in the Sierras close to one of the trails where your birds nest, Shabina, parents and a toddler? The woman had two sisters. They were triplets—the two of them and the woman who died. The two sisters stayed in one of my cabins during the investigation. The husband had gone off trail, and they got into the section where that fire had been. The trees were burned, and there was no canopy. Then we got hit with so much rain, and the ground turned into a marsh. After that, the temperatures soared."

Vienna nodded. "That was so horrible. It's always bad when a child is involved."

"It was extremely hot," Harlow added. "They weren't carrying adequate water. They were avid hikers but weren't prepared at all for the hot weather."

"No one was prepared for the weather," Vienna said. "So many patients came to the hospital with heatstroke. It was a bad time."

Shabina remembered that as head of Search and Rescue, Vienna had been called when the family hadn't been heard from, and their car had been found seemingly abandoned. She'd organized search parties, and the bodies of the three were found four days later in a very unlikely area. Shabina had been heartsick for the family of those dead and just as heartsick for the ones finding and caring for the bodies. Everyone was distraught over the deaths.

Shabina knew that area of the forest very well. The trail was faint, nearly obscure. It had been marked for rehabilitation. Wildlife and weather had damaged signs. She could see how anyone unfamiliar with the trails would get hopelessly turned around. Once they were off the trail and into the section with the damaged trees, it would be even more difficult to know which way to go. Without adequate shade, it would be burning hot.

Shabina sighed. "The two women came into my café often, and I'd sit and talk with them. I felt very bad for them."

Stella nodded. "They mentioned you several times, Shabina,

and how kind you were to them." She smiled. "And they remembered how amazing the food was. They've come back to have a memorial ceremony. I think you'll be seeing quite a bit of them. They wanted to spend an extended vacation here. They've booked one of my nicest cabins for a month, and they've been here nearly a week, exploring all around Sunrise."

"That surprises me," Harlow said. "What with losing their sister here, I would have thought it would be difficult to come back."

"They want to learn about all the things she loved. One of the things they want to do is go on Shabina's bird-watching tour. I've got you completely booked for Tuesday. There are students from a university who are very excited to go on that tour too. Will you be driving up Monday night after work?"

Shabina managed not to bite down on her lip. Raine never missed details and she was already assessing Shabina closely. "Yes, but I'm going to camp. It's still an hour's drive from Sunrise Resort, so if I'm camping in Yosemite, I can get a little more sleep and also run the dogs before the shuttle brings my clients."

The dogs were always her best excuse for anything. Her friends had companion dogs and saw to their needs. They understood the dogs would want to run.

Zahra snuggled the ball of fluff in her lap. "This one wants to run all the time." She gave an exaggerated sigh. "You know how much I detest running."

Shabina found herself laughing with the others. Zahra might sound like she was complaining, but she loved that bundle of fluff.

"Raine, I may as well take Daisy with me when I take the little monster out. I can swing by and pick her up."

Raine's Jack Russell was very active and loved to run along the canal three times a day. Raine's shattered leg was healing slowly, preventing her from going for the long runs she would normally take with her dog. She walked, but it was still very painful for her, and Daisy tended to stay close to her rather than run like she needed to.

Raine's face lit up. "Zahra, you really wouldn't mind? I try to take her for walks, but Daisy won't leave me when we go out. You know how she is; she needs tons of exercise."

Zahra waved her hand. "I have to take this naughty one out anyway. And it will be good for them to become friends."

CHAPTER TWO

did have something I wanted to run by all of you," Shabina said. She kept her voice carefully controlled, but her friends instantly fell silent, waiting, as if they knew this wasn't as casual as she was trying to make it sound.

She couldn't help laughing. She was so lucky. "You women. I can't get anything past you. You knew all along I wanted to talk about something important."

"It's been obvious you're upset about something, Shabina," Stella said, her voice gentle.

"Your dogs are on edge," Harlow pointed out. "Whether they're picking up your mood or there really is something wrong, it's apparent something is out of sync. We've just been waiting for you to share."

Shabina took a deep breath. Now that she was going to articulate her fears, they seemed silly. What evidence did she have that anything was wrong? She found herself hesitating. If it got out that she was worried, her parents would insist she come home. They'd keep her locked in their house, surrounded by security. She wouldn't be able to move or breathe without permission or having half a dozen guards around her. All the things she loved doing wouldn't matter.

"I'm not exactly sure how to start. Now that I'm going to say it out loud to someone, I feel a little ridiculous," she admitted.

"Shabina." Raine sounded more than gentle. "Take your time. We're your friends. You don't have to worry about how you sound. Just tell us what's bothering you."

Shabina sank to the floor so she wouldn't be tempted to pace. She'd worked hard to appear relaxed and calm at all times. The moment she sat on one of the cushions scattered on the floor, Malik lay down on one side of her and Sharif on the other. They pressed against her thighs, crowding close, feeling her inner agitation. She had to keep reminding herself these were her friends and they had her best interests at heart.

"You know my father puts out oil fires all over the world, that he's considered the best in the business, right?" She knew they were aware of her rather famous father, but she had to start somewhere. "I told you that when I was fifteen, he took my mother and me to Saudi Arabia to put out fires there and I was kidnapped. It was a strange time. Quite a few kidnappings had taken place, and my mother and I were coached on how to behave if it should ever happen to us. We were told ransom would be demanded. It would be paid, and we would be freed. We were instructed not to resist. Not to try to escape. Not to agitate our kidnappers in any way. We were told repeatedly that sometimes negotiations broke down but not to worry, they always resumed."

"How strange that would be," Vienna said. "Having to worry all the time about being kidnapped, so much so that you're given instructions on how to respond."

Harlow exchanged a long look with Shabina before she admitted to the others that she'd also been given strict instructions. "I grew up with a father in politics. We had security around us all the time, but obviously, my training wasn't as intense as Shabina's."

Shabina sent her a small smile, thankful someone understood the pressures of having to be constantly on alert for danger. "My mother and I went shopping at this little market. It wasn't like we weren't heavily guarded; we were. The next thing I know there was shouting and jostling and guns waving at us. My mother was grabbed by our security guards and they made a run for the armored vehicle. I was on the other side of the table of a fruit seller's stand. I remember looking at the oranges exploding all around me and then at my mother's back as the men shoved her into the SUV. My guards threw me to the ground, and we rolled under the table with all the fruit."

"You must have been so frightened," Stella said.

"I mostly remember being worried about my mother. I didn't like being separated from her. She didn't look back either. That felt so strange to me. She didn't call out or look back. She let them push her inside the SUV. I told myself if my mother could be that calm and do what we were told in the situation, I should be able to do it too."

Raine let out her breath. "You were fifteen, Shabina. Separated from your mother in the middle of gunfire. No one would have blamed you if you panicked."

Shabina shifted her gaze to Raine. Raine could be a firecracker if she thought one of her friends had been misjudged—or in this case, was taking on guilt that wasn't hers. She found herself smiling again, the heaviness in her heart lifting a little.

"The thing is, Raine, I didn't panic. I just told myself the security team had gotten my mother out of there, and mine would get me out."

"But they didn't," Stella whispered. She wrapped her arms around Bailey's neck.

Shabina pressed her palm against her thigh, high up, where sometimes the muscle refused to stop aching. Like now. She told herself it was psychosomatic, not real, all in her head. No matter that she ran daily and stretched endlessly, that pain from the scarring never quite left her body.

"No, those men with guns were everywhere. My team didn't want to start a war and get everyone in the marketplace killed, so they opted to lie down with the rest of us when they were told. Two of them tried to cover me, but it was my mother and me they were looking for. I was taken along with six other prisoners. Two women in their thirties, both from France, and three men from London in their early twenties, and a woman from Argentina who was close to sixty. I didn't put up any resistance. No one had been killed. I think a couple of people may have been wounded, but for the most part, when they left with us, the market just had to be put back in order."

"The fact that you weren't the only one kidnapped was reassuring to you?" Harlow inquired.

Shabina nodded. "So much so that when the older woman, Kathryn was her name, began to cry, I whispered to her not to resist, that they would negotiate for our release. I was certain they wouldn't hurt her. I spoke in Spanish, hoping our captors wouldn't understand me and be angry that I was reassuring her. I had been told to stay very quiet and not draw attention to myself, but I didn't like seeing her in such distress."

"That's so you, Shabina," Raine said. "You have the most compassionate heart. You clearly had it even then."

"I would have been too petrified to move," Vienna said.

Shabina couldn't help laughing. Vienna hung off cliffs rescuing total strangers. "I doubt that. I think what I'm trying to say is we were treated with kindness. No one hit me or any of the others. They took us to a place with tents, gave us food and water and explained the rules. We were told we were being held for ransom and once that ransom was paid, we would be freed. It was more or less a profitable business for them, just as we'd been told by our security team."

"There were others in this camp?"

"Even some of their women. Old and young. The leader was a man named Salman Ahmad. He was soft-spoken, but what he said was law. No one disobeyed him. He didn't torture or murder, but he meant what he said. He had each of us make a video to plea with our families to pay the ransom. There were no political statements, just simple business transactions. Then the entire camp was moved."

Shabina rubbed her aching left thigh. The muscle pounded with the throb of her heartbeat. "I should have tried to escape. I don't know why I didn't. The truth is, I didn't feel as if I was in a camp with kidnappers. That first year, I was treated with kindness by the women and mostly ignored by the men. I learned so many things and found everything about their lives fascinating. I was able to help with the children and was taught to sew and cook. I perfected my language skills. Kathryn was the first to go, and even she hugged a couple of the women and me when she was escorted away."

Tears burned behind her eyes, tears for those women and children she'd come to love. They had been like family to her. "I thought about my parents, but it felt as if I'd been sent to one of the many camps or boarding schools while the two of them went off alone together. This was nicer than the summer camps. I learned to play musical instruments and sing their songs. The birds were so beautiful, and I could coax them to come right to me. I practiced each note any bird would sing until I could duplicate it exactly. I studied their beliefs and found them to be fascinating. In most ways, they were a quiet, peaceful, loving people. The men always wore the traditional garb, as did the women. I did as well."

The lump in her throat threatened to choke her. She found she was rocking, self-soothing, something she had tried very hard not to do.

"Shabina." Raine's voice was gentle. "You don't have to tell us."

"No, I do. I was responsible for what happened. I should have tried to escape. The Frenchwomen were ransomed a few months after the first one. We moved often, but it was always the same: a nice setup and everyone seemed so peaceful. There were two babies born. The three college students left. Salman Ahmad came to me one day and said it would be my turn. He said I was too good with the children, teaching them different languages and playing games with them, and no one wanted me to go. I overheard him telling his men that each time the ransom was to be paid, it was intercepted. He didn't know if my father was deliberately keeping the money or if they had a traitor among them, someone taking the money before it got into their hands. Either way, he couldn't keep me much longer. I knew I would be going home."

She touched her tongue to her suddenly dry lips. "But then they came. He called himself Scorpion." Without thinking she wrapped her fingers just above her left wrist. "He said his name was Al Aqrab Jabrir Birvul Fareed. He claimed he was likely named after the star, but he prides himself as the Deathstalker Scorpion. He even referred to himself that way. He has a special brand he puts on his captive women to claim to the world they belong to him."

Shabina realized her friends were watching her closely, and she forced her hands to relax and drop once more to the dogs pressed close to her.

"He wore a mask, but I realized fairly quickly he wasn't from the Middle East. His name wasn't really Fareed. The men he surrounded himself with were mercenaries, and they were nearly as sadistic as he was. They used automatic weapons and mowed down the men. It didn't matter the age of the women; old or young, they were raped before they were killed. They killed every single person in the camp, babies included. Everyone." She whispered the last word because her voice refused to go any louder. "I thought I would be raped and murdered as well. I was part of them. They had become my family."

"Oh, Shabina," Zahra whispered. "How terrible you had to witness such a massacre."

"I know you might think I have some kind of Stockholm syndrome from being kidnapped and held so long by Salman Ahmad, but I know it isn't that. To him, kidnapping was simply a business transaction. He was a good man. A wise man. He led his tribe with fairness and kindness. Not just his men but the women and children. They followed their traditional beliefs, and while I was with them, I tried to learn as much as I could and followed them as well. Scorpion was just the opposite, and he is a true sadist."

"I've heard of him," Stella said. "That name has been in the news numerous times. He's an international serial killer. Most people suspect he's an airline pilot because he's killed in so many countries."

"There's little trail left behind," Raine added, "because he murders everyone he comes into contact with. He usually keeps a young girl for about six months, tortures her and then kills her in some sadistic way, leaving his brand on her arm."

Shabina resisted rubbing her forearm beneath the long-sleeved shirt she wore.

"He's killed in the United States," Stella said. "In France. In

Argentina. Costa Rica. Egypt, Belgium and I think one other country besides Saudi Arabia. He was reputed to have massacred several villages or very small towns in each of the countries."

"He insisted everyone around him address him as Sheik Fareed," Shabina said. "A sheik is a holy man, wise, an advisor, someone for everyone in the tribe to look up to. Scorpion didn't earn his title. He took it, when it wasn't his to take. He doesn't practice the beliefs he pretended to outsiders to have. He doesn't have one ounce of respect for any of the people, the land, or even the royal family. He truly is a serial killer, and so far, no one has been able to catch him. When I realized he wasn't from the Middle East, I did my best to find out his true identity. At least to figure out where he was from."

She rubbed her aching thigh. It was throbbing now, her heart beating in tune to that pulsing pain. "I heard him speaking French more than once with several of his top commanders. He called them his cabinet. I won't go into what happened to anyone who dared to cross him, or what he did to me, but he was no holy man. He was a total fraud, and he hated me and yet seemed obsessed with me. I couldn't do anything right. I pretended not to know his language and made him speak French or English to me. That earned me quite a few punishments, but after a while, the mercenaries he'd hired locally grew careless and talked in front of me. His command of both those languages was excellent."

"You don't have to go into detail," Raine assured. "And no one here thinks you have Stockholm syndrome in regards to Salman Ahmad. He sounds as if he was a good man and did his best for his people."

She appreciated Raine all the more for being understanding. Not even her parents understood how well she'd been treated or how the tribe had integrated her into their families. They'd shown her respect, and in turn, she respected and grew to love them. It had all started with their leader, Salman Ahmad. She'd seen the difference between a true leader and practitioner of his traditions and a power-hungry sadist out to get everything he could for himself. Scorpion had robbed the tribe and murdered the members.

She knew they weren't his only victims. She had become aware, through all the questioning she'd been subjected to when she'd been rescued, that the man who called himself Scorpion was an international serial killer determined to create as many headlines as possible with the sadistic massacres. He would disappear for months or a year, and then the killings would start up again in another country. His name was never the same, only Scorpion and the signature brand on the wrist of the young girl he kept for six months before murdering her.

She had to get to the present and push the past far away from her mind. Close the door before it creaked too far open.

"Four days ago, two men came into the café. They said they were from France. That isn't unusual. We get tourists from all over the world. Ordinarily, I wouldn't have thought too much about it, but they looked familiar to me. Their features. You know I don't forget faces. I was fairly certain I hadn't seen either of them before, but I knew I had seen their features. Their eyes and foreheads. Neither of them looked directly at me. That's unusual too."

She didn't want to sound vain—she wasn't. She dressed modestly at all times. She covered her skin. It was a habit and necessity as far as she was concerned. Her friends had never questioned why she wore the clothes she did—the long sleeves even in the heat. She never wore shorts. But men looked at her. She'd looked in the mirror, and she knew by most people's standards she was considered beautiful.

She had her mother's flawless skin and thick, rich gleaming

hair so black it could shine nearly blue under the lights. It fell to her narrow waist, usually in a roped braid. Her eyes were large, a deep blue with hints of purple, ringed with thick black lashes. She was on the shorter side, barely reaching five foot four with her shoes on, but she had curves. Men looked at her. Noticed her. It didn't matter that she dressed modestly.

"They talked quietly, were respectful when they ordered and paid for their food. Nothing about them should have stood out, yet everything did. The longer they were in the café, the more this really bad feeling grew. They spoke to each other in French, but their accent didn't ring true. I have an ear for sound, and there was just something off."

"You do realize," Vienna said very gently, almost soothingly, "you are always going to have triggers. Those men easily could trigger PTSD from the horrific trauma you suffered. You said Scorpion spoke to you in excellent French. That alone could trigger you."

As if she didn't already know that. It was all she could do not to roll her eyes. Vienna sounded much the same as her therapist. She'd been seeing the therapist for several years, and yet the woman didn't seem to think Shabina would be able to remember from one session to the next the tools she'd been given to cope when she had a meltdown. And that voice. Soothing. As if Shabina were a child and didn't understand what was happening to her. It had been happening for *years*.

She swallowed every retort, reminding herself these were her friends and they were trying to understand and help. There was no way to explain her built-in radar for deception and danger after six months of living in hell with Scorpion.

"That's one of the many reasons I didn't rush to any conclusions," she agreed. "But they looked like two of the cabinet members working for Scorpion. You have to remember, they wore masks, so I only saw their eyes and foreheads. The shape of their chins. They spoke excellent French, but I wasn't certain that was their first language."

There was a brief silence. "Have you talked with your therapist?" Stella asked. "It might be a good thing to call her just to check in."

Shabina was torn between laughter and tears. She'd known this was going to happen. Raine met her eyes again. She sent her a little smile of encouragement.

"No one ever knows the right thing to say in these circumstances, Shabina. We know you've done these things. You've been through panic attacks and triggering events probably multiple times. You're a very disciplined person. We know you've got the tools to deal with each crisis when it comes, but that doesn't mean those tools always get you through. That leaves us with nothing to offer you but our love and friendship."

The others nodded. "And our faith in you," Stella added. "We may play the devil's advocate and argue the other side, but that's just to give you every perspective. Whatever you choose to do, we're with you all the way."

These women. How could she not love them? They'd offered her unconditional love and friendship without knowing her past, almost right from their first meeting her. She had issues, and yet they didn't seem to care. They remained steadfast in their resolve to help her.

She had been stoic as a prisoner, refusing to cry no matter the inventive tortures of Scorpion and the seven men he referred to as his cabinet members. Or the mercenaries he'd hired to help him destroy small villages. Now she was a bundle of volatile emotions. Tears burned behind her eyes. She was so grateful and so lucky for the friendships. She might despise thinking of her past, but in doing so, she was reminded of the good people she'd lived with who had treated her as part of their family. Scorpion's mercenary guards, who had risked their lives and the lives of their families to give her as much aid and comfort as possible under horrific circumstances. She never wanted to forget the goodness and compassion of those people.

"What else happened?" Raine encouraged when Shabina fell silent.

She took another deep breath and forced herself back to the present and what had occurred to set her off. "Two days ago, I found something lying on the back steps of the café when I got there to bake. It was just before four in the morning."

She patted the dogs, rose to her feet and went to a low cabinet with several drawers in it. She'd slipped the feathers in a Ziploc bag. "I found these on the top stair. Three feathers." She handed the bag to Stella.

"These look like the feathers from the mourning dove, Shabina. I know four a.m. is early, but why would these upset you?" Stella passed the bag to Harlow.

Harlow frowned as she studied the feathers. "They do look like mourning dove feathers, but they don't have spots. If I recall, don't those doves have brown or black dots on their wing feathers, Shabina?" She handed off the bag to Zahra. Vienna looked over Zahra's shoulder.

"I wouldn't know," Zahra admitted. "Just looks like regular feathers to me."

"Me too," Vienna agreed. She pulled the transparent bag closer. "Is that blood on the feathers? And on the shaft? Were the feathers pulled out of the bird?"

Raine held out her hand, and Vienna placed the bag in her

palm. "Definitely drops of blood. Birds aren't my field of expertise, Shabina, they're yours. What type of bird?" Raine carefully
handed the bag back to Shabina. Shabina's hand shook as she
placed it carefully in the drawer. To her, the feathers were evidence she wasn't losing her mind.

Shabina pressed her palm against her thigh hard. "There's a
species of bird, beautiful, pigeon-like, called the laughing dove.
It looks similar to the mourning dove, but it has a very long tail,
and the body is pastel pink and brown edged with blue. They
mate for life. Most of the time, they walk along the ground hunting for food. They're called laughing doves because they sound
much like a human laughing."

She kept her gaze fixed on Raine. If anyone believed her, it
would be Raine. Shabina knew birds. She didn't have a single
doubt that these feathers had come from a laughing dove. That
didn't mean someone couldn't have dropped them outside and
they'd blown in the wind and found the way to the steps of her
café. That seemed an unlikely coincidence, but then three feathers?

"What significance would these feathers have between you and
Scorpion?" Raine asked. "There must be a tie for you to be upset."

"Scorpion was gone a lot. He'd leave behind orders to torture
me but not kill me. Despite his hiring mercenaries, there were a
couple of good men in his camp who didn't like what he was doing to me. We'd move every three or four days, but I was always
in bad shape. There was one guard, a man called Iyad. He never
participated in rape. He was always rough with me, and a few
times he was forced to beat or whip me. I understood. He was
risking his life to be kind to me. He would sneak me water or a
small bite of food when I was at my worst. I was forced to walk
every day to keep my endurance up. He knew I liked birds, so he
would deliberately find a flock and take me in that direction. He

rarely spoke or made eye contact, and I was careful to keep my gaze fixed on the ground. It was a protection for us both."

"They had eyes on you all the time," Harlow guessed.

"Yes." Shabina inclined her head. "We moved every few days, and it wasn't like before with Salman Ahmad and his tribe. This was only a small group of Scorpion's paid soldiers."

"Do you think those men knew Scorpion's true identity?" Raine asked.

Shabina shook her head. "I know the majority didn't. He always wore a mask. He had the seven men he referred to as his cabinet members who may have known. They stuck close together, and those men also wore masks. Sometimes I would hear them speak in French to one another. If Scorpion was present, he would always shut that down."

"I'm sorry I interrupted," Raine said. "Please continue."

"They'd throw tents together, and that's where we'd stay and then move on. That morning, Iyad had taken me for a walk, and Scorpion arrived with no warning. He was really angry. That meant he was at his most dangerous. Even his men were afraid of him when he was like that. He began shouting and cursing at everyone. Something had gone wrong with the money transfer. Unfortunately, at that very moment, the doves took their opportunity to chime in, and it did sound very much like human laughter. I must have smiled. I was so disciplined by that time and always kept my head down and eyes averted from Scorpion, but he must have seen me."

Her heart accelerated, remembering that moment. It felt as if time stood still. She knew Scorpion would beat her to death. He was more than capable in his blackest moods, and there was no doubt that he was in one of his killing frenzies. She had lifted her chin, determined to goad him into doing it, killing her. Getting it over with. She'd had enough. She was already weak and felt hopeless. Her body was worn out and so was her mind.

Her guard, Iyad, had instantly recognized the danger she was in and what she planned to do. Maybe all the men had. It was that silent. Only the wind blew and the sand swirled lightly around them. Iyad yanked her around to face him, slapped her face, and forced her to the ground, yelling at her to kneel before the sheik. He began to viciously whip her back, over and over, all the while cursing and admonishing her to respect Scorpion. Instantly, in one of his infamous mercurial moods, Scorpion stopped Iyad from beating her and said he knew a better way to teach her manners.

Just uttering those words sent that same sinister chill down her spine. Shabina couldn't help looking out her windows again. Was he out there watching her right at that moment? Watching her friends? He couldn't see into her home. She shivered and crossed her arms over her chest.

"To make a long story short, that night, he had several laughing doves killed in front of me and cooked for my dinner. When I refused to eat, he decreed I couldn't eat anything until I'd eaten what he'd put in front of me. Little did he know he'd given me the perfect out."

No one could be more stubborn or more disciplined than Shabina when she made up her mind to something. If starving was the only way to escape Scorpion, she would take it gladly. She knew it wouldn't take long. These men had abused her to the point her body had few reserves left.

"How did you survive?" Vienna asked when she fell silent again.

Shabina had presented her case regarding the laughing birds' feathers and their connection to her. She didn't see how anyone would call finding them on her doorstep a coincidence. She hadn't planned to continue talking about her time with Scorpion.

She sighed. "When it was clear I was going to die and no threat was enough to force me to eat, no beating could induce me to eat, and nothing he did or said worked, in the end, he turned his wrath on my guards. He threatened that if I died, he would give them a slow death, not only them but their families as well. Two of the four guards assigned to watch me day and night had been decent. In a camp that size, two wasn't many, but they were good men just doing their best to stay alive. Both had risked their lives several times to give me small respites from pain or to give me encouragement. I knew Scorpion meant what he said. He would have taken great pleasure in hurting them, although they'd served him well. I felt I had to live for their sake."

Shabina was done reliving her past. She forced her gaze to meet Raine's. "I don't know why those two men claiming to be from France are here, but I think he sent them. I know he's still alive because I would have been informed if he had been killed."

Raine confirmed her suspicion by nodding her head.

"Scorpion and his seven cabinet members were the worst of the men who assaulted me during the six months I was with them. I know they're on an international wanted list, but without really being able to identify them, how are they going to be caught?"

Shabina was certain they were being actively hunted. She wasn't supposed to know, but she did. She just felt that it was impossible to find a man capable of assuming identities in various countries and committing the kinds of sadistic massacres Scorpion did. He could be anyone. Any nationality. Well, almost. She had narrowed his accent down to a couple of countries. She had a good ear for accents, but what did that get her when he could assume the identity of anyone?

She would have been informed if Scorpion had been captured

or killed, and so far, no word had come in. She had hoped, after all these years of silence, he would leave her alone.

"Did you call your head of security?" Stella asked. "Because you didn't contact Sam."

Sam had worked for Special Activities Division, the same as Zale, Rainier and Rush still did. Vienna's birth father, Elliot Blom, was the director of that program at the CIA.

"No, I didn't because I wasn't positive that it was a threat to me. I'm still not. I don't want my parents freaking out and insisting I close my café and come home. I'm doing my best to live a normal life. If this is just some strange coincidence, then I don't want to panic early."

"I don't think you're losing your mind." Zahra got right to the point. "I'd be worried."

"I can run the two men through a facial recognition program," Raine offered. "I'll get their faces from the security feed from your café. It will take some time, Shabina, especially if they aren't known terrorists or known to be connected to Scorpion."

"Thank you. Running that program won't put you in jeopardy in any way, will it?" Shabina felt as if she were responsible for enough people's lives ending without having to worry about Raine as well.

"No, I'm very experienced at what I do. I'm a 'ghost' in a computer." She flashed Shabina a mischievous little grin. Using the word *ghost* was a play on the word. There had been times when Sam and Zale had been referred to as ghosts.

Shabina returned her smile, nearly sagging with relief. She'd told her friends, and it had lifted her burden just a little. She even felt better.

"Thanks for listening. It was getting so I couldn't sleep. I start thinking too much."

"Don't wait so long," Raine advised. "I'm on a forced vacation and going a little crazy just sitting around doing nothing. It will give me something to do."

"Who exactly is this 'General' who calls you during your vacation and insists only you can get him the information he needs?" Harlow asked. "If he's very young, he can't be a real general, can he? And he sounds like he's a bit of a spoiled brat."

Raine burst out laughing. It was impossible not to laugh with her. "He does sound like a spoiled brat now that you say that. I would never have thought of him in those terms, but he does throw temper tantrums until he gets his way. Can you imagine being married to him?"

"I can't imagine being married to anyone," Harlow said. She gave a little shudder. "Stella and Vienna are so brave."

"Stella is," Vienna corrected. "I'm still vacillating. When Zale's with me, it's a solid yes. When he's gone, it's a 'maybe I need to think about this for a long time.'"

"I'm fortunate because I have Sam," Stella said. "He's dreamy."

Zahra held up her hand. "Don't start. None of us have had enough drinks to listen to you carrying on about how dreamy and sexy Sam is. I would have to put in earplugs."

"We could quote you, Stella," Shabina added. "You said those things for two years before you ever started a relationship with him."

"But everything I say is the truth," Stella insisted. "As my best friends, you should be able to handle me giving you factual information about the man in my life."

"The only factual information we want is when you and Sam decide you're going to have a baby," Harlow said.

"A baby?" Stella choked on her ice-cold beer. "Not yet."

"Ticktock, ticktock," Vienna said, her tone mischievous.

"I don't think you can say very much," Stella pointed out.

"We're the same age, aren't we? Doesn't Zale want children? As in more than one? I'm sure I overheard him talking to Sam."

"He's not home to help raise them," Vienna said. "I'll think about marriage and children when and if Zale retires."

Stella sobered immediately. "Vienna, I thought you were okay with Zale working even if you were married."

"I'm trying to be okay with it. I believe Zale should do what he loves. If he needs to work for my hideous birth father, I'll do my best to be supportive. I want to continue doing my jobs. I wouldn't want him to tell me what I can or can't do. On the other hand, I don't want to be a single mother. I don't have the first idea about raising children. If he wants to have them, he needs to be part of their lives, not an occasional father who comes and goes."

That made sense to Shabina. She was the youngest of the women. The man she wanted was unattainable. Not only was he out of her reach, but he was older than her by over ten years. He thought of her as a child. More, after all she'd been through, she wasn't certain she could be in a physical relationship with a man, although she was attracted to him. Like most things in her life she had no control over, she pushed thoughts of partnerships and children from her mind.

"That's totally understandable," Zahra said staunchly. "I'd be the same way. I think men should participate in raising their children." She snuggled Misty closer to her. "And I don't mean just discipline them."

Harlow blew her a kiss. "Different generations were taught various things. Same with other countries and cultures. Hopefully, things are changing and we're all evolving into better human beings."

"I certainly saw evidence of that," Shabina said. "There were so many people good to me. As parents, Salman Ahmad's tribe all seemed to participate in raising the children. They treated them lovingly. The boys and girls were separated for education and a few other things, but they were treated with love by both the men and women in the tribe."

"What were their religious beliefs?" Stella asked, curious.

"They followed the basic pillars of Islam. They were Muslim. They also followed the laws of the country. Women are subject to their fathers, brothers and husbands. In that tribe, it didn't appear to be a hardship. The elders of the tribe and the women's fathers appeared to have their best interests at heart. I was there a year and didn't see a single woman beaten. I didn't see a child struck."

She missed them. Each of them. The men and women. It was strange because she loved her parents, but hadn't spent nearly as much time one on one with them as she had with the female members of Ahmad's tribe. They taught her so many things. She had always been curious, her brain active, and they encouraged her questions. They taught her practical and survival skills. Crafts. They taught her to play with the children. There seemed to always be laughter and singing.

When she was at home with her parents, her father was away at work, and her mother often traveled with him. She had a nanny and tutors. She and her mother shopped together, but her extracurricular activities and classes took up a great deal of her time. She lived in a loving home and didn't lack for anything, but once she was with Ahmad's tribe, Shabina realized she wanted to be the kind of parent who spent time with her child.

"What a difference it must have been to go from his tribe to being a real prisoner of a man like Scorpion," Raine said.

Not just a difference. A shock.

CHAPTER THREE

T his is crazy, Shabina," Vaughn Miller said. "You're going to
have to hire more help. We can't keep up. Every table is full
both inside and outside and we have a line waiting." He grinned
at her, eyes bright with happiness.

Vaughn had first come to Knightly three years earlier to climb,
camping out of a beat-up van, one of the many "dirt baggers"
who lived to climb boulders and hike. Like quite a few others,
he'd fallen in love with the small town and wanted to stay but
needed to find a way to make enough money to rent one of the
few coveted vacant places. The rentals went fast, and very few
gave them up once they'd moved in.

He'd jumped at the chance of working for Shabina and her
business had grown fast. She was great about sharing profits. The
more money she made, the more she paid him. He was completely loyal to her and determined to help her any way he could.
Together, they'd interviewed and hired one dishwasher, Nellie
Frost; one waiter, Tyrone Michigan; and two waitresses, Patsy
Daily and Chelsey Sarten. They were still swamped. Tyrone and
Patsy were quickly moved up to head waitstaff, and Nellie became a waitress out of necessity. They all pitched in to do dishes.

Shabina sent Vaughn an answering smile. "We can't fit in more tables and chairs, and even outside we don't have room to expand. I don't want to get any bigger. If we did, we'd lose the personal touch. This is as big as we're going to get."

"I guess I'll be okay with that." Vaughn studied the room. "Who are the five in the corner booth? I don't recognize them."

"The new crew to rehabilitate the trails in Yosemite. They'll leave straight from here and head up. The crew chief said they've been hired for the summer."

"Climbers?"

Shabina laughed. "How ever did you guess?" There were three men and two women on the trail rehabilitation crew. It was a never-ending job to keep the popular trails open and in good condition.

"And the three smart-looking newbies with Sean Watson?" Vaughn didn't bother to hide his dislike of Sean.

Sean was one of four local men who came into the café, ate the food and then often complained loudly that it was terrible and refused to pay. He harassed Shabina often at the café and at the Grill, a local restaurant where live music was played and Shabina and her friends went to dance.

"Fish and Wildlife interns. He's mentoring them or something. If I go near their booth, they harass me. The one with the sandy-colored hair is named Deacon, and he can't resist making childish kissy noises. Naturally, Sean encourages him. He's asked me out three times already."

"We should have banned Sean from ever coming back here. I know he was one of those who graffitied the crap out of the café. He did it with his little band of friends, Jason Briggs, Bale Landry and Edward Fenton. We should have banned them all."

Shabina privately agreed with him. The four men were a menace, and they'd taken a strong dislike to her. They believed she didn't belong in the United States, despite the fact that she'd been born there and her father was American. She did have the Saudi Arabian features of her mother. She didn't care what set their prejudices off; they didn't like her and went out of their way to make her as uncomfortable as possible.

"So far, they haven't managed to get under my skin," she said truthfully. When a woman had been tortured and abused, verbal harassment with taunts and insults about her cooking skills wasn't going to make her fall apart. "My philosophy is to kill them with kindness."

"The twins?" Vaughn nodded to the two women sitting at one of the prime tables beside the window where one could get a good view of the sun rising.

"They were here last year. That's Felicity Garner in the red and Eve in the purple. They lost their sister, Freda, who made them triplets. She died of dehydration with her husband, Emilio, and her daughter, Crystal, last year in Yosemite. There was a big investigation."

"I remember that," Vaughn said, dropping his voice. "That was so sad, Shabina. You spent a lot of time with them. I see Raine is here with Vienna. How is she doing?"

Shabina sighed. Although Raine didn't show it, she knew her friend was in pain. "I think she's going to need quite a lot more rehab."

"She has her leg thanks to all of you," Vaughn pointed out. He flicked a towel at her. "You'd better make your rounds before the next wave of customers comes in. I see Jason Briggs is sitting in a corner with Bruce Akins instead of with his friends, Bale and Edward. That's new."

"Not so much. Jason agreed to work at the Brewery with Bruce.

Bruce wants someone to come in as a partner, and Jason wants to stay in Knightly permanently, so they're working together."

"Does Bruce seriously want to be partners with a man who treats women the way Jason does?" Vaughn sounded shocked.

Shabina gave a little shake of her head. They were in the kitchen looking out through the half wall at their customers, but she was taking no chances of being overheard. Vaughn was a huge asset to her. She had been around men who were seriously deranged, and she knew Scorpion was a sadistic psychopath who wanted the reputation of someone in history such as Vlad the Impaler, who had murdered over eighty thousand people. She thought he was well on his way to trying to match the number of tortures and murders of the historical figures he admired so much.

Bale, Edward and Sean could get ugly. They would threaten and even get into fistfights, but they weren't the type to pull out a gun and shoot someone. Still, they could make Vaughn's life a living hell. They certainly did their best to make hers that way. She wasn't the only one either. Zahra was raised in a small village in Azerbaijan. Any woman who appeared to be or was from a different country was looked down on and treated with disrespect by the men. That was why it was a little shocking to see Bruce, who had always crushed on Zahra, with Jason, who was good friends with Bale, Edward and Sean.

"I'm going to make my rounds and give the personal touch to the customers. I want to check in with Eve and Felicity to see how they're doing. Keep everyone moving. We've got to clear the tables fast, Vaughn."

"We're on it."

Fortunately, most of the food for the café was prepared in advance. She served a limited menu each day. The customers were aware of that before they entered. She posted the menu outside on the wall so it was easily read before they chose to eat or just get coffee and pastries or sandwiches for travel.

As she went down the line of booths and tables, she stopped to greet the customers and see if they had any questions about the town or places to shop or just ask if they were on their way to Sunrise Lake or Yosemite. She was fortunate in that she easily retained names and faces and spoke several languages so she could make her customers feel welcomed and at ease within a few short minutes. That was what she loved most about having her café.

"Hey, gorgeous," Deacon called out as she bypassed their table. He leaned out with a long arm in an effort to grab her wrist.

Shabina glided away from him, but half turned to look at him over his shoulder. "Did you need something, sir?" She glanced around the café. "Your waiter is Tyrone. Let me call him for you."

"I need something from you," Deacon countered, winking at the other men at the table.

Sean grinned like an ape. "We all could use a little something from you."

Shabina lifted an eyebrow, shook her head and signaled to Tyrone, but she kept walking. It was too bad Sean was teaching his ways to impressionable young interns. Deacon made his kissy noises, and his two friends and Sean uttered a couple of catcalls. She didn't turn around.

"Are they always like that?" Felicity asked. She pulled up a chair from a nearby table and patted the seat. "I know you're super busy, but sit for a minute."

Shabina glanced around the room. Her staff had things under control, breaking down tables and seating new customers. "Unfortunately, there are a couple of locals who have taken a dislike to me, although they come here frequently to eat. That's their form of harassment. I don't like seeing it taught to the students they mentor."

"Those kids aren't younger than you, Shabina," Eve said staunchly. "They should know better than to act that way."

Shabina forced an easy smile. "I've made a lot of mistakes in my life, so I do my best to give people the chance to grow and learn from their mistakes." She gave a little wave of her hand as if dismissing the conversation. "I want to hear how you're doing."

The two women exchanged a look. Again, Felicity answered. "We're contemplating making a move here. It's so peaceful. And Freda loved this area so much. She talked about it all the time. Just the time we've been here makes us feel different. When we're back in Galaxy, Maine, it seems like we don't have the time to take a breath."

"Galaxy? What a nice name for a town," Shabina said.

"Very small town," Felicity said. "Here, the views insist you sit back and enjoy them."

"The sunsets," Eve added. "And the sunrises. We feel closer to Freda here."

Felicity nodded. "We're trying to learn as much as we can about hiking from guides and books, but I still don't understand fully what happened to that section of trees where Freda and her family were found. Why would they go there? The trees were black and twisted, with no leaves at all."

"We were told that trail had been closed. It was grown over, but we didn't see any sign saying the trail was closed," Eve added. "When we read the final report, it said they had entered a trail that had been marked closed."

Shabina had hoped she wouldn't have to discuss their tragedy, but clearly, they were trying to understand.

"We don't want to make the same mistakes," Felicity said. "We don't have Emilio and Freda's hiking experience. We're going on trails that are on the maps, and we do ask others, but it doesn't make sense that Freda got so far off trail if it was closed to hikers."

"Maintaining trails is difficult in the wild," Shabina explained as gently as she could. "Crews are hired, but it requires money and it's a lot of work. Not all trails can be rehabilitated right away or kept up. The main trails are first priority. The trees were compromised by some change in the underground water. I don't honestly remember what happened off the top of my head, but in that area the trees and all the brush died. A fire swept through the area not long after that. The trail was closed as soon as it happened. There were clear signs put up warning the trail was closed. As time went by, the trail became overgrown."

"Where were the signs?" Felicity pursued.

Shabina sighed again. "We do have an abundance of wild animals in Yosemite. Bears like to scratch on some of the signs. Weather plays a part as well. It isn't entirely impossible that a bear managed to break the sign apart and no one noticed. A park ranger or Fish and Wildlife might go that way every few months. If that trail wasn't scheduled for rehabilitation, no crew would have gone there to see the closed signs were down. Anyone getting off trail would be in trouble. Without a canopy and that intense heat wave bouncing off the rock, the temperatures would be unrelenting."

The women looked defeated. "There just seems so much to learn," Felicity said. "If experienced hikers can get into trouble, I don't see how we can learn all this."

"You're trying to go too fast. Right now, stay on the main hiking trails. It's my busiest time right now, but eventually things will slow down. If you've still decided you want to stay, I can show you some of my favorite trails and give you a few tips. Again, there are much more experienced backpackers than me, but if you start out slow and end up really loving it, I'm sure you'll meet others who love it and are willing to help you out as well."

Both women brightened. "That's so generous of you to offer, Shabina. We're also considering learning to boulder since Knightly is so famous for it. Do you climb?"

"Sadly, I could be the worst climber in this café. I do try though. I have friends who are very good climbers. They boulder and trad climb. Stella would be the one to ask if anyone is taking out a group. She could arrange something for you."

Again, the twins exchanged a long look. "We should have thought to ask her," Felicity said. "She seems to know so much about both Knightly and Yosemite."

"She likes to keep her clients happy," Shabina said.

"Shabina, whatever kind of name that is," Bale called out from across the café. "I want to talk to you about this food you served us."

"Are you trying to get the attention of Beanie Baby?" Sean asked in an overloud voice. "She's talking to her lesbo friends. You know she prefers women. Can't take manly men. They scare her."

Raine and Vienna both looked up quickly from their table. A sudden hush fell over the café. Vaughn stepped out from behind the counter. Shabina held up her hand to him and shook her head.

"Are they talking about us?" Felicity asked.

Shabina smiled at her as she stood. "I believe so. You have to ignore the riffraff. All kinds come in and I try my best to be welcoming. We do have security cameras on them, and if they get out of hand, we'll make a complaint to the sheriff. They think if a woman turns them down for a date or any kind of sexual activity, she must be a lesbian. Not that that should matter. By chance, did either of them proposition you? They're so manly their egos can't take rejection."

Although she spoke in a sweet tone, the café was silent enough that the amusement could be heard.

Felicity nodded. "Last year, when they found my sister, her

daughter, and her husband dead, and there was an investigation. We went to the Grill one night, and Bale and his friends wanted to have a night of fun with twins. We thought it was a bit inappropriate when we'd just lost our family members but thought perhaps they weren't aware."

Shabina turned back to face Bale and Sean, all trace of amusement gone from her features. "They knew; they're on the Search and Rescue team. Bale, after that revelation, I don't feel like dealing with your crap this morning. Your waiter can talk to you about your bill, but if you ate the food, you're paying for it."

Bale's features twisted into a malevolent, hate-filled mask. She refused to be intimidated, although a chill went down her spine. Maybe she needed to rethink what Bale was capable of. She turned back to the twins, dismissing him.

"I hope I see you both again very soon."

"We're heading to Yosemite today, but we're taking your bird tour on Tuesday. After we do some more exploring, we plan on looking around Knightly for a few days, so we'll be in every morning for breakfast," Eve assured.

Bale cursed loudly. She heard him stomping as he and Edward left the café. She was a little shocked he hadn't put up more of a fight and that Edward hadn't backed him up. Sean had been the one to aid in the harassment. It bothered her that Bale hadn't said even more than he had. She would have to watch her back. Enemies seemed to be stacking up.

"That was pleasant. I assure you, most people here are wonderful. I really have to make my rounds, but will see you later."

The women gave her a quick assurance they would be back to the café and see her Tuesday for the bird-watching tour. Shabina moved on to the next three tables, talking to the customers to ensure they enjoyed their meal. She made her way to Raine and Vienna.

"You really need to ban Bale and his followers," Raine said bluntly. "His behavior is escalating."

Shabina pulled a chair from one of the tables a server was cleaning and sat down. "If I banned him, he would only get worse. He's that type."

"He is getting worse," Raine insisted.

"Remember how bad he was with Zahra? He was mean and spiteful to her all the time. He never stopped saying nasty things and trying to intimidate her. But she just rode it out, and now he's given up. I'm his current target, but he'll get tired and find someone else."

Vienna shook her head. "That isn't altogether true. Bruce made it plain that Zahra was to be left alone. Sam backed him up. That happened every time Bale got drunk at the Grill and got out of line with her. You haven't let us talk to Sam. He'd put a stop to it."

Shabina sighed and rubbed her temples. She had the beginnings of a headache just thinking about dealing with Bale. "I guess the bottom line is, I've dealt with so much worse, putting up with him seems easy in comparison."

"You shouldn't have to put up with any harassment, Shabina," Vienna insisted. "No one has the right to treat you that way."

"Certainly not in your place of business," Raine agreed. "I can't imagine what Rainier would do if he heard Bale or anyone else talking to you like that."

Shabina's heart felt as if it skipped a beat. She pressed her palm over her chest. "Why would you even think that? Rainier checks on my security. So far, everything has been fine."

"Is that the only thing he checks on?" Raine asked.

Sometimes Raine talked in a code Shabina didn't understand. Maybe the other women did. She'd missed out on having girlfriends growing up, and she didn't always catch the innuendos the other women seemed to find humorous.

"I have no idea what you're talking about," she admitted freely. "If you want to clue me in, now is the time."

"I think Rainier checks up on you quite often because you're very special to him," Raine explained. "In fact, I'm quite certain of it."

Shabina might wish that were the truth, but she knew better. "I'm an obligation. His responsibility, and trust me, Rainier always takes care of his responsibilities."

"Well, trust *me*, if Rainier heard Bale talking to you the way he does, Bale would be in more trouble than he could handle," Raine assured.

Shabina didn't doubt that. Rainier could be a very violent man. She'd seen him explode into action. He was sent out on assignments others would never take. He always got the job done. "I think it's better if no one talks about Bale to Rainier."

Stella was married to Sam Rossi. Vienna was engaged to Zale Vizzini. Both men had worked at the same agency with Rainier. They knew him and were friends with him. It hadn't occurred to her that when she confided in her friends about things that disturbed her, they might tell their men, who in turn might relay those concerns to Rainier.

"I wouldn't want anything I say to you to be repeated to Sam or Zale. It would definitely get back to Rainier." She forced herself to look directly at Vienna. "I'd feel as if I couldn't confide in anyone, and there are times I need to talk things over with friends."

"I doubt that would ever need to happen unless we felt your life was in danger, Shabina," Vienna said. "Then we would have no choice."

That left her with nothing to say. Shabina sighed and looked around her café. The early morning sunlight streaked in through the windows. The murmur of the various conversations peppered

with laughter instantly lightened her mood. She understood why
Eve and Felicity found peace in the Sierra. She certainly had. For
the most part. Unless she allowed her past to creep in. Determined not to allow that to happen, she went about her rounds,
going from booths to tables, talking to her customers, helping to
clear dishes and bringing food out to new customers.

Her café was very popular, and although they officially closed
at two, if customers had waited in line to get in, they weren't
turned away. Vaughn, her manager, and Tyrone and Patsy stayed
late with her to serve the customers and break down the tables
after. She had two other waitresses, newly hired that season, Nellie and Chelsey. Both were cheerful and hard workers. She felt
very lucky to have them. They mostly waited on the outdoor tables.

The nice thing about having so many customers was it forced her
mind to concentrate on the busywork. She didn't have time to dwell
on Bale and why he chose to target her or Zahra. Or if Scorpion was
really stalking her again after all the years that had gone by. Or that
Sean might be teaching young, impressionable minds to be disrespectful, racist and sexist. Instead, she worked hard and laughed
with customers, getting to know them as she made her customary
rounds, answering questions and asking a few of her own.

It helped that she spoke several languages and could put people at ease. She attributed that trait to her time spent with the
women of Salman Ahmad's tribe. They had a warmth about
them and a way of making anyone, even those kidnapped for ransom, feel safe and among friends.

By the time they managed to close the café, it was after three
and nearly four thirty when they finished thoroughly cleaning
tables and the kitchen.

"I wish I could give you time off," Shabina told the three that
always stuck with her. "I can't since we're in the middle of our

biggest season, but I can give you extra bonuses. You deserve them too. I can't tell you how much I appreciate you. I honestly don't know what I'd do without you. If you have suggestions for making things easier, please feel free to share your ideas. And any days you absolutely need, let me know in advance if possible so I can make arrangements to cover your shifts." She really hoped none of them needed time off. They were fast and knew how to handle every emergency that cropped up.

"I love this job," Patsy said. "Greg was able to get a job right away with Carl Montgomery, the local contractor. Greg's a really good carpenter. With both of us having good jobs we were able to rent a nice house."

"You're staying for sure, then?" Tyrone asked.

Patsy gave them a huge smile. "For certain. It's always been our dream to live in the Sierra. We both love to climb. We're passionate about hiking. We just had to find a way to make it happen."

"My parents were born here," Tyrone said. "Both of them were. I grew up on a ranch, hunting and fishing. My brother and I climbed from the time we were about two. Then Dad had a stroke and my mother a heart attack. Both died within two months of each other. Tristan and I were sent to an aunt, our only relative. She lived in a city in Ohio. Didn't want kids and gave us up to foster care. We were lucky in that they kept us together and we landed with some really good people. Still, we were used to being wild and free, not in the city. We couldn't wait to get back here."

"It's a miracle you managed it," Vaughn said.

Tyrone flashed a grin at the others. "Money is always a problem when you want to move. We decided to live out of a van and join the dirt baggers who come to climb the boulders and use the hot springs. We both hoped to score good jobs, save money and find a place we could eventually buy."

"What is your brother doing?" Shabina asked. Tristan had no interest in food other than to eat it. He'd come in several times, and Shabina always fed him. The man could put away food. She didn't mind. When he came in, he did so at the end of the day and asked what she had the most left over. He always offered to pay. She didn't let her employees pay, and she wasn't about to allow Tristan to pay when she knew the brothers were working toward owning their own home.

Most of the leftover dishes were carefully packed and taken to the homeless shelter, where volunteers distributed them along with other donations.

"He has a job making cabinets. Loves it and he's good at it," Tyrone said with pride.

"Good for him," Vaughn said.

"If Chelsey or Nellie ever bring a complaint to any of you, that any of the customers, including Bale and his crew, say anything out of place to them, harass them in any way or touch them inappropriately, let me know right away. That's for certain when we'll ban them from the café," Shabina said. "That same goes for the three of you."

"Bale's homophobic as hell, but so far he's not bothered me much," Tyrone said.

"You'll ban him for harassing us, but not for yourself," Vaughn added. "That's not right, Shabina."

"I'm hoping it doesn't come to that, but it may. Bale and Edward have lived here all their lives. Sean as well. They have extended family here. If I can somehow resolve the situation peacefully, I would prefer to do that."

"I don't understand why they insist on continuing to come back to the café so much. They're here all the time," Patsy said.

"No one serves better food," Tyrone said. "That's the truth."

"I wish they were coming for the food," Shabina replied. "I think Bale needs to humiliate others to make himself feel like a big man. Edward and Sean seem to need the same thing. I haven't made my mind up about Jason. He never seemed to fit in with them. More and more he's pulled away from them, especially since he's been around Bruce."

"I looked at him when Bale was yelling at you," Vaughn said. "He was really unhappy. So was Bruce."

"So were a lot of the customers," Patsy pointed out. "That's the trouble with having those men in here acting that way. We're taking the chance that they drive our good customers away."

"Or worse," Tyrone said. "Some of the men wanted to stand up for you. They didn't like the way he was talking to you. That could lead to fights."

"Bale would like that," Vaughn added. "Breaking up your furniture and dishes. Blaming you if he got punched in your café. He'd probably sue you for every penny you have."

"That would be his style," Patsy agreed.

"You all paint a grim picture of my future," Shabina said. "Unfortunately, you may be right about him. I'm going to give it a lot more thought. All of you, go home and rest. I'll lock up. My pack has been patient. They want their workout. I'm behind schedule."

Vaughn lingered to ensure she was safe as she locked the doors to the café. He walked her to her car before jogging to his.

Her first stop was the agility course that she'd set up for her dogs. They loved working the course, going up ladders, banking off high walls, crawling through tunnels—even the steep swaying bridges didn't slow them down. From there they went into a training area for obedience, where she put all three dogs through various commands from close range and distant, using both verbal and hand signals.

She chose the gun range next. It was important to her to practice every day with a variety of weapons. She was an expert marksman from just about any distance. She wanted to be smoother bringing her pistol up and aiming straight at the target without thinking. Her goal was for the movement to be automatic, a muscle memory. She knew if she ever faced Scorpion or any member of his cabinet again, there was every chance she might freeze. She didn't want to worry that she couldn't pull the trigger. She'd rather be dead than ever allow any of them to get their hands on her again.

Shabina spent a good two hours practicing and then took the dogs running along the canal. It was one of their favorite times of the day. She kept her body in good condition. The running helped keep the dogs in condition as well. It was later than usual, and the sun had already set over the canal, but she still had plenty of light to see, and she knew the path well.

Eerie shadows, cast from the trees lining one side of the water, fell across the narrow trail in macabre ribbons that swayed when the wind blew in short gusts. A sense of unease crept down her spine. Just as her radar system gave her a warning, the dogs swerved into her, circling to shepherd her back in the direction they'd come.

Shabina ran smoothly, not missing a step. The dogs had caught the scent of something they didn't like, but it very well could have been an animal. They hadn't alerted in the way they would have if a threat was immediate. She didn't question the decision of the highly trained dogs. That was why she'd paid the amount of money she had for their training. She was willing to follow their appraisal of a given situation.

She drove straight back to her house. The iron gates opened for her, but she slid out of the car to retrieve a small package that sat on a bench just outside the gates.

Malik bared his teeth and gave her a low warning growl. Shabina instantly reacted, halting, heart pounding, hand sliding down the zipper of her jacket to retrieve her favorite pistol. Keeping the gun concealed against her body, she gave the signal to the three Doberman pinschers to be on guard. They instantly settled into guarding positions.

"Bale," she greeted, grateful for the small things. She'd much rather face him than Scorpion or his accomplices. She noted Bale had come alone. She was certain that was a bad sign. He normally had one or more of his friends with him. If he came alone, he didn't want a witness to whatever he planned on doing or saying. "I didn't expect to see you here this time of night."

"I'll bet you didn't after your little show this morning."

His eyes shifted to the Dobermans, and he cursed aloud. "Do you think you can scare me with your mangy pack of dogs? A bullet can stop them before they get within eight feet of me."

She lifted an eyebrow but refrained from responding. She'd shoot him the moment he pulled out a gun. Were they within hearing of her cameras? They were definitely in recording range for video, and the cameras above the gates were aimed straight at them. She wasn't certain of audio range.

Bale's face twisted again into that same mask of malevolent hatred he'd shown for a brief moment in her café that morning. "Why don't you pack up and leave? This is my town. I was born here. Raised here. We don't want your kind here."

"What exactly is my kind?"

"You know what you are. You stink of foreigners."

"How strange, since I was born right here in the United States. My father was born and raised in Houston. His parents were born and raised there. His family goes back generations. Not that it should matter. Have you looked into your ancestry? Where you came from? Bale, your prejudice makes no sense." She knew she wasn't getting through to him. She could see the anger spreading by the redness creeping under his skin.

"No woman should be talking to me like you do, let alone someone like you. When I say anything to you, you shut the hell up and just listen. You do what I say. If you don't, you may find your little café burnt to the ground with you and your wimp dogs inside it."

"I'm reporting the threats you've just made to the sheriff."

"Go ahead. I've got family in local law enforcement. Who do you think they're going to believe? Me? Or you? You'd better get in line or you're going to find yourself in a world of hurt."

"It won't matter. It will be on record, and if you burn down the café, they'll know who did it, won't they?"

"You'll still be dead."

Shabina shrugged. "We all have to die sometime, Bale."

"You are really in for trouble. I'm going to make your life miserable," he promised.

She didn't reply, just watched him storm away. When she heard the roar of a vehicle start up, she stared down at the package on the bench. Had he put it there to lure her out of the car? Did she dare bring it into her house? What if it was some type of explosive?

She leaned down to sniff it and instantly recoiled. Oud perfume. The scent of Saudi Arabia. The powerful, sensual scent was produced from the aquilaria or agar tree. She stepped back, her hand shaking. There was no forgetting that scent. It could be found everywhere in the marketplaces. Luxury perfumes were made from it, as well as small packets for tourists. She opted to leave it right where it was, but she knew it was going to haunt her all night. The package was more upsetting than Bale, and he was bad enough.

CHAPTER FOUR

News traveled fast in Knightly. The café was buzzing with the latest gossip. Vaughn tried to keep from smirking as he faced Shabina over the counter.

"Sean lost one of his newbies. Mr. Fish and Wildlife big shot lost his protégé on the trail." There was a tiny bit of a taunt in his voice.

"Vaughn, it's a serious situation," Shabina reminded. "I know you don't like Sean, but it isn't about him. Think about that kid lost out there. He's been gone overnight, and no one has found him yet. They've launched a full search for him."

"I know. I do know I shouldn't feel gleeful over Sean looking like a fool, but I can't help it. He's such a jerk all the time," Vaughn admitted. "I'm a bad person, Shabina. I'll admit it. And so far, I haven't said that a night spent in the spooky woods alone might do that Deacon person some good. He needs a few manners taught to him. If he wants to be Fish and Wildlife, surely he has some skills in the forest."

"You would think so, but apparently his skills weren't so good because he did get lost."

"Um, Vaughn." Patsy leaned in close, whispering as she picked up two plates. "You actually are saying that a night in the woods would do Deacon good because he needs to learn a few manners."

Vaughn snorted. "Color me bad. I'm sure they'll find him today, crying for his mommy."

"Let's get to work," Shabina finally managed and turned back to the floor. She had no idea what else to say to that. Vaughn wasn't going to give Deacon or Sean any sympathy.

She made her way to Raine's table. This time Raine was alone. Vienna was head of Search and Rescue. She was the one who had organized a search party for the missing intern and was leading the search party now.

The café had been built with the exact intent to show off the sky's colorful display. In Shabina's eye, the building was a work of art and had captured her dream exactly. Sitting at any booth or table in ninety percent of the café, one could see the vibrant colors spreading across the sky. If a storm came in, those darker purples looked amazing and quite beautiful.

Patsy escorted a group of four men to one of the premier tables near the bank of windows showcasing the rising sun. For a moment, Shabina's heart dropped. Three of the four men wore the traditional garb of men from the Middle East. Her mouth went dry, and her hands went clammy. She forced air through her lungs. They had visitors from different countries all the time, and she didn't have problems with any religious beliefs. What was wrong with her? Stella had already advised her that students were coming from the university. They would be on her bird-watching tour as well.

"I guess I should work too," she told Raine.

She waited until they had gone over the menu before she approached the table. The men were speaking to one another in Arabic. Two had Algerian accents, one sounded as if he might be from Turkey, and the last, she was certain, was from Belgium. That meant nothing. As usual, she asked if they had any questions on the menu. When each answered, she listened carefully to make certain she was correct about their accents and where they might have originated from. Only the man from Belgium had a French accent.

Disregarding her natural inclination to wait until they asked questions, she chatted as if she knew little about their culture, asking if they'd met at the university and had been friends a long time. The answer was important.

Jules Beaumont had met the three others at Sunrise Lake. They'd found they were attending the same university, although none shared the same classes. Emar Salhi and Jamal Talbi were from the same tribe in Algeria and were furthering their education in the hopes of modernizing many of the agricultural techniques to help their people. Deniz Kaplan, from Turkey, had met the two at the university and become friends. He'd decided to take the opportunity to vacation in Yosemite with them. They were pleased that Shabina was going to be their guide for the bird tour on Tuesday. They were looking forward to it.

Shabina couldn't find fault with any of the four. They treated her respectfully. Everything they said made sense. It shouldn't be a red flag that Jules Beaumont hadn't known the others prior to coming to Sunrise Lake Resort and that he spoke fluent Arabic along with French. Shabina spoke Arabic, Italian, and French as well as several other languages.

Many university students vacationed there. Most were climbers or hikers. Some enjoyed fishing. Sunrise Lake was the halfway point between Yosemite and Knightly. Staying there in one of the cabins or the campgrounds with showers and bathroom facilities was a good compromise. Getting permits to camp in the park was becoming difficult, and Knightly didn't have a lot of accommodations.

She waited tables and made her rounds all the while keeping an eye on the four men. None of them seemed to take special interest in her. They didn't sneak out their cell phones and snap pictures of her. They didn't seem to be talking about her, but they lingered longer than most customers did.

The table across from theirs held the five young people who had been hired to rehabilitate the trails in Yosemite. The two women were in their early twenties. Both had dark, straight hair pulled back into ponytails.

"I'm Georgia, and this is my sister, Mandy." The older of the two girls introduced them. "We're from West Virginia and started out hiking the trails in the Appalachian Mountains. It's so incredibly beautiful there. We always wanted to hike Yosemite and saw the job come up and applied immediately."

"Do either of you boulder?" Shabina asked. It was unusual for anyone to come to Knightly and not want to attempt to climb the famous boulders.

The two girls looked at one another and burst out laughing. It was Mandy who answered. "No. I guess we're in the minority. We're avid backpackers. We've already mapped out so many trails we want to hike through Yosemite on our time off."

"At least we won't have to worry about you getting lost like that poor dude who didn't make it back to his group last night," said a blond man.

Shabina recognized him from the year before. She gave him a bright smile. "Pete. It's nice to see you again. You too, Billy." Like the women, they were also in their early twenties. They'd frequented her café the year before so much that she remembered their routine orders for both breakfast and lunch. They were definitely climbers, both boulder and trad climbers. She wasn't surprised that they'd taken jobs at Yosemite again.

Both men beamed at her. "Do you remember everyone?" Billy asked.

"Only my special customers. I try my best to forget the ones that give me trouble." That was strictly the truth. She did try her best. It was impossible, but she gave it her best shot.

"I'm Charlie Gainer." Charlie held out his hand to her. "I lived in New Orleans most of my life." He had an accent. Southern? Cajun? French was spoken in New Orleans.

She shook his hand without hesitation. She'd learned that was one of the many things one did when owning a business. Even so, she found herself leery of him. She had to acknowledge she was becoming more paranoid by the moment when simply meeting new men made her nervous.

"How did you end up here?"

"Got the wander bug and set out to see the United States. Worked my way from park to park and landed here. I went backpacking in Shasta and ran into some people who couldn't say enough about the Sierra. Saw the advertisement for work and hopped on it."

Shabina liked all of them. They were heading up to Yosemite that morning and eager to start work. She liked their enthusiasm. She'd found quite a few of the newer hires for trail rehabilitation were genuinely nice people who cared about the parks and keeping them preserved for future generations.

"Have you checked out the trails in Yosemite yet?"

"Pete and I camped there last week," Billy said.

Mandy laughed. "Georgia and I rented camp space up at Sunrise Lake and drove up to Yosemite to hike the trails daily. We did camp there, but just for the one night. Sunrise Lake spoils you, and I knew we were going to be working hard for the next few weeks, so I wanted to hit the spa."

"Spa?" Charlie nearly spewed his coffee over the table. "There's a spa at Sunrise Lake? I can't believe the two of you were camping in the lap of luxury. I hit the hot springs just outside of Knightly. That's my one luxury."

Mandy lifted one eyebrow. "We can't help it if we already know all the great places to hang out."

Billy nudged Pete. "We used to go to those hot springs after we went bouldering. Now, too many people are there. It isn't quite as nice as it used to be."

"Don't tell me you go up to the Sunrise Lake spa too," Charlie said, disgust in his voice. "I won't believe it."

"No dirt under my fingernails." Billy held out his hand.

Shabina couldn't help laughing. She noticed Billy hadn't claimed he went to the spa. He just couldn't help taunting Charlie.

"I hope you enjoy your food. Patsy is your waitress. Please let her know if you need anything at all, and thank you for coming in."

Shabina moved on to the next table. The four men from the university were still at their table. She noted the two men from Algeria were drinking mint tea. The one from Turkey had ordered an Arabic coffee. The man, Jules Beaumont, from Belgium had ordered her *qahwa*, a roasted coffee ground with cardamom and flavored with saffron. He'd also ordered her specialty *ma'amoul*, cookies stuffed with nuts and dates, and seemed to be enjoying them.

The cookies and coffee were nostalgic to her. She didn't make them often, and when she did have them, they sold out fast, but they were always a bridge between her lost, massacred family in Saudi Arabia and the present. It had been Mama Ahmad who had taught her how to bake and cook.

She quickly looked away before she drew Beaumont's attention and engaged the people at the table she'd stopped beside in conversation. It took another hour to make her way to Raine's table.

"Mind if I sit down for a minute?" Shabina asked. "It looks as if you're working, so feel free to say no." A part of her hoped Raine would say she was too busy. The more upset she got, the more likely someone would tell Sam. He was such a part of their group, he was almost considered one of the girls. Raine was extremely perceptive. She didn't miss details, not even small ones. Shabina knew she wasn't going to get much past Raine.

"Shabina, I always want to visit with you. Why do you think I stayed so long?" Raine flashed a little smile. "That and your apricot scones. They're so good. I could eat a dozen of them. I might have already." She closed her laptop. "Why aren't you sleeping? I thought we put your fears to rest for a little while, long enough for me to work on facial recognition."

"I felt better after all of us talked," Shabina confirmed. "I really did. A couple of things have happened since then." She hesitated, dropping her hand below the table to rub at her left thigh. She would have to learn to break that particular very bad habit. It seemed the moment she got rid of one, a new, much worse behavior took its place.

Raine leaned toward her. "Tell me."

"There was a small package on the bench beside my gate, where packages sometimes are left. I exited my car. The dogs always come with me and they alerted instantly. Bale confronted me. The cameras were recording; we were right in front of them. I haven't checked to see if audio was on. I thought it better if I had you do that. I'm okay at handling them but not the best. I want to make sure that we have the best recordings. He threatened to burn down the café with the dogs and me inside. He told me he intended to make my life a living hell, and this time I believed him. He really hates me, Raine."

"Were you afraid for your life?"

"I think if the dogs hadn't been there, he would have attacked me. I had my gun and would have shot him. He was armed. There was no doubt that he was. Had he pulled his weapon, I would have shot him. He left, but I know he's planning something big to exact his revenge for what he considers me humiliating him."

"I can get the security video and audio, no problem. I've been collecting proof of his harassment from the feed here at the café. I have permission from Alek Donovan at the Grill to collect the feed there as well."

"Does Lawyer know you're doing it?" Lawyer Collins had been the person to install Shabina's security cameras in the café. Not at her home, but he'd installed most of the security networks in town. He'd been born and raised in Knightly, which meant he'd known Bale Landry since they were boys. Lawyer sold laptops, cell phones and computers out of his store as well as repaired them. He was brilliant when it came to technology. He was always open and friendly. He often came into the café to eat and recommended it to everyone. Shabina liked him, but she didn't altogether trust him. But then she didn't trust many people. Lately, that trait in her had worsened, she feared, growing straight into paranoia.

"You aren't telling me everything." Raine made it a statement.

"I know. I'm thinking what to say about the package. I just left it sitting outside my gate there on the bench. I really did think Bale put it there to get me to stop when the gates were open, but now I don't."

Raine, being Raine, just waited. Shabina pressed her fingertips into the aching muscle of her thigh. She could count her heartbeats there.

"In Saudi Arabia, oud is a perfume created from the aquilaria tree. It's considered a luxury perfume, and many of the top brands are extremely expensive. You can go into most marketplaces, and you'll smell oud everywhere. Small packets of oud perfume and chips are sold as souvenirs to tourists. The scent of oud is said to strengthen the body and mind, so it's used often for aromatherapy."

Raine's intense blue eyes moved over her face, missing nothing. Shabina was certain that her friend could see she hadn't slept at all. It hadn't been Bale's threat of burning down the café, although it should have been; it was the idea that Scorpion had sent his agents to kidnap her. She was certain he wouldn't just kill her outright. He would try to put her in the worst state of fear possible. He was a true sadist and took great pleasure in watching others suffer. He would want to see her slowly losing all confidence—just as she was—before he had her taken.

"When I smelled the package, I identified the oud fragrance immediately. I left the package on the bench. I didn't know what to think. Bale has no way of knowing what that scent would trigger in me. At least, I don't think he does. And what if it's something else? A bomb? Just the outside packaging might have been tainted with the scent. It wasn't heavy. It was subtle. Faint. But it was definitely oud. There was no mistaking it."

"I'm sure after all the time you spent in Saudi Arabia, you would recognize such a familiar scent, faint or not. There's no doubt the package had that perfume on it. It will be easy enough for one of my guys to pick it up. We can scan it, see what's inside, and if it's harmless, return it to you."

"Will you have to report it to anyone before we know?"

"Meaning Rainier? He oversees your security."

"I feel like I have to be certain something is really threatening me before I involve him."

"That isn't the way he feels."

A shadow fell across the table, and both women looked up. Zahra, as always, looked sophisticated dressed in her professional clothes, her hair windblown and her wide smile giving her a slightly seductive look. "I'm *dying* of starvation. I called in my order for your famous zucchini sticks and then added a hundred other items. Now I'm going to be late for my meeting. Sheesh."

Shabina couldn't help laughing. Zahra was always hungry, ate an impressive amount of food but didn't seem to gain weight. She wasn't in the same category as Raine, who could put away food impressively, but Zahra was no slouch.

"Do you need me to speed your order up?"

"No, they've got it under control. I just wanted to make sure you got the package I left you. I put it on the bench by your gate last night. I was going to text you, but I forgot. I found your bracelet. You left it at my house, so I wrapped it up and put it in a little box, but you weren't home and I was in a hurry. Then I got worried because it was outside the gate."

Shabina nearly slumped over the table in relief. "You left that package? It didn't have a label on it, and I couldn't tell who it was from. I didn't open it."

"Oh no." Zahra put her hand briefly on Shabina's shoulder. "Did I scare you? I should have texted you right away, but I got distracted playing with Misty and forgot everything."

"No, everything is fine," Shabina lied to reassure her friend. "Vaughn is waving like mad. I think your order is ready. We can't have you fainting on the floor for lack of food."

Zahra laughed. "I doubt it would happen. I used to want to

faint like a heroine in a movie, but I never could manage it." She waved cheerfully and rushed over to the counter, gathering up several carryout bags.

"She's like a little tornado," Shabina said.

"She is," Raine agreed.

"I'm so relieved she came in when she did. You don't have to go to all the trouble of anyone looking at the package." Shabina was very grateful there was no chance Rainier would be informed.

"I'm glad Zahra had an explanation for the box, Shabina," Raine said. "But what about the fragrance on the outside of the packaging? Someone else had to have tampered with the wrapping. I don't want you to dismiss this incident so lightly."

"I could have been mistaken." But Shabina knew she wasn't. She snuck a quick look at the four men from the university sitting at the table near the windows. They didn't appear to be paying the least bit of attention to her. Neither was Charlie Gainer. He was laughing and joking with his friends, his accent very heavy.

"It's easy enough to check through the feed to see who else went near that parcel. They didn't have a big window of opportunity between the time Zahra dropped the package after her work and when you arrived home. Bale was already there. If he didn't do it, someone had to have done it just before he arrived."

"Raine, is there a way to tell if someone else can tap into my security cameras? Could someone be watching me through my own cameras?"

Raine glanced around the café. "Here? With Lawyer's system? I do it, so any really good hacker could. Your home is covered by an entirely different system, Shabina, so it isn't likely. I'm not saying it would be impossible. Nothing is ever impossible, at least not in the tech world. There's always something more to learn. There's always someone better."

That didn't answer the question. In fact, Raine made the idea sound entirely possible. Shabina sank back in the chair. Suddenly, after the elation of finding out Zahra had been the one to give her the small package, she felt a dark shadow creeping back in.

"Why don't I drop by tonight after you get off work, Shabina?" Raine offered. "We can talk things out. Daisy can run in the gardens with your boys and get more exercise that way. I'll be grateful. Even with Zahra taking her out, little Misty can't possibly keep up with the running Daisy needs."

Shabina knew that was true. Jack Russell terriers had all kinds of energy. Raine had always taken Daisy backpacking for miles. They ran together. The dog was used to a tremendous amount of exercise. With Raine unable to take her, the little Jack Russell had to be getting restless, even agitated.

"I'd like that, thank you, Raine."

Shabina pushed up from the table and went back to ensuring her customers had a good experience at her café.

RAINE BROUGHT THE news that Deacon Mulberry's body had been found on an overgrown trail that hadn't been used in years. Clearly, the killer had taken time with him after the brutal murder. It appeared as if he'd been ambushed, his skull smashed in with a rock—or rocks. A ritual of some sort had been performed. The sheriff had no idea what kind of ritual it was supposed to be. There were feathers, candles, sticks, stones, flowers and gourds filled with water, all on a flat rock altar. The area around the body had been cleared of vegetation, scraped away by small branches that had been left behind at the scene. The cleared area was extremely small, no more than a few inches surrounding the body.

Deacon was fully clothed, but his face was unrecognizable due to the repeated smashing from the rocks. The two good-sized rocks used to bludgeon him to death were left behind. His body had been covered with insects, but they were lucky in that no predator had found him.

"That doesn't sound good," Shabina ventured. "If whoever murdered him performed some kind of ritual, they very well could repeat it. I don't know all that much about this kind of thing. Stella is the one to talk to about serial killers, but I don't like the sound of a ritual."

Scorpion had never used any kind of ritual before he killed. His idol was Vlad the Impaler, and he wanted the same kind of fame. One kill wasn't his style. But still . . .

"I put various beliefs in the computer to search for similar rituals, and nothing came up with an exact match," Raine said. "The computer is still searching, but it isn't a voodoo ceremony or satanic or any other that might involve a blood sacrifice. Naturally, they don't want to release details to the public. The problem is they had so many on Search and Rescue that enough people saw the body and talked about what they saw in spite of being told not to."

"The sheriff will call in the FBI, won't he?"

"That would be standard. And they'll warn park visitors to stay alert and in pairs. You have to be careful, Shabina. You go out on your own often."

"I have the dogs with me, and I'm always armed." She sounded confident because she was. She knew the trails, and she knew her dogs. They would alert the moment anyone came close to her. She didn't get lost or turned around. No one could sneak up on her and bash her over the head.

Shabina did worry about the various tourists that had come into her café. They had all been eager to go backpacking and exploring in Yosemite. It wasn't that many months earlier that a serial killer had been stalking victims in the Sierra, people she knew. Friends. It had been an extremely troubling time for her and her friends, particularly Stella and Vienna. The serial killer had turned out to be someone they knew and had targeted both women.

"I still think it would be a good idea for you to stay off the trails until the murderer is caught," Raine suggested.

Shabina made a face. "When I'm alone in the forest with just the birds, I find peace there I can't find anywhere else. I wish I could explain it to you. I have an affinity with them. It isn't just that I can sing their notes or identify them by their feathers or the sounds they make."

She hesitated again, afraid of sounding crazy. If anyone would believe her and understand, it was Raine. "Sometimes I can fly with them. I don't know how I can connect with them, but I do. Maybe it's all in my imagination, but they seem to be able to take me with them into the trees, where I can look through their eyes down onto the floor of the forest. Or we soar in the sky, and I can see for miles. It's true freedom when I never feel free."

Raine rubbed at the bridge of her nose for a moment. "I can see why you would want to continue going out when you have that. Who wouldn't?"

"You, more than anyone else, know what I've been through. You at least saw the photographs, but there's no real way for you to experience what it was like to live in the kind of terror Scorpion subjected me to on a daily basis. Seeing him torture and kill men, women and children. Not just him but his demented cabinet and the mercenaries he surrounded himself with. He took such delight in what he did and more delight in forcing me to witness his sadistic depravity."

A shudder went through her body. She wrapped her arms

around her middle and found herself rocking back and forth in an effort to self-soothe. "I do my best to lead a normal life. I *want* to be normal. I want to have my dream café and friends I care about. I know all of you love me. I do know that. I love all of you. But the truth is, I feel alone every minute of the day. There's no way for anyone to understand me. I can hardly understand me or my reactions to things on any given day. How would any of you be able to? When you ask me if I've called my therapist because I'm getting nightmares or flashbacks? Of course I have. Am I implementing the tools I've learned to counteract the PTSD negativity? Yes. The answer would be yes. I've done every single thing I'm supposed to do."

Raine's blue eyes filled with compassion. "Honey, you do realize there is no possible way for you to lead what you think is a normal life. Not after the things that happened to you. You suffered severe trauma. And no, none of us can understand what you went through. We do love you, and we'd do anything to help you, but we don't know what to do. We say and do things that must sound ludicrous to you because we have no way of knowing what to say that would help."

Shabina tried to force air through her lungs. "I'm so terrified Scorpion has found a way to watch me and he's tormenting me. He has money. So much, Raine. You know he does. He seems to travel the world at will. Even if he isn't a pilot, and I don't think he is, he's most likely got a private jet. For all I know he has his own satellite and that helps him plan his kills. He's probably known where I am for the last couple of years. As far as I know, I'm the only survivor of those he's targeted. Do you really think he's going to let that go? He knows I can identify him if I ever see or hear him again."

"It's more than probable that if he's keeping an eye out for you, he knows where you are," Raine admitted. "I'm not going to lie to you about that."

"I never feel safe. Never. Not unless Rainier is with me." Shabina sighed. "I *detest* that I put that on him. He doesn't need me to cling to him like a little child, but honestly, that's what I want to do. I want him with me all the time. Never out of my sight. Please don't ever tell anyone I admitted that. It makes me feel so weak when I swear to you, I've worked hard to be strong."

"I know you *are* strong, Shabina. You're in crisis right now. We'll sort out what's happening."

"I know I'm already asking so much of you to look at the security and see who might have tampered with Zahra's package by spraying oud on it. But if there is a way to find someone spying on me through my own security or any other way, without putting yourself in jeopardy, I'd really appreciate your doing that too."

"You know that's the kind of thing I do. It isn't a problem." Raine had her laptop out and was already typing away.

Shabina found it fascinating how fast Raine's fingers could fly across a keyboard. Not wanting to disturb her, Shabina wandered over to the bank of windows to watch the dogs as they zoomed madly around the huge gardens. Daisy was in her element. Much smaller than the Dobermans, she could cut through areas they had been taught to maneuver around. She noted that her guard dogs took turns playing, with one always on patrol. She found the fact that the animals had their own hierarchy, in terms of leadership after her, captivating. The dogs were very intelligent, and it showed in every aspect of their interaction.

"Come look at this, Shabina," Raine urged. "There is someone coming up to the gate. They were there when Zahra drove up. They watched her jump out of her car and leave the package on

the bench. You can barely make them out. See, right there."
Raine indicated a darker shade of gray in the gray shadows of a
giant hydrangea bush to the right of the gate.

The figure was stooped down or he would have been taller
than the bush, and that bush was tall and widespread. The hydrangea was very healthy.

"Definitely a man," Raine murmured. "Look at his shoes."

Shabina tried to make him out. The figure looked ghostly, his
clothing blending into the shadows and the plants. His shoes,
when she stared, appeared to be loafers with pointed toes. A
man's shoe. Zahra's car came into sight. She drove up to the gate,
opened the driver's side door and leapt out, placed the package on
the bench and jumped back into her car to drive away in her usual
whirlwind of speed. That was Zahra, either all blazing energy or
pure laziness.

The man in the shadows waited a few moments before emerging.

"He's aware of the camera," Raine murmured. "He's made no
attempt to stop it recording, but he's making certain he can't be
identified. Notice the way he's angled his body and head." She
studied the screen. "He's put his body between the package and
the camera so we can't see what he's doing, but there isn't a doubt
that this is the man who put the scent on the outside of the parcel, not Bale."

Fear had a taste to it. Shabina knew it all too well. She'd spent
months with that taste in her mouth. Now her mouth was so dry
she couldn't speak at first when she tried to form words. Her gaze
was glued to the screen, desperately trying to identify who had
been sent to torment her.

"Shabina." Raine's voice was gentle. "I know this must be
frightening, but the truth is many people know about your past.

They know your mother is from Saudi Arabia. Just because it wasn't Bale who did this, doesn't mean Scorpion sent someone. The worst thing you can do is jump to conclusions."

She knew Raine made sense. If she panicked, her brain would shut down and she wouldn't be able to think. Scorpion would win whether it was him or not.

"You're right," she conceded. Still, that didn't calm her pounding heart or stop the coppery taste of fear from choking her.

"I can't run him through facial recognition because there isn't enough of him to run."

That implied he was a professional. Shabina tried to superimpose the men from her past, Scorpion's cabinet members over that blurry figure. They didn't seem to fit. He had seven friends he took with him to every massacre no matter where in the world. She did her best to attempt to fit those images over the man on the screen even though she only saw them with masks. One or two might fit.

She groaned and covered her face with her hands. She was going to make herself crazy. Would Scorpion go so far as to kill someone in a fake ritualistic manner and leave them on a trail in Yosemite? There were a few very rare birds nesting that were kept from the public. Shabina had identified the birds and sent in the locations to be documented. Had Scorpion hoped she'd be the one who would discover the body? It would be something his devious mind would conjure up.

Shabina groaned. The idea that she would be responsible in any way for more deaths was abhorrent. Scorpion reveled in telling her how she was the one who held the sole responsibility for every member of Salman Ahmad's tribe being massacred. Intellectually, she might know it wasn't so, but that teenage girl who had been forced to stay awake, been beaten, raped, and told repeatedly that she was the cause of those deaths—deep down, she believed.

"Shabina, what is it?"

She raised stricken eyes to Raine's. "It's possible that Scorpion is the one behind Deacon's murder. He might have left the body for me to find on that trail. Few people hike those obscure trails, but I do when I'm documenting rare birds nesting. If he's been watching me, he might know that."

Raine sat back in the very comfortable cuddle chair and regarded Shabina steadily. As much as Shabina wanted Raine to deny that her wild thoughts could possibly be true, she knew Raine would give the idea serious consideration. She had an analytical brain.

"We can't discount that possibility, Shabina, but it's slim."

"Do you know where he is? Where his friends could be? Could you find their locations?"

Raine sighed. "Shabina, you know you're getting into very sensitive, highly classified matters I can't possibly discuss. No one knows who they really are."

"But this is about me. You know it is. The only reason Blom began looking for them in the first place was because of me. They know Scorpion is watching me, don't they? They know he's going to come for me sooner or later, and that's why Rainier is always checking on me."

Raine sighed again.

"If you know where any of them are, I need to know."

CHAPTER FIVE

Raine regarded Shabina for a long time in silence. Eventually, she heaved a sigh. "Do you have any idea what you're asking?"

Shabina nodded. "I'm sorry, Raine. I wouldn't ask if it weren't important."

"Have you been threatened? Tell me the truth, Shabina. Have you received an actual threat from anyone other than Bale?"

Shabina shoved her hand through the thick dark hair at the top of her scalp. "It's just that I *feel* threatened. I can't sleep. I know you're going to talk to me again about PTSD. I've heard it all. I told you that I talked to my therapist. I've taken all the precautions. I've done everything but turn myself over to a hospital. I might be losing my mind for real, but then again, what if I'm right? What if Scorpion is stalking me right this minute? What if he is looking through my own security cameras? What if that man you just saw coming out of my hydrangea bush is one of his men?"

"Why haven't you contacted Rainier?"

Shabina twisted her fingers together in her lap, out of sight. "Our relationship is complicated. I don't want to go running to him and look like I've lost my mind when it's only smoke and mirrors. I've messed up his life enough."

"I don't think you messed up his life. Rainier goes his own way. No one controls him, Shabina. No matter how much they'd like to, no one has found a way."

"I'm asking you to tell me if you know who or where these men are. If they're nowhere around here, I'll know I'm being paranoid."

She wouldn't tell Raine that Scorpion had money enough to hire someone to harass and kidnap her if he wanted to at any time; Raine already knew. Raine probably knew more about the man than she did.

Reluctantly, Raine raised the lid of her laptop. "This could get me in trouble."

"I don't want you in trouble. I would never want that, and you know I'd never put you in this position if I didn't need this information. I feel as if I'm going insane, Raine." She couldn't think clearly anymore. She needed sleep desperately.

"It isn't like you can do anything with the information," Raine said. "But you can't share, not even with the others. These men are all on a wanted list, and although our government, along with many others and Interpol, have done their best to find out his identity and that of his companions, we weren't the ones to do so."

"You're saying Scorpion is on a secret hit list," she interpreted. Maybe that was wishful thinking. She knew that Elliot Blom ran a special division in the CIA. His agents were very well educated. Each of them had been an officer and trained in special ops. They were highly motivated, spoke several languages, and could operate easily alone in any environment. Some called them ghosts. Few people ever saw them, but they got the job done, taking out terrorist cells, the heads of drug cartels, in a hot zone, opening a way for a unit of soldiers pinned down to escape. They recruited agents and then brought those agents to safety if their cover was blown. They were also the men sent after killers like Scorpion.

Raine brought up a file and opened it. "We found these two kills only because an assassin known as Deadly Storms tracked them down. He's notorious in the Middle East. Several countries hire him to get rid of men like Scorpion.

"I don't have his identity for certain, but these two kills, which have been kept under wraps, pointed toward a diplomat from Canada. He travels with his own people when he goes to another country. I'm telling you this in strict confidence, Shabina. We don't know for certain who he is. He's under suspicion, but the fact that he's a diplomat for a foreign country makes it very difficult. We have to have irrefutable evidence that this man is the serial killer."

"He's a mass murderer," Shabina whispered.

"The two men, Cole Caron and Saul Charpentier, were Canadian and they worked for a diplomat named Darian Lefebre." Raine began to close her file.

"Wait." Shabina stopped her. "Everyone knows the ambassador Darian Lefebre. I can't imagine that he would be involved. I need to know how the men who worked for him died. Why they would be linked to Scorpion?"

Raine sighed again. "Is that necessary? They're dead, Shabina. They can't get to you."

Shabina lifted her chin. "How did they die, Raine? How do you know this Deadly Storms killed them?"

"What I'm telling you is classified. Very, very classified. This assassin was named Deadly Storms because he comes out of the sand and takes the intended target right under the noses of an entire camp. No one ever hears or sees him. He's a ghost. He vanishes, and so does his target. He found both men and he took them."

Her heart jumped. Skipped a beat. An assassin who came out

of the sand and took targets out right under the noses of an entire camp. A ghost. No one hears him. No one sees him. She knew someone like that. She kept her face averted from Raine just in case she gave herself away, but her fingers dug hard into her thigh.

"Is he one of ours?"

Raine didn't respond, just shrugged. When Shabina remained silent, looking at her, she sighed. "They know Deadly Storms is an assassin for hire in the Middle East."

That definitely didn't rule out Rainier.

"How did he kill them?"

"You don't want to know. He doesn't always kill cleanly. In this case, both men were tortured. They bore identical marks on them."

Shabina frowned. Considering. "How do you know the same man killed them?"

"He left behind his signature tattoo just above their left wrists. The tattoo signifies Deadly Storms. It isn't a tattoo as if he spent time with a needle tattooing them. He burned the tattoo into their arms like a brand."

Her heart leapt. More and more she was certain the assassin was Rainier. She resisted rubbing the tattoo on her left arm, scant inches above her wrist—the one she never allowed anyone to see. When she swam, she wore a swim shirt over her bathing suit to ensure scars and the tattoo of a scorpion were covered and she wouldn't get questions.

If Raine had the photographs of the dead terrorists, she very well could have the photographs of sixteen-year-old Shabina Foster, scars, tattoos and all.

"Do you have photographs?"

"I'm not showing them to you. I will say this: if you were to take transparent paper with a map of the wounds on your body, including every violation done to you from head to toe, and place it over their bodies, there would be an exact match. Is that what you want to know?"

"Yes." She wrapped her arms around her middle and held on tight.

"Rainier." She whispered his name to herself. Her anchor. The one person who kept her safe. He had come when there was no hope. He'd been like the desert storms, sand whirling like tornados, rising out of nowhere and passing fast, leaving devastation in their wake.

He'd hunted down two of the men who had tortured her. Two of the men who had massacred an entire tribe. She knew him and his ruthless, single-minded purpose. He wouldn't stop until he found each of the men threatening her.

"You know the identity of Deadly Storms, don't you?" Raine asked, her voice gentle.

Of course Raine would know. The way he'd killed the two men was a dead giveaway. Blom might not put two and two together. He probably didn't want to know, but Raine knew.

"You can never tell anyone, Shabina," Raine cautioned. "Not ever. Take that to your grave."

"I took his life away from him," she confessed. "I didn't mean to, but it happened. I took everything from him."

"You didn't, Shabina. You take on the world. Scorpion did that to you. He made you think you were guilty, responsible for everything he did. Rainier makes his choices, he always has. No one runs him. No one. That man can't be controlled by anyone."

Raine didn't know the entire story. Shabina nodded her head because what else could she do? Raine had just gone against her code to help, showing her classified files. That went above and beyond friendship.

"Thank you, Raine. I really appreciate what you're doing for me."

"Just because those two men were Canadian doesn't mean Lefebre is involved," Raine cautioned. "The men traveled extensively and were often in countries setting up for Lefebre's arrival weeks before he arrived."

A shiver went through her body. She wasn't much closer to knowing Scorpion's true identity.

"Just get some sleep, Shabina. You aren't going to be able to function if you don't sleep. I'll work on identities and also to find out if anyone has infiltrated your security feed. I don't think it's possible without alerting us, but I'm not taking chances. Sleep."

Shabina watched Daisy leaping into the car and going into her crate before the lights faded as Raine drove down the drive and out the gates, once more leaving her alone. She paced long into the night and finally fell into a fitful sleep.

Shabina woke choking back a cry. One didn't ever make a sound and draw the attention of the guards, or worse, Scorpion or his cruel cabinet members strutting around camp shoving others out of their way and spewing orders right and left. Most of those Scorpion took on his raids were men like him, sadistic and cruel, but not all of them. Still, even those raiding with him were afraid of Scorpion and his cabinet.

She rolled off the bed, heart pounding. Sitting on the floor, pressing herself against the wall, drawing up her knees, she made herself as small as possible. The dogs pressed close to her on either side. Malik made the rounds, both at the bedroom windows and then throughout the rest of the house. When he was finished, Sharif took over patrolling and then Morza. They traded all night. She didn't move until the alarm went off to tell her it was time to go to the café to bake the day's pastries.

THE MAIN TOPIC of conversation in the café was the murder. She couldn't blame the locals or the tourists for their curiosity.

"I feel terrible," Vaughn greeted. "I was pretty flippant the other day after he went missing. This should teach me to keep my mouth shut."

He looked so glum Shabina couldn't help but try to cheer him up. "You didn't mean anything, Vaughn. You certainly had no idea he was dead."

"I know, but I shouldn't have said anything at all."

"He hadn't been very nice. Sean had encouraged him to act like a hostile, belligerent jerk, and you were just defending me. You can't get down on yourself. Let's just try to keep our customers happy. We don't want them thinking they're going to get murdered if they go to Yosemite."

Patsy picked up two plates. "But they might. Who knows? I heard maybe there's a coven of satanic worshipers or something making human sacrifices."

Shabina was horrified. "I hope you aren't repeating that. Who in the world told you that? Because it wasn't the sheriff."

Patsy looked slightly ashamed, but a small grin hovered. "No, Nellie did. She's very gullible. Sonny Leven, you know, one of Stella's security guards up at Sunrise, was in this morning teasing her. I think he has a crush on her."

"Great. That's all we need. That Sonny has more tales than anyone I know," Shabina said. "He'll feed her all kinds of nonsense."

Vaughn scowled. "He'd better not lead her on. Nellie's pretty innocent, and he's older than she is."

Shabina winced. Rainier was older than she was by more than ten years. She knew her parents would object just on the age difference—let alone the work he did for Blom. Rainier couldn't see her as anything but a child. Part of that was her fault. Every time he came around it was because she was falling apart.

"There isn't anything wrong with an age difference, Vaughn," she countered. "And Sonny isn't that much older than Nellie. He's a good man. He's local, born right here in Knightly. He had a full scholarship to attend Davis, from what Stella told me, but his father had a stroke and couldn't work. He stayed home and supported the family."

"He flirts a lot," Vaughn pointed out.

"You think everyone flirts," Patsy said.

"They do. The entire world revolves around flirting."

Shabina shook her head and picked up the next order to carry it out to her customers. Business, as always, was brisk. She found the murmur of conversation and low laughter comforting. She loved the way the blend of locals and tourists came together, the locals often giving the tourists advice on where to shop for the best gear, or where the easiest boulders were if they were new to bouldering. Sometimes they asked Shabina where they could go to find really great coffee after her café was closed. Or where to go for nightlife.

It felt good to be able to turn conversations away from the murder and put the focus back on everyone having a positive time. Her crew delivered meals and drinks with smooth efficiency, busing tables and serving new customers, so the lines outside that always gave her a bit of anxiety lessened quickly. She knew she should be grateful that customers were willing to wait for openings, and she was, it was just that she wanted everyone to feel welcome. She didn't take reservations. It was always first come, first served. She found that was the best way to get the most people served.

Stella and Raine came in just before closing and indicated they preferred to sit at one of the tables in the back that seated four. Shabina quickly cleared one for them. Vaughn shouted the phone was for her and it was urgent.

Paul Rafferty was the local sheriff. After closing, he wanted to bring two FBI agents to the café to meet with her to identify the feathers found at the crime scene. Rafferty hoped she would agree to aid the FBI in the capacity of the local ornithologist. There were petals from flowers there as well. Rafferty knew she was considered an expert in the local flora and fauna and hoped she might aid them with identifying the flowers that were used in the ritual. Stones had been on the altar. Shabina frequented obscure trails few others, even park rangers, hiked, and Rafferty hoped she might have seen these stones before.

Shabina seated herself at the table with Stella and Raine. "That was Paul Rafferty, the local sheriff, on the phone. He told me he was bringing two members of the FBI with him to ask me to identify feathers and flowers for them. They also have rocks, but I did tell them that isn't my strong suit."

She studied her friend's face. "Why don't either of you look surprised?"

"I knew Rafferty was going to ask you," Raine admitted. "You are the acknowledged expert here in the field. It wasn't much of a leap that they'd come to you. I've asked one of our lawyers to join us, just to be on the safe side."

Raine indicated the man in a gray suit coming toward them. "This is Raymond Decker. He's an attorney. If he tells you not to answer anything, don't."

Shabina frowned. "What's going on? Why should I be worried about being questioned? I thought this was just about me classifying feathers and flowers for them."

"I'm aware," Raine said. "We're just taking precautions. I always prefer to keep everything aboveboard. We'll identify Mr. Decker as a lawyer immediately. If they read you your rights, that changes everything and you don't say a word. Not one single word."

Shabina shook Decker's hand and politely thanked him for coming. She still didn't understand. She glanced at Stella. How in the world was Raine aware that Rafferty would call her to ask her to identify plants, bird feathers and possibly rocks?

"Are you two going to stay here with me?" Now she was nervous to talk to the sheriff when she hadn't expected to be. Identifying feathers and waiting to be accused of having something to do with murder were two different things.

"Of course," Stella said. "I'm not about to leave you alone."

"I don't see how they could possibly think I had anything to do with Deacon's death, Raine. I work in the café and everyone saw me here. Deacon was in Yosemite. It isn't like I could have jogged up there and back in a few minutes." Shabina was stuck on the idea of needing an attorney present.

"It's just a precaution," Raine assured. "I'm that person. Always covering every base. I've seen so many interrogations, honey. They start out nice and easy, friendly, asking questions that seem benign, and then the questions veer in a completely different direction. I don't want that to happen. You've been through enough. I don't want you to be uncomfortable when you don't have to be."

Stella nodded. "We're just looking out for you."

"I'm grateful that you're here." Shabina forced herself to look directly at the attorney. She had no idea where he came from, but his rigid posture and short haircut told her he was either CIA or from one of the branches of military Raine did contract work for—if that was what she did. Shabina was never certain.

Decker's nod was friendly enough, but his gaze was on the café's door as Paul Rafferty entered along with two men dressed in tailored blue suits. The sheriff brought them straight to the table.

"Shabina Foster, Special Agents Len Jenkins and Rob Howard," Rafferty introduced the two men.

Both men showed her a badge and then looked expectantly at the others at the table. Raine introduced Stella, Decker and then herself to the agents. Both raised an eyebrow when they were told Decker was an attorney.

Shabina waved them to chairs. "What can I do for you?"

"We would like to record this conversation," Jenkins said, once the three men were seated. He placed a recorder between them. "If you would state your name, date of birth and where you were born, please."

Decker stirred but didn't disapprove.

Next, they wanted to establish her credentials. From which university had she received her degrees that made her an acknowledged expert in ornithology as well as biology in the area. She answered easily, and Decker offered no objections. She had received her bachelor's and master's from the University of California, Davis, in wildlife biology and avian sciences.

Shabina kept her hands folded in her lap. She'd learned discipline from being a prisoner for a year and a half. Even more from trying to hide the results of that trauma from her parents. She managed to appear calm and composed as the three men from law enforcement faced her.

It was Rafferty who produced three transparent bags and laid them in front of her. Each contained two bloodstained feathers.

"May I?" Shabina's hand hovered over the bag closest to her.

Again, it was Rafferty who nodded. The two agents watched

her intently. Shabina lifted the bag and turned it one way and then the other, back and forth, studying the feathers. Then she took the second bag and held it up to the light. The feathers were a reddish-pinkish brown. One had faint blue markings along the very edge, while the other three had black dots scattered across them.

Her heart accelerated, but she kept her breathing even. She had a great deal of practice looking composed when she really was terrified.

"These come from two different species of birds. They appear to be from the same species if you just take into account their coloring, but the feathers with the black spots are from a bird called a mourning dove. They're native to California. That bird appears to have been killed sometime after the other one. You can see the drops of blood are much fresher."

"And the fourth feather?" Jenkins prompted.

"That one makes no sense. I believe the last feather is one from the laughing dove. See the blue markings just on the edge there? The color is different as well. More of a pinkish cast. The laughing dove isn't native to California. It's found in Saudi Arabia, which is why this doesn't make any sense. This bird has been dead for some time. You can see the color of the blood is far different. It's possible I'm wrong about this—I can't be certain without studying it under a microscope—but I don't think I am."

She placed both bags carefully on the table in front of Rafferty and sat back in her chair, once more folding her hands in her lap. She didn't dare look at Raine or Stella. Her mind began to race with possibilities. She couldn't slow it down or push down her panic.

What if the FBI searched her home and found the feathers she'd kept as proof she wasn't losing her mind? What if the feathers were no longer there? Someone could have broken in and stolen them while she was gone. That feather could very well be one of the ones she placed in the baggie in a drawer in her house.

"A bird from Saudi Arabia?" Rob Howard murmured softly. "Isn't your mother from Saudi Arabia?"

"You were kidnapped and held in Saudi Arabia for nearly two years," Len Jenkins added. "Is that where you encountered this laughing dove?"

"That isn't pertinent to her credentials as an expert, and she isn't going to answer anything that doesn't pertain to what you need to identify your items," Decker said before Shabina could answer. "And if you bring up my client's past trauma, this meeting will be terminated immediately."

She glanced at the attorney, still afraid to look at Raine. Her mouth went dry as Rafferty produced two more transparent bags. The evidence bags held several small blossoms still intact as well as petals from at least two other species of bright flowers. They had been carefully preserved. The flower was shriveled, but the bright pink petals looking like smooth velvet were distinctive to her. That flower was very popular in Saudi Arabia despite the fact that it was highly toxic. In Africa, the poison had been used to coat arrow darts. The name of the flower was kudu or desert rose.

Was someone trying to frame her? Sean? Bale? Both of them? Or was this really Scorpion up to his old tricks of murdering innocents to watch her slowly lose her mind before he sent his agents to kidnap her? Was he torturing her? That would be like him.

She forced her mind back to the other petals. There was a mixture of meadow flowers and high-elevation flowers, all natural to the Sierra. What was the killer trying to say?

"You're frowning," Rafferty observed. "And shaking your head."

"The mixture of flowers is strange to me. It's like they were collected from all over. That's fireweed and asters, which you might find in Tuolumne Meadows. That's called a swamp onion, and it is found at a higher elevation."

She frowned again at the flower and the scattering of white petals throughout the mixture of other petals. Recognizing the beginnings of a headache, she rubbed at her temple. "To me, the white petals look a bit like a white iris, but that particular species doesn't grow in Yosemite." She bit down on her lower lip.

"Do you know where it came from?"

"White iris is fairly common in many countries." Including Saudi Arabia. The cemetery iris was popular there. She didn't say that. "The pink flower is called kudu or desert rose. It grows in Saudi Arabia and is very toxic."

She pushed the bags across the table toward Rafferty and dropped her hands into her lap. So far, she'd been able to keep all evidence of trembling from the sharp-eyed agents, but she feared that wasn't going to last if the interview went on much longer.

"You had a bit of an altercation with Deacon right here in the café the morning he went missing," Rob Howard stated. "I'd like to hear about that."

"We're done here," Decker interrupted decisively. "If you want anything else from my client, you contact me and I'll set up an appointment for her to meet with you."

"We have rocks here," Rafferty said. "They were scattered on the altar, and some were formed in a semicircle around the feathers and flowers." He placed the transparent bags in front of Shabina on the table.

She glanced down at them but made no move to touch them. She just shook her head. "This isn't my field of expertise." Her mouth was so dry her tongue wanted to cling to the roof of her mouth. She recognized the Qaisumah diamond, named after the

Saudi village where they were first discovered. They weren't true diamonds, but a variety of quartz. When cut and polished properly, the brilliance and luster were identical to carbon diamonds.

Shabina wasn't about to admit to recognizing one more item from the altar of the ritualistic slaying as coming from Saudi Arabia, especially after Jenkins had brought up the fact that Deacon had been taunting her in the café the very morning he had gone missing.

"Gentlemen, you'll have to find another expert for your rocks," Decker said immediately. "I believe Miss Foster has identified the feathers and plants for you to the best of her ability. We're done here."

"I've typed up an accurate, word-for-word report, Sheriff Rafferty," Raine said. "I'll send all three of you copies after Shabina reads it over and signs it."

"Thanks, Raine," the sheriff said.

Shabina agreed with the lawyer. "If that's everything? I don't want to hurry you, but my dogs have been waiting patiently all day to go out."

Decker stood. Shabina followed his example. Stella smiled at the three men as she stood, leaving the others little choice but to rise as well. The men gathered their evidence bags, and after a brief exchange of goodbyes, they left. Decker followed them out.

Shabina threw herself back into the chair opposite Raine. "What is going on?"

"I don't know. I don't have any idea what to think. You're positive that flower was from Saudi Arabia?" Raine asked.

Shabina nodded. "And I think the iris was as well. There was a Qaisumah diamond in the other evidence bag along with the rocks they'd gathered off the altar." She rested her forehead in her palm. "I can't imagine why anyone would want to kill Deacon."

"Bale did make threats," Raine pointed out. "It isn't like your kidnapping isn't common knowledge. It's on the internet if anyone wants to dig up your history. Sean could have killed Deacon and left him on the trail for you to find."

Shabina bit down on her lip. "That did cross my mind. Still, Sean's a jerk, but is he really a cold-blooded killer? I can imagine Bale doing something like that—and that's a stretch—but Sean? A ritualistic murder doesn't fit with his personality."

"None of us thought Denver could possibly be a killer. I didn't think so," Stella admitted, "right up until the very last moment when I was looking into his eyes. My heart stood still. Even then I didn't *want* to believe it. Sam saved the day, or I would have given myself away completely. In the end, he was aware I knew, and he decided to kill me." She pressed her hand over her heart. "It still hurts. I still have a difficult time believing he would do such a thing. I considered him one of my best friends. If he could do something like that, then Sean is just as capable."

Shabina had looked into the face of evil every day for months. Sean was twisted, but she wasn't convinced he could cold-bloodedly plan and carry out a murder as heinous as Deacon's had been. Sean had been in charge of the young man. Just that alone would put him on the suspect list. He was an intelligent man. Sean didn't make sense to her as the killer.

"I think we need more facts before we can reach any real conclusions," Raine said.

"I hate that Deacon was murdered," Stella said. "No one has told us if he was robbed. It's the weird ritual that bothers me because that indicates the killer might strike again. We don't need another serial killer." She gave a little shudder. "Honestly, Shabina, it's no wonder you're having trouble sleeping. All these references to Saudi Arabia."

"I think you should call Rainier," Raine said. "I know you don't want to, Shabina, but this could turn into a mess very fast. I think it already has."

Stella looked up sharply. "Wait, what? Rainier Ashcroft? I know he's headed Shabina's security for a long time, but I thought he was out of the picture. He made her cry when we were in Vegas. I wanted to stab him with a fork."

Shabina couldn't help laughing. Even Raine had to smile. The idea of Stella attempting to stab Rainier with a fork was hilarious, but then when Stella had a bit too much to drink on a backpacking trip, she came roaring out of her tent in lingerie ready to take on a bear with her karate moves.

Stella looked affronted. "I don't know why you two would laugh. He might be a badass, but no one makes my friends cry and gets away with it. He *deserves* to be stabbed with a fork."

"He probably did deserve it at the time," Raine said. "But I think you missed your opportunity. You can't just decide months later to attack the man willy-nilly."

"'Willy-nilly'?" Stella echoed. "No one says that, Raine. And the only way I'd have a chance of skewering him is a surprise attack."

Shabina couldn't believe she had gone from despair to laughter in such a short time. She really needed to spend more time around these women. They were good for her. She didn't dwell on the worst-case scenario every minute.

"Stella Harrison-Rossi, it sounds as if you have been planning to skewer him since Vegas," Raine accused, doing her best to look outraged, but succeeding in looking as if she might fall off her chair laughing.

"Well, as a matter of fact, I have been." Stella's nose went in the air. "I *dream* about retaliation. He's so sure of himself."

"Does Sam have any idea that you carry grudges forever?" Raine asked.

"Unfortunately, yes." Stella heaved a sigh. "I try to keep him with illusions, but he sees all. He always has. He doesn't seem to mind that I have these little flaws."

Shabina couldn't help laughing again at the sigh in her voice. "I think Sam loves what you call your 'little flaws.' In any case, you have the wrong impression of Rainier. I don't want you to think he's some terrible brute. The truth is, I totally ruined his life. I destroyed his career. I lost him the one woman he loved. He's on a dozen hit lists because of me."

"Shabina," Raine said, her voice gentle. "Stop taking on the responsibility for Rainier's choices. There was no gun pointed at Rainier's head."

"You weren't there. You didn't see me. He did. I gave him no real choice. I was barely sixteen and in a terrible state. You may have seen pictures they took of me when Rainier returned with me, but that was after he'd treated me for two weeks. My father was furious with him for not bringing me straight back and did everything he could to ruin Rainier's career, even after Rainier risked his life to get me out of that hellhole. Rainier was the one to figure out where I was by watching the videos. He realized I was sending coordinates in each one when no one else did. Still, that didn't matter to my father. It didn't matter that I'd told Rainier that I would commit suicide before I would ever allow anyone else to see me in the condition I was in. He knew I'd meant it, and again, he risked everything to take me somewhere safe and treat me himself."

There was silence while the two women did their best to comprehend what Shabina told them. She'd spared them the details—those were too grim to share.

"Rainier listened to me when no one else could hear me. Again, my parents didn't want him near me, but no one else could make me feel safe, and he came to me when the nightmares wouldn't stop. He was the one who taught me to use a gun. When I begged to learn self-defense and my father said it was not necessary, that I would have security day and night, Rainier taught me self-defense. When he wasn't around, he provided me with good teachers. Even then, I didn't feel safe if he wasn't with me. I saw a handler working dogs and wanted to learn how to do that for myself. Rainier talked my father into it."

"What you're telling me is," Stella said, "Rainier is a good guy despite the fact that he makes you cry."

Shabina nodded. "I turn into such a baby when he's around. I want him to see me as a woman, but that's impossible when he only comes around when I'm in the middle of a crisis. I do my best to get strong and stand on my own feet, so one day he can either let go completely or view me in a completely different light."

"Shabina," Stella breathed her name out in a shocked whisper. "You're in love with him."

Shabina didn't know if it was love. She knew there was no one else for her. There never would be. Others would always say she had developed feelings for him because of the extreme circumstances they'd met under. It was probably true. Whatever the reasons, her feelings ran deep, and she knew they weren't going away. Rainier was everything to her. She didn't even know when she became so utterly dependent on him. It had been a gradual realization that she couldn't do without him.

She worried about him. A big part of the reason she had moved out of her parents' home was because she felt they treated him so unfairly. Rainier didn't seem bothered by the way her parents acted toward him, and their behavior never stopped him from coming to her when she needed him. Still, it bothered her so much she felt eventually it would drive a wedge between her and her parents. They worried that she was so close to him. Maybe it was because they knew she needed him, and they wanted her to need them.

"You should be very, very careful," Stella murmured. "Really know what you're getting into before you take that leap."

Shabina gave her a fake smile as they all stood to leave. "He doesn't look at me that way, Stella, so don't worry about it."

"I just want to caution you again, Shabina," Raine said. "If Rafferty or either of those agents contact you with more questions, don't answer without Decker present."

"I'll be heading up to Yosemite to camp for a couple of nights," she pointed out. "I don't think they'll be so eager to talk to me that they'll come looking to find where I'm camping."

CHAPTER SIX

Shabina got a very late start to make the drive to Yosemite. The dogs had been patient and needed their run. She wanted to go to the gun range and practice. Maybe she was putting off going home and checking to ensure no one had broken into her home and the feathers were still there. She'd already packed for her trip. She always had her backpack ready with supplies for the dogs, a first aid kit for them and everything she would need for survival should anything go wrong. She believed in being prepared for the worst-case scenario.

Once she'd assured herself her home had remained secure and the bag with the feathers was untouched, she decided she needed a better place to keep them. She should have given them to Raine. If Shabina's house was searched or someone broke in, the feathers could be found easily, even though her home was enormous, and she had a safe room. Two of them. That had been at Rainier's insistence.

Rainier. She'd finally admitted to two of her friends her feelings for the man. Sooner or later, they were going to give their honest opinion on what they thought about that. They'd most likely talk it over with Vienna, Zahra and Harlow. They were that close. She'd known when she'd disclosed how she felt that they'd talk it over, but it was time. She wanted the truth out in the open. She couldn't give them everything, but she wanted to share more of herself with them, as much as she could. And she didn't want them to continue to think of Rainier as an ogre.

Driving time from Knightly to Sunrise Lake was about an hour. From Sunrise to Yosemite was another hour. She didn't stop at the resort as she normally would have. Stella would have tried to persuade her to stay in one of the cabins and go up in the early morning, but she wanted to have her campsite set up for the night and the dogs settled. She'd decided she needed to sort herself out. She hadn't slept for more than an hour or two in a couple of nights, and she'd had nightmares. She hoped being outside under the stars would lull her into a peaceful sleep.

She loved the Sierra. On her days off, she took the dogs, rain or shine, and spent her time hiking every obscure trail she could find looking for birds. There the forest had its own music if one listened. The wind played through the needles and leaves of the varieties of trees and foliage creating various notes. Some sounded mournful, others joyful. There was always something new to discover.

For Shabina, the Sierra felt like a magical, uplifting place each time she walked through it. Light streamed through the canopy overhead if she was in thick forest. Birds flitted from tree branch to tree branch, calling out to one another and singing. Squirrels were busy gathering food to store for the winter. There was the ever-present skitter of lizards, deer mice, rodents and snakes through the leaves, mushrooms and debris on the forest floor.

The fresh scent of the outdoors felt cleansing to her. This was the place she came to reset. Recharge. She found a semblance of peace in the beauty of the vistas and gorges. The meadows, with an abundance of wildflowers, ever changing with the seasons and elevations, were as inspiring and gave her just as much balance as the wild of the forest.

She had three favorite campsites, all far from the ones popular with the public. They weren't well-known and were off the beaten path. She set up her tent and took the dogs for a short run along a narrow path she was familiar with that looped back around to her campsite. When she returned, to her astonishment, Zahra's SUV was parked down from hers, and she was just arriving with her backpack and tent strapped to her back. The Dobermans rushed to her side, eager to greet her.

Zahra looked grumpy, which, on her, translated to adorable.

"Zahra, what are you doing here? You despise camping. I didn't know you had time off. What did you do with Misty?" Shabina couldn't believe her eyes.

The last person she'd expected to see was Zahra Metcalf. The woman would rather cut off her fingernails than camp—and she loved her perfectly manicured fingernails.

"Don't even talk to me," Zahra said as she shook out her small tent and placed it a few feet from Shabina's. "We aren't friends right now." She stuck her nose in the air. "I'm not certain we can ever be friends again."

"But what are you doing here?"

"You do realize there is a *perfectly* good spa at Sunrise Lake with cabins and decent beds. Right this very minute we could be getting a massage in the lap of luxury, eating a five-star meal, but what are we doing? Camping in dirt. Eating insects. Shivering with cold. Looking out for bears." Zahra looked suspiciously around her into the trees. "There are bears here, aren't there?"

"All the food goes into the bear containers," Shabina assured.

"If they were to come around, which they won't because the dogs are here, we would be safe."

Malik and Sharif both pushed their heads against Zahra's thighs, nearly knocking her over. It was all Shabina could do not to burst out laughing, but at the same time, tears burned behind her eyes. Zahra looked indignant and truly annoyed. Only one thing would have induced Zahra to find someone to watch her new puppy and go out into a cold night to go camping—her friendship with Shabina. No matter her posturing, she had dropped everything to support her friend.

"Thanks, Zahra," she said simply but very sincerely.

Zahra flashed her million-dollar smile. "I did pack food, not trail mix. And chocolate. And treats for the dogs." She scratched the dogs' ears until they were leaning into her, nearly moaning with happiness. "No grumpy bear is eating our chocolate tonight. I suppose we'll have to eat it all in one night. I brought enough for two nights if you're staying that long."

Two nights? Zahra had come prepared to camp for the two nights Shabina was staying. That meant she took two days off from her work, all to do something she didn't enjoy that much so she could support Shabina.

"We can use the bear container to ensure the chocolate is safe," Shabina said. "Even if they come around, which I'm really sure they won't, they wouldn't be able to get to the chocolate."

Zahra wasn't supposed to eat very much chocolate. She always carried it, claiming she needed it in case her blood sugar dropped too low. Mostly she carried it to share with the others. She knew each of her friends had their favorites, and she brought those particular types along on their backpacking trips or on the nights they got together.

"It won't be safe from Stella," Zahra said, setting a lounge chair in front of the ring of rocks surrounding the firepit, which wasn't lit.

"Stella?" Shabina echoed. "Is Stella planning on camping with us? She can't do that. She has to make sure her guests are on the right shuttles tomorrow morning."

Zahra shrugged. "She has staff to do that if she decides to take a couple of nights off."

Shabina didn't know what to say. The idea that Stella would come camping as well made her happy but also put a huge lump in her throat. These women were good friends to her, offering unconditional friendship, and what was she giving in return? She shut the thought down. Zahra was there, and she wasn't going to waste time feeling guilt. She was going to enjoy her company instead of second-guessing everything going on around her.

Two more cars drove up, one following the other. Harlow and Vienna. That was crazy and made Shabina laugh. How they'd both managed to get time off to come camping at such short notice, she couldn't imagine. They both had to have called in so many favors with other nurses at the hospital—all for her.

Harlow went over to Vienna's car, opened the back passenger door and ducked inside. Shabina's breath caught in her throat as Raine wrapped her arm around Harlow's neck to allow her to pull her out of the vehicle. Raine? She shouldn't be camping yet. Her doctors would have a fit. She couldn't imagine what they would say to her.

"Zahra, Raine's here."

Zahra shrugged. "You know no one can stop her when she wants to do something. I'm sure she didn't tell anyone. She just signed off, closed everything down and left."

"We could have four branches of the military looking for us." Shabina was only half joking.

"That's true, but Raine's probably found some way to shield us from discovery." Zahra didn't sound too worried about the possibility of troops showing up. She could handle irate men with ease.

Vienna hurried ahead to arrange a chair for Raine to sit in. Shabina and Zahra helped carry backpacks and tents and set them up. Vienna was the one to start the low fire in the deep pit. She put a screen over the flames to ensure no embers could fly up to the leaves in the trees.

"Raine decided to join us," Vienna announced while the others fussed over Raine's leg, adding a chair to elevate it. "She's going to get in so much trouble." The last was said gleefully.

"Unlike the rest of you, I don't answer to anyone," Raine objected.

Harlow burst out laughing. "I'm not sure that's true. I've heard a certain doctor bossing you around."

"If you're speaking of Rush, he bosses, but that doesn't mean I listen." Raine rubbed the bridge of her nose. "Unless he's talking about my leg. I do listen to him when he's giving me medical advice. Anything else is pure nonsense, and I have no intention of allowing him or anyone else to tell me what to do."

"How did you know where I was camping? I didn't tell Stella which campsite I was using."

This time she got the Zahra mysterious smile. "I'm psychic and I told everyone."

"Or Raine was spying with some kind of satellite," Shabina guessed, glaring at Raine. "She pinpointed my phone, didn't she?"

Zahra laughed. "I still found my way here, which is a miracle."

That was true. Zahra could get lost in a parking lot. The others joined in with Zahra's contagious laughter.

"What did everyone bring in the way of food?" Harlow asked, opening her pack. "I'm starving. By the time we've got everything ready, Stella should be here."

"If I'd known everyone was coming, I would have brought food," Shabina said.

One of the first things she'd learned to do was cook over a campfire. Mama Ahmad had begun teaching her almost immediately, and she'd soaked up every bit of knowledge she could. Almost all of the cooking and baking had been over campfires or in outdoor ovens Mama Ahmad and the other women had constructed. They moved camp so often that it was necessary to learn to build fires and ovens quickly wherever they went.

"Don't worry, Shabina," Vienna said. "I think I remembered everything you like to have on hand when you're cooking, and I brought it with me so you could whip up one of your famous camp dinners in like twenty magical minutes."

"And her bread," Zahra added. "She always does that flatbread."

"I can't just conjure up things out of thin air."

"Seriously, I brought everything I've seen you bring," Vienna insisted. "Raine keeps a running list for us. We figured anything we didn't use we'd lock away in the bear canister and take back to Sunrise Lake for Stella to use or donate to your café. Since you're the master chef, we could purchase the ingredients and make the side dishes."

Shabina couldn't believe it when Vienna unloaded the grocery items. Vienna had somehow procured her flat stones, the ones she kept for camp cooking. Within minutes she organized what she had to work with and began making one of the dishes she knew the women were very fond of. She put the flat stones on the embers and laid out the chicken after rubbing the pieces with oil and spices. The rice was seasoned while it cooked on the grill. Harlow had brought a pasta salad and Raine a green one. They would have enough food to easily feed all six of them. Stella drove up just as the chicken was pronounced done.

"It smells so good," Stella greeted them. "The moment I parked I knew Shabina was cooking. I'm starving."

"Grab a plate," Harlow said. "Raine, I've got your dish. Don't try to get up." Raine was a vegetarian, but she would eat everything but the chicken.

"Thanks, Harlow," Raine said.

"Are you comfortable enough?" Vienna asked. "I brought more pillows. We can prop your leg up higher."

"I'm good for now, thank you," Raine said, taking her plate.

Zahra leaned back in her lounge chair, the firelight playing over her face. "I've been giving our bear situation quite a bit of thought."

"Our bear situation?" Stella asked. She looked around at the other women who appeared just as puzzled. "Is there a bear situation here? I didn't see any warning signs up."

Zahra waved her hand airily and then took a bite of her chicken, closed her eyes and made orgasmic noises. They all had to wait until her food appreciation was over. "See, that's the problem with all of you. *Of course* there's a bear problem. They run rampant here in Yosemite. We've seen them. The aroma of this food is bound to bring them in herds."

"Zahra, bears don't run around together in herds the way deer or horses do," Harlow said.

That got Harlow a dismissive hand and the rest of them another round of her moaning appreciation of the chicken and rice.

"In this case, the bears will come in herds. I believe in being prepared. None of you are thinking ahead, which we need to do because Raine can't run. She's going to be just sitting there in that chair. Bear bait."

Raine raised an eyebrow. "Ugh. That doesn't sound fun at all."

"Believe me," Zahra said. "I looked up bear attacks. They're no joke. They've ripped faces off. It isn't pretty stuff. But I formulated a plan of action while the rest of you were worried about your stomachs."

"I see you weren't worried at all," Vienna said. "We're so grateful you've thought this plan of action through for us."

"No need for sarcasm, Vienna," Zahra replied, waving around a forkful of flavorful rice. "There are no grizzly bears here, which is a good thing. Only the American black bear. The name is silly since the majority are brown, not black." She took several bites and did more moaning, clearly appreciating her food.

"*Zahra*," Harlow hissed impatiently. "Now you've got me worried about a bear attack. Stop enjoying your food so much. You're so loud, you won't draw bears. We'll have every male camper for miles trying to find us."

Shabina couldn't stifle her laughter no matter how hard she tried. Zahra looked indignant.

"If there are male campers close enough to hear me moan over Shabina's cooking, then they can smell it. They'll be here right along with the bears anyway."

The others were laughing just as hard as Shabina. "She has a point," Shabina said. "Thank you for the compliment. It's nice to know I can still throw a meal together."

"Speaking of men," Stella began.

"We were speaking of bears," Shabina corrected. "The American black bear, to be exact. We have to listen to Zahra's plan since she went to all the trouble of making one to save Raine." She wasn't quite ready to have the women give her their opinions on whether she could possibly really be in love with Rainier Ashcroft, and she knew that was the direction the conversation was veering to.

"I do get saved in the end, don't I?" Raine asked. "Because I don't want my face ripped off by a bear." She gave a delicate little shudder.

"I wouldn't let you get your head bit off by a bear," Zahra assured. "According to everything I read, the bears aren't aggressive unless you happen to come between a mother and her cubs or them and food." She looked a little smug. "Food. Which is why I'm eating so much. You should all thank me for saving you."

"Is that your excuse? I thought you were showing off," Stella objected. "Everyone knows you can eat twice as much as anyone else and not gain an ounce."

"Um, that's my one and only claim to fame, and I'm not giving it up," Raine protested. "I can eat more than Zahra. I love you, Zahra, especially since you have a plan to save me from a bear, but I can't let you take my eating crown from me. It's all I've got."

Zahra waved a magnanimous hand. "The crown is yours. The bear should be afraid if we make ourselves big and yell quite loudly. Ordinarily, we could back slowly away, flapping arms and retreating as we told the thing to go away. But someone has to stay and defend Raine. Stella can't be the one because she married Sam. I objected strenuously to babies, but I've had to rethink my position on that subject. I've decided Stella and Sam need to have a baby or two running around driving Sam crazy."

"Sam crazy?" Stella nearly squeaked it. "Sam never goes crazy. He's always calm and steady. I'm the crazy one. Don't be wishing babies on me now after all your objections."

"I was just jealous," Zahra admitted without the least bit of embarrassment. "I didn't want to lose you. I should have known I wouldn't. I just gained Sam."

"Silly. You've always had Sam." Stella blew her a kiss.

It was dawning on Shabina what true friendship was. She'd never had that before. She'd been in boarding schools, but she'd never gotten close to other students for a variety of reasons. When her father began taking her with him on some of his trips, they went from country to country, and she had tutors. After she'd been kidnapped, she stayed to herself until Stella, a force to be reckoned with, had come into her life. Stella had brought the others.

These women had been around her for several years, but she'd always held herself apart from them, believing herself so flawed she couldn't possibly fit in. They couldn't understand her. She couldn't really understand them. What was real friendship? She was sitting right there in the middle of it. They didn't seem to mind flaws—in themselves or each other. They were just there for one another when they were needed. They gave honest opinions—sometimes not wanted but valued nevertheless.

"Vienna needs to marry Zale. The man is crazy about her, and someone has to save him," Zahra declared. "Shabina's been through enough for ten people. Harlow saved me once already. And we're not sacrificing Raine because she's too amazing. So, sadly, it's me." She heaved a sigh. "If the bear comes and collectively we can't scare it off, Vienna or Harlow has to pick up Raine and get her to one of the cars. I'll keep the bear's attention centered on me while you all make a run for it."

She slumped back in her lounge chair a bit dramatically like the heroine in a movie and forked rice into her mouth with another moan of appreciation.

Shabina coughed into her sleeve and busied herself rolling the last of the chicken in foil to keep it hot. She had to remove the stones from the embers once they burned clean. It gave her something to concentrate on to keep her laughter at bay. Zahra might be a drama queen, but she was absolutely serious.

"Good plan," Harlow said. "But you are kind of small, Zahra. If we're supposed to make ourselves huge to scare the bear, I think you might need a couple of us to make the bear think we're enormous."

Zahra lifted an eyebrow. "Did you not listen, Harlow? I said *if* the bear didn't respond to our collective noise and size, then you make a run for it."

Harlow nodded solemnly. "Yes, yes, of course. I think that plan's a good one, although we should add in there that Shabina should sprint to her car and drive it up so you can have a fast escape. That would give you a better exit plan."

"We just have to make certain all the food is put in the bear containers and all the smells are covered," Shabina said. "We don't want to attract them to this site. We can clean everything up carefully, Zahra. I'm used to scrubbing the stones and cooking pots so there isn't evidence of food left for the bears."

"*Now* can we talk about men?" Vienna asked. "Or one man at least?"

Shabina continued to work clearing the food. Stella and Harlow helped. They wanted the camp pristine from all food sources. Shabina kept her head down. She knew the inevitable had been coming. The women had come to support her so she wouldn't be alone, but they were going to weigh in on whether her feelings for Rainier were realistic. She didn't think talking about it mattered one way or the other since he didn't return her feelings. If he knew, and maybe he did, he would consider her emotions juvenile. That would be even more painfully embarrassing.

"If I get a vote," she said without looking up, "I vote no."

"We've all had to endure the endless talks on men," Stella pointed out. "Look at all the times we talked about Sam."

A collective groan went around the campfire. Zahra covered her eyes. Harlow her ears. Vienna attempted to do both.

"Sam is dreamy, we get it," Raine said. "No more Sam discussions or you get fed to the bear, baby or no baby."

"I'm *not* having a baby," Stella said decisively. "Stop saying that. You'll jinx me."

"Even if the baby looked like Sam?" Zahra asked, her mischievous expression very much in evidence.

Stella paused before she answered. "Well, if it could be guaranteed the baby had his eyes and his laid-back manner, then I'd have his child in a hot minute. But it would be a girl with a nasty little temper and she'd give me attitude night and day."

"Which you would deserve," Zahra said.

"Thank you, bestie." Stella glared at her.

"What are friends for but to point out the obvious?"

Another round of laughter, which Stella took good-naturedly, told Shabina she was going to have to be okay with being in the hot seat next. It was all part of the friend's creed.

She huffed a little, sank back in her chair and faced them. "Fine, then, but just know, this conversation is beside the point, Rainier has absolutely no feelings for me whatsoever other than he believes it's his responsibility to keep me alive. In fact, he looks at me like a thorn in his side, kind of a child that falls apart at the drop of a hat."

"I doubt that," Harlow said. "Look at everything you've accomplished. You live on your own. You have a very successful business. You're recognized as one of the leading ornithologists studying birds in the wild in North America, especially the Sierra. You graduated with honors from UC Davis, getting your bachelor's and master's degrees in well under the time it would have taken most people."

Shabina found herself smiling at the staunch support of her friend. "Where do you get all this information? Raine? Have you been telling tales about me?" She knew better. Raine didn't break confidences.

Harlow smiled at her, but there was an apology in her eyes. "I'm a senator's daughter, Shabina. I make sure anyone I let into my circle of friends is someone we can count on."

That told Shabina that Harlow was as wary as she was when it came to letting others into her inner circle.

"I do sound a little impressive when you put it that way, but I'm not sure Rainier would pay the slightest attention to my degrees. Just my security. He makes certain I keep up with self-defense, weapons practice and training of my protection dogs. He oversees all of that and occasionally checks out the security cameras to ensure they are working. Other than that, he's out doing whatever it is Rainier does."

Being the assassin Deadly Storms when he wasn't doing the same kind of work for Blom. She didn't add that. She didn't want to think about it too much.

She found she was rubbing at her thigh again, something she had been so determined she would stop. It was more of a self-soothing gesture than to alleviate the ache. The scars didn't hurt as bad anymore. Time, running and stretching had helped. It was one of those telling nervous actions Rainier—or Scorpion—would notice immediately. Scorpion would take advantage. Rainier would coach her until she was rid of it.

"You don't know," Zahra said. "If I were any man, I'd be falling all over you. Not only are you a successful businesswoman, but you're gorgeous."

Shabina laughed. "I'm not exactly thin."

"Men like figures, Shabina," Raine said. "Believe me, I know." She was extremely thin.

Shabina gave a little snort of derision. "Weren't we just talking about all the men who are courting you?"

"Courting you?" Harlow echoed.

Attention immediately swung to Raine. Shabina smirked.

"Oh no you don't," Raine countered. "Do you see what she's doing? That's called manipulation. She's directing attention toward me so you won't talk to her about Rainier."

"Are you trying to outsmart Raine?" Zahra lifted an eyebrow as she passed around chocolate bars.

"For a moment, I may have lost my ability to think clearly." Shabina went for humor. "Just the thought of Rainier does that to me."

Harlow rolled her eyes. "The thought of Rainier with you scares me to death. Sam is sweet, but he does have that aura of danger surrounding him. Zale is quieter and gives the impression that he could very quickly go lethal, but Rainier has an altogether different vibe. He doesn't even try to hide what he is."

Shabina tried not to bristle or come to Rainier's defense. Harlow wasn't saying anything that wasn't true. Rainier didn't bother to hide who he was from most people, not unless he was playing an undercover role.

"We don't know Rainier." Raine unexpectedly came to Rainier's defense. "Since none of us do, we can't fairly judge him, can we?"

Shabina didn't look at her, but she wanted to throw her arms around Raine and hug her.

Zahra pouted openly. "Well, that takes all the fun out of every-thing. What are we supposed to do now?"

"Discuss the murder and what could be happening, other than what it appears," Stella suggested.

"Do we have to talk about the murder?" Zahra protested with one of her most dramatic groans. "We're going to sleep in tents where anyone can creep in and bash us in the head with a rock."

Stella glared at her. "That was the assignment, Zahra. We were all going to think of different reasons this killer would have an altar with mixed feathers and flowers, including some from Saudi Arabia. Instead, you were researching bears."

"That wasn't my fault. I didn't understand how the body wasn't found by a bear when there was blood. Shouldn't a predator like a bear or mountain lion have scented it? Essentially, even if I don't want to think about it, a body is meat. Once I looked up what bears eat, I began to worry about all of us here and the scent of food and how to protect Raine. That's a logical progression." She was indignant.

"I can see how that would happen," Shabina soothed. "I get caught up in research all the time. I'm sure Raine does as well. And Harlow must with her photography. We all get sidetracked when we're interested in a subject."

Zahra sent her a winning smile. "I did think about the murder and why the bird feathers and flower could have been mixed in with the ones from here. Also, the fact that the body was found on a trail that was overgrown and no backpackers use. It was closed, wasn't it?"

"Yes," Shabina said. "Mainly because it leads to one of the rare bird-nesting sites. The park shut down that trail two years ago. Only a very few avid backpackers ever go that way. It's steep, with a lot of twists and turns. The trees grow closer together. A small stream crosses the trail in three spots, and it can be very muddy. It's high altitude, so the snow doesn't melt as quickly as in other areas. The ground can be very wet for the month of June and even July."

"But you go there," Vienna said.

"I discovered the birds nesting there and photographed them. I don't go often because I don't want to take a chance of disturbing them, but I was interested to see if the female would lay an egg. They are extremely slow to reproduce. If they do, it's only one egg and normally only every other year. It's been a rare opportunity to study them," Shabina said.

"What kind of bird?" Stella asked.

Shabina hesitated. "It isn't something we talk about because there are so few left alive. They became extinct in the wild sometime around the 1980s. The last of them were brought in to try to safeguard them and keep the species going. A few have been released into the wild fairly recently. They're magnificent."

She sighed as they all waited expectantly. "There's a mated pair of California condors several miles up that trail. Most of the time they nest in the crevice of a cliff or a cave, but they found a burnt-out hollow in one of the trees. They don't breed in the wild until they're at least seven, or that's the understanding. That's what's so amazing about discovering them nesting right here in Yosemite in a burnt-out hollow of a tree."

There was no way to keep the excitement from her voice. "The adults take turns incubating the egg, changing places regularly every few days. Their wings, from tip to tip, can be nearly ten feet across. Seriously amazing. They can weigh twenty pounds and soar very high in wind thermals, but have such great eyesight they can spot food easily. They can easily fly up to a couple hundred miles a day. It's the find of a lifetime."

"Congratulations, Shabina," Raine said. "You must be elated."

"It's so difficult to stay away," Shabina admitted. "I don't want anyone to discover the pair and disturb them. It would be horrible to lose this opportunity. I was able to record the courtship and the best part, the male's display dance. They did eventually have one egg, which just hatched late May or the first of June. I wasn't there to catch it when it happened, but the egg arrived on the last day of March. I did my best to stay away to keep anyone from finding them."

"How many people know you use that trail?" Stella asked. "There had to be people you informed about the pair."

"I documented them officially, yes, but it was considered best that we didn't reveal the exact location until it was determined if they actually bred and produced an offspring. If anyone knew I was using that trail, they would have had to follow me. The dogs would have alerted me."

"Think back over the last few months, Shabina," Raine said. "Did you go up there when it snowed? You would have left tracks. No one would have had to be close."

Shabina frowned. She'd always loved that particular trail. She nodded. "Yes. More than once."

"Jason Briggs warned you not to go off by yourself bird-watching, remember?" Stella reminded. "When all the murders were happening before. We'd gone to the Grill after James Marley's body was found, and I went outside to get some air, and he walked up to me and warned me to tell you to stop going into the forest alone."

That was true. She had always brought more than one gun after that. "I worried that Bale and the others were watching me."

"No doubt they were. They watch Zahra as well. Just because they leave her alone at the moment doesn't mean we haven't caught them keeping a close eye on her," Raine said. "They're horrible with women anyway, and if the woman is perceived to be from a different country, they consider her prey. You stand up to them, Shabina. Bale can't take that. What you did in the café the other day will make him crazy. He'll dwell on it."

"How would they be able to get flowers or feathers from Saudi Arabia, let alone a Qaisumah diamond? I recognized that as well."

"Mail order," Raine said. "I looked it up. You can get anything on the internet."

"Even flowers from Saudi Arabia?"

"Well, they wouldn't necessarily have to come from there. They could be grown in a greenhouse here in the States and billed as exotic flowers. Or toxic ones," Raine explained. "Birds aren't that difficult to come by on the black market. You know that. If Bale wants to frame you, and Sean was helping him by getting Deacon to act like a jerk to you in front of everyone, the idea could have been for you to find the body, not Search and Rescue. Bale and the others are part of the Search and Rescue team. For all we know, they were directing others away from the trail."

Everyone looked to Vienna, who was the head of Search and Rescue. "I gave out the assignments. Bale and Edward each headed a search party because they have so much experience. Neither was assigned to that elevation. I didn't notice them trying to push their way into leading those groups, but I was so busy, I doubt that I would have."

"We just can't rule them out, Shabina," Harlow said with a sigh. "All of us need to be on alert. Everyone knows Sean is obsessed with you, and not in a good way."

"Bale threatened me at my house," Shabina admitted. "He was waiting for me the other night when I came home and even told me he would burn down the café with the dogs and me in it. I definitely made an enemy there."

"Did you call the police?" Harlow was outraged.

"I'm pulling every incident from the security tapes at the local businesses and her café over the last few months," Raine said. "His family is in law enforcement. Rafferty, the sheriff, is his uncle. He's always gotten away with everything. This time, I want him absolutely nailed dead to rights." She shifted in her chair. "Before I head to bed, did you bring those feathers with you?"

Shabina shook her head. "I didn't want them anywhere near me just in case the feds serve me with a warrant to search my house. I did put them where they couldn't be found. When I get back to the house, if you come over, I'll transfer them to you."

"I think that would be best for now," Raine agreed. "For Zahra's sake, make certain no bear can even think we have food here before we turn in."

CHAPTER SEVEN

S habina met with the bird-watching tour group in the lower parking lot far below her campsite. It was a larger group than she had expected for the half-day tour. Five people had signed on at the last moment. To her shock and horror, Bale Landry, Edward Fenton and Sean Watson had booked the tour. They'd each claimed their fitness level was top of the chart. She avoided looking at them, just continued going down the names of people, checking them off the list and ensuring each person was physically in shape enough to make the planned hikes.

Eve and Felicity Garner smiled and waved excitedly. They had their backpacks with binoculars attached and were almost jumping up and down, happy to see her. According to both women, their fitness level was fairly good. They'd hiked extensively but weren't used to steep terrain as of yet.

Shabina checked off their names and went on to view the four men from the university. Jules Beaumont from Belgium was present, and her heart dropped. He stood just a little apart from the other three students. Today he was dressed in hiking attire. The other three men, Emar Salhi and Jamal Talbi from Algeria, and Deniz Kaplan from Turkey, were also dressed in loose clothing. These men were climbers and backpackers, according to the brief information they'd provided about their state of fitness.

Three women had come from Washington together, vacationing. Two were in their late thirties, with one, Theresa, being in her early forties. Theresa Nelson, Val Johnson and Janine Hale. All claimed moderate to good physical condition and appeared to be. The three kept looking at Edward, Bale and Sean and then smiling at one another.

A family of four, Oscar and Leslie Myers were attending with their teenage daughters, Pamela and Cindy. The parents were early forties in moderate physical condition, and the teenagers, one sixteen and one fifteen, were in good shape, both athletes. The girls eyed Sean and giggled quite a bit.

The last two on the list were Ellis Boucher, a thirty-six-year-old physically fit man, and his thirty-four-year-old business partner, Rhys Cormier, claiming equal fitness, both from Paris. These were the two men who had come into her café. Up close to them, she realized their features were familiar to her. She had been with Scorpion for six months and studied his every expression and his mannerisms. She could have sworn that both men had his all-too-familiar mannerisms. She told herself she was paranoid, but her heart beat like crazy. Worse, their eyes and foreheads seemed more familiar than ever.

Shabina's breath caught in her lungs as she raised her gaze to take in the two men. She'd asked Raine to look back through the security footage to see if she could identify them. Shabina knew she'd seen their features before. They claimed they were from Paris. Just the fact that their mannerisms and expressions reminded her of Scorpion, and they spoke French, it was all she could do to keep from having a panic attack. Twice she saw them laughing and talking with Jules Beaumont, all three speaking French.

Harlow had decided to come with her on the tour, and she was grateful. Vienna had taken Raine back down to Knightly. Zahra and Stella had returned to work since Shabina assured them she was going home after the tour. At least she had Harlow with her. It made her feel not quite so alone. Was she being paranoid or were those men Scorpion's men? Her head was beginning to pound.

She knew Bale was there to cause trouble. No way would he ever want to go bird-watching. He'd brought Edward and Sean along to aid him in harassing her. She decided the best way was to circumvent the problem before it began. She just needed inspiration.

She gave her talk on safety, sticking together, staying quiet and letting her know if anyone was having a difficult time with the terrain. She asked if anyone had any questions.

Bale was the first to make himself heard. "I read that there's no degree to be a bird expert, so how do you get to call yourself one?" He smirked at her, looking pleased with himself.

Shabina flashed him a high-wattage smile. "Thank you for bringing that up, Bale, I always forget to explain to everyone. Just so everyone knows, we have three locals taking the tour today. We're very lucky to have them. Bale Landry is one of our most prominent senior members of Search and Rescue. He's a diver, skilled climber and skier. If any of you have a problem today, rest assured, Bale is quite able to help you."

The ladies and the two teenagers all murmured appreciatively. Bale looked a little shocked and lifted his hand, not quite knowing what to do.

"Next to Bale is Sean Watson. He works for Fish and Wildlife and knows Yosemite inside and out. He also is a valued senior member of Search and Rescue. Sean has incredible skills when it comes to climbing and bouldering. He also dives and skis, and,

Sean, you work with avalanche control, don't you?" She poured admiration into her voice.

Sean dipped his head to acknowledge that he did.

Shabina beamed at him. "Sean is another man you can count on if you have any problems. And Edward Fenton is with them. He is also a local and a senior member of our Search and Rescue team. Edward is a helicopter pilot, and his skills are invaluable when we have rescues requiring a helicopter. He owns the local flying service. If you want to learn to fly or book a really cool trip to see Yosemite from a bird's-eye view, he's the man to call. He also climbs, dives and skis. I think we're in good hands today."

Edward's smile was the biggest she'd ever seen. He even puffed out his chest a little as the ladies cooed over him. The men from the university carefully wrote his name down, as did the Myers family, probably with the idea of booking a sightseeing flight over Yosemite with him. Shabina could tell Eve and Felicity liked the idea as well. She hoped she hadn't gone too far in promoting the man. She didn't want him shoving the men from Algeria, Turkey or Belgium from his helicopter or harassing the Garner sisters. She tried not to think about shoving the men from Paris out of the helicopter. It wasn't like she knew for certain they were members of Scorpion's cabinet.

She glanced at her watch. She had to get everyone moving before first light. "As for my education. Bale is correct: there isn't a specific degree for being a bird-watching expert." She gave a little self-deprecating laugh. "I pulled off a double major at the University of California, Davis, getting both my bachelor's and master's in wildlife biology, and I'm working toward my PhD. I also have a bachelor's and master's in botany. I'm working toward my PhD in that as well." She gave a little shrug. "What can I say? I like to learn things."

"You look very young to have earned such degrees already," Jamal Talbi said. "I'm going to the university and have a workload I thought was heavy."

Shabina snuck a quick glance at Bale. He hadn't expected her answer or the group's reaction. He had no idea what to do. She'd called attention to the three men and described them as heroic. If they made their snide comments to her or any of the other women, they would look bad. She'd also answered questions about her education in a way that was totally unexpected. Bale hadn't done his research on her at all. Now the group looked at her as if she was a superstar, especially the ones from the university.

"We need to get moving if we're going to see the birds we'd like to observe this early. You have to remember to stay as quiet as possible. I don't usually have such a large group."

She started up the narrow trail toward the first wide meadow where they would be able to catch a variety of early morning birds calling out to one another. If they were really lucky, in the dim light before dawn really broke, they might catch a glimpse or two of one of the owls that had been nesting close by. There was also a pair of red-tailed hawks nesting in close vicinity of the meadow. It was the first time she'd seen a pair of the hawks there. That meadow wasn't large, and usually, the hawks preferred a larger open area to hunt prey. The group might get lucky enough to spot the male high up in the branches of a tree, watching for prey.

She took them along the trail leading to the meadow, and when they reached the edge of the trees, she halted the group so they could spread out. Each of them had brought along binoculars and little earbuds, allowing them to hear when she spoke to point out a bird or tell them about it.

Shabina had been giving tours for the last year and a half, and she found it easy to slip into the role of instructor. She had a

group, including the teenage girls, that seemed to be very interested in the various species. They studied them and took photographs. Before moving on to the next site, she would answer
questions. They asked very good ones.

The two businessmen claiming to be from Paris didn't speak
to her during the walk as most of the others did. They seemed to
be, like the others in the group, caught up in the different types
of birds as they went from meadow to rockier terrain and then to
forest. There were a few times when she caught one or the other
watching her instead of the birds, giving her a very uneasy feeling.

During the break for lunch, she kept her distance from Bale,
Edward and Sean, gratified to see they were surrounded by fe-
males asking them questions and generally being admiring. Every few minutes, Bale would lift his head and stare at her across
the distance, a malevolent look on his face. With a sinking heart,
she could see Bale was working himself up to something. She
knew the afternoon wasn't going to be quite as easy as the morning had been.

She made her rounds, Harlow by her side, visiting with each
of those on the tour and answering specific questions they had. It
took effort to approach the students from the university, but she
called on the months of discipline, not allowing her hands to
tremble or her facial expression to be anything but absolutely
calm.

They were friendly, asking about various species and what had
gotten her interested in the study of birds. The question threw
her for a moment. She's always had a special connection to birds,
even as a young child. She tried to answer it thoughtfully without
sounding as if she was out of her mind. She just told them she'd
always dreamt of flying, and watching birds and listening to them
brought her a sense of peace and happiness.

Deniz Kaplan asked her if she'd lived a long time in Saudi Arabia and how she'd learned to cook such delicious food. He asked her the question not in English but in Arabic. She didn't hesitate to answer him in the same language. She wasn't going to pretend she didn't understand or speak Arabic.

Her heart ached the way it always did remembering that she'd spent a little over a year and a half in Saudi Arabia and had met a wonderful woman who had treated her as a daughter. She'd taught her to cook, bake and grill. She knew the four men and Harlow heard the love and sorrow in her voice, but she didn't care. Mama Ahmad had been a huge influence on her life. She missed her every day. She also told them her mother was from Saudi Arabia.

All four men complimented the woman who had trained her. She took that as the highest praise they could give her.

Jules Beaumont asked her where she'd learned to speak French and if she spoke other languages. She shouldn't have been unsettled by his question or the piercing stare he gave her, but she was. She managed to smile and tell him she had a gift for languages and had learned at a young age. And yes, she spoke several different languages.

She moved away from them to the relative safety of the Garner sisters. Felicity and Eve were high energy and helped to keep her fears at bay while she answered the dozens of questions they always had.

It took every ounce of courage she possessed to join the two businessmen. They greeted her politely, both speaking in French. She answered them in that language and then introduced Harlow. No one ever pointed out that Harlow was the daughter of a senator, but in this case, she was tempted. She wanted the men to know Harlow was protected. They made her even more nervous than Jules Beaumont, but she wasn't sure why. She was fast becoming a wreck for no apparent reason.

Both men were polite, assuring her they were having a good time and learning about the things they were most interested in. She thought that was an odd way to phrase it. She noted that Beaumont joined them for lunch and the three men seemed easy in one another's company.

There was no getting around facing Bale, with his flock of women hanging around him. Edward surprised her by asking about a couple of the birds they'd seen. He seemed genuinely interested. Bale gave a loud snort of derision, and Edward looked away. Bale made a snide comment about Shabina's cushy job staring at birds all day. One of the women voiced a protest. Shabina flashed a cheerful smile and walked away.

Throughout the rest of the tour, each time she spoke, Bale had something derogatory to say, mostly implying that he doubted she had accurate information. A few of the others objected and asked him to stop. He glared at them, trying his best to intimidate them. She noticed Edward walked a little ahead of him, joining the three women vacationing from Washington. He didn't once look back at Bale, or if he did, she didn't catch him. Sean didn't follow Bale's lead by interrupting her or making nasty comments, but he stared at her constantly. That alone gave her the creeps.

Shabina was mentally and physically exhausted as she made her way with Harlow back to her car. "That went fairly well, considering it was such a large group."

"What do you think Bale and his buddies were up to?" Harlow asked. "I did text Raine that they had come and also sent her pictures of everyone on the tour."

"Bale is really beginning to worry me," Shabina confessed. "I don't know what he's up to, but if he's involved in that murder, he very well could have been looking for another way to involve me, although I don't see how."

"You were brilliant the way you handled them. They were definitely confused," Harlow said. "But I'll admit, they made me so nervous, I couldn't concentrate on anything you were saying. How did you manage to keep going all day? Especially with the way Sean kept staring at you. Did you notice?"

She had noticed. How could she have missed it? But Bale had been worse. It was clear he was planning something. Mostly she'd been concerned about Rhys Cormier and Ellis Boucher. She had the bad feeling their business had something to do with her. It was the way they both avoided looking at her. They knew she spoke French. They had come to her café and known she had spent a great deal of time in Saudi Arabia just by the food she had on the menu. Her name meant "eye of the storm." She had built-in radar, and it was going off big-time. On the other hand, she had so many triggers the flashbacks were creeping far too close. Physically, she had all the symptoms. It was only the discipline she'd acquired during her time as a captive that allowed her to appear calm, even serene.

"I don't understand Sean at all. If he really has a thing for me, why would he act so obnoxious? Does he think that's going to win him points? If he ever once had the chance to date me, it ended the first time he threw a fit in my café insisting my food was bad." Shabina lifted her chin. "My food is *never* bad. Had he said he didn't like what he'd ordered and asked if he could try something else, I would have gladly switched the items for him."

Harlow leaned against her car. "You know what I think? Bale calls the shots and the others dance to his tune. I think he told them to start harassing you. Bale's been the ringleader since they were kids, so they follow his lead blindly."

"Like sheep. Great. Our Fish and Wildlife ranger is a sheep." Shabina rubbed her temples. Her headaches were coming back in force. She used to get them all the time, but after finding her way to Knightly, the headaches had slowly begun to disappear. "Worse, Sean believes he's a predator."

"Well, we know he's not," Harlow said staunchly. "If he's so ridiculous as to be part of a scheme to try to frame you for murder, we definitely can outsmart him, and he'll get everything he has coming to him."

Shabina hoped she was right. "What do you think about Jason? He's always with them, or at least he used to be."

Harlow sighed. "I honestly don't know what to make of him. He went to college with them and came here and fell in love with the Sierra. My impression is he doesn't like the things they do. If you notice, he rarely says anything when the others are harassing women. Sometimes he just walks off. More and more it seems as if he is separating himself from them."

"Were you surprised when Bruce offered him a job at the Brewery? Because it shocked me. And I think it shocked Bale." Shabina rubbed at her thigh. The dogs pushed closer to her, another sign that they knew she was becoming more anxious.

"I think everyone was shocked, especially Zahra. In the end, that, more than anything else, really made up her mind that she wouldn't wait around for Bruce to man up and ask her out. If he could become close to a man who surrounded himself with the kinds of friends Jason had, the ones who taunted her and harassed her, she wasn't going to wait. You know Zahra, she just fades away."

"Bruce appears to be still pining."

"That's on him. If he's too dense to realize what he's done and that he's lost his opportunity, then it's too bad for him," Harlow reiterated. "At least Jason isn't hanging around Bale so much, taking his command as absolute law like Edward and Sean."

"No, he doesn't seem to be."

Shabina knew Bale wasn't giving up his anger and whatever revenge he had planned, whether it had anything to do with the murder or not. She'd felt his eyes on her several times, and when she'd looked his way, he'd been looking at her with open malice.

"Why do you suppose men despise me so much?" She intended to ask Rainier the same question the next time he turned up. "What is it about me that causes them to hate me so much that they're willing to do such despicable things, Harlow?"

She'd asked the question of herself so many times, she didn't even feel sorry for herself the way she had when she was a teenager. Scorpion had reminded her a hundred times a day every torture, every death was on her head. She didn't understand why. When she asked, he beat her and told her she should know. She should be able to figure it out if she had a brain. She knew she was intelligent, but logically she couldn't put it together. Why his cabinet despised her. Why he did. Why most of the mercenaries had. Now Bale and his friends.

"You have to know it isn't you, Shabina," Harlow said. "How could it be? There isn't anything you do or say that could possibly make anyone dislike you. You're friendly to everyone."

That was the standard reaction. It didn't explain anything. Her therapist had given her that same exact answer. Raine had given it to her. It was always the same, and yet, men seemed to be driven to commit heinous acts because of her. At least, they claimed it was because of her.

Her head began to feel as if it were being crushed in a vise.

She had to stop thinking so much about Scorpion, or she would be too sick to drive home.

"Last night I had such fun with all of you, and I felt that I could get through the next few days, that maybe all of us together could figure out what was really happening. That we could make sense of it. But just a few hours in the company of Bale and the men from Paris and the one from Belgium, and I'm a mess all over again. I'm so paranoid I suspect everyone."

Her dogs pressed close to her in an effort to comfort her. Harlow touched her shoulder gently. "Honey, today would have been difficult for anyone. It was pure torture with Bale and his crew coming, and you handled it like a pro. On top of that with the murderer doing some sort of ritual sacrifice that involved items from the Middle East, naturally you would be upset. I'm upset and very leery. I certainly don't want you to come alone out in the forest the way you always do."

Shabina shook her head, which sent a piercing jab of pain straight through her temples. "I think about all the times I sat in my café and visited with students and tourists from various countries, happy to see them. I was happy to be able to serve them food I knew brought a little bit of home to them. I loved to hear them talk about their homes and their families. Just the conversations would make me feel closer to Mama Ahmad. I'd be sitting there in the café, surrounded by the fresh-ground coffee and the cookies I'd make from her recipes, and it would make not only them happy but me too."

"That's beautiful, Shabina."

"But it isn't that way now." Her right hand crept up to circle two inches above her left wrist. Her thigh throbbed and burned. "Now just seeing those men, hearing their voices, I find myself terrified. I really am, Harlow."

"Then I admire you all the more. You didn't act it in the least. In fact, you were composed the entire tour. Your voice was calm and controlled when you delivered the information on the various birds and their habits. I know you, and I wouldn't have guessed that you were triggered by the presence of the men at all."

Shabina despised the word *triggered*. Her therapist used it often when she referred to post-traumatic stress disorder. She was well aware she suffered from PTSD and that she was experiencing an ever-increasing episode, no matter how hard she tried to stop it.

She had the now-familiar physical symptoms: shaking, pain throughout her body, nausea, even sweating. She couldn't sleep, and when she did, she had vivid nightmares. She had heightened sensitivity and awareness of her surroundings. Paranoia. All were definite signs of PTSD. She was having flashbacks, intense flashbacks, as if the trauma were happening to her right at that moment. Those were brief, but so severe the experiences seemed real all over again. She couldn't eat anything. When she tried, it came right back up. She'd been lucky that her friends hadn't noticed that while she cooked for them, she hadn't done more than push food around on her plate.

She had wanted to isolate herself but was grateful that her friends had sought her out, although she'd worried that she might have a nightmare and wake them. Not that she screamed. She had learned not to give Scorpion and his men the satisfaction. There were times she couldn't stop tears, but most of the time they were silent. The more she could do to defy Scorpion's expectations, the stronger she felt.

Scorpion despised resistance. He didn't want anyone standing up to him, especially a female. That meant he wanted to enjoy her suffering. If she didn't scream and cry, how could he possibly get the satisfaction he needed?

"Harlow, I really think the FBI and Rafferty suspect I had something to do with the murder. I think they already had someone identify the flowers and feathers."

Harlow didn't just dismiss her concerns. "Raine is worried. If she's worried, there's good reason, although you have an airtight alibi. You couldn't have committed the actual murder. You would have to have had an accomplice."

"If Bale is the one behind this, one of the students from the university would provide the perfect fall guy, wouldn't they?" Shabina speculated.

"Or Zahra."

"She could prove she was at work. And everyone knows she doesn't hike unless we drag her around with us," Shabina protested. "If Bale is really orchestrating this, he wouldn't consider implicating Zahra. It would never work. He'd think an outsider from another country would be perfect."

Again, Harlow took her time thinking it over. "I would hate that Bale could be that sick, but I know it happens. Sometimes people are twisted, Shabina."

She sounded as tired as Shabina felt. Worn out. Shabina studied her features. Harlow was a beautiful woman. She rarely dated. The friends she had were the same ones Shabina had. Harlow stayed in that tight circle. She was always friendly. Always gracious. She was an amazing photographer, and her name was growing in the art world. Even the few pieces of pottery, which she didn't care to show others, sold for a mint when she did allow a gallery to display them. She was creative, yet she had a reputation for being one of the best surgical nurses on staff.

Her mother came twice a year to visit her. She didn't go home for holidays but spent them with the other women and Shabina. Shabina didn't go home for the holidays either. Her mother didn't ever celebrate them, so it was a good excuse to stay home and be with her friends. It just seemed odd that Harlow never wanted to go home. Her father was very active in politics, and yet she never went to see him. If anything, she avoided all contact with him.

"If I get arrested, Harlow, you'll have to make sure my father knows. He'll come roaring to the rescue, as much as I'd hate that."

"Raine isn't going to allow that to happen," Harlow assured. "She's brilliant. Far more intelligent than anyone gives her credit for. She's always three steps ahead of everyone else. If Bale, the FBI or Rafferty think they're going to pin this on you, they're in for a shock."

Shabina rubbed at her thigh again. "One of the biggest problems I have right now isn't Bale or the FBI. It's me. I'm really heading straight for a breakdown. That would help Bale and the sheriff and his friends do whatever they wanted. Pin the murder on the woman suffering flashbacks. She doesn't know reality from illusion."

Harlow smiled at her. "You have friends, Shabina. We'll keep you grounded."

Shabina was just grateful that they would try. She didn't know if it was possible. "I'd better start back to Knightly. I have to run the boys before we call it a night."

Her vehicle was parked beside Harlow's. She opened the back door and gave the signal for the dogs to load up. As she walked around the front of the car, she noticed a small package sitting on the hood.

A chill went down her spine and she looked around her carefully, searching the parking lot and then the surrounding brush. Was someone watching her? All of a sudden it felt like it. There was a tingling between her shoulder blades. She froze and glanced over at Harlow, who had already slid behind the wheel of her car.

Harlow pushed open her door and immediately hurried over to her. "What is it?"

"On the hood." Shabina didn't know why she whispered it. There was no one else in the parking lot. They were the last two to leave. That didn't mean they were really alone though. Scorpion could have his spies watching her. Or it could be the murderer. Maybe he was out there watching.

"Don't touch it. Let me," Harlow said. She strode right up to the hood, leaned over, and keeping her hands in her pockets, nudged the lid from the box with the edge of her jacket. The lid slid right off revealing several frayed twigs, each packed in a single bag of cellophane.

Harlow frowned. "Do you know what it is?"

Shabina nodded slowly. "Yes. Those are miswak sticks. They're made from the Salvadora persica tree, or arak trees. They're used several times a day on the teeth like a toothbrush and flosser before prayers. They have antibacterial properties."

"I take it these are used in Saudi Arabia," Harlow said.

"Yes." Shabina was back to whispering. One hand went to her throat. Her heart was beating too fast. Her skin was clammy. She couldn't quite catch her breath.

"I'm going to take a guess, Shabina, and say if anyone else turns up dead, these sticks will be on the little altar dedicated to their sacrifice. You can't touch them. I'm going to take them in my car and give them to Raine if it's all right with you. I'd prefer that you aren't anywhere near them."

Shabina didn't want to touch them. "Maybe we should just leave them here, Harlow." Her voice sounded faint. Tinny. She had to pull it together.

"I know you've had a problem in the past with PTSD," Harlow

ventured. "I'm wondering if Bale found that out and is doing every-thing he can to trigger another episode. Did you end up going back to Houston after the last one? Maybe that's his endgame, to drive you away."

"Murder someone just to get me out of town?" That sounded too farfetched, even for Bale.

"Who knows what motive a murderer has? Just remember, these sticks can be bought on the internet, just as the other items can be." Harlow sounded practical, as was her way.

"Do you have the eerie feeling that someone is watching us right now?" Shabina asked because that ominous shadow refused to fade. It was easy to slip into paranoia in the midst of a PTSD episode. She was already having trouble distinguishing reality from illusion.

Harlow again waited before answering. She nodded once. "I don't know if it's real or not, Shabina. We're both a little spooked by this, but I don't like being so exposed out here. I'm grateful for the dogs. Are you armed?"

At least Harlow admitted she was uneasy. That made Shabina feel a little better.

"I always carry a gun. In this case, I have more than one on me."

"I'm going to take this package in my car, and I'll follow you back to Knightly. If you need to stop at Sunrise to let the dogs out or for a bathroom break, just signal. I'll stop with you. I'm going to text Raine as soon as I can and ask her to meet us at your house. We can turn this over to her."

"I don't want anyone going after Raine. She's been through enough." That was one of her biggest worries—bringing danger to her friends.

"Raine has more protection than the rest of us. She'll know exactly what to do to keep you safe from any charges if you're being set up. You can't have any evidence in your home, Shabina. Bale's a big man in a small town. He has no idea of the kind of power someone like Raine can wield. She's a woman. She's very small and delicate looking. She's quiet. Bale doesn't understand real intelligence, especially in a woman. He understands brawn. That's the only thing he respects."

Shabina knew everything Harlow said was the truth. The only problem she had with it was, suppose her opponent wasn't Bale? What if Scorpion was creating this mess just to torture her? Although, to be honest, when she really thought about it, he would be more likely to use one or more of her friends as the murder victim. He would know that would hurt her far more, and he would revel in her suffering.

She stayed silent because there wasn't anything more to say. Speculation only went so far. They had no idea who really had killed Deacon Mulberry or why the bizarre altar had been set up. They didn't have enough details about the actual murder to put any more clues together. The authorities were keeping some information away from the public.

Harlow carefully wrapped her jacket around the small package and took it to her car. Both women slid behind the wheels of their respective vehicles and began the long trek home.

Shabina flooded the RAV4 with calming music. She needed her mind to stop racing the way it was. It wouldn't help to replay every nasty insult Bale had given her or the harassment he and his friends had subjected her to when she'd gone out dancing at the Grill. Once in the last year, she had gone to work in the early morning hours to find someone had painted filth all over the outside of her café. There was an investigation, but no one was arrested. That was when she had Lawyer Collins install a better security system with more cameras outside and inside.

Thinking about Bale was better than having her mind dwell on the nightmarish six months she'd endured with Scorpion before Rainier had appeared out of the sandstorm, rising up like some specter, slaughtering her enemies and carrying her to safety. But that thought brought her mind to fixate on Rainier.

Thinking of Rainier was a two-edged sword. She knew she had to find a way to break her reliance on him. He didn't—and couldn't—return her feelings. No one, including him, thought her feelings for him were real. They believed she had established not only a dependence on him, but as a teenager she had developed a crush on the man who had rescued her.

Shabina knew that wasn't true. As a teenager, she hadn't crushed on any man, let alone Rainier. He was older and as hard as nails. He was intimidating and demanding. He was the only one who didn't coddle her or want to keep her locked away from the world, especially when she wanted to retreat into complete isolation. He made her face what had happened to her and the consequences. He believed in the truth even when she didn't want to hear it. Now, she appreciated that quality in him. As a teen, it had been very hard to take at times.

She'd found it difficult to be around any man other than Rainier when she'd first come home. Even her father. That could have set the stage for the two to have such an adversarial relationship. She really didn't like the security guards always watching her. It was difficult to leave her room even for physical therapy. Only Rainier could get her to go out and only if he was with her. That hadn't been a crush; that had been a necessity for survival. She knew the difference.

Did she have a dependence on him? Back when she was a teen? He was the only person she fully trusted, so yes. Now? Same answer. When her life fell apart and she couldn't distinguish reality from insanity, she depended on Rainier. She tried not to. She wanted to have a completely different relationship with him. Unfortunately, he didn't return those feelings for her. She was also fairly certain she wasn't going to suddenly be miraculously "cured" of PTSD, no matter how much counseling she underwent.

As for the way she felt about Rainier now, those feelings for him had developed over time. She hadn't known it was happening at first until it was too late to protect herself. She was the kind of woman who had intense, powerful emotions. Her loyalty, once given, was unswerving. It was the same with her love. And she knew she loved the man. He didn't have to return her love; she wanted the best for him. That was one of the reasons she tried so hard to fight calling for him when she was in a downward spiral.

She'd wrecked his life once. She could only hope he was rebuilding it. She wanted that for him. It was the same with her parents. They'd been so close. The house filled with laughter and love when they were together. Once she was back home, there were constant tears, whispered arguments and a dark pall that had never been there before. She wanted her parents to find their happiness together again.

Shabina did her best to keep her mind centered on her friends and the way they were doing everything they could to help her. She was very grateful for them, especially when she pulled up to her gate and found Vienna had taken the time to drive Raine to her house. Raine was still having difficulty driving. She told everyone she could if the situation was dire, but no one wanted to test that theory.

Once in the house, Harlow immediately told the other two about Bale, Edward and Sean joining the bird-watching tour. She also AirDropped Raine pictures of Ellis Boucher and Rhys

Cormier, the two businessmen from Paris, as well as Jules Beaumont from Belgium. For good measure, she threw in Charlie Gainer. She included more photographs of the university students as well, worried that if they were wrong about Bale, one or more might have been sent by Scorpion to break Shabina down before either killing her or attempting to kidnap her again.

While Harlow explained things, Shabina let the dogs run free in the gardens, feeling guilty that she hadn't taken them for their usual run by the canal. She was tired, and it was late. She was grateful her friends were there to support her, but she also wanted to curl up in the fetal position and pull the blankets over her head and disappear. She knew she shouldn't be alone, but that's exactly what she wanted.

After she retrieved the plastic bag containing the feathers she'd found on the steps of the café and gave it to Raine, she busied herself making food for the others while they went over much the same thing Harlow and she had earlier in the day— whether Bale was involved.

She understood. Even though she considered him one of the worst human beings a man could be, he was still someone in their community who contributed when things went wrong. He really was a senior member of Search and Rescue, and he had never once shirked his duties.

Sean hunted, and, like many others, he provided meat for the elderly in Knightly. Edward cultivated a garden, indoor and out, and his winter greenhouse helped more than one older couple survive the winter. Grudgingly, she had to admit, the three men had a few good traits.

CHAPTER EIGHT

Shabina had very few days off that she kept strictly for herself. Usually, when she did have them, she was in Yosemite searching for birds. She wanted to find a way to relax, and she doubted being in the environment where the murder had taken place would allow her to do that.

She hadn't gotten much sleep again, and her increasing anxiety had been conveyed to her dogs. They were restless, patrolling the entire house continually, going to the windows, insisting on being let outside to patrol. She was reluctant to let them, afraid if someone was watching, they might take the opportunity to hurt or kill her dogs.

Her Dobermans had been trained never to touch food anyone had tossed into the yard. If someone attempted to bribe them with food, that stranger would be met with a full-on attack. She wasn't worried about poison, more like a bullet. Bailey, Stella's Airedale cross, had been attacked and stabbed repeatedly with a knife. She would never forget that night of waiting at the vet's, anxious to hear Bailey would live. She couldn't imagine if that had been one of her dogs.

Her favorite early morning run was along the Knightly Creek Canal. She started the nearly four-mile run where the scenery was the most beautiful. Very large deciduous trees lined one side of the canal with beautiful panoramic views of the Sierra Nevada mountains in the distance. The scenery was breathtaking, and she never got tired of it.

Great blue herons with sticklike legs walked in the water, hunting for fish or frogs. They were majestic birds, standing around four or four and a half feet tall, but she knew they had hollow bones and weighed no more than five or six pounds. These beautiful birds could fly up to thirty miles an hour.

Her dogs knew better than to go near the canal when the birds were in it. They ran beside her or just ahead or behind her on the dirt road. After crossing a cattle guard, the terrain changed to grass and wildflowers. The grass was a mixture of brown, yellow and green stalks interspersed with brightly colored flowers. Occasionally a cow lay in the field close to the road, and a few others grazed in the grass. Again, the dogs paid no attention to the cows but stayed close to her as she ran.

She left the canal to follow a gravel road along the lane and kept running until she hit the four-way junction. She made a left turn, looping back along the dirt road following a small waterway ditch. Brush and grass grew in abundance along the ditch. At times she lengthened her stride here to pick up the pace, but Malik suddenly spun away from the ditch toward the brush. Morza went on full alert, matching his pace to hers exactly, as if his body could absorb any attack coming at her.

Sharif aimed his body across hers to block her progress, and she halted immediately, taking a long, slow look around her, one hand sliding into the pack at her waist, fingers curling around the familiar butt of her gun.

"What is it, Malik?" she asked softly.

Releasing the safety, she kept her weapon in close, moving within the center formed between Sharif and Morza as she approached the third Doberman. He stood over a large bush, his teeth bared, hackles up. She moved closer, half expecting to see a snake, although her dogs generally didn't react to any form of wildlife unless it was a direct threat to her.

As she got closer, she could see a few of the leaves and thin branches of the bush had a dusting of what appeared to be various spices. She crouched down to smell them. Black lime, cardamon, saffron. Her heart began to pound as she caught sight of the torn packages. She bought many of her spices directly from a spice souk in Saudi Arabia. When she couldn't get what she wanted directly because of restrictions on shipping, she knew of a store in the States owned by a family from Saudi Arabia who somehow were able to get very high-end spices.

She caught sight of one date stuck to a leaf toward the center of the bush. An Ajwa date from Saudi Arabia, which she considered one of the best dates in the world. She purchased the dates from that same shop in order to make the cookies she served with the Arabic coffee.

This wasn't a coincidence. Someone had broken into the café and gotten into her kitchen—unless . . . Her thinking trailed off. She didn't want to believe that anyone working for her would betray her. Would they help Bale? Or Sean? Many of the women in town had really fallen for Sean, and the newer, younger waitresses flirted with him. If he asked them to get a little of her spices and a date or two, would they think it was harmless?

If another murder occurred and the spices and dates coming straight out of her kitchen were found on the altar, she was in real trouble. There was no way for anyone, not even Raine, to save her from being arrested. She backed away from the bush. She wasn't touching it.

Calling the dogs to her, she flipped the safety on, shoved her gun back into her pack and began to run along the dirt road looping back toward the canal. She forced her mind away from panic and attempted to sort through the possibilities. Bale? Or Scorpion? Those were her two main suspects. She just couldn't wrap her head around the senseless murder of an innocent man to frame her, not from either of them.

Nothing Scorpion had done made the least bit of sense to her. As far as she was concerned, he wasn't merely a serial killer, he was a mass murderer. He just hadn't been caught at it. If his government knew he was the one raiding and killing, they chose to turn a blind eye because he was a diplomat. That didn't make sense either, not when he could cause an international incident. And truthfully, she didn't know if Scorpion was who Raine said the government suspected. She didn't understand why they hadn't arrested him if they thought he'd committed such heinous crimes.

She'd been a teenager when she had been rescued, and the truth was, she knew very little about Scorpion's life. Raine had said her people didn't know for certain who he was, but that wasn't necessarily the truth. Shabina understood classified. She also understood that under the cloak of diplomatic immunity he was protected.

Once back at her car, she loaded the dogs and drove straight home. It had always been a sanctuary for her, much like the Sierra. Now she felt vulnerable. Her café wasn't safe either. She knew she needed to ask Raine to check the security feed at the café. She didn't know if she was becoming more paranoid by the minute or if the danger to her was real. Would the conspiracy to implicate her include members of her own staff? She was absolutely positive the spices and date had come from her supplies at the café.

To her horror, Bale's car was parked in front of her gate. He had the engine running, but the moment she drove up, he leapt out of the driver's seat and approached.

She gave the command to alert the three dogs and once again pulled her favorite pistol with the cherrywood handle and dropped her hand out of sight, but where she could easily bring it up to defend herself.

"Bale," she greeted.

Studying him, she realized he appeared as if he'd been in a physical altercation. There was swelling around his jaw and under one eye. The knuckles on both hands were scraped and swollen. He definitely had been in a fight.

"What did you think you were doing yesterday?" he demanded. His eyes were filled with hate, with malice. "If you think you can turn my friends against me, you're wrong, you little bitch."

"I have no idea what you're talking about, Bale. I gave my regular tour. I didn't do anything out of the ordinary."

He stepped closer to the car and all three dogs gave a low warning growl.

"Step back," she advised.

"Don't you *ever* tell me what to do. I'm not afraid of those mangy mutts. I've told you that before." He lifted two fingers as if he had a gun, aimed them at each dog and acted like he was shooting each one in the head. "That simple. They're gone. You're going to be running along the canal, opening your café or hiking a trail and all three will be dead in a matter of seconds."

A chill went down her spine. He meant it. She heard the resolve in his voice. First, he had threatened to burn her café down with her inside it, now he was admitting he planned on killing her dogs.

"I don't understand why you hate me so much, Bale. What is it that I did to you?" She knew better than to engage him in conversation. The more he talked to her, the angrier he seemed to get. Just looking at her provoked him.

"You're one of those high-and-mighty bitches that think the world revolves around them. Look at this place." His arm swept wildly around to encompass the high fence and gates protecting her home. "Keeping the riffraff out. Everyone you look down your nose at." His voice got louder. Spittle burst from his mouth along with his accusations. "Born with a silver spoon in your mouth, spending Daddy's money and teasing men with your face and body because you think you can get away with it."

She swallowed her protest. She dressed modestly. She didn't flirt with men. She didn't go on dates. Sometimes she thought about it, but she knew it wouldn't be fair when her heart was already taken. She wasn't the kind of person who was going to fall out of love. Her feelings for Rainier had grown stronger, not diminished, even though at times, his behavior toward her hurt. She wouldn't lead other men on. Still, she didn't defend herself.

"Now you think you can use your body to lure my boys away from me." He clenched his fists. "They know a little slut when they see one."

He narrowed his eyes at her. Accusing. Certain of his facts. "Did you think I wouldn't find out all about you? Flaunting yourself in some foreign country when you were a kid. Tempting those men. Naturally, you blamed everything on them. Daddy paid hush-hush money, but you probably ran off with some boy and got yourself into trouble. No one is gone for a year and a half unless they want to be gone. You were playing house. Or whoring yourself out before Daddy could get you back."

Shabina froze. She hadn't expected Bale to bring up her time in Saudi Arabia. She had no idea why she'd been that naïve. Maybe she couldn't bear to face it, to have it come out in the open. Her father was a big deal. The kidnapping might have been kept under wraps, but the rescue hadn't been. Once she'd been returned, reporters had gotten ahold of the story, although they didn't know the details, only that she'd been held captive by the notorious serial killer Scorpion. There had been interviews with her father. He'd been grim-faced in front of the cameras but refused to give details, protecting her. She'd been surrounded by security and hidden away in their large estate, where no one could get to her, no one other than Rainier.

She knew she paled. She couldn't stop that reaction, but she stayed composed. She had too much discipline to allow her distress to show.

"You may think you're going to win, but you won't. This is my town. These are my boys." He hit the side of her door with his palm so hard it shook the vehicle.

Malik reacted instantly, leaping across Shabina's body to block access to her. At the same time, he shoved his head through the open window, his teeth snapping viciously at Bale.

Bale escaped a nasty bite only because he had stepped back as he hit the door, presumably because he'd hurt his already injured hand. Sharif and Morza roared a challenge, rushing the back windows. All three dogs easily could have launched themselves from the car. Shabina gave the command to hold. She knew if Bale suffered a bite, he would immediately go to the authorities and demand her dogs be put down. Even if that didn't happen, they would be quarantined, leaving her without protection.

Bale swore savagely, reached into his jacket and dragged out a revolver. He stepped back again, aiming it at Malik—or her—

she wasn't sure which. She raised her gun and made certain he knew exactly who she was aiming at. Her hand was rock steady.

"I suggest you leave, Bale. The security cameras have caught everything you've said and done from the time you first pulled up. If you dare to pull that trigger, I'll kill you. Even if you get me, you'll be dead. I don't miss. Not ever. I was trained by the best. The gates might be right here, but you're on my property. It will be self-defense." She kept her voice very calm.

She hoped Rainier never viewed the footage. He would be furious that she hadn't shot Bale. He'd told her a million times if she had to pull her weapon, not to hesitate. To shoot. He would have killed Bale by now. If he witnessed half the things Bale had done or said to her, she would be very concerned for Bale's life.

Bale glanced around him, looking for cameras. For a moment, he looked as if he might try to shoot out the camera over the gate, but he thought better of it.

"This isn't over by a long shot," he snarled. "And if you think those recordings are going to help you, forget it. Lawyer Collins has been my friend for years. He'll destroy every scrap of anything you have on me." He spoke with absolute conviction.

She didn't deign to answer him, nor did she lower her pistol. He spit on the ground, shoved his gun back in his jacket and stormed to his Jeep.

She sat for a long time, head on the steering wheel, too shaken by the encounter to move. Just finding the spices and date was bad enough, but then facing Bale's malevolent hatred was horrific on top of that. Worse, he'd brought up her past, bringing the memories far too close, threatening to open those doors she kept barricaded closed.

She had no idea how long she stayed in her car before she became aware of the dogs' distress. They pushed around her, heads on her shoulders, Malik all but sitting on her thigh. She took a deep breath and forced herself to open the gates. Rainier had drilled it into her to put security first. She didn't know if someone had broken into her home and stolen spices and dates out of her kitchen or if they had done so from the café.

Almost on autopilot, she allowed the dogs in the garden first, giving them the alert command to patrol. She stayed just inside the gates, her weapon in her hand. She'd already texted Raine asking for her to check the security feed at the café and at her home. She also asked her to make certain she had her own recordings in case the ones in the café and at her home were wiped out.

Shabina was careful how she worded her request to Raine, not knowing if the FBI could already be monitoring her phone. Could they legally do that without her knowledge? She didn't know. That was another question for Raine. She feared she was becoming that needy friend. She was so dependent on Rainier, now she felt she was putting too much on her friends.

She was sweating but cold. Shivering. Her legs felt stiff, every joint painful. Her thigh throbbed with increasing agony. Leaning her weight against the gate to help hold her up, she tried to breathe deeply to slow her pounding heart. Her heart was racing so fast her chest hurt, making her nauseous. She concentrated on staying on her feet and keeping air moving in and out of her lungs, trying not to think too much about the suddenly all-too-vivid details of her time spent with Scorpion, his hideous cabinet and his mercenaries.

When the dogs returned to her without alerting, she sent Malik and Sharif into the house. Morza stayed with her, as was protocol in a situation where it was possible her home had been broken into, although part of that protocol was to inform Rainier there was a possibility of trouble. She didn't do that. She knew if she did, he would drop whatever he was doing and come. He always did.

The temptation to send for him was nearly overwhelming. The only reason she didn't was because she loved him. She truly loved him, and she wanted him to have a life. If she kept calling him and forcing him to drop everything and rush to save her sanity, he would never be able to find happiness for himself. Above all else, even her own happiness, she wanted that for him.

She could barely stand. Her body felt so painful, as if she'd been beaten mercilessly, and there wasn't an inch of her that had been spared. She didn't dare look at her left thigh, which she covered with her palm. The fabric separating her hand from her leg felt slick with blood. There was so much that she knew if she looked at the wounds inflicted in one of the many fits of rage Scorpion had, her thigh muscle would be gaping open. She'd lived with that, with the infection that followed for weeks. That had been one of the worst times. The beatings, the skin flayed from her back, her thigh stabbed numerous times to make a point. When something triggered flashbacks, she felt every one of those wounds and hallucinated that they were open all over again.

Shabina had wanted him to kill her, but Iyad had intervened and reminded Scorpion she would die. She'd lost too much blood. Shabina could see the sadistic insanity in Scorpion's eyes. His men could see it too. Most turned away to protect themselves, knowing he was quite capable of turning his wrath on them. She couldn't believe Iyad had risked his life by interceding on her behalf. She didn't want him to, but she was too far gone to say so. She couldn't speak, going in and out of consciousness.

Malik and Sharif returned, pulling her partially out of the dark abyss threatening to swallow her. Both dogs were relaxed, which meant there had been no intruder in her home. Stepping inside, she quickly closed the door and sagged against it, making another deliberate attempt to slow her pounding heart.

She slid down the doorframe to the floor, drawing up her knees and resting her forehead on the tops. The flashbacks were becoming more vivid. More intense. That was a bad, bad sign. She rubbed her pounding forehead back and forth over the tops of her knees as she hugged her legs tightly, folding in on herself, making herself as small as possible.

The pain in her body made her feel physically ill, but she refused to give in to her lurching stomach. She'd been having trouble eating for the last week, and once she started being sick, she wouldn't be able to even look at or smell food—not a good thing when she owned and operated a café.

Just the idea of facing her staff and customers was daunting. She couldn't bear the idea of seeing anyone, especially when she was certain one of her staff had betrayed her. The spices had to have been stolen from the café's kitchen. She considered calling Vaughn and telling him they would need to close the café for a few days, but that would mean her staff wouldn't be paid. She couldn't afford to pay them if she didn't have the café open.

Malik rushed to the window and gave a short bark, jerking her out of her internal monologue. It wasn't his alarm bark, or a challenge, but more a greeting. She pulled out her phone and looked at the camera with a little sigh.

The trouble with having friends was they just showed up when you absolutely didn't want to see a single soul. What happened to the call-ahead policy? Hadn't they always done that? She couldn't remember. They all had the code to her gate, and no one thought a thing about using it.

Her back was to the door. They were just going to push their way right in, sweeping her against the wall. Maybe they wouldn't see her behind the open door. There was no way to hide the state she was in. It wasn't as if she could pull herself together and go whip up a meal for everyone in the next half hour. She scooted on her butt away from the door but just stayed on the floor.

Zahra shoved open the door, and Daisy bounded in. The little Jack Russell leapt at Shabina's raised knees in an attempt to get into her nonexistent lap, giving her location away immediately. Zahra hesitated but turned back to help Raine into the house. As usual, Raine had her computer bag with her. Zahra had Misty on a leash and brought her crate in after she helped Raine to one of Shabina's comfortable chairs.

"Have the dogs been fed?" Zahra asked, all business. She put Misty in the crate and pulled the dogs' beds from the closet where she knew Shabina kept them stored.

Shabina silently shook her head.

"Give me a minute and I'll get that done. I know where everything is. Raine, you'll have to direct Daisy to her bed unless you want me to go ahead and feed her now as well."

"She hasn't eaten either," Raine confirmed. "I would appreciate it, thanks, Zahra." She pulled her laptop from the bag and began to set it up. "I'm sorry for the invasion without calling first, Shabina, but after your text, I received a very alarming call from Lawyer Collins."

Shabina hadn't thought anything could bring her out of her dark well of memories and back to the present, but at the mention of the man who had installed the security system at her place of business, she lifted her head and looked at Raine.

"Bale obviously believes Lawyer installed your home system as well as the one at the café. He called Lawyer tonight and demanded he destroy all the feeds, the recordings and every bit of stored data you might have here and in the café," Raine announced.

Zahra came all the way out of the kitchen. "Bale did what? Seriously?" Not only did she sound outraged, she looked it. "Why would he think Lawyer would do that? If others using his security system found out, they'd drop him. He'd go out of business."

"Exactly what I asked," Raine replied with her usual calm. She waited until Zahra returned to the kitchen and her task of filling dog dishes.

Shabina threaded her fingers together and hugged her legs tightly, chin on the tops of her knees, gaze steady on Raine.

"Apparently, when they were kids, Bale and his merry little band were into robbing people, specifically in the parking lot after a football game once most everyone had gone home. He despised his football coach, who was a young man at the time with a couple of kids. The coach didn't make much money, but when they surrounded him and demanded his money, wearing ski masks of course, he refused to give them his wallet. Bale and the others beat him up and he ended up in the hospital. Lawyer was there that night. It was the only night he went with them, but Bale had a camera set up somewhere to record the robberies. He claims he kept the footage and insists if Lawyer doesn't do what he says, he'll expose him to everyone in Knightly. The coach and his wife still reside here, although he's retired now and has grandchildren."

Shabina was stunned. She didn't know why she was. More and more, she was beginning to believe Bale was capable of murder. Not only of cold-blooded murder but of masterminding a plot to pin a series of murders on her simply because he hated her. His reasons didn't have to make sense to anyone else, only to him.

"How old was Lawyer?" She whispered the question because her voice didn't seem capable of rising above that volume.

"He said he was sixteen. He was so shocked at the level of violence he just stood there and didn't help the coach. He claims he didn't hit the man or kick the man, but he did pick up the wallet and hand it to Bale with the idea that Bale would stop kicking the coach," Raine said.

Zahra called the Dobermans to her. Shabina hastily gave them a release signal so they knew they were free to take the food from their friend.

"He wants Lawyer to destroy any recordings from here because he was waiting for me after my run. He threatened to kill the dogs again, called me names, and then when he hit the driver's-side door with his hand, Malik rushed him through the window. He pulled a gun, but I had mine out, so it was a standoff. I reminded him he was on my property and cameras were recording everything he said and did."

She couldn't bring herself to put any animation in her voice. She was exhausted. Sick of trying to keep her head above water.

"You have to report him," Zahra insisted. "This has gone on long enough."

"Rafferty is his uncle," Raine reminded. "Every piece of evidence against Bale disappears. You know that, Zahra. When we make our complaint, it's going to an outside source, and we're going to have ironclad evidence against him. I've been gathering it for a while from the Grill, the café, here and even the grocery store. Don't worry, I have permission from the owners."

"If Lawyer didn't install Shabina's security system, who did?" Zahra asked.

Shabina sighed and rubbed her chin on her knees. "Who do you think?"

"Rainier had the cameras on this property installed," Raine

answered for her. "They're high-tech, and there is no way Bale could destroy any of the recordings, not where they're stored."

"Someone is *spying* on us?" Zahra asked. "Can Rainier see what Shabina is doing whenever he'd like?"

"If he could," Shabina said, "it would have been nice for him to have been watching the Bale show."

"It wouldn't have been nice for Bale," Raine objected. "In any case, what Bale is unaware of is that Lawyer told his parents what happened a few days after the incident. He refused to name the other boys, but he went to the coach, admitted he'd been there and apologized. He said he would take the blame if the coach wanted to turn him in. Regardless, he was going to work off the money that was stolen. The coach didn't give the sheriff Lawyer's identity. Lawyer was certain the coach suspected Bale, Edward and Sean were involved, but he didn't ever say. He accepted the money with the interest Lawyer's father insisted be paid to him."

"Bale and the others don't know?" Zahra said. She put a treat in the crate for Misty so the little puppy could have something while the other dogs ate and then gave Daisy her food.

"No. The coach never said a word and neither did Lawyer. Over the years, Lawyer told me he became friends with the coach and his wife, and he still looks after them," Raine said. "He was extremely concerned that Bale has centered his attention on you, Shabina. He's known Bale a long time, and he's obviously worried. He said the man is vindictive."

"That's not news," Zahra said.

"If that isn't bad enough," Shabina said, "I think someone broke into my café and stole spices and dates from my kitchen. I buy them specifically from Saudi Arabia or from a shop here in the States that carries them. Some of the spices and dates were dumped in a bush where I run along the canal. If someone else is murdered and there is some kind of ritual altar with spices and dates on it, that would point straight back to me."

There was absolute silence. "No wonder you wanted me to sort through the recordings from the café," Raine finally said. "This is bad, Shabina. It does sound as if you're being set up."

The alarm indicating someone was at the gate sounded, and Shabina nearly jumped out of her skin. She caught up her phone to stare in a kind of dazed terror at the two men sitting in their car, waiting for permission to drive up to her house.

"Get in the shower, Shabina," Raine said. "Zahra will let them in. I'm armed. I won't look like a threat to them because I look injured with my pathetic little leg. I can turn on the cameras in here as well. Take a quick shower and come out looking your usual composed self. We won't leave you alone with them. Whatever they want they can say right in front of us."

Shabina wasn't certain she could stand up, but she gave her phone to Zahra so Raine could use it to talk to the two men at the gate.

"Raine O'Mallory here. What can I do for you?"

Two IDs appeared on-screen. One man was Ellis Boucher the other Rhys Cormier, both claimed to be Interpol agents from Paris. Raine immediately took a screenshot of the men's identifications and went to work on her computer.

"We'd like to speak with Shabina Foster," Boucher said.

"She's in the shower at the moment. Let me have our friend ask her if it would be all right for you to come up to the house. Give me a moment, please." Raine was very good at stalling. She sounded sweet and reasonable.

Shabina managed to make it to her feet. Wrapping her arms around her churning stomach, she hurried to her bathroom, where she allowed the hot water to pour over her, hoping it would revive her. By the time she emerged, dressed in fresh clothes, her hair wet but braided in a thick rope, she felt a little better. She put the dogs on alert but sent them to their stations, three different corners of the room, where they would have the advantage should they have to attack. Daisy was crated for safety.

"Are you armed?" Raine asked Shabina.

Shabina wouldn't have walked into the room without being armed. She nodded and put in the code to allow the gates to swing open.

"I want a weapon," Zahra said. "Just in case."

"In the kitchen, taped under the center island." Shabina made her way to the front door. Each step felt like she was wading through quicksand. Why would Interpol want to talk to her? It was bad enough that the FBI and Rafferty were looking at her as a suspect, but now Interpol?

She took a deep breath and opened the door, steeling herself to handle the situation.

Both men had their IDs out to show her at the door. She waved them inside but indicated Raine. "You'll have to show your identification to Raine. She can't get up at the moment, but she works for the government and will be acting as my official counsel."

The two men exchanged a look but entered, both looking around carefully to take in the position of furniture and windows and seeking the location of her protection dogs. It was no secret that she had them and that they were always with her.

Raine looked their IDs over carefully and nodded before Shabina invited them to take a seat.

"This certainly is a surprise." She chose her chair, making certain to present the most difficult target and the angle that would not hinder Raine if she needed to take a shot. "What can I do for you?" She folded her hands in her lap.

Her revolver was tucked into the side of the cushion, only inches from her fingers. She was extremely proud of her voice. Steady as a rock. No trembling. She kept her gaze fixed on both men, noting every breath, every movement. Having Raine and Zahra there gave her a measure of confidence. She wasn't entirely alone.

"We know that you spent some very unpleasant months with a man referred to as Scorpion," Boucher opened. "I'm sorry if this conversation is uncomfortable for you, but we've been attempting to gather evidence against him and one of his associates."

Cormier took up the narrative. "Many people we've questioned believe Scorpion doesn't act alone."

She didn't move, not even when her stomach knotted and churned. These men were investigators from Paris trying to build a case against Scorpion, and yet warning alarms were shrieking at her. She had no idea why. Both spoke in gentle tones. Both were polite. She kept her hands still and her features composed. So far, they hadn't asked a question. She'd learned, when she was a teenager, never to speak unless she had to.

"Scorpion works with a master assassin. This man at first was thought to be a myth. When others spoke of him, they did so in whispers. He came to our attention, the stories building a picture of him. He's been killing for Scorpion for at least ten years," Boucher said.

Both men watched her closely. Shabina had been in Scorpion's camps for over six months. They moved constantly. He wasn't always with them, but his orders were followed. She had never once noticed that he had a special assassin he sent out. He had his cabinet. They specialized in cruelty and murdered often, as did the mercenaries he left behind to run his camp when he was gone. But an assassin? Scorpion preferred to do his own killing.

It was all she could do not to rub her left wrist, where the tattoo was branded into her skin. The hated scorpion. She kept it covered at all times.

"This man is very familiar with every terrain. He knows the desert and the hills. He knows the cities. He moves with the wind. If one ever catches a glimpse of him, they do so before they die," Boucher added. "In all the time you were in those camps, did you see such a man? Could you identify him?"

Shabina forced the air to move through her lungs at an even rate. She didn't want to think about those days or remember any of the men other than the few who had been decent, risking their lives to try to aid her. She remembered them. Their faces. Their names. She kept them and their families in her heart.

She shook her head. "I'm sorry. I have no idea what you're talking about. All of the men who rode with Scorpion killed. I didn't notice any one man standing out above the rest."

Boucher frowned. It was the first time he appeared to be annoyed. "It is said he comes when the sandstorms come. That's when he strikes, sometimes leaving behind many dead, not just one."

She shook her head again, but this time she couldn't keep her heart from racing. She didn't dare look at Raine. Could he be referring to Rainier? No one knew Rainier was the master assassin Deadly Storms. Not even Blom. Was Interpol looking for Rainier? Why weren't they asking questions about Scorpion?

"They call him Deadly Storms," Cormier added. "Had you ever heard this name in the camp?"

"No." She hadn't. That was strictly the truth.

"Around the time you were rescued, there was a sandstorm,"

Boucher said. "Do you remember? It was one of the very worst in the region in a long while. It came in fast, and when it passed, every man in that camp was dead."

Raine cleared her throat, drawing their attention away from Shabina. "Am I understanding your implication? Do you believe this assassin killed all the men in this camp?"

Boucher was silent a moment. "We have to investigate every possibility, and the men all died by his signature kill."

"I'm not sure what you're saying. If this assassin works for Scorpion," Raine continued, "why would he kill Scorpion's men? Weren't those men the ones he rode with on his raids?"

"Like I said, we're just investigating every possibility. Scorpion hires mercenaries, and he often disposes of them and their families once he no longer has a use for them." Cormier turned his full attention on Shabina. Both men did. She could feel their gaze piercing her. These men were used to interrogating others. They hadn't expected Raine there. "What happened that night? You had to have seen whoever killed those men."

Shabina took another breath and pressed her fingers to her mouth. "I'm sorry, this is really difficult to talk about. I try not to look back on that time. I was in very bad shape. Close to death. They had whipped the skin from my back. I'd been raped multiple times. I had deep stab wounds in my thigh. A raging infection. I was sliding in and out of consciousness most of the time. Scorpion had demanded they keep me alive before he left, and someone set up an IV with antibiotics. I do remember that much."

Shabina paused and stroked her fingers down her throat, appearing to struggle to bring up memories. "I think they gave me some kind of painkiller. I vaguely remember someone coming and whispering to me to stay quiet; that's hazy like a dream. He just wrapped me up in a sheet and gave me a shot of something. I woke up later in a safe house with a doctor attending me."

The two men exchanged a frustrated look. They asked her several more questions, but she made it clear she had little memory of that night, and as far as she knew, everyone was alive when she was removed from the camp. The man taking her out had whispered the need for silence. To her that meant he feared they would be caught.

Shabina watched the gates swing close after their car exited her circular drive. She leaned against the door and looked helplessly at Raine.

"They said Scorpion often killed the men he hires to aid him when he's massacring entire villages. That means some of the men who were good to me might be dead. They weren't in the camp that night. Are they dead, Raine?"

Pressing one hand to her temple, she thought about the two guards who had risked their lives to try to aid her.

"I'm sorry, Shabina," Raine said quietly.

Shabina turned away from her, not wanting to face her. Not wanting to see the compassion. Of course, Scorpion would have to kill the men aiding him. He wouldn't want to pay them or risk any of them identifying him.

"I'll have to do quite a bit of work to pull all the feed from the café," Raine said. "But I'll get it done as soon as possible. I'll come to the café just before closing, and we can go over anything then. I will tell you this though. Those two men aren't Interpol agents," Raine announced. "I don't know who they are, but those IDs are fake. Good fakes, but they're fakes."

CHAPTER NINE

Trail crews camped in Yosemite, and oftentimes supplies were brought to them. Rehabilitating the trails took time and a tremendous amount of work. The distances were long, so it made sense that the crews stayed in camps until they had days off. Many of the young men and women working on the trails came back each summer. All of them had a love of the outdoors and a passion for maintaining the beauty and nature of the Sierra.

Shabina had met most of them. Often, before they went to Yosemite to camp for weeks on end, they would drop by the café, laughingly calling out to her that they were eating their last great meal for a long time. They usually ordered double portions in order to pack another dinner with them to eat later.

She missed the laughter and good-natured camaraderie of the younger crowd before they made their way to their campgrounds. She needed their joy and upbeat personalities in her café after the long night she'd had with no sleep.

Not only did she have to worry that Bale was setting her up as a murderer, but she had to worry that if he wasn't, he planned on killing her dogs and burning down her beloved café. She had no idea who the fake Interpol agents were, but she was afraid they were trying to uncover Rainier's identity. She didn't know for who or why. Then there was Scorpion. Did he have spies watching her every move?

She looked around the large room. It wasn't that the café was empty, in fact, it was absolutely full and had been since she'd opened, but there seemed to be mostly tourists, and she was so paranoid she could barely function, let alone talk to strangers as if nothing were wrong. It was her way to go to each table and welcome everyone, to ensure they enjoyed their meal. It was part of the experience in her café. She just wasn't able to do that and hadn't during the first shift either. She knew Vaughn had noticed because it was so out of the ordinary for her.

They'd cleared quite a few tables, making room for customers who had been waiting in line. She was grateful these would be the last ones before closing. She wanted to take the dogs and go running, get away from everyone. Not think about who in her café might have betrayed her.

She'd gone over the inventory in the kitchen when she'd first arrived to get the baking done before opening. It should have been impossible to tell if someone had just taken a pinch or two of her spices and a few dates, but they'd been in a hurry and had used the same cup to dip into each marked bin, transferring spices from one bin to the next. Two of her special dates had been dropped on the floor. The thief had been in a hurry and was afraid of getting caught. In their haste, they hadn't been very stealthy.

She'd taken photographs and sent them to Raine before cleaning up the mess. Vaughn came in before the rest of her staff, the way he always did, cheerful and excited to start the day. She couldn't imagine that he would be the thief, not after all he'd done to help her make a success out of the café.

Raine had texted back one word. Fingerprints. Shabina didn't want to think about pressing charges against one of her staff.

"Are you going to tell me what's wrong, Shabina?" Vaughn asked. He took the two plates of food right out of her hand. "I'll take these to the table for you. I've never seen you like this before. Are you sick?"

That would be such a perfect excuse, but if she was sick, she had no business being in the café where she could expose her customers. She shook her head. "I promise to tell you about it later. I don't want anyone else to overhear us."

Vaughn had been a big part of her café since the very beginning. He'd sacrificed right along with her. She was certain he wasn't involved in a conspiracy against her. She couldn't allow herself to become so paranoid she became suspicious of all her friends.

Sean came in with Edward, and Chelsey sat them at one of the tables with the best views. Patsy was sure to have a word with her. It wasn't Chelsey's job to hostess. She worked the outside patio with Nellie. Patsy or Tyrone seated the customers. Shabina found herself watching Chelsey's interaction with Sean and Edward. She was very flirtatious, touching Sean on the shoulder, giggling like a schoolgirl and leaning in to whisper to him.

When the young waitress moved away, light spilled through the window onto Sean's face. Shabina's breath caught in her throat. Sean had a black eye. There was no getting around it: the eye was swollen and bruised. His lower lip was split. Sean didn't seem to care if anyone saw it either.

Shabina immediately came to the conclusion that Sean had been the one to get into a physical fight with Bale. Her gaze followed Chelsey speculatively. Was he dating her waitress? Or at least acting interested in her, so interested that she might do a favor for him, such as get a few pinches of spice out of Shabina's kitchen? Would Chelsey do that? When she'd applied for the job as waitress, during the interview she'd confessed she was desperate and living in her car. She'd had no money left and didn't want to return home. She had implied it was a very bad situation there.

It didn't exactly follow that Chelsey would show Shabina loyalty over a man she hoped to date just because Shabina had given her a job and found her a safe place to live. Shabina knew people were flawed. She was flawed. She couldn't expect everyone else to be perfect when she was well aware it was impossible, but she valued loyalty. She didn't like to think her judgment had been so skewed.

Tyrone, Shabina's head waiter, seated three women who had been on the bird-watching tour, Val Johnson, Janine Hale and Theresa Nelson, two rows over from Sean and Edward. The women waved at her in excitement. There was no getting around the fact that she was going to have to speak with them. Ordinarily, she would have enjoyed a follow-up visit, but just moving seemed to be difficult, let alone forcing conversation.

Truthfully, she didn't want to move around the café and call attention to herself, not with Sean and Edward in the building. She didn't have the energy to put up with any harassment from either of them. She might fall on the floor in a pitiful heap and cry in front of everyone. If she did that, she'd never be able to face her customers again.

She waved back to the women, plastering a smile on her face, and when they indicated for her to come over, she took water glasses and set them on their table. "What a lovely surprise," she greeted.

Janine glanced across the room toward the table where Sean and Edward were seated. "Edward raved about the food here. He said we shouldn't miss it. Stella told us the best dancing was at a place called the Grill, and when we asked Edward about it, he said not only was the dancing fun, but they served good food as well."

Shabina was shocked to hear that Edward had recommended her café. He came there often to eat breakfast. Most of the locals did. But she hadn't thought he would ever recommend the Sunrise Café to tourists.

"Stella said your café was the best as well," Val agreed. "We thought it would be fun to spend a few days in Knightly and do many of the fun things Stella had in her brochures. We booked at the local hotel. We're going to do a tour of the brewery. I'm not so much into beer, but Theresa really likes it."

Janine glanced across the room toward the table where Sean and Edward were seated. Shabina was surprised to see she was looking at Edward with interest not Sean. Sean was undoubtedly handsome. His job as a Fish and Wildlife officer gave him status. Edward rarely spoke when Sean and Bale were around. He faded into the background. He had zero social skills; in fact, Shabina was certain he fought a stutter on occasion. He certainly wasn't a ladies' man, yet there was no doubt Janine had her eye on Edward.

"I hope you really enjoy yourselves. The brewery is fun to see, and I understand the beer is amazing. As for the Grill, my friends and I go there often to dance. It's our favorite. If you have any questions about the menu, let me know or get Tyrone's attention. He can help you too."

The three women nodded, and Shabina moved away from their table, avoiding Sean's and Edward's gazes. The Myers family, Oscar, Leslie and their two teenage daughters, Pamela and Cindy, were seated two tables down from the three women from Washington. She paused to greet them.

"The girls and I are very excited," Leslie said, handing Shabina a brochure that Stella customarily left in all the cabins at Sunrise Lake. "A pottery class. I've always wanted to take one and this is a beginning class."

Shabina knew Tom and Judy Rosewood, an older couple, had a gift shop. They sold pottery, embroidered hats that were sought after and a few of Harlow's sculptures. The couple were beloved in Knightly. Although in their seventies, they were extremely active. She knew they occasionally gave pottery classes.

"You'll love Tom and Judy. Everyone does. And they're very, very good at their craft. If you get the chance, pick up one of their embroidered baseball hats. They're only sold here in Knightly, and everyone who sees them wants one. It's a very exclusive item. They might not have any at the moment if you don't see them," she advised, handing back the brochure.

She chatted with them a few more minutes and was relieved to see Raine and Vienna come in. That gave her a good reason to excuse herself. She was able to seat her friends at one of the more secluded tables in the back. She took their orders and told Vaughn she was taking a break. If he needed her, just give a sign. Vaughn seemed happy that she was going to sit for a while with her friends.

"You didn't sleep again," Vienna greeted.

Shabina sent her a wan smile. "You should be more polite, seeing as you're my friend. You're supposed to boost my confidence."

"I'm a nurse and your friend. It isn't good for you not to sleep, Shabina."

"I'll get right on that." She did her best not to sound sarcastic, but really? If she could sleep, she would have been sleeping. She was terrified to close her eyes. Nightmares were too close. Flashbacks were making it difficult to distinguish reality from illusion.

She ducked her head and shoved at an imaginary stray strand of hair. She had to put her hand down beneath the table because it was trembling.

"I'm sorry. I know you're just trying to take care of me." She was ashamed of herself for snapping at Vienna. She was in the pushing-her-friends-away stage. She knew that was what she was doing.

"I think you already know who the culprit is," Raine said.

"Chelsey Sarten." Shabina dropped her forehead into her palm. It hurt. She hadn't expected the betrayal to hurt so much.

Raine nodded. "She comes back into the café using a key after hours. Does she have her own key?"

Shabina shook her head. "I have one, Vaughn, Tyrone and Patsy. Rainier has one. And there's a spare set kept in a drawer in the kitchen."

"In a drawer?" Raine echoed. "Does everyone who works here know about the spare set?"

"It has the keys to the outside building housing the freezer and larger refrigerator. The freezer is kept locked, and so is the refrigerator, just in case children accidentally manage to get in there. The answer is yes, at some point everyone has had to go out to get something from the fridge or freezer."

"What about customers?" Vienna asked.

Shabina shook her head. "They would have no reason to know."

"But Chelsey easily could have pocketed the keys during her shift at any time, and no one would have noticed," Raine said.

"That's true," Shabina admitted. "It never occurred to me one of my staff would help someone set me up to take the fall for murder."

Her head was pounding all over again, and she felt physically ill. "I'll check to see if the keys are in the drawer when no one's around. I don't want Chelsey or Sean to know we have them on the security cameras." She lifted her head frowning. "When I saw Bale, his face and jaw were swollen and his knuckles were scraped. He'd clearly been in a fight. Look at Sean's face. He has a black eye."

Both women looked toward the table where Sean and Edward were seated while trying not to appear as if they were staring.

"He's definitely been in a fight," Vienna agreed. "With the accusations Bale hurled at you about trying to break up his friendships with his boys, I'd say you might have been a part of their disagreement."

Raine nodded slowly. "Sean is an intelligent man. He might have agreed, at first, to get the spices and dates for Bale to somehow incriminate you at the scene of a murder, but he had to know he would also be incriminating himself. Chelsey would know she stole those spices from your kitchen and gave them to him. If they were found with a murder victim, do you think she would remain silent and allow you to be accused of killing someone?"

Shabina rubbed her pounding head. "I didn't think she'd steal from me, so I can't honestly answer that."

Vienna looked out the long window to the patio, watching the young waitress as she laughed and talked with her customers. "I'm going to go with Raine on this one. Stealing might be appalling, just to try to get laid, but I don't think she'd go along with framing you."

"She'd probably think Sean was the murderer," Raine added. "If he thought this through, he was the one most likely to throw the spices and dates away. Bale would have been furious, not only because he didn't have the items to implicate you, but because he's beginning to feel as if he's losing control of the men who always did whatever he said. They just went along with him, and now suddenly they're rebelling."

Patsy placed the food in front of them, including a plate of zucchini sticks. Shabina's café was famous for her zucchini sticks. "Vaughn sent these to you, Shabina. And this smoothie. He says you're losing weight and he's getting worried. He doesn't want to have to wrestle you to the ground and force-feed you, but he will."

The thought of Vaughn trying to wrestle her made her want to laugh. That was unexpected. Just the fact that she could find it in herself to laugh she thought was a good sign. Maybe she wasn't as far gone as she thought. But then she couldn't seem to stop. Vienna and Raine stared at her with a kind of horror.

"Honey, I'm not going to tell you it's going to be all right," Raine said quietly, "because I know it doesn't feel that way to you right now. Take some deep breaths."

Out of control. She was never out of control in public. Because she had to do something to stop the hysteria, she drank water, big gulps of it. Naturally, it went down the wrong way and she coughed and choked. Her lungs fought for air.

"Just talk to me. Were you able to find out anything more about Boucher and Cormier? Who they really are. They speak in fluent French, but the accent isn't exactly right. And what about Beaumont?" That was a gift she had—languages. She heard the slightest little nuance in pronunciation. Her ear was so good she could tell regions people came from in the same country.

Shabina felt the thin chain around her neck pulling tighter and tighter, constricting her airway. Harsh, taunting laughter erupted around her. The walls of the café rippled and faded, morphing into a high rocky cliff. Beneath her feet, the floor faded away, turning to sand. Splashes of crimson striped the sand like a bizarre painting.

Rolling thunder boomed in her ears, drowning out everything around her until she was only aware of the beads of sweat trickling down her face. Her lungs were raw and burning for air. The feel of blood seeping through her clothing was all too real.

"Shabina." Raine's voice penetrated the strange roaring in her ears. Calm. Steady. "Honey, look at me. Concentrate on looking at me. Don't touch her, Vienna." That was Raine's firm voice.

Shabina recognized Raine in the midst of the strange sensations she was experiencing. The fading in and out of reality. She forced herself to listen to Raine's voice. It didn't matter what she said, it was her tone.

Inside her head, she found herself screaming for the one man who could make this all stop. *Rainier.* She knew she could never allow him to come near her again. The two men pretending to be Interpol agents had been hunting him, not Scorpion. They were hunting Deadly Storms. Even more than Raine's firm, steady voice, it was the thought of Rainier in danger that brought her back to reality. She laid her head on her forearms for a brief moment.

"I'm all right. I'm okay," she murmured, more to reassure herself than her two friends. "I'm sorry."

"Don't apologize," Vienna said. "There's no need. This type of trauma is a burden you're going to carry on your shoulders for the rest of your life. You're not just going to shrug it off, Shabina. All the counseling in the world is not going to remove it. It helps to have tools to deal with it, but it isn't going away. I think you know that."

Shabina lifted her head to look at her friend. She did know it.

She was just a little shocked that Vienna knew it. Most people thought anyone could put trauma in the past with a little effort, especially if they went into therapy. She'd been in therapy since she had come home, but there had been many episodes of PTSD. This one was proving to be severe, and she was very scared. She didn't admit that, not when Vienna and Raine were doing their best to help her.

"You already know," Raine said gently, "you learn to live with the trauma and what it's shaped you into. That's okay because it can make you stronger."

Shabina didn't feel stronger. She felt worn out. Exhausted from fighting back and trying to stay alive when she wasn't certain why. Sometimes she tried to write down reasons. She had a notebook she kept for that purpose. Reasons to live. Beautiful things in her life. She told herself she had so much. She had good friends. She lived in one of the most beautiful places on earth, but she could no longer see it. The beauty was fading and she could no longer find peace.

"I've never had a flashback in public before." She tried to force her voice to sound normal. She had tremendous control and discipline. She just needed to find it. This was her place of business. She couldn't make a scene here, especially when there was so much at stake.

"We're in the very back of the café, and you didn't make a sound," Vienna assured. "Vaughn looked this way a couple of times, but he couldn't possibly have known you were in distress. I think he was checking to see if you ate anything."

Her stomach lurched at the thought of trying to eat. She forced herself to sit up straight. Her entire body ached— every joint, every muscle. That wasn't unusual when her flashbacks were so vivid.

"You might have to eat the zucchini sticks, Vienna," she said and pushed the plate toward her friend. "Raine, if Boucher and Cormier aren't really Interpol agents, who do you suppose they work for? Do you think Scorpion sent them? Or the government? They said they were from Paris." She didn't believe they were from France. Something was just off about them.

The thought of Rainier being in danger was terrifying. She knew those men were hunting him. Fortunately, the story she told couldn't be discounted. If they were aware of her condition prior to the rescue, she would sound believable.

"I'm still checking into them, Shabina. One of the biggest problems is the fact that they could be working as Interpol agents, but also be agents for Scorpion. You're well aware many people in all kinds of high positions can be corrupt."

"Look at Rafferty," Vienna said. "I always thought he was a good man. He seems like he is, until you throw his family into the mix. Evidence disappears the moment a member of his family is charged with anything. That's corruption."

"He'd call it loyalty," Shabina said.

"Not when he's helping pin a murder on someone," Vienna said.

"We don't know if he is." Raine was the voice of reason. "He did bring the FBI agents here, but that's his job. There is nothing to suggest he's persuading them to believe Shabina had anything to do with the murder."

Vienna made a face. "Maybe not, but I think he's corrupt. That's just my opinion."

"You're upset on Shabina's behalf," Raine pointed out. "I wish some of these programs didn't take so much time. I've been searching to find Boucher's and Cormier's real identities. I have to use facial recognition. And so far, I haven't turned up anything on Charlie Gainer or Beaumont that would incriminate them . . . Well." She hesitated.

Shabina held her breath.

"I can't locate their whereabouts at any of the times Scorpion struck in the countries he murdered in."

Shabina forced air through her lungs. "I appreciate you trying," she said.

Vienna didn't—and couldn't—know about Rainier and the danger he was in so Shabina couldn't ask questions of Raine in front of her. She wanted as many details on the two men claiming to be Interpol agents as fast as possible. She would have to warn Rainier to stay away from her. They would need to cut all ties. It was the only way to ensure his safety.

The thought of never seeing Rainier again was devastating to her. She knew he wouldn't ever love her the way she loved him. She accepted that. But never seeing him again? Knowing when she was at her very worst, she could never call for him? That was one more thing to cross off her "to live for" list.

It didn't help her uneasiness that Raine couldn't rule out any of them from being associated with Scorpion or his mass murders.

Patsy collected the dishes, and Vienna ordered coffee with orange cranberry scones. Raine ordered tea and said she'd eat Vienna's scones. Patsy clucked at Shabina as she cleared away the uneaten zucchini sticks and smoothie.

"Vaughn is going to lecture you," she cautioned.

"I know." Shabina tried to sound as if she were laughing it off. "I'm getting used to his lectures."

"I forgot to tell you," Vienna said, as Patsy walked away. "Harlow called this morning and said Edward came around to her studio. He had a sketch book with a few drawings he'd done of birds. She said she was shocked at how good he was. He told her he hadn't drawn since high school, and he was struggling with proportions. He had really good photographs, she said, and she didn't think his drawings were that far off, but he was very critical of them and frustrated. She thought Stella was the best person to talk to. You know she's an excellent artist, even though she never shows her paintings to anyone but her closest friends—and Sam."

"Oh no," Shabina said softly. "Another reason for Bale to be angry at me. I did notice Edward was really paying attention during the bird-watching tour. He asked questions even when Bale made fun of him. At one point, it was pretty clear Bale was annoyed with him for being interested. I had no idea Edward was an artist."

"Like I said, Harlow indicated Edward said he hadn't drawn anything since high school. She was even more impressed with his work because of that," Vienna said.

"Bale would really feel as if he were losing control of his boyhood friends if Sean refused to do what he wanted and then Edward acted in the least friendly way toward you," Raine said.

"I wouldn't say he was friendly," Shabina objected. "Just not hostile."

"To Bale that would be the same as friendly," Raine said. "That would be a betrayal, in his opinion. In his eyes, you're stealing Sean and Edward. Jason already left him. I would say Bale is getting desperate and will do just about anything to assert his dominance over those men and everyone else around him. He's spiraling. I wouldn't want to work for him."

"He'd make a terrible boss anyway," Vienna stated. "I can't imagine what he's like now, when he's acting so out of control."

"Once I've collected all the evidence against him for harassing and threatening you," Raine said, "I'll have you swear out a complaint and ask for a restraining order. We can bypass the judge here with just cause. Fortunately, some of his harassment occurred on federal land and earns him a federal charge."

Shabina shook her head. "If I get a restraining order against him, Raine, and I'm at the Grill for a night out with all of you, he won't be able to go into the building. That isn't going to sit well with him."

"That's his problem, not yours," Vienna said. "He brought that on himself if it happens. You didn't ask him to treat you like dirt or threaten to burn down the café."

"Or threaten to shoot your dogs," Raine added.

Patsy returned with coffee, tea and scones. Just as she set Vienna's coffee and Raine's tea on the table with the scones they'd ordered, Vienna's alarm went off. As head of Search and Rescue, she was nearly always the first to be called when someone went missing. She frowned as she read the text.

"One of the members from the trail rehabilitation crew, Charlie Gainer, didn't make it back to camp last night. The other crews searched for him through the night and most of this morning, but they haven't been able to find him. They've asked for help." She was already getting to her feet.

Her eyes met Shabina's. Shabina could see the apprehension. The dread. Shabina tasted fear in her mouth. She didn't want to think it was too late for Charlie Gainer, but that dark roiling in the pit of her stomach told her he was most likely the latest victim of the murderer. Why? Why Charlie Gainer? Was he murdered because he knew something about Scorpion? The thought was terrifying.

"Good luck," Raine said.

"Do you want me to have the staff pack food for your team while you're putting out the word for everyone to meet?" Shabina offered. "We can get someone to take it up to your base if you send us the location."

"Thanks, I'd appreciate it. I'll let you know when we have everything set up." Vienna abruptly turned and strode from the building.

"Charlie Gainer was here in the café before he went up to the camp," Shabina told Raine unnecessarily. Raine had researched him. Shabina drummed her fingers on the table. "He was with Pete and Billy. You know them; I think you've even bouldered with them. There were also two women, Mandy and Georgia from West Virginia. They were excited and laughing. All of them seemed to be very nice people." She was ashamed that she'd been fearful of Charlie simply because he spoke French. Half the world spoke French. She pressed her forehead into her hand and breathed deeply.

Sean and Edward stood up as abruptly as Vienna, both looking worried as they stared at the alerts on their phones. Edward tossed a handful of bills onto the table, and the two men hurried out. She couldn't help but notice that Sean looked back at her. It wouldn't be long before word was out to all Search and Rescue volunteers, and they would make their way to the base camp Vienna would set up prior to sending them in grid patterns to search for the missing man.

Unless one spent a great deal of time in the Sierra, it was difficult to understand the scope of trying to find a missing person in the vast wilderness. It was possible Charlie had gotten turned around on the trails but not probable. Not when he had maps and his supervisor had gone over the trails with him.

How had he gotten separated from the rest of his team? Shabina didn't want to think about the young man being murdered and dragged somewhere secluded, far away from everyone, to be found with ritualistic objects scattered around an altar.

"I suppose Vienna had to include Bale in her text," Shabina said.

"He's a valuable senior member of the Search and Rescue team," Raine said. "Once the alarm goes out, it goes out to everyone."

"Hopefully, he won't bring evidence to incriminate me with him, unless he killed Charlie and has already staged the crime scene."

Raine broke off a piece of scone. "You need to really think about calling Rainier, Shabina." She sipped at the tea, her gaze meeting Shabina's steadily over the rim of the cup.

"You know why I can't. It's too risky. You heard Boucher and Cormier. There might not be proof of who the assassin is they're referring to, but I'm not taking any chances."

"There is no proof," Raine said quietly. "No one knows for certain, Shabina. When I say that, I mean no one. There may be suspicion, but there is never evidence left behind. He's that careful."

"It isn't careful when he leaves a signature," Shabina whispered, leaning across the table toward Raine and covering her mouth just in case. She'd learned many people could read lips. Who knew if her café was bugged? She wasn't about to take chances with Rainier's life.

"He's only left that signature on a couple of kills. They know the other work is his because of the sandstorm and the way he's so silent and deadly. He's been at this for years. And it isn't just in the Middle East."

"He can't leave a signature again," she hissed, trying not to sound angry.

It was unreasonable to be upset with Raine when she couldn't control Rainier. She wasn't even in touch with him. Shabina didn't think Rainier's boss could control him. She didn't even know if he still worked for Blom or if he just went out on his own. That would be like him. If that was the case, he wouldn't have any protection at all.

She groaned and rubbed her temples. "He makes me crazy."

Raine laughed. "Doesn't he say that about you?"

"Probably, but I never do anything. I run a café."

"And hike the Sierra alone on trails that are closed to the public."

"I have three highly trained protection dogs with me, not to mention I'm armed to the teeth and very skilled in hand-to-hand combat if it came down to it."

"I think he would prefer it didn't come down to it. My point is, he wants you to always have a bodyguard with you."

Shabina rolled her eyes. "The last time he said that to me, I told him I thought he needed to have more than one bodyguard with him."

"I'll bet that made him happy."

Raine laughed softly, but Shabina could see that she was really assessing her condition. Shabina hoped she had pulled herself together enough to manage to look composed. She wasn't. She was a mess, but she would hold it together long enough to make certain Rainier was safe. That was what she cared about more than anything else.

Vaughn approached the table. "Shabina, I saw Vienna, Sean and Edward leave abruptly. If Search and Rescue was called, do you want Patsy, Tyrone and me to start preparing food to take up to the base camp? Chelsey and Nellie can clear tables. They won't mind."

"Thanks, Vaughn. I'll help in a few minutes. We'll need the usual. Sandwiches, the stew, the salads, everything on the menu to sustain them through the rest of the day and night. You know the drill. You've done it enough times."

"Let's hope the outcome is better than the last time." He hesitated, obviously wanting to ask if she knew any details.

"One of the trail rehabilitation crew didn't make it back to camp last night. That's not for public knowledge. Don't pass it on to anyone," she cautioned.

Vaughn knew that was an extremely bad sign. A lost tourist would have been better. "Anyone we know?"

"He was here a couple of weeks ago with Pete and Billy and a couple of women. They were all traveling to their camp together."

"I'm sorry, Shabina. I know this has been a lot for you lately. Stay with Raine for a little while longer and let us close the café and start getting things ready."

Shabina watched him talk to the others and set everything in motion for her. She was grateful she had taken a chance on him. It had been difficult trusting a man to come into the café in the early morning hours before anyone else arrived to help her set up. She wanted to go to him and tell him she felt it was such a privilege to know him. If she couldn't hold on, she would write him a letter.

CHAPTER TEN

The low hissing brought Shabina out of her half stupor. She'd heard that sound before. It was no snake slithering through the desert sand toward her. The increasing sound was layers of sand being lifted and driven ahead of the wind. Her heart accelerated in time with the gathering force. It was now or never.

Scorpion had made his first mistake and it was huge. He'd been called away, and this time, along with his cabinet, he'd taken the two men who were good to her. He had tasked those left behind with keeping her alive. She was in bad shape, far worse than Scorpion wanted to believe. They were giving her blood, feeding her intravenously and even providing fluids because she was too weak after his last furious assault on her to survive on her own.

Before he left, Iyad pressed a knife into her hand as he bent over her supposedly to check that she was still breathing. He whispered that he was sorry and that the shame was shared by all his people. He thought he knew what she intended to do. She still wanted to protect him. She didn't know if the knife could be traced back to him.

The sound of drums joined the hissing, swelling in volume. She tore the lines out of her arms, heedless of the pain. She barely noticed it with the agony she experienced with every tiny movement of her body. She *had almost no skin on her back, and the stab wounds in her left thigh were still open. When the sandstorm hit, anywhere on the human body that wasn't covered, the sand could take the skin right off. With open wounds and no clothing, she would be in trouble. That was to her advantage. No one, least of all her guards, would think her capable of moving, let alone attacking them during such an event.*

The hissing and drumming increased as she rolled from the thin pallet onto the desert floor. Black spots played behind her eyes as she hit the ground. Agony sent bile rising so that she retched over and over. She was used to pain, but trying to get on top of this was horrendous. She had no idea if she could do it. Consciousness kept coming and going as she began to drag herself across the sand toward the men in the distance, as they hurried to wrap themselves in blankets.

A roar grew, swallowing every sound. The dim light of a partial moon was snuffed out to be replaced by total darkness. The sand hit, abrasive, cruel, cutting into her already-torn body. She rolled, trying to escape the whipping particles as they roared into the camp at a good sixty miles an hour.

SHABINA FOUND HERSELF on the floor of her bedroom, her dogs pushing against her as she buried her face in her hands. Her chest felt on fire, and the pain in her left thigh was intense and throbbing. She couldn't stop the horrific memories from flooding her mind.

"I can't do this," she whispered to the Dobermans. "I just can't do this anymore."

She dragged herself up to her bed and sat on the edge, rocking herself back and forth. She had to make it all stop. Her face was wet, and she continually wiped at it with shaking hands. "You have to go outside, boys," she whispered. "I can't have you in here."

She couldn't have them in the house with her. She had no idea what she was going to do. She didn't trust her judgment. The dogs crowded around, and she scratched, patted and petted them, all the while crying silent tears. So many tears running down her face.

She had no idea how much time passed but she managed to force her stiff, painful body up. She was impossibly weak. She didn't think she would make it to the front door, so she let the dogs into the garden through the side door and relocked it before going back to her bedroom.

Her favorite pistol was where she kept it at night, under her pillow. Once more she slid down to the floor, drawing up her knees, making herself as small as possible. Placing the gun beside her left thigh, she pulled out her cell phone. She had to get it over with. She had to call Rainier. Once she'd warned him, she could try to clear her mind enough to think straight.

Shabina knew she shouldn't punch the number into her private cell, not when she was this far gone, because he might know. She was completely falling apart, but she had to warn him.

Rainier knew her better than anyone else. She had never called him before. It would be so unlike her. And she intended to thank him for everything he'd done for her. And give him his life back. He deserved that. She just had to find a way to sound completely composed for a few minutes while she spoke with him.

This wasn't a government number. She wouldn't be calling in an army. No one else would know or hear their conversation. She needed help, and the only person who could help her was at the other end of that line, and she couldn't ask him to come. There would be no one later to listen to a recording and analyze her voice.

Shaking, chin on her knees, she waited for him to answer. It took less than three seconds.

"Are you safe?"

On the heels of Rainier Ashcroft's demand came a distinctive feminine laugh. "He's occupied, honey. Call back later."

Shabina pressed her fingers over her mouth to shove back the sobs threatening to escape and froze like a little mouse. Not again. She was *always* ruining Rainier's life. It was never going to end.

He was with someone. A woman. Unlike her, he had a life. He deserved to have a life. She thought she'd taken that from him. Ruined everything for him. Now it was happening all over again. How stupid to think he wasn't living with a woman. Why hadn't she considered that? It was what she'd always wanted for him, so why did it hurt so bad? Why did she feel absolutely shattered?

Rainier swore, the words ugly and merciless, so like him. The woman shrieked. "What are you doing? I don't have my clothes. You can't throw me out naked. I'm sorry. I'm sorry."

"You're lucky I don't cut your throat. Get out and don't ever let me see you again."

That was very distinctive and so like Rainier. He was on the move. Shabina could tell. She broke the connection between them and hugged her knees tighter, rocking back and forth. She had no one. *No one.* She was slowly losing her mind. There was nowhere to go. She would never find her way out of this minefield alone. She'd tried everything she could think of on her own. She was so tired of being alone.

Her cell announced a text. She lifted the phone, knowing if she didn't answer, all hell would break loose, but she didn't know if she could speak to Rainier and convince him she was perfectly fine. She could barely breathe as she read his text.

You fucking better answer and code
in or I'll be sending every branch of
the service and special units your
way in ten seconds.

The phone buzzed. She took a deep breath and did her best to sound normal. "Rainier, it's your private cell, not the panic cell. Stop being dramatic. I'm fine."

"Code, damn it." A door slammed. He was already moving. She heard him murmuring orders into another phone.

She had to take another deep breath to keep a sob from escaping. "Sandstorms cover secrets." Whatever orders he was giving, she hoped he rescinded quickly.

"Are you alone?"

"Rainier." She couldn't say anything else. Of course, she was alone. She was always alone. She pressed the phone to her forehead, trying to think of a way not to sound pitiful. "I have to end the call. I'm fine now. I just had a bad moment."

"I'll be there in a few. Don't shoot me, *Qadri*."

"No. No, that's why I called. You can't come here." A sob welled up, and she jammed her fist in her mouth to cover the sound before she took another choking breath.

"Keep talking," he said tersely.

He was still moving. She hadn't stopped him. She needed to. "Please, for once in your life, listen to me. I never call you. I wouldn't have if this wasn't absolutely imperative. Two men claiming to be Interpol agents came here asking questions about an assassin they called Deadly Storms. They said they were from Paris, but I don't believe them. They claimed the assassin worked for Scorpion, but their story didn't make any sense. They weren't asking about Scorpion, only Deadly Storms."

"When did they talk to you?" His voice was clipped. Imperious. So Rainier.

"Yesterday. The day before. I don't know. I'm mixed up. Just take your life back. Thank you for everything. I would never have gotten this far without you. You mean the world to me, Rainier, but I want you to live your life free of worrying about me. Be safe."

There was that lump choking her. Tears wouldn't stop. She was sick to her stomach. Rocking like a two-year-old. Grateful he couldn't see her. She could hear the engine of a car, and he was snapping more orders into another phone.

"You didn't call me the minute they questioned you?" Now his voice dropped even lower, always a bad sign with Rainier. "These men are extremely dangerous. Were you alone?"

"No, Raine and Zahra were here."

She was terrified she was going to be sick, her stomach lurching terribly. Her skin was sweaty, but she was freezing, shaking with cold.

"I'll be talking to Raine, asking her why she didn't call. One of you should have."

There would be no stopping Rainier once he made up his mind. How many times had she screwed up his life? So many times. She groaned and curled her palm around the familiar cherrywood handle of her pistol. No matter how much work she put into standing on her own two feet, he thought of her as a child. This was why. She fell apart and couldn't pull herself back together no matter how hard she tried.

"I didn't want Raine to call you. I told her I would. Please don't blame her."

"But you didn't."

When she needed him to hear her and believe her, he ignored her. "Rainier, please don't come. Please let me go."

His breath hissed out, a long slow exhale. She wiped at the tears on her face, but they kept falling. How could she save him, when she couldn't save herself?

"Where are the dogs, *Qadri*? I need to know where your dogs are."

His voice, soft like velvet, penetrated the black fear.

"I'm so tired of fighting, Rainier. Of being alone. I really despise pity parties. And crying and feeling sorry for myself. I'm tired of being terrified every minute of the day."

"Tell me where your dogs are, Shabina."

She opened her mouth to answer him. A sob escaped. He had to have heard. She tried again. "Outside. In the garden. I put them outside."

She heard the brakes on his vehicle shrieking, as if he had been going full speed and slammed them on at the last minute.

"Do you remember when we first talked, baby? I told you there would be times like this. They come, but they always go away. You hang on, ride it out. I'll be there soon."

"I'm tired, Rainier." The moment the words came out of her mouth, she felt pathetic, but she always told him the truth.

She was tired of fighting against the inevitable. Scorpion had left her alone for the last few years, but she knew he was out there, and he would come for her. Rainier knew it too. She worried about everyone around her, fearing Scorpion would use them against her. For one brief moment, the idea of simply surrendering to him entered her mind. At the thought, her entire body shuddered, rebelling. Bile rose. Her fingernails bit into her skin. She couldn't breathe with the roaring in her head. No, she couldn't face him ever again. It would be better to be dead.

Her hand tightened around the grip of her gun. She just had to make the decision. She'd put the dogs out for a reason. She wouldn't end her life with them inside. She just needed to get a clear head and think things through, but she was too terrified. Too long without sleep. She wasn't certain what the right decision was.

"Rainier." She whispered his name. For him. She had to make certain he was safe. If she was in the world, he never would be safe because, like now, he would come to her when she had a problem. She would always have a problem. One didn't get over her kind of trauma. "You need to be safe. I have to make sure you're safe."

"Do you have your gun with you, *Qadri*?"

"Yes." She could barely get the word out.

"Where is it?"

She choked back another sob. "I've got it in my hand."

She heard dogs and then the murmur of another man's voice. The engine of a plane roared to life. Her heart nearly exploded in her chest.

"I want you to put the gun down and push it away from you."

That voice. Low. Firm. Absolute command. She always did what Rainier asked her to do, even when she didn't like it. But this was for him. To keep him safe. To give him a life.

"You don't understand. You'll never have a life. Never. You'll never be safe." She tried to make him understand. He *had* to understand.

"You *are* my life, Shabina. I need you to do what I tell you."

She shook her head. "I can't go back to my parents. You don't know what they're like, what I've done to them. They used to be so happy. All my mother does is cry when she looks at me, and my father consoles her. I can't breathe there. They watch me every minute of the day. Sometimes I think they look for an excuse to put me in a hospital."

She wiped at her tear-wet face, the barrel of the pistol nearly hitting her cheek.

"You don't have to go back to Houston."

Rainier. So firm. But he didn't understand. How could he? He was always strong. He could face anything. She'd seen him. He was like an avenging dark angel rising up in the worst of the sandstorms to take her away from Scorpion when no one could ever move in a sandstorm.

"I can't be alone anymore, Rainier. That sounds so pitiful, I'm embarrassed. I have good friends. I do. They all rallied around me, gave up work to be with me. They did. They were so wonderful. But I always feel apart from them, no matter how hard they try to bridge that gap between us. I know it isn't their fault, it's mine."

She curled into herself and let herself cry. She couldn't have stopped if she tried.

Rainier was silent for a moment, and then his voice turned commanding. It was the one she recognized when he was finished arguing and he expected everyone just to do what he said.

"Shabina, I'm coming to you now. I'm close, so it won't take long. I need to know you've put the gun on the floor and pushed it away from you. Do it now and confirm to me that you've done what I've asked you to do."

She heard another man's voice shouting. She could have sworn there was more than one man's voice in the background. It would be like Rainier to bring a full security crew even when she'd told him repeatedly she didn't want bodyguards. Only him. She only wanted him.

Rainier called back, and this time his answer was distinct as he replied to whoever had spoken. "Give me a minute. Shabina, we're going to take off. I need to know you've put the gun on the floor, and you're just going to sit there and wait for me. We'll talk when I get there."

"How can I stop you?" she whispered. "How can I save you if you don't let me?" He just wouldn't listen, and she was so tired and confused. Her brain didn't seem to function.

"*Qadri*, you saved me a long time ago. Confirm that you put the gun down."

She complied with his demand because she didn't know what else to do. There was no stopping him. "It's on the floor."

There were the briefest moments of silence and then he spoke again. "I'll be out of communication for just under half an hour. When I get there, don't pick that gun back up and shoot me."

Ordinarily, she would have tried to joke with him, but she didn't have it in her. She hugged her legs tightly, rested her cheek on her knees and cried. She should have known she couldn't stop Rainier. He was a force every bit as powerful as the worst of the sandstorms in the desert. What had he meant by she'd already saved him? He didn't say things he didn't mean.

Her head was pounding, the ache vicious. She couldn't think clearly or sort through her thoughts. There was so much pressure in her chest that it felt as if her heart were shattering. It couldn't be because the moment she realized she couldn't keep Rainier away, it occurred to her that he might be walking into a trap where she was the bait, and her heart had broken into a million little pieces right then.

She'd destroyed so many lives. Her parents. The unity of her family. There had been a time when they'd all been happy. She hadn't known another way of life except boarding schools and summer camps, traveling occasionally with her parents when her father was working outside the country.

Never once did she think her parents were worried while she was with Salman Ahmad and his tribe. When a video was made demanding ransom, she knew she looked healthy. She honestly hadn't thought they would be concerned about her. It had been drilled into her that kidnappings were simply a business and not to fight it. She hadn't.

When she was away at boarding school, they didn't seem particularly worried about her well-being. But she'd been a young teen then, not viewing the kidnapping from her parents' perspective. Life with the tribe had been an adventure. She'd seen the others ransomed successfully and wasn't in the least worried her turn wouldn't come.

Shabina wiped unsuccessfully at the tears. She *never* cried like this, but she couldn't stop no matter how many times she told herself to get control. She had lived in the desert with Scorpion, his cabinet and his mercenaries for just over six months. In that time, she'd experienced torture and rape, she'd witnessed the murders of innocent men, women and children. She hadn't cried on the outside. She hadn't given Scorpion or his men the satisfaction. On the inside, she'd screamed until her lungs and throat were raw, but she refused to give into tears.

She thought she was frozen inside, unable to cry real tears. She was wrong. She must have stored up years of tears because they were all being shed and there didn't seem to be a thing she could do about it.

There was no sound. No alert from the dogs outside the house. Not a single alarm went off outside, not on the fence, the gate, in the gardens, or on her doors or windows, but she knew the house had been penetrated. Her head went up alertly. She wasn't alone. She shoved her fist into her mouth to keep from making any noise. The intruder was in the room with her. A shadow only. She heard a pack fall to the floor across the room from her and then metal clacked together as another, very heavy pack that might have had weapons in it was dropped to the floor.

"Just me, *Qadri*. Don't panic. I'm coming to you. Keep your gun on the floor."

She put her head back on top of her knees. Rainier. She was a sorry mess. He was the one person who always saw her at her very worst. She didn't even care. There was nothing she could do about it. He knew what to expect. She'd told him not to come, but he hadn't listened.

Rainier crouched beside her, lifted her into his arms, and sank down onto the floor, cradling her on his lap. His arms tightened around her like a fortress, and she burrowed into him just the way she had when he'd taken her to his safe house because she'd begged him not to let anyone see her in the condition he had found her in.

He didn't say anything at all at first, he just held her and let her sob. For some reason, his presence made her tears increase, not lessen. She always said Rainier treated her like a child, but at least he heard her when no one else did. When she first was returned to her parents, she was terrified Scorpion would find a way to get her back. She begged her father to allow her to learn to shoot a gun, to start some form of self-defense lessons. He simply told her she was surrounded by security. Only Rainier heard her desperation.

Shabina didn't know how he got away with defying her father's decree, but Rainier insisted on teaching her self-defense. He was the one who first started instructing her to shoot a gun. He ignored the dictates of her parents and took her to a gym and taught her escape moves until she was proficient at them.

She rubbed her face against his chest. He had removed his jacket, dropping it on the bed as he made his way across the room to her so tears soaked his soft shirt. He was armed to the teeth, holsters and sheaths over and under his clothing. That was familiar to her, a part of Rainier. She couldn't imagine him without dozens of weapons. She knew he was a weapon without guns and knives and whatever else he had on him. His chest was dense, and when she rested her head there, it wasn't as if she had a soft pillow, but that didn't matter. She was always comforted by his presence.

Rainier rocked her gently, his chin resting on top of her head. He murmured softly to her but made no attempt to get her to stop crying. That was another thing, he just let her feel whatever she was feeling when everyone else told her what she should be feeling. Or how to cope with her feelings.

When she had panic attacks and horrendous nightmares, and in the beginning, when she first returned home that was all the time, despite the heavy security in her parents' home, he would suddenly appear in her bedroom and hold her, just as he was doing now.

Shabina tried to concentrate on his voice in the hopes she would find her control. She felt him brush kisses in her hair and then down along her temple. No one ever saw Rainier's sweet side. They didn't know he had one. Most of the time, he didn't even show it to her. He was abrupt and bossy and bordered on rude. But when he was like this, he stole her heart. She ached for him. Needed him desperately.

"I'm being selfish." She didn't know how she managed to get her voice to be heard above the coughing, sobbing hysteria.

"No, you're not," he denied. "You'd be selfish if I jumped out of a plane in the dead of night and you refused to let me comfort you."

There was just the slightest trace of emotion in his voice, but she couldn't tell what he was feeling. She wrapped her arms around his neck, pressing her wet face into his neck, taking in deep gulps of air, drawing his familiar scent into her lungs. "How did you get here so fast?"

"I have private planes and pilots ready to go at a moment's notice. I just parachuted in with my three Belgian Malinois and my equipment." He kept rocking her. "I'm always ready to get to you from wherever I am. I just happened to be closer this time than usual."

"All three dogs?" Three? She knew his dogs were trained for military, security and protection purposes. They had far more training than her Dobermans. "How could you get them to the ground safely and still have the gear you do?"

"Practice. And friends."

She didn't know if that meant others had parachuted in with him and were somewhere out in the night guarding the house, but she wasn't going to ask.

"Private planes and pilots?" She echoed his first statement, trying to figure out what he meant by always ready to get to her. "As in more than one?"

"Some time ago, I started my own security company. I hire men I know are good at their jobs yet have a difficult time fitting back into society. I have money and resources, sometimes more than I know what to do with. I still work with Blom but spend the majority of my time taking security jobs and training recruits."

His chin settled on the top of her head and rubbed. She remembered him doing that each time he held her close. She found it comforting. She closed her eyes, breathing him in. His strength, his scent, everything Rainier.

"When was the last time you slept?"

She shook her head or tried to. Her head wanted to explode if she moved it. Her eyes burned from crying so much. "Days," she managed to mumble.

"*Qadri.*" He whispered the endearment like a reprimand. "Why didn't you call me?"

"Nothing can happen to you." Her lips were against his throat, the only time she dared to show him how she felt. Just the thought of putting him in danger brought a fresh flood of tears. "I can't bear the thought of anything happening to you, Rainier."

As confessions went, it was rather silly. She wasn't certain he could understand between the sobs still escaping, the hiccups and gasping for breath. Her voice sounded strangled.

His fingers fisted in her hair. "Has it occurred to you, Shabina, I can't bear the thought of anything happening to you? We agreed you'd talk to me when things start to go bad. What happened to that agreement?"

What was she going to say? That she'd ruined his life already? "I should have tried to escape from Salman Ahmad's tribe," she confessed in a low tone. Ashamed. That was where it had all started. "Even if they caught me, I doubt if he would have punished me severely, if at all."

"This is the reason you didn't call me?"

She nodded, wiping more tears on his neck. "My father's security people told us not to resist if we were kidnapped, but looking back, I was very comfortable with Ahmad's people. I grew to love them."

A fresh flood of tears cascaded, and Rainier shifted her in his arms, careful to keep her close to his chest but where he could tip up her face to his. She tried to avoid his piercing gray eyes by burrowing tight against his chest.

"Keep going, baby. This sounds important."

Rainier, willing to listen when it was too late. He would try to make sense of her garbled ramblings. Of her guilt. Of the reason she couldn't call him.

"It didn't occur to me to try to escape because I really grew to think of many of the women and children as family. I saw others leave when the ransom was paid and waited my turn. I honestly didn't want to go. I was learning so many things. Not just that, I felt like I actually had a home."

That confession would tell him too much about her home life with her parents. She felt as if she was betraying them all over again. She moaned and tried to cover her face, but Rainier caught her wrist and held her hand down.

"Don't, *Qadri*. I need to see your face when you tell me this. It's clearly important."

Only Rainier would realize how important it really was. He would see her with those eyes that could see right into a person's heart. She had too many sins to want him to see her so clearly.

"If I had just escaped then, Rainier, Salman Ahmad, Mama Ahmad and all the members of his tribe, men, women and children, all of them, would still be alive today. There would have been no reason for Scorpion to attack them."

"Is that what you think?"

"I don't think it, I know it," she said decisively. "I can barely look at my parents, I'm so weighed down with guilt. They want me to live with them, and I just can't do it. I can't live in that environment with the two of them so sad and depressed. I've ruined their lives, Rainier."

"I disagree that Scorpion wouldn't have attacked them. They had money. He's a sadist, and he targets smaller towns or villages. They were most likely on his radar."

She shook her head. "He knew about the ransom my father tried to pay and he prevented that money from reaching the sheik. He didn't stop any of the other ransoms. And the things he did to me were very personal."

She knew she wasn't the first teenage girl he had taken prisoner and tortured, but his hatred of her was far too acute to be anything but personal. She fell silent, biting her lip, not knowing how to convince him or even if it mattered.

His fingers began a slow massage of the nape of her neck. "Keep going, Shabina. You haven't gotten to the part where you feel you can't call me when you're in trouble."

"You're a brilliant man, a brilliant doctor. You could have done anything, but that night, when you came for me, I was such a mess. You knew what I planned to do. You caught me crawling across the sand in the middle of the sandstorm. They were giving me antibiotics and blood and even trying to feed me intravenously. I'd pulled the tubes out because for the first time, Scorpion had made a mistake."

He remained silent, his fingers continuing that strong massage on the nape of her neck. She wiped her tears on his shirt.

"He'd taken the two mercenaries with him that had been good to me. I knew when he came back and found me dead, he'd kill some of the men he'd left behind. He's truly insane. Iyad had given me a knife, and I was going to kill as many as I could before one of them killed me or I died from loss of blood. I'd planned my death out very carefully."

She raised her gaze to his, her eyes meeting his. Her heart stuttered. Clenched hard in her chest. "You came out of the storm like an apparition. An angel of death. *Rainier.*" She breathed his name, once again caught up in the terrible memory of that night.

Scorpion's mercenaries had forgotten all about her, busy protecting themselves against the sandstorm. They hadn't thought— or cared—to protect a helpless girl.

"You're here with me now, *Qadri.* You're safe, far from him."

She shook her head. "I'm terrified Scorpion will make good

on his vow to me—that I can never escape him. That he'll come for me and anyone around me will be in danger. My friends. My parents. Now I know I'm bringing that same danger to you."

"He's the one afraid for his life."

Rainier's assurance was delivered in that same calm, steady voice he'd used when he'd taken her to his safe house and meticulously addressed each of her wounds. He didn't sugarcoat anything when he talked to her about her wounds or the infection she had or what she would experience in the future with the trauma she'd suffered. He didn't do that now.

"You've always believed you influenced my decision to kill those men holding you prisoner because you were so determined to do it, but that isn't the truth, Shabina. I cut off all emotion when I'm sent out. That's the only way I function in the field. Finding a sixteen-year-old girl nearly dead, tortured beyond what I'd seen in some of the worst cases, I was grateful I didn't feel. Knowing your guards abandoned you in that sandstorm while they protected their own skin would have made anyone go a little insane, but I don't operate that way."

He trailed his lips down her cheek following the path of tears. Her heart clenched and then pounded in reaction. He'd never done that before in all the times he'd held her. That was new, and she liked it far more than she should.

"I had already planned to kill those men. I had taken a contract to find and kill Scorpion and any of his associates. That contract was with several countries, none of which, at that time, was the United States. It just so happened that my rescue mission brought me straight to his camp. Unfortunately, he was gone and so was his inner circle."

Shabina frowned, trying to think back. Her memories were hazy. She'd been so ill. "He was so angry. He often was, but he'd gotten a message and told everyone that he had to leave immediately. He usually left behind at least two of the men he called his cabinet, but this time he ordered all of them to go with him. At one point, I think he considered taking me, but I was so far gone, he was afraid if he moved me, I'd die."

"You know for certain he received a message before he left?" There was speculation in Rainier's voice.

She nodded. The tears were beginning to finally slow, leaving her hiccupping. She was *such* a mess. She took the tissue he handed her. Rainier always seemed to be prepared for any emergency.

"He was so angry after reading it. Most of his men were afraid of him, and as soon as he began to rage at everyone, they got as far from him as possible. I wanted to make him angrier. I hoped he would kill me. When he was that angry, he looked for any target, and I was often his favorite. I did manage to draw his attention, which normally would have brought him straight to me. He would have beat me with his fists, but he'd already stabbed me multiple times in the thigh and had his men take turns with a whip."

"Why was he so angry with you?"

"I tried to escape. I was very weak. He'd gone through his starving-me phase, and that hadn't made me comply. For me, it was just another way to maybe leave the world. A couple of his men had stopped him before he killed me after he dragged me back to camp, but the punishment was the worst I'd ever gone through. Again, his men stopped him, or I know I would have died. He had turned calm after the camp medic told him I wasn't going to live. He told him if I died, the medic and his entire family would die."

"That's Scorpion calm?"

Her body gave a shudder as she took a deep breath, doing her best to regain control. "He isn't a calm man." She looked up at him. "He killed the guards that were so good to me, didn't he?" There was despair in her voice.

"They were dead the moment they signed up to work as mercenaries. All those men were. He'd planned to kill them all along. Deadly Storms just helped him out. In any case, baby, those guards participated in raiding other small tribes and killing innocent people. They may have objected to how far Scorpion was going to torture a young teenage girl, but don't forget they were paid to kill innocents."

He was right. She hadn't thought about that. She should have. It was just that they were the only ones to show her any kindness.

Rainier stroked a hand down the back of her hair. "Let's get you cleaned up and comfortable, Shabina."

Instinctively, her hands tightened on his shirt. That usually meant he was going to leave. He needed to leave, but it was the last thing she wanted.

CHAPTER ELEVEN

Shabina shook her head. "Don't go yet, Rainier. I know you have to, but not yet. I'll be able to deal with all of this in another few minutes. I've almost stopped crying. I don't even know where that came from."

"I didn't say anything about leaving, baby." His arms tightened around her. "You always demand too much of yourself. Here's what we're going to do. I'm going to carry you into the bathroom and run a bath for you. Hot water will help your body relax."

Every muscle and joint in her body felt as if she'd been hit by a truck. The idea of hot water sounded good but being away from Rainier, even for a few minutes, was terrifying. After the ordeal of the past few weeks, she didn't want to let go of him. She felt safe for the first time in months.

Compulsively, her fingers clutched in his shirt. When she was with him, she felt she could find her strength to fight on, even if it was just for a short period of time.

He stood smoothly. A Rainier move. He was a big man, all muscle, but when he moved, he flowed across the ground, almost as if he glided above it. Shabina never understood how he could so easily lift her when she wasn't small. She might be on the shorter side, but she had curves. He acted like she didn't weigh anything at all. He carried her right through to the master bath and sat on the edge of the tub, turning on the taps with one hand, keeping her secure on his lap with the other.

She wasn't surprised in the least that he knew his way around her home as if he lived there. He probably knew the layout better than she did. When she first moved to Knightly, Rainier refused to turn her security over to the men her father provided. He went over the property she'd purchased, had two safe rooms and cameras installed inside and outside. He had been meticulous about ensuring the windows were bulletproof. He made certain she could see outside but no one could see in at night.

"I detest this, Rainier, interrupting your life the way I always do. You were with a woman, and, as usual, I managed to mess that up for you with my panic attack."

"You saved her life, Shabina. I was just waiting for her to make her move. It never occurred to me you would call. You've never once called. I used a burner, but I made certain it had the ability to patch you in if you called. I knew she was an agent the minute she approached me. I gave her every opportunity to steal my phone or try to kill me. She was dead either way."

Shabina looked up at the hard lines in his face. "She was there to kill you?" She whispered the words, one hand cupping the side of his jaw. So hard, no give, just like him.

"Don't look like the world is coming to an end. My identity as Deadly Storms isn't known. This had to do with my work with Blom. It happens every now and then. Most of the time, no one knows who I am or where I am. I have a few personal enemies. I've been in this business a very long time. She's affiliated with a small cell that began to make noise in Colombia about eight years ago. I was sent in. She's a cousin in the family seeking revenge."

Her thumb slid along his jaw, tracing the strong line. "Why didn't you just protect yourself immediately?"

"I thought at the time I would get information from her. Who was behind the hit, how many, where they were and how they were able to get my name and location. It would make it easier down the line when I could turn my attention to tracking them down. Also, Blom has suspected for the last few months that someone on the inside was selling information on his men."

She pulled herself up straight, horrified. "Those two men who came here, the ones lying about being Interpol agents, what if they know who you are and were trying to confirm it by questioning me?"

"They're looking for someone else, an assassin, not a government agent."

Shabina frowned at him. "Wouldn't whoever is leaking information know who the assassin is?"

"Why would they? That information is not known. Blom might suspect, but I started gaining my reputation back home before I ever signed on with Blom."

"Your life, Rainier, is so awful. And then you have me clinging to you. You seem to be my lifeline." She rubbed her face on his chest again. She had to give him the truth. She owed him that much. "You *are* my lifeline."

"Funny thing, that, Shabina. I think of you that way. Lifeline. Destiny. Reason to stay alive. All those things. Stop looking as if it's the end of the world. I'm here now."

She leaned into him again. "Sometimes I don't think I can stand one more second feeling alone, and I need you desperately. I know that's terrible and puts so much pressure on you. I don't mean to do that to you. I don't want to do it to you. I swear, I've tried to build a life and be strong, so you feel like you're free of me." She couldn't stop her confession, the words just kept tumbling out, no matter how hard she tried to remain silent.

He brushed another kiss on top of her head, one hand testing the temperature of the water. "Who said I wanted to be free of you? I never once told you I wanted to be free of you, Shabina. I've never acted that way. Where the hell do you get these ideas?"

His tone was gruff. Matter-of-fact. Low and steady. So Rainier. She couldn't always tell what he was thinking or feeling, but there was a slight hint of exasperation in his voice. Was he becoming impatient with her? She wouldn't blame him.

"Why do you feel alone? You have friends, Shabina. I thought you were happy here. You've made a life for yourself."

"They try to understand. They all try to know me, but how can they? Even Raine. She comes the closest, but only you really know. Everyone tells me how I should think or feel about what happened to me, but they didn't experience it." Another sob welled up, and she pushed her fist into her mouth, refusing to start crying again when she'd just gotten herself under control.

She took a deep breath. "I'm not being fair to my friends. They try very hard to understand. When they were worried about me, they took time off work to be with me. They've been amazing friends. It isn't them. It's me. I feel so apart from everyone."

"Why haven't you told me this before now?"

Convulsively, her fingers tightened in his shirt. "I know how you are. You don't think anyone knows you, Rainier, but I do. If you hear me whining and crying, confessing I feel alone unless you're around, you're going to move heaven and earth to find a way to be with me." She forced her stricken gaze to meet his. "You would, wouldn't you?"

"In a heartbeat." He trailed more kisses down her wet cheeks. "Stop crying now. You're safe. I've got you safe."

"The only time I feel safe is when you're with me. The only time I don't feel alone is when you're with me. It isn't fair to you, but it's the truth." She lifted her head, forcing herself to look into his eyes as she made her confession. "I'm sorry. I know that only makes things worse for you. I swear I'm doing everything I can to learn to be okay, but I can't seem to get there. Not without you."

Rainier cupped her chin, his steel-gray eyes studying hers. "Do you mean that? You only feel safe when I'm with you?"

"I hate it when you're away from me." She was truthful.

"And you didn't think to tell me this either? You felt alone all this time and you haven't felt safe?" He didn't sound happy.

Shabina shook her head. "Not for one single minute of the day. I'm not going to live with my parents, Rainier. And I don't want a security team here. I'll get stronger. I will." She did her best to pour determination into her voice, but she didn't believe she could do it anymore. She'd been trying, physically, emotionally, spiritually, all of it, to build herself up. She would do fine for a period of time, and then she'd crash and burn just like now. This time had been the worst of the episodes she'd experienced. Had he not come, she had no idea what would have happened.

"You should have called me right away, *Qadri*. We're supposed to talk about things. You promised me you'd be honest with me."

"You don't like clingy women." She tried a watery smile. "And don't pretend you don't mind them. I know you better than that."

His lips ran down her wet cheek again. "You're absolutely right, Shabina. I wouldn't tolerate any other woman trying to cling to me, but you aren't just any woman. You can cling all you want, and you should have been honest with me."

Shabina wasn't certain how best to respond to him. His answers surprised her. Shocked her, even. The feel of his lips on her skin sent little sparks of electricity skittering down her spine and hope blossoming in her heart. She did her best to ignore hope. She tended to misread Rainier's kindness to her because she desperately wanted him to care for her the way she did him.

"I want you in the tub, Shabina. We'll talk about all this when you're not shaking like a leaf and your body isn't hurting quite so bad."

Steam rose from the bathwater. Rainier believed in hot water. More than once he'd put her in a hot bath or taken her into a hot shower. He was a great believer in a cold shower as well. That wasn't her favorite, and she didn't want him to get any ideas. The hot water was far more appealing to her.

"I'm going to bring in your dogs. My three will be in the garden to ensure everything stays quiet. I've got to make certain they have water and the gates are secure and locked." A hint of a smile touched his mouth. "Not that they couldn't escape if they wanted to, but they'll stay."

Panic was instantly overwhelming. Involuntarily, her fingers curled into fists in his shirt, holding him to her. She shook her head. "You can't leave, Rainier. You can't go anywhere."

"I'm not going anywhere." His voice was steady. Firm. "I'm putting you in the tub, taking care of the animals, and then I'll be right back. Your muscles are going to lock up if they haven't already." His hands dropped to the buttons of her blouse, and he began to slip them loose from the buttonholes. "I'm not leaving you." He slipped the blouse from her shoulders. "Where are the pins you keep in here so I can put your hair on top of your head?"

Shabina looked around a little helplessly, forcing herself not to clutch at him. She was doing all the things she'd promised herself she wouldn't do. She wasn't embarrassed as he gently lifted her to her feet to strip her trousers from her hips. He had seen her completely nude numerous times. She wished he weren't so impersonal, but he always was. It would be nice to think she could seduce him, that he would be interested in her other than as a patient he needed to care for medically or as someone who needed him to provide her with security.

Her muscles and joints were far too locked up for her to stand on her own. Rainier had to lift her into the deep tub and help her sit in the hot water. Nothing had ever felt so good. He kept her hair in his hands to prevent it from falling into the water, twisting it on top of her head and pinning it in place with an expertise that reminded her he had done so many times. How he'd found the pins for her hair, she had no idea.

"I'm glad you aren't cutting your hair, although I'm a little surprised. It's heavy. You have a lot of hair. Your mother has beautiful hair, you inherited it from her, but she's very modern. She doesn't wear it long like this."

He hadn't exactly asked her a question, but she knew he was curious. "Scorpion chopped it off. Remember when you first rescued me?" Although he might not have noticed when her body was such a mess and she was close to death.

"I remember."

"Chopping my hair off was part of his punishment. He wouldn't let me have hair because he claimed I didn't know how to behave correctly as a woman." She had tried hard to close the door tight against those memories. "I prefer to have my hair long. Mama Ahmad wore her hair in a long braid most of the time and covered it. She showed me how to do quite a few different braids and how to wrap them on the back of my head or on top so I could cover my hair."

"She made quite an impression on you."

"She was wonderful. She taught me so many things, from cooking and baking to henna tattooing. I never heard her complain. If visitors came, she welcomed them and made them feel at home."

Rainier's hands were on her shoulders, his strong fingers massaging her muscles to loosen the tight, sore knots. "She sounds like she was a very impressive woman. She would have been proud of you, Shabina. You turned out very much like her. Warm, welcoming. You treat everyone who comes to your home or café with that feeling of warmth that makes them want to return."

His praise thrilled her. That was the thing about Rainier. He didn't just hand out compliments on a regular basis. That wasn't his way, but he managed to make her feel good about herself in unexpected moments. In unexpected ways.

"Thank you, Rainier. It means a lot that you would say that to me. I loved her. I miss her every day. I always ask myself what she would say or do in each situation when someone is being nasty to me in the café."

His fingers ceased motion, tightening on her shoulders. "What do you mean by that? Do you have customers who get ugly with you?"

Shabina couldn't help herself; his reaction made her want to laugh. She tilted her head back to look up at him. "Rainier, be serious. Anytime you're in a business dealing with the public you're going to have to expect to run into people with bad attitudes."

Some dark emotion moved through his eyes. "Perhaps that business isn't one you should be in, *Qadri*."

"I love my café."

He stood up, and immediately tendrils of panic began to unfold in the pit of her stomach. She pressed her fist against her churning abdomen resisting the urge to bring her knees up. She would *not* be so pitiful that she couldn't trust that he would return in a few minutes.

"Get warmed up. It won't take me long to settle the animals and ensure security is tight."

She nodded, wishing she could muster up the strength to tease him about his commanding tone. He always used it. He always would. She knew it irritated her friends, but she didn't mind; in fact, she found the way he spoke reassuring.

Rainier wasn't arrogant, although he came off that way to most people. She knew her father thought he was arrogant. She had always found it funny when her father accused Rainier of arrogance because the majority of people dealing with her father considered him extremely arrogant. Her father had always gotten his way in negotiations—until he tried to pay the ransom for her.

Shabina couldn't help herself, she drew her knees up to her chest and wrapped her arms around her legs, contemplating the things Rainier had revealed to her about the night he'd rescued her. He claimed that she hadn't been the reason he'd killed the men in the camp that night, that he'd been sent there for that purpose.

Her mind turned that information over and over. Rainier was Deadly Storms, the assassin so often whispered about, and he told her he was there to dispose of Scorpion. If that was true, had it been a bonus that he'd rescued her? She'd always thought he had come to the camp specifically for the purpose of retrieving her. He knew she was there. That hadn't been a surprise to him.

Assassins didn't allow others to know their identities. Never once had she felt threatened by him. She was dying when he'd found her. He easily could have left her there to die after he'd killed the mercenaries. The direction her mind was taking her made no sense at all. Paranoia was once more creeping in.

"You're crying again."

His voice was low. Gentle. So much so that he didn't startle her. He reached down to open the drain plug and lifted her, uncaring that she was soaked and would get him wet.

"Am I?" She hadn't realized. "I don't really cry. I think somehow the faucet turned on and I don't know how to turn it off."

He was being impersonal again as he dried her off. That was enough to make her cry.

"Now you're beginning to laugh. Don't get hysterical on me." His tone turned grim.

He'd already pulled pajamas from one of the drawers in her closet. He dragged the top over her head. It was a short camisole in a dark rose made from soft cotton fabric. The matching long drawstring pants were very comfortable. He hadn't retrieved the little jacket that went with it. Instead, he just took her through to the bedroom and, after yanking back the covers, put her in the bed.

She couldn't look at him. "I'm not a child, Rainier. I know it may seem like I'm acting that way now, but I'm all grown up."

"I've never treated you like a child, Shabina. I don't view you as one. I didn't even when I first rescued you. How could I after what you'd gone through? Your childhood was ripped away from you." He sat on the edge of the mattress. "I'd had experience with that and knew what it was like."

"It feels like you do."

"Am I too bossy with you?" He sounded a little sad. "I'm serious about your security because I don't lie to you and pretend you aren't still in danger. You are. You're going to be in danger until that bastard Scorpion is dead. Not captured and put in prison but dead. I don't play games with your safety. I never have and I never will."

"I'm aware of that, Rainier. I appreciate that you look out for me. It isn't that."

"I'm never going to be able to change who I am. I wanted to, for you, but I'll always be that man talking to you like this. I'll take charge when I think it's necessary to protect you and anyone else we care about. That's who I am."

"I'm well aware of that." She looked down at her hands. "You make me feel safe. The only time I ever feel safe is when you're with me. I shouldn't admit that to you, but I don't want you to think it bothers me that you take charge. It doesn't. It makes me feel safe."

There was a long silence, and then Rainier caught her chin and forced her head up. "You've said that before. You don't feel safe without me around."

She felt the color creeping under her skin. What difference would it make if he knew how she felt about him? He probably already did. "I never have. I detest it when you leave. I feel alone and can't sleep." She moved her chin from his hand with a little shake of the head. "I don't have PTSD episodes all the time, Rainier, but I don't like being away from you. That has nothing to do with PTSD. And please don't be like everyone else and try to convince me it's because you rescued me and I'm dependent on you, that I'll get over it. I'm not ever going to get over it."

Rainier pushed a stray strand of hair behind her ear, his fingers gentle as they traced her earlobe. "I wish you would have felt confident enough to tell me this months ago. Why didn't you?"

She sighed again. "I overheard you say you lost the one woman you loved. I believed it was because of me. I also feared you ruined your chances of moving up the ladder in your career. You rescued me and went a little insane when you saw what those men had done to me. I blamed myself."

"I had no idea all this time you felt guilt for something you didn't do. First, let me set the record straight once and for all. I was called in to try to find the camp where you were held. I watched the videos and figured out you used birds to send the location of the camp, but I also knew you were moved as soon as the videos were sent. Sadly, it took time to work out your code. Once I had it, I moved fast."

"But you said you were sent after Scorpion and his men."

He nodded slowly. "That is true. That was two separate missions. I have a standing contract with several countries Scorpion and his men committed crimes in. He's considered an international serial killer. No one knew his identity. My boss in Special Activities has no idea that before I ever joined, I had already established myself as an assassin in the Middle East."

"I suspected no one knew you were Deadly Storms, although Raine definitely is suspicious. Or just plain knows." She hadn't known for certain and she'd witnessed him in action.

"It just so happened that you had been kidnapped by Scorpion and his men. Blom and everyone else believes I rescued you just before the sandstorm hit, and the assassin struck after we were already gone. Killing those men had nothing to do with you and didn't impact my career as you seemed to believe. I didn't want to move up the ladder. I had freedom to do the things I was good at and at the same time look after the woman I love."

Her heart jumped. Stuttered. Her gaze met his. What was he saying to her? She didn't dare jump to conclusions, but she *had* to know. She needed clarification.

"Rainier, what are saying?" Her voice refused to go above a whisper.

"You're the only person in my world who doesn't seem to know. If you want me to stay, all you have to do is say so, but you'd better mean it. If I stay, I stay permanently. There isn't any going back. You go into the relationship with your eyes open. You know who I am and what I do. I've waited a long time for you, but it has to come from you."

Shocked, she blinked up at him, not comprehending what he was saying to her. He didn't repeat himself. His gaze didn't move from hers.

She gathered every bit of courage she had. "If I had my way, Rainier, you'd always stay with me."

"Don't just say it because you're having a difficult time. Your father will do everything in his power to put every roadblock imaginable in front of us. If you choose me, you very well could be separating yourself from your parents."

There was that overwhelming guilt weighing her down immediately. When it came to her parents, she felt as if she'd destroyed their lives.

"Why does my father dislike you so much?"

"We can talk about that after we talk about us. You'll have to make your decision based on how you really feel about me, Shabina. If you want me to stay, you need to want the same thing I do, a permanent relationship. Marriage. The two of us having each other's backs. It won't be easy with me. I'm no prize, but I've always shown you the real me."

"I have so many issues, Rainier. I want you to be with me, but I can't imagine why you would love me. And I want to be loved by you."

"Baby, look at me." He caught her chin and tilted her head up. "I can assure you without any reservations, I love you. There isn't anyone else, and there never will be." He pressed a brief kiss to the corner of her mouth and let her go.

"Why would you? How? When?"

"I've always known we were meant to be together. You think I saved you, but that isn't true. Until I met you, I thought that my childhood had shaped me into a bitter, relentless psychopath."

"I've seen true psychopaths, Rainier. You're not that."

"If I'm not, it's because of you. You brought humanity back into my life. After all the things done to you, there was such compassion in you. Such gentleness. You truly loved the people. You would lie awake beside me and tell me about the men risking their lives and the lives of their families to give you a drink of water. Or to find a way to take you for a walk among birds. They would do you small kindnesses knowing if they were found out, Scorpion would torture not only them but their wives and children. You painted a vivid picture of men walking such a tightrope with not only one madman but several in order to aid you. It made me rethink the way I thought about people. I had to spend quite a lot of time meditating and thinking over my life and what I'd become."

Shabina was afraid to believe he might want to stay with her. That he could really love her knowing what a mess she was. Even hearing him attribute the changes in him to her seemed unbelievable. She didn't think of herself as extraordinary. She couldn't see the vision he had of her.

"I knew if I wanted to be with you, I would have to learn to be a better man. I'd have to learn that same compassion and depth of humanity you have. You see people as individuals, and you give them respect until they prove to you that they no longer deserve it."

She shook her head. "I'm really not that kind and compassionate. I wish I were." She bit her lip. "If I had my way, Rainier, you'd move in and stay with me forever."

"Even if you lose your parents over it?"

She took a deep breath. She knew that it was a possibility, but she didn't know why. At the back of her mind, there was a little nagging thought she kept shutting down. "Yes." Her voice wobbled. She wanted it to be stronger. Her resolve was strong, but she despised hurting her parents, and she knew this decision would.

"Be sure, Shabina. I move in, I stay. We get married immediately and quietly. I wouldn't put it past your father to try to hospitalize you if I'm called out of town. It would be like him to do something like that to get you away from me."

She wanted to deny it, but it was the truth. "You keep saying I have to be sure, Rainier. You need to take a good look at what you're getting. Please look at the real me, the one falling apart every few months. Do you really want me for the mother of your children?"

"I told you. I've built my life around yours already. I've started a business, so when I decide to retire, I'll have something I can pass on to others, training and giving jobs to men like me who need somewhere to go when they've had enough of government work."

"It's settled, then. You're moving in with me. There's an entire side of the closet empty." She felt extremely courageous telling him so matter-of-factly when she was shaking inside.

His palm smoothed over the back of her hair. For just one moment his eyes lit up and a very brief smile softened the cruel edge of his mouth. "Brought the necessities with me, and I can easily get the rest. I do still have work to finish. I've got a lead on a couple of the men I've been hunting. The last place they were seen was in Jordan. As soon as I know you're going to be fine, I'll go after them. I need to have solid intel first because I'll have to get in and out of the country without detection."

The idea of his leaving her alone again terrified her, but she tried to cover the reaction by crossing her arms over her chest and hugging her body tightly.

"I'm not going until I know you're one hundred percent, Shabina." He unfolded his large frame and sauntered over to his duffel bag. "These customers of yours that aren't always nice, maybe we should talk about them."

Shabina considered pretending she was so exhausted she couldn't continue with their conversation, but Rainier would never allow her to get away with that. He disappeared into the closet, but when she remained silent, he stuck his head back out, raising his eyebrow.

"That bad?"

"You'll be upset that I didn't tell you before this. Raine has been collecting video from the various establishments to prove harassment. I can't go to Rafferty, the local sheriff, because Bale Landry is related to him. Evidence always disappears. We have a plan in place, but we need to gather all the evidence before I file a restraining order."

She tried to give him the explanation fast. Now that he was standing in front of her again, his hard features grim, those piercing eyes looking like steel, she thought it was a big mistake on her part not to have informed him.

"Don't leave out any details."

Shabina told him everything, starting with the way Bale, Edward, Sean and Jason had harassed Zahra and her almost from the very beginning when they'd moved to Knightly. At first it had been snide comments, but lately the behavior had escalated. Not from Jason, but mostly from Bale and Sean. She tried to keep emotion from her voice when she related the details of the graffiti on the walls of her café. The many times they came in and complained about her meals, refusing to pay and even going so far as to file a police report saying she tried to poison them.

Rainier was still, his features expressionless, but his gray eyes had gone a scary mercury. That didn't bode well for the men. He didn't interrupt to ask questions, so she continued to tell him about the recent murder and how Bale had threatened her both at the café and at her home.

She kept her gaze fixed on his. His stillness gave him the illusion of fading into the background—something difficult to do for a man as large as he was. But the color of his eyes changed radically. Gray went to mercury. Mercury went to a darker silver. She could see a black ring around the silver. A storm, a desert storm, one with lightning and thunder, all right there in his eyes. A little shiver of apprehension slid down her spine.

"Rainier, these men are regular civilians." She felt the need to remind him. "They're creepy, and Bale has gone way too far, but I think once I pursue legal action through the proper channels they'll stop."

Rainier bent down to brush his palm over her cheek. "Do you really believe that?"

She swallowed the first three things she would have said just to placate him. She had to be honest. "No." The admission was made in a low tone. "The others, yes, but not Bale. Raine thinks losing control of the others has made him desperate."

She told him about the murder and finding the feathers and how Chelsey stole the spices from the café. How she found the spices and dates in a bush along the canal where she ran every day.

Rainier regarded her steadily. "Murder. Threats. The FBI questioning you. A corrupt sheriff. Two men pretending to be Interpol agents. It took how long before you decided to call me?

And not for your own safety but because you were worried about me." He shook his head. "What am I going to do with you?"

She flashed a tentative smile. "It does sound kind of bad when you put it all together like that. I thought Scorpion might have sent someone here to implicate me in a murder."

Rainier shook his head. "Not his style. He'd target your friends if he was going to murder anyone and do his best to make it look like you're guilty. Anyone can get birds or flowers from places here in the States if they know where to look. If someone is looking to frame you, it's a shit job. You can prove you were in Knightly when the murder took place. The most they can do is try to find a way to implicate you as an accomplice, which would be difficult and ludicrous."

Relief left her shaky. Other than her fears for Rainier, her worst fear had been that Scorpion was close. She trusted Rainer's judgment. If he said Scorpion wasn't leaving feathers on her doorstep to torment her, she believed him.

"That leaves the questions, who would leave feathers on the steps of my café, Rainier, and why? How would those same feathers be used on an altar at a murder site?"

"We'll find those answers, *Qadri*. In the meantime, I'll get together with Raine and take a look at the security footage. It's possible I can spot something she hasn't, although, as far as I can tell, not very much gets past her."

Shabina was happy to hear Rainier praise Raine. They had seemed at odds on more than one occasion. Raine was brilliant, and she was a good friend. Shabina wanted Rainier to like her friends. They were important to her.

"I've got a ring. I've had it for a very long time." He leaned down to take her hand. "We can drive to the courthouse in Independence on your next day off and get our marriage license."

She raised an eyebrow. "You've been planning this."

"For a long, long time."

Rainier slipped the ring on her finger, and her heart went into overdrive. It wasn't huge, which was perfect for her. She didn't want huge. The color of the diamond was a vivid greenish, nearly royal blue, cut in multi-facets. It was extraordinarily beautiful.

"As soon as I saw this stone, I knew I had to have it for you." He brushed his lips gently over the ring. "Never think you aren't loved, Shabina."

CHAPTER TWELVE

S habina." Eve Garner waved at her, smiling widely. Her sister gestured for Shabina to join them at the little table where Tyrone had seated them.

Shabina excused herself to the Swedish climbers she was speaking with and made her way across the room to join the two women.

"You won't believe the little house we found to buy," Felicity told her, excitement edging her voice. "It's so perfect for us. It has a yard where we can grow vegetables, but it isn't too big, so it should be easy to take care of."

"And a patio with a built-in firepit right off a sliding glass door," Eve added. "We've already started the paperwork. The agent said if the loan goes through, and it will, we can move in after the first."

"I'm so happy for you." Shabina genuinely was. The two sisters were glowing. It was such a difference from when she'd first encountered them.

"We feel so much closer to Freda here," Felicity said. "It's nice to learn all the things she loved to do. We ran into the local vet, Dr. Sanderson, and she recommended Miguel Valdez to teach us to climb. He's a personal trainer. Do you know him?"

Shabina nodded. "He's very nice, but exacting. If you hire him, he works, and he'll expect you to." She laughed. "Unless you're Zahra. The rest of us work our butts off, but somehow, and we've never quite figured out how, she manages to get out of the workout."

"Zahra is legendary," Felicity said. "I hear her name all over town."

"She's the chief administrator at the hospital. Without her, we wouldn't have the amazing trauma center that we do. No one is better at securing grants and fundraising than she is."

Tyrone seated the four male students from the university at one of the window tables, handing out menus and chatting briefly before leaving them to their waitress. Shabina had the same reaction to the four men she'd had before Rainier's arrival. Her heart accelerated. It was difficult to breathe. She instantly felt on guard.

Shabina was disappointed in herself. She kept her mask on, murmuring her replies to the two women with a smile before she took her leave and went on to the next table to greet her customers. She would have to say hello to the men from the university. They had come into her café several times now and had taken the bird-watching tour. It was clear they enjoyed the cuisine she included from the Middle East as well as the specialty coffee. They ordered it each time they came in. Jules Beaumont had switched from the Middle Eastern cuisine to her Belgian waterzooi, a creamy stew made with chicken, cream, vegetables and eggs, at lunchtime. He seemed to really savor the dish. She had put it on the menu when he'd mentioned that he came from Belgium.

Raine and Zahra entered the café, and Vaughn hurried to help Raine to their favorite table in the back. Shabina brought them their usual drinks, grateful for their reassuring presence.

"Can you sit a moment?" Raine asked. "I want to catch you up on the latest."

"I only have a few minutes. We're filling up," Shabina said, slipping into the chair beside her.

Raine leaned close to her. "A member of the rescue team didn't check in last night. They always search in groups, and they check in with one another and their team leader."

Cold fingers crept down Shabina's spine. "It's too soon. He must be lost. The murderer wouldn't kill again this soon, would he? And how would he find the opportunity with so many people searching the trails?"

"We don't know for certain he's been murdered." Zahra was practical. "He could have gotten turned around."

"You don't believe that," Shabina objected. "Who, Raine? He must be local, or he wouldn't be on the Search and Rescue team."

"Lucca Delgotto. He's a waiter at the Grill. His family moved to Knightly when he was eight. Two brothers, one sister. Both parents are alive." Raine had no expression in her voice.

Shabina scrubbed her hand down her face. She not only knew Lucca, but she knew his entire family. "Has Vienna been in touch?"

"Only to send news of Lucca," Raine said.

"And to tell me she needs more time off. Harlow returned to cover at the hospital," Zahra interjected.

"We've got to figure out who's doing this," Shabina said. "We can't wait for the FBI or Rafferty. Raine, we have to put the clues together and stop him. I know we can do it; we're smart. If we all work at it, we should be able to figure it out."

Patsy arrived to take their orders. "Sorry it took so long. We're one waitress down, and I'm covering outside as well." She gave Shabina a sober, questioning look. "Your partner took Chelsey outside for a talk. It didn't go well. He looked scary. She cried a lot. She apparently was fired?" That was a question.

Shabina nodded. "Yes. I've got three interviews this afternoon after work. I've talked to them before, and all three seem good candidates. I'm sorry I didn't have time to warn you, Patsy. I'll get moving in a minute."

Patsy waved the suggestion away. "We can handle it right now. You visit for a minute. If we get too overloaded, I thought we might tell Mr. Hottie he has to wait tables." She winked at Shabina. "Can you imagine the women fainting when he walks in?"

"I can't imagine anyone telling him to wait tables," Shabina said. "That idea leaves me a little faint."

Patsy laughed again and hurried away to put their orders in. Silence followed her departure. Shabina felt color rising under her skin and creeping up her neck and face. She tried not to look at Zahra and Raine, but it was impossible.

Raine regarded her with a mixture of amusement and what could have been satisfaction. Zahra had her infamous expressive eyebrow lift and shock on her face.

"Partner?" she challenged. "You have a partner, and your besties don't know?"

"We were discussing murder." Shabina tried her best to be nonchalant.

Zahra waved the subject away. "Not nearly as interesting at this time. Explain the partner."

"You aren't the most observant woman in the world, *little mama*," Shabina said, calling her by the familiar endearment she often used for her. She placed her left hand on the table between them, so that her ring caught the light. She had no doubt that Raine had seen the ring the moment she sat down.

Zahra caught her hand to nearly jerk her out of her chair. "Is that thing real? It looks like a blue diamond. Tell me it isn't real. And who is your partner?" Abruptly she sat back, her expression changing rapidly. "Not Rainier. Don't tell me you're engaged to Rainier Ashcroft. Because if you are, we need to have an intervention immediately."

Shabina burst out laughing. "Prepare to intervene, not that it will do you any good. I'm not giving him up. If he tried to run away, I'd sue him for breach of contract or whatever it is I could do to hold him to his word."

Raine joined in her laughter. "I hardly think that's a possibility. Rainier's built his entire life around you. He isn't going to run off because Zahra doesn't like him."

"I didn't say I didn't like him," Zahra objected. "I'm reserving judgment until I have all the details."

Shabina and Raine both laughed. Zahra had the most expressive face. She managed to look innocent and skeptical at the same time.

"I think the instant response of stating we need an intervention might show your feelings toward Rainier are negative," Raine pointed out.

Zahra waved that away. "I suppose my statement could have a negative connotation, if you really wanted to stretch the imagination. The man has the good taste to choose Shabina. That does say something for him."

Shabina and Raine exchanged an amused look but didn't dare reply. They both were afraid they'd erupt into gales of laughter.

"When did all this come about?" Raine asked.

"He parachuted in last night with his three Malinois because, you know, drama suits him." Shabina knew Zahra would be impressed. "Those dogs are no joke. He tries to act tough, but you should see him with them."

"Parachuted?" Zahra echoed. "Three dogs?"

"And lots of equipment. You know, the usual. Guns, knives,

grenades, C-4, maybe a mortar gun or two." Shabina just managed to keep a straight face.

"He parachuted? At night? Why?"

"I was having a hard time, and I called him. He came right away," Shabina explained. "We sorted out how we both felt. He already had a ring for me. Apparently, he's had it for a while. Am I the only one who didn't know how he felt about me?" She looked directly at Raine.

Raine smiled at her. "It was evident to me that he was building his entire life around you. I didn't say anything because I wasn't so certain of him. After Zale and he weren't forthcoming about the knowledge they had of Vienna's father, I wasn't exactly thrilled with him."

"Neither was I," Zahra said. "In fact, I wanted to kick him really hard. Did he have an explanation for his silence?"

"We didn't talk about that," Shabina admitted. "I had to fill him in on the murder, Bale's creepy behavior and the fact that one of my servers stole from me. He wasn't happy that I'd waited so long to call him."

"You just remember that men who are bossy don't get better over time, Shabina," Zahra cautioned. "They often get worse. Rainier strikes me as an extremely take-charge man. Have you taken that into consideration?"

Shabina nodded. "I'm well aware of Rainier's personality."

"There's an age difference too," Zahra pointed out. "He might always think he can act like he knows so much more than you do just because of that. And wasn't he raised in the Middle East? If so, it's very possible he has that attitude that men can rule women. I'm not being judgmental; I'm just saying these are points to consider. Your backgrounds are very different. There are cultural differences as well as economic differences to consider."

Shabina appreciated everything Zahra brought up. Each argument was a well-thought-out concern. Zahra didn't have all the facts about Shabina's upbringing or Rainier's. It was impossible for her to know what Shabina needed in a relationship. Still, Zahra struggled to understand and be supportive of her friend's choice even while she pointed out the possible pitfalls.

"He was born in the United States but raised in the Middle East. I honestly have taken all those things into consideration, Zahra," Shabina assured. "The thing you don't know about Rainier is that he puts me first." She rubbed her thigh. "I worry that I'm not going to be a good partner for him in the bedroom after all the trauma I've been through. He doesn't seem worried in the least. He just tells me it will happen when it's right. Not to rush things or feel we need to. He makes me feel safe and loved. I don't feel those things unless he's with me."

"Then he sounds like he's right for you," Zahra said.

"I'm going to have to get to work. It's getting super busy in here, and my staff has been amazing to let me sit and visit."

"They're most likely terrified of Rainier's wrath if you're upset in any way," Raine said.

Shabina couldn't argue with that assessment. "Did he contact you already about viewing the security footage? Is that why he confronted Chelsey?"

Raine nodded. "I received a call from him early this morning. Does he sleep?"

Shabina had fallen asleep with Rainier's arms around her. He'd held her against him, his arms that fortress she remembered from all the many years when he showed up, sliding into her bedroom when she needed him the most. She had no idea if he slept because she always fell asleep first, and he was out of bed early, caring for the dogs and doing a thorough security check.

They'd gone running together, taking all the dogs with them before returning his three, Mick, Sonar and Bomber, back to the house to guard while they went to the café so she could do the early morning baking. Rainier had disappeared for a short time. When he returned, he took his laptop to Raine's favorite table and stayed out of the kitchen. It hadn't occurred to her that Rainier would contact Raine so soon and ask to view the security footage for the café and her home. She'd brought him Arabic coffee and date cookies once she had them fresh from the oven but left him to his work while she did hers.

"That's a good question," she answered Raine as she stood up.

"Did you hear the gossip about Lawyer?" Zahra asked her quickly. "He gave an interview to a local reporter and told them a story about how when he was a teen, he had been involved with other boys and they'd robbed and beat up their football coach. He confessed to the coach and paid him back the money. He made the coach out to be a hero. I know his is one of our local families you take food to in the winter, Shabina."

"Wow, Lawyer is such a good guy," Shabina said. She smiled at the two women over her shoulder and then hurried to help the waiters and waitresses take orders and get food and drink out to her customers. She knew exactly why Lawyer had made his confession. He was circumventing Bale from using what he thought was damning evidence against him.

She was a little surprised to see that the three women from Washington were still in town. Janine, Val and Theresa waved to her and indicated when she had time they would love to chat. They were friendly and clearly enjoyed bird-watching and hiking, but climbing wasn't one of their passions. Most visitors prolonged their stay in Knightly to boulder.

Lucca's sister, Avita, and one of his brothers, Pablo, came in for breakfast. Both had clearly been up all night. She took their order. "I'm so sorry to hear about Lucca," she whispered. "I know they're keeping it under wraps, and I won't say anything, but we get all the latest news because we send supplies to the volunteers."

She didn't know what to say, so she felt she said too much. Avita teared up, and Pablo put his arm around her.

"We're heading up to the base camp. If you need us to take anything up there, we can do that," Pablo said.

"We want to be closer just in case," Avita added.

"I'll see if we can have the supplies ready in time before you leave," Shabina said.

"Oh, Shabina," Avita suddenly said, tears spilling over. She stood up and flung herself into Shabina's arms.

Shabina held her tight for a few minutes. To her consternation, Pablo stood as well and wrapped his arms around his sister and her. She was uncomfortable with men touching her, even men she knew. It wasn't as if Pablo was a stranger, and she had empathy for him, but every cell in her body rebelled. It was all she could do not to stiffen, especially when he put his head on her shoulder.

There was a sudden hush in the café. Rainier appeared beside them in that silent way he had. Pablo stepped back, as did Avita. Rainier gave them an easy smile, holding out his hand to Pablo. "Rainier Ashcroft, Shabina's fiancé and partner here in the café." His voice was pitched low, impossible to hear other than by the two members of the Delgotto family. "I wanted to let you know we're putting together supplies to take up to the base camp. If there's anything we can do for your family, please let us know." His arm swept around Shabina, and he pulled her protectively beneath his shoulder.

Pablo shook his hand. "Thanks, man. We appreciate everything you're doing for us. Shabina has always been a good friend to our family, particularly to our parents."

Rainier waved the two back to their seats and indicated for Patsy to bring them their drinks.

"Mom was very sick last winter," Avita revealed. "When Shabina found out we were having trouble getting her to eat, she brought her different kinds of soups and smoothies and shakes. She also brought meals for our entire family. Dad was working and also trying to caretake our mother. He didn't like leaving her, so he was stretched pretty thin. I was away at school, and they didn't want me taking a leave of absence." She flashed Shabina a smile. "Shabina went over nearly every day."

She felt color creeping under her skin. She didn't like the spotlight on her. "I wasn't the only one. Zahra, Harlow, Vienna and Raine took turns as well. I just brought food. Your parents are wonderful. We feel incredibly honored to have them as friends."

"Again, please let us know if there's anything we can do for you," Rainier reiterated. "In the meantime, your breakfast will be out shortly. We're a little short on staff today, so we're running late, but we're catching up." He turned, taking Shabina with him as he made his way back to the kitchen.

"Are you all right?" His hand swept down the back of her neatly braided hair. "Raine texted me about the family, and when I looked out of the kitchen and saw them putting you in a bear hug, I knew you would be uncomfortable."

"I really despise that I'm like this, Rainier. It shouldn't be such a big deal. Pablo is hurting every bit as much as Avita. They're both scared for Lucca. I should be able to get over my aversion to being touched by men."

"Stop, *Qadri*. It's perfectly reasonable for you to have the reaction you do. You're too hard on yourself. You allowed him to hug you, and there was no way anyone in that room, including him, could tell you were uncomfortable."

"You could."

He pressed a kiss to her forehead. "We have a strange connection, one I'm grateful for. Are you going to be okay to go back on the floor? If I tried to carry orders out, it would be a disaster. As it is, Patsy is secretly laughing at me about the way I do dishes."

"You're lucky it's secretly. They openly laugh at me if I screw up," Shabina confessed. "I'm fine now. You keep up with the dishes, and I'll keep up with the orders and customers."

"You need me, just give me our birdsong."

She loved him just for that alone. He knew birds and their individual calls to one another. He had perfect pitch. Sometimes at night when she was falling apart alone in her room in Houston, he slipped in, singing different birdsongs, and she would have to identify them. It became a game, a distracting one. He knew so many. Later, when she found out he was the one who realized she used the birds in the video to send the coordinates of the camps, she wasn't in the least surprised. Rainier noticed the smallest details.

For the next hour, she worked fast to get orders out, keeping an eye on the outside patio. Nellie was amazing, covering for Chelsey's absence with the occasional help of Tyrone or Patsy. She was extremely proud of her staff and Nellie in particular, making a note to herself that she would have to give them a bonus for the extra work.

Albert and Sally Chavez, who owned the local cleaning service, came in when the café was packed. The only table available was the smaller table just behind the four university students, leaving Shabina no other option. She led them to the table and took their drink orders, stopping for a minute to chat with them.

The cleaning service took care of offices, businesses, rentals, Airbnbs, and the occasional house when asked. They had a full cleaning service and did a brisk business. As she went to turn away to take the order to the kitchen, Albert stopped her.

"Shabina, we have a huge favor to ask. We took on a massive job, not realizing it was going to be such a large undertaking or that it would take so much time or manpower. Edward Fenton hired us to completely go through his home and clean every room. To be fair, he boxed up a tremendous amount of the old clothes, personal items and knickknacks, things he had trouble getting rid of after his mother passed. He even pulled down the old drapes in all the rooms and had a dumpster brought in to make it easy to throw things away. Still, he has an enormous house, and I'm not certain it has seen the light of day for years."

Sally took up the narration. "To make a long story short, he's on the Search and Rescue team and has been gone for a couple of days, so hasn't been home to help us. He told us to keep going, that it was important to him to have the house cleaned and aired out. We know what they may find, and we want to do this for him, but it's taking so much time. Our crew usually cleans your café at six each night. Would you mind if we come much later? Albert and I will come ourselves. It could be extremely late."

Shabina glanced over at Raine, unable to help herself, although she couldn't possibly have overhead. What were the odds that Edward suddenly had an interest in painting? In changing his house, which he'd kept the same for years? And Bale's escalating behavior toward her? Had this change in Edward started on the bird-watching tour? Before? She tried to think back. Were there signs of Edward pulling away from Bale the way Jason had? Jason separating himself from Bale could have paved the way for Edward to take the steps to do the same.

"I have no problem with you coming in late," she assured.

"Thanks for your understanding," Albert said. "This is a big break for us. He'd like us to clean every week. We clean his office at the airport, but the contract for a house that size would allow us to keep more of our workers on through the winter."

Shabina nodded her understanding and forced herself to greet the four university students at the next table. It would have seemed rude if she'd skipped them. Since all four spoke the language, she greeted them with the traditional Arab greeting, using flawless Arabic. She repeated a greeting in French to Jules Beaumont. They answered her solemnly in the same languages. She asked if they needed anything. Deniz Kaplan from Turkey complimented the coffee and the breakfast dish she'd made specifically for him— fried eggs made with minced ground beef topped off with pepper and tomato paste, olive oil and parsley. It went perfectly with Turkish bread.

Emar Salhi and Jamal Talbi from Algeria both asked her to make a traditional Algerian breakfast for them. It consisted of eggs, peppers, tomatoes and onions. She served their breakfast with plenty of toast and their favorite coffee.

Jules Beaumont preferred the more traditional breakfast of potatoes and sausage. She'd served him *stoemp* (mashed potatoes) and pork sausage with gravy.

All four had seemed to savor the breakfasts from their homelands. She was happy to be able to provide them with something from home. She just wished she wasn't so paranoid. Having Rainier close helped tremendously.

"Where did you learn to cook these dishes?" Deniz asked. "My mother would praise such an ability and want to keep you in the family. She would tell me to bring you home. *Mashallah.*"

Keeping her hands together, Shabina gave him a tentative

smile. "*Mashallah.*" She returned the blessing. When he continued to look at her expectantly, she forced herself to answer the question. "I was fortunate enough to live in Saudi Arabia with a family for a year. In that time, I was given many valuable lessons I'll never forget. Baking and cooking were just a very small part of what I was taught."

Before she could turn away, he asked another question. "Would you consider returning?"

A note in his voice and the speculation in his eyes set her heart pounding. "My life is here. My family, my fiancé, this café."

"That's too bad. I can feel your love of the country in the food you cook. Perhaps you would change your mind if you came back."

There was nothing to say to that. She did have love for the people. She gave another smiling half bow with her hands folded and wished them a good day as she moved on to the next table. She could feel Deniz's gaze following her. He wasn't alone in his staring after her. Jules did the same. What was it about him that bothered her so much? What did he want from her? Was Deniz simply interested in her because of her cooking skills? She had known men like that.

She greeted the three visitors from Washington, doing her best to push Jules and Deniz from her mind. The women were finished with breakfast and lingering over their coffee with scones in the hopes of having a word with her. Their faces lit up when she stopped at their table.

"It's so lovely to see you again," Shabina greeted them. "I certainly hope the food met your expectations this morning."

"Favorite place to eat *ever*," Val said. "Stella told us we'd love the food, and she was so right. It's amazing."

"I wasn't sure about waiting in line, no reservations and no standard menu," Theresa added. "But I am so glad Val and Janine insisted we give the café a try. I think I'm learning to be adventurous."

"Wasn't that the point of this trip?" Janine asked. "To prove to ourselves we could still do things we wanted to do, like we used to? Only in a much more mature fashion?"

The three women exchanged a look and then burst into laughter.

"I don't know how mature we've been," Val admitted, "but we've certainly had fun."

"That's wonderful. How long have you been friends?" Shabina asked.

"We lived in the same neighborhood as children and went to the same schools," Theresa supplied. "I'm a little older, so I tell them I'm the boss."

Janine nodded very solemnly. "She's *so* good at being bossy."

"I've had quite a bit of practice," Theresa said. "These two get out of control. I never thought I'd see the day Janine lost her mind over a man, but she has. Now, here we are, still in Knightly while she does her best to reel him in."

Janine tried to look innocent, but it was very clear Theresa was telling the truth. "Okay, they are the best friends *ever* to stay with me while I explore the idea of actually being in a relationship with someone after saying I would never do it."

Shabina was almost afraid to ask. "Who is the lucky man?"

"You know him. Edward Fenton. He owns the helicopter service in town. He's the most wonderful painter. It took me forever to get him to show me his work. I love to paint, but I don't compare to his work."

"Janine is really good," Val said, breaking off a small piece of scone. "But I agree with her, Edward is amazing. We all went out to the canal together to paint last week."

"There were blue herons," Janine said. "Just walking along the canal. Edward captured them beautifully. Mine weren't the best. He thought they were good, but his were vivid and looked so elegant and real."

"We ran into Sean," Theresa added. "He seemed very upset that Edward was painting with us. The two of them walked off together and seemed to be having a heated exchange. Then they moved where we couldn't see them and were gone for a bit of time. When Edward came back, he was alone, and it looked as if they may have gotten into a physical altercation. We asked Edward about it, but he said not to worry, that Sean got into moods."

"I think he made fun of Edward painting with us," Janine said.

"Why did you think that?" Shabina asked.

Val nodded in agreement. "Edward said disparaging things about his painting after the run-in with Sean."

"The way he talked about his painting made us think Sean had influenced him negatively," Theresa said. "Edward had admitted to Janine he hadn't made any real attempts at artwork since school. He was already feeling very shy about his work."

"I try not to say bad things about people," Val said, "but I think Sean needs a therapist."

"That's not a bad thing," Janine said. "I think everyone needs a therapist, but then I am one." She laughed at her own joke.

"He may have been having a bad day," Theresa pointed out. "We don't know what goes on in someone's life. We can only try to treat them with kindness and hope they benefit from good energy."

Val rolled her eyes. "Theresa, I swear you're the only reason we're going to make it through the pearly gates if there are gates. You'll pull us on the top of your wings."

"You're such a heathen, Val," Theresa said, but there was amusement in her voice.

Janine burst out laughing. "You've stumbled onto an ongoing argument between the two of them. Val is our scientist, and Theresa is a woman of faith."

"One doesn't exclude the other," Theresa said.

"No, it doesn't," Val agreed, "but common sense tells me when men like Sean are mean to everyone around them, kindness doesn't win out. If that were true, at his age, he would already be a decent human being."

"Maybe," Theresa said, "but I think we should all try kindness before we resort to being mean ourselves."

"Telling someone they need therapy isn't being mean, Theresa," Val said. "It's helpful advice. I could have said something entirely different, which is what I was really thinking."

Shabina struggled to keep a straight face despite hearing the information that Edward and Sean had been in a physical altercation and both had been at the canal near the same place where she had discovered the spices and dates dumped in the bushes.

The three women's friendship reminded her so much of what she had with Stella, Raine, Harlow, Vienna and Zahra. She might not have known her friends as long, but she knew that relationship was strong and lasting. It was clear to her that these women knew they could count on each other, and they always backed one another up.

Theresa was the one to roll her eyes. "Ignore her, Shabina. She sounds awful, but she truly has a heart of gold. We'll be regulars in your café for breakfast or lunch for the next couple of weeks. Stella is helping us find a place to stay in Knightly. She knows so many people."

"She has a line on a little guesthouse—it's only two bedrooms, not three, but it's still ideal for us," Janine said. "A kitchenette and living room and, best of all, it has a pottery studio right on the property. The couple give pottery classes. If I end up staying longer, the couple will consider extending the lease."

"You must be talking about Tom and Judy Rosewood. They're incredible and so kind and thoughtful. Their property is beautiful. Have you seen the guesthouse yet?"

"Not yet, just pictures," Val said. "But it looks picture perfect. The gardens are impressive."

Shabina had to agree. "I'd better get busy, or my own staff will fire me. I really do hope you get a chance to meet with Tom and Judy. They're very special people."

She gave a friendly wave and returned to quickly breaking down tables and setting them up for new customers. She stayed on automatic pilot as she turned the information she'd inadvertently gotten from the women over and over in her mind. She wanted to talk to her friends and Rainier about what she'd discovered.

She helped pack supplies in the SUV Avita and Pablo were driving up to the base camp. Rainier stood with one arm around her, making it easier as she hugged them both goodbye. Shabina had a terrible feeling in the pit of her stomach that their brother was gone. She could see the despair on their faces. They both felt the same way. The fact that Rainier shook hands and assured them that the café's staff would do whatever they could to help, rather than offer platitudes of hope, convinced her that he had that same bad feeling in his gut as well. Even Vaughn looked grim.

"This is a bad situation," Tyrone said. "They have to catch this guy."

"They will," Rainier said. He did sound confident about that. "Let's get back to work. All of you have been amazing. I can see why Shabina has nothing but good things to say about you."

"After we close, I still have to interview a couple of potential waiters and waitresses," Shabina reminded. "And the cleaning crew is coming in late tonight."

"Whatever you do, Shabina," Patsy said, "don't do your bleeding-heart thing."

"I'm not like that."

"Yes, you are," Vaughn, Tyrone and Patsy said simultaneously.

Rainier nuzzled the top of her head with his chin. "She is," he agreed.

CHAPTER THIRTEEN

Lucca Delgotto's body was discovered two days later. Vienna had found tracks that appeared as if he'd gone off trail to check on something he might have seen or heard, and he was struck and went down. There was dried blood in the grass and leaves and a jagged rock with dark stains on it. She surmised that he'd been killed or knocked unconscious in that spot and then dragged away from the location.

The terrain was steep and wild, very difficult to negotiate. Sean and Vienna unraveled the tracks over the next day, following the very faint trail. Whoever was committing the murders had attempted to cover their tracks, leaving only a few bruised and twisted leaves despite carrying or dragging the deadweight of a fully grown man.

Lucca's body had been laid out in his bloodstained clothes, a makeshift altar built on a flat rock just to the right of his head. Feathers, candles, sticks, flowers and gourds of water were on the altar in a precise pattern. A few inches of vegetation around his body had been cleared away, leaving the ground bare. The body was covered in insects, but no predator had gotten to it.

Forensics took over the crime scene, leaving Search and Rescue to continue looking for Charlie Gainer, the missing member of the trail rehabilitation crew. Vienna insisted that her search crews stay close together, that no member was to go off on their own, even for a brief moment.

A pall hung over the café when the news came in. Lucca had been well-liked in Knightly. His family had lived there for years. Even when they brought the body down the mountain to the medical examiner, it wasn't released to the family. And Charlie Gainer was still missing.

Shabina and others brought food to the family. There was little else they could do. There is no comfort when experiencing a loss as grave as the Delgotto family had, especially in such a violent and senseless way. Many of Lucca's friends gathered at the Grill in the evening just to try to support each other.

The café and the Grill sent food to the base camp for the Search and Rescue volunteers. Three days after Lucca's body was discovered, Charlie's body was found by Sean and Vienna. Along with their five-man search team, they had laid out a grid that included the overgrown, closed trail that was no longer visible leading to the burnt section of trees where the California condors were nesting.

The park had shut down the trail several years after the fire had occurred. As soon as Shabina had discovered the nest, the park had completely closed off the section to all hikers and tourists with posted signs and gates blocking off anything that appeared to be a semblance of a trail. There were warning signs up everywhere to stay away.

Vienna and Sean had searched the section staying in constant touch with the other three members of their team, who were searching another trail. Sean pointed out Shabina's tracks multiple times. She left very little evidence of her passing, but they could see it occasionally. Once they found a paw print from one of her dogs that had dried in mud.

Sean was the one who discovered the dried blood several yards to the left of the trail. Vienna surmised that Charlie had somehow learned of the condor nest and decided to try to find it. He must have run right into the murderer, or the murderer had stalked him. They found the rock that had been used to kill him. He'd been hit several times with it, crushing his skull. Whoever hit him had stood in wait for him and used a good deal of strength when they swung the rock. Charlie had been facing away from his assailant when he'd been struck.

Charlie had been dragged well off the nearly nonexistent trail. He'd been treated just as the other murdered men had. He'd been fully clothed. All damage had been done to his skull. The amount of bare ground scraped free of vegetation around his body was extremely small and had to have been difficult to manage due to the thickness of the thorny berries growing on the spot the murderer had chosen to construct his altar.

There was a wide, flat rock which might have determined his choice, but looking at the ground cover, the rocks and thick brush, it wouldn't have been easy to set up whatever the ritual called for. The altar was covered in feathers, stones, candles, gourds of water, sticks and flowers. The site had also seemingly been chosen to keep the altar out of the wind.

Charlie's body had not only been attacked by insects, but predators had gotten to it as well. It wasn't the first time Vienna and Sean had found bodies in that condition, but it was never pleasant.

The body was found the day before Shabina's two days off, and she was grateful the café would be closed. Having the townspeople mourning Lucca and now finding Charlie felt overwhelming.

She knew everyone who knew them would congregate at the Grill during the evenings and at her café during the mornings. She was thankful she would be closed that day.

RAINIER DROVE HER to the courthouse in Independence to obtain their marriage license. "You're certain you want to marry me, Shabina? There's not one doubt in your mind?"

Shabina glanced up at him from under her long lashes, trying to guess if he was asking because he was having second thoughts.

When she didn't answer him immediately, he reached over and took her hand, threading his fingers through hers. "It's a yes-or-no question, *Qadri*. In a few years, I don't want you to suddenly wake up and realize I railroaded you."

"Is that what you're doing?"

"I haven't yet, but I'm considering it. We can get our license and go to another window and get married. It isn't a big wedding like you probably dreamt of, surrounded by your friends and family, but it affords you protection." He paused. "And it will make me feel a hell of a lot more secure."

"Wait. Are you saying you think we should get married today? Can we do that? Is it legal?"

"I called and asked. California has a same-day marriage policy. It's called an express marriage and can be done at the courthouse if you request it ahead of time. The Clerk-Recorder's Office can provide a witness, and we can be married right there. Today."

Shabina touched the tip of her tongue to her upper lip. Rainier had checked into an express marriage. For some reason that shocked her because it meant he really did want to marry her. He'd put thought into how they could be married quickly.

"A license is only good for ninety days. We would have to get married in that time frame. If you prefer, I can arrange a service at the house with your friends attending. I have a friend who could marry us."

She shook her head. "We could ask them to come to the house in the evening and we'll tell them we got married. We don't want gifts, so we can't tell them ahead of time why we're inviting them."

"That's a good idea."

"Unless this isn't a very good time. Vienna is going to be decompressing. It's so hard on her when she finds the people she's searching for dead. In this case, two of them, and she knows the Delgotto family very well."

"She may need her friends around her, Shabina. It's been a couple of days. She will have talked to the people she needs to. She might just want to go somewhere safe with the people she loves and trusts the most."

He was correct about Vienna. She practiced self-care. She not only made certain her volunteers were taken care of, but she made certain she followed protocol herself.

"If we let Vaughn, Tyrone and Patsy know, they'd cater for us."

She shook her head. "No, I wouldn't want them to have to work. If they come, they're guests. I can pull the food together for a small gathering, or we can have one tomorrow night, which will give me more time to put things together."

"Thanks, baby."

Shabina tilted her head up to look at him. "For what?"

"For being willing to marry me."

"Rainier, I *want* to marry you. I want to be with you. I've always wanted to be with you."

"When you call your parents, they're going to be very angry with you."

"I've never understood my parents' objection to you, and

frankly, I truly don't care. It's unreasonable. They've never taken the time to know you."

"Your father knows me—don't kid yourself, Shabina. He sees the real me, and more than once he's come up against my ruthless side. When it comes to protecting you or taking care of you, I put you first. He found that out very early on."

That same ominous shadow crept into her mind that had begun to visit her far too often when she thought of her father, and the door to her memories creaked open. She had kept that particular door closed and barricaded because she didn't want to know the truth about the choices her father had made during those times.

She had a brain demanding answers though. Once a puzzle presented itself, her subconscious insisted on working on it. Even if she tried to shut it down, in the back of her mind, she continued to work for the answer. Why had an assassin been sent to her exact location when she was supposed to be rescued? Was he supposed to kill her? She'd asked Rainier, and his reply had been abrupt and didn't answer her question. *I don't kill innocents.*

That didn't mean her father hadn't tried to hire the notorious assassin to kill her. He certainly had the means to reach out to an anonymous assassin. But then, if he had, he couldn't possibly know Deadly Storms' true identity. No one knew for certain. She doubted if her father would even guess. Rainier was a doctor. An officer. He worked for Blom in the Special Activities Division of the CIA. That was all factual and could easily be verified. She doubted anyone would suspect him of being a notorious assassin. Rainier had confirmed that fact. If her father did know, he would use the information to get whatever he wanted. There was no way he knew the identity of Deadly Storms.

The story of her rescue prior to the assassin striking during a sandstorm was plausible. Rainier had kept her with him while she was partially healing because she'd begged him not to allow anyone else to see her in the condition in which he'd found her. Again, he'd concocted a believable story, one his agency bought, that they had been trapped by Scorpion as he'd searched the desert for his captive, believing it would be impossible in her state to transport her a far distance quickly.

Rainier had convinced Blom it had been impossible to use a helicopter because of the strength and duration of the sandstorm. Shabina had been in such bad condition that once he took her to a safe place, he had to treat her in order to keep her alive. That had to be his first priority. As soon as he knew it was safe to contact his people, he had, but he hadn't allowed transport until he knew she would survive, and no one could come to them because he wouldn't chance exposing their position. It had all been very plausible.

Shabina couldn't imagine how that would incur her father's wrath. She sighed and tapped the back of her head against the seat. "Why does my father dislike you so much, Rainier? It isn't some small thing between you."

He brought her hand to his mouth, kissing her fingers and then bringing their joined hands to his chest directly over his heart all the while keeping his eyes on the road. "No, baby, you're correct, it isn't a small thing. It's quite a few things." He pressed her hand tighter to his chest. "Do you really want to know hurtful things about your parents on your wedding day?"

She had been avoiding the truth for years. Hiding like a child with her eyes closed, covering her ears, trying desperately not to allow her brain to give her answers because all along nothing added up.

"My father despised you, and he still does. He went out of his way to turn me against you. Even now, after all these years, every chance he gets, he says disparaging things about you. If he could, I think he would do his best to ruin your career."

"He tried. Jack found he doesn't have that kind of clout. I shut him down after that. I warned him to quit trying to mess with my career. He stopped. I would know if he did anything stupid."

"Weren't you worried he'd turn me against you?" She'd always been curious about that.

"You're one of the strongest people I've ever met. You stick to your own convictions and judgments. You don't let someone else make up your mind for you. You're fair. When I first got you out of Scorpion's camp, you talked to me about the people you'd met, the good ones. The brave ones. You were determined to beat Scorpion at his own game. There's fire in you."

"I was dying. I wanted to die."

"Baby, you had a raging infection. You'd been tortured. Raped. Through all that, you didn't arbitrarily convict every man, woman and child born in that country. You told me about the ones who helped you. Nothing I said was going to change your mind. *You* changed *my* mind. I had turned myself into a sword of revenge, but by listening to you, I learned to be a better person—at least I hope I have."

Rainier gave her compliments when no one in her life had done so. Mama Ahmad had praised her when she was learning to bake or apply henna tattoos, but it wasn't the same. He didn't sound as if he was trying to build her up or flatter her. He sounded offhand, matter-of-fact, as if he were simply stating a truth.

"The way you say that, it sounds like you don't believe you're a good person, Rainier. I know you. Inside, where no one else sees." She cupped his jaw briefly. "I'm so grateful that you let me see the real you."

"That's what I counted on when I knew your father would do

his best to turn you against me. You don't let anyone persuade or intimidate you into thinking the way they do. If anything, the more he talked against me or demanded you have someone else head your security, the more I knew you'd defend me. You're faithful to the people you believe deserve your loyalty."

"The security on the estate was so tight, not just the alarms on doors and windows, but guards everywhere. Still, you always knew when I had vicious nightmares, and you'd slip inside the house. I don't know why he didn't turn you in to the cops. I worried so much about that. I'd feel guilty when I'd make you stay with me, and then my father would find out you were there."

"You should have told me you were worried. I would have reassured you. Jack wasn't about to call the cops on me. He might want to, but he's a brilliant man."

Shabina studied his profile. He was all angles and planes. A strong jaw with a dark shadow that never quite left him even if he shaved. He was the most intense individual she'd ever met. He could be so still; he could blend into the background or exude such lethal energy everyone around him froze in place, fearful of moving. He commanded a room simply by walking into it. Even his dangerous demeanor wouldn't stop her father.

"You knew something damaging about my father." She murmured the statement aloud, more to herself than to him. Puzzling. That wasn't necessarily right. "No, he would be more inclined to protect my mother than himself. Or the two of them together. Something to do with my kidnapping."

Rainier kept his gaze fixed on the road, his expression giving nothing away. He might as well have been carved from stone.

"A year passed, and the ransom still hadn't been paid to Salman Ahmad. It was a simple business transaction. All the other ransoms had been paid easily, and the other prisoners had been released. Ahmad was worried, so much so that he had decided to release me without being paid. I overheard him tell his men, and then he came and told me not to worry, I'd be going home soon."

"Do you know why the ransom money hadn't been paid?"

"I know they went to collect it on at least three occasions but came back empty-handed. We would break camp immediately and leave the area. Men would stay behind to cover our tracks."

"What did Ahmad think happened to the money? Or did he believe Jack wasn't paying?"

Shabina had been secretly happy the ransom hadn't been paid. She hadn't realized how much she wanted to be with someone like Mama Ahmad, learning from her, sharing chores, telling stories, holding babies and looking after the children. There was always joy and laughter from the time the sun came up until it went down. She hadn't been concerned about why her father wasn't paying until the day she realized Salman Ahmad was worried. Then she paid attention and tried to gather information quickly.

"My father claimed to Ahmad that he'd paid the ransom three times and Ahmad hadn't delivered. Ahmad said no one showed to give them the money. He was very uneasy, and that's when he told his men he was releasing me."

"You believe that Jack paid the ransom?"

"Yes." She did believe it. "Like I said, we were told that if we were ever kidnapped, it was treated as a business. Cooperate. The ransom would be paid. There can only be one explanation. Ahmad had a traitor in his camp. Scorpion must have intercepted the ransom each time it was paid. He took the money. He had to know when and where it was being delivered, and he got there first or had his mercenaries there to intercept. The only way he could do that was if someone tipped him off."

"That's logical," Rainier agreed.

"When Ahmad said he would release me, word must have been sent to Scorpion, and he and his men came and murdered everyone. It was a total massacre. No one was prepared. They didn't have a chance."

Just thinking about that day tore her up. She didn't want to see the images crowding into her mind, so she slammed that door closed the way she always did the moment vivid pictures formed.

"Qadri." Rainier breathed the name he often called her. Destiny. "I'm with you."

That was all. *I'm with you.* So simple, but it was everything to her. She wasn't alone. She never would be as long as she had Rainier.

"I can do this, Rainier," she said, more for herself than for him. She was determined to solve the puzzle once and for all. To know the truth.

"Scorpion and his cabinet *hated* me. It was personal. Very, very personal. I'd never met them. I tried to stay quiet and do exactly as I was ordered, but it didn't matter. Scorpion was determined to torture me. He didn't need excuses. He took great pleasure in finding ways to not just physically but emotionally hurt me. I asked myself why a million times."

Rainier kept his gaze on the road. "Baby." There was caution in his voice. "Be sure you want the answers."

"She didn't look back." The sudden lump in her throat nearly choked her.

"Who didn't look back?"

"My mother. Her security team pushed her into the armored SUV, and they drove away. I was looking straight at her, and she didn't even look over her shoulder at me. I took that to mean she was confident in the system, that I'd be ransomed easily. It was just business, and I should be calm. But that wasn't the reason, was it?"

Rainier cursed under his breath. He brought her fingertips to his mouth and bit down gently. "I feel as if I'm always bringing bad news. I hate doing this."

"*I'm* doing this, not you. I need to face the truth, Rainier. I can't keep hiding from it. That's part of the reason the PTSD episodes are so severe. These are things I can't talk about to anyone else."

She didn't trust anyone enough other than Rainier. She loved her parents, and she didn't want anyone else to know anything she uncovered that would put them in a bad light.

Rainier was silent for a moment, and then he sighed. "I understand, baby. You need to talk about this, we talk about it."

How could she not love him? His reluctance and his reasons were clear, but for her, he would do it. More than ever, she knew she was making the right decision to spend her life with him.

"Scorpion hated my mother, didn't he? He intercepted the ransom because he was making his own demands. That was what was happening, wasn't it?"

"Yes."

Rainier sounded terse. Grim. The tension inside the car grew.

"Was he making her part of the negotiations? Money and my mother to get me back? If Scorpion did that, my father would never agree. He'd surround my mother with ten million guards." She wasn't really asking, because how could he possibly know? Could he? She was musing aloud the way she often did when she was piecing together a puzzle.

Rainier didn't utter a single word.

Shabina refused to be a coward any longer. She hadn't trusted Talia Warren enough to explore her worst fears with her. Her father had hired the therapist, and, although she'd explored going to a few others, she didn't like repeating the story, so in the end, she'd stayed with Talia. Even though she was told often everything she said was confidential, for all she knew the therapist reported every word to her father. Her father had enough money to buy a tremendous amount of loyalty, and she'd been pretty messed up when she'd first come back. Who was she kidding? She still was. She probably always would be.

Shabina considered whether the silence from Rainier meant he knew the answer to her question. He was astute, very intelligent, and he had access to various sources of information she never would. She decided not to press him. Her mind was already coming up with answers, and she was certain she would find the truth without forcing him to reveal anything he was reluctant to say, especially if it made her parents look bad.

"My mother's family is from the Middle East. Since I was a very little girl, I've never seen them or heard from them. My mother always speaks of them lovingly, but she doesn't visit them, and they don't come here, although my father could afford to bring them here."

Why hadn't she ever put that together? Her thigh ached. Her headache began to return with a vengeance. She tasted copper in her mouth. That meant she was coming very, very close to a revelation she should have put together long ago.

"Arranged marriages are very common in Saudi Arabia, especially in the smaller villages, either through a matchmaker or family. My mother comes from a family where they most likely promised her to someone." Her voice sounded strangled, even to her own ears.

Of course, her mother had been promised in marriage to a man. Her father would have had many offers for her. Yasemin was beautiful, strikingly so. She had been raised in a traditional family. She was quiet, submissive and made the perfect wife.

Her father had married Yasemin when she was very young. An oil fire was raging in one of the prince's main oil fields, and no one had been able to put it out. Jack admitted he met her mother in Saudi Arabia and once he laid eyes on her, he had known she was the only one for him.

"Yasemin was promised to a friend of the prince, a man who brought with him ideas for a particular irrigation system for those farming in the desert," Rainier said abruptly. "The prince was especially fond of him, and once the young man saw Yasemin, he asked for her in marriage. He lived in another country, and that must have terrified her. She was very young, and she'd never been out of the country."

"You know who he is." For some unexplained reason, her heart began to pound. Identifying Scorpion was paramount, yet she was reluctant to learn more. It didn't make sense, and she was determined to overcome the barrier her mind continued to erect. She knew it was to protect her, but knowing who Scorpion was should alleviate some of her worries and paranoia.

"I suspect. I don't yet have enough proof, and I don't kill innocents."

He stated it as an absolute.

"My mother isn't outgoing at all. She's quite shy," Shabina said. *Timid* might be the proper word to describe her mother.

"At the time, Darian Lefebre was considered a brilliant young man who spent a great deal of time going to countries in need of finding a way to get water into dry lands."

Her breath caught in her throat. She knew the name Darian Lefebre. Everyone did. He was an ambassador for Canada. One of the good guys. Charming. He had his hand in many charitable organizations worldwide. He was known for his mediation when things got heated between countries. The name Lefebre was synonymous with kindness and benevolence. He was beloved in his country and nearly everywhere he went.

She found herself shaking her head. "Rainier, that can't be."

"Your reaction would be the world's reaction," he replied. "He's charming. Has charisma and despises your parents with every breath he takes. He's also a sadist. That's a well-kept secret, but in following him, it wasn't difficult to find the very young women he abuses."

Her hand crept to her thigh. "Are you certain that he's Scorpion?"

"If I were certain, I would have taken him out already. Once I'm completely satisfied he's Scorpion and I can leave proof behind on his body, I'll take him out."

She bit down on her lip trying to equate the man who gave speeches on peace, the man who led others by being first to put up money for hard-hit nations when natural disasters struck, with the sadistic, vicious mass murderer. Scorpion took pleasure in torture. In killing. In leading others to kill. How could it be the same man?

"How did my mother come to be with my father and not Lefebre?"

"Your father was needed to put out massive oil fires. He saw your mother and the two met secretly several times. Your father negotiated with the prince to make her part of the deal to put out the oil fires. Lefebre was a nobody with too much money at the time, not the diplomat he is today. The prince had plenty of money and little need of Lefebre. He needed the fires put out. What was the giving of one woman to a man who could save him millions of dollars?"

Shabina understood. The prince would view the exchange as

a simple business transaction, whether Yasemin agreed or not. Even if Yasemin had loved Lefebre and wanted to stay with him, the prince would have offered Lefebre money for his loss, but he wouldn't have changed his mind. His word was absolute law. Yasemin would go to Jack, so Jack Foster would put out the fire in his oil field.

"Jack and Yasemin were married immediately. The prince hosted and attended. It was a huge event. Lefebre was humiliated. Although he was invited to attend the wedding, which took place at the palace, he refused. Jack and Yasemin made a bitter enemy. I doubt that Yasemin knew, but Jack certainly did."

She knew Jack. Her father would have been so arrogant as to taunt his rival. More, once Darian Lefebre entered politics, Jack would have waved his marriage to Yasemin like a red flag.

"Jack has opposed Lefebre in nearly every possible way he could over the years," Rainier added. "A man like Lefebre would take special delight in torturing Jack's daughter. Jack taunted the diplomat, unaware he was an international mass murderer."

"How were you able to prove that two of his friends were part of Scorpion's cabinet?"

Rainier's set features hardened even more. "The proof was irrefutable." His voice was grim. "I'll catch Lefebre the same way."

Her mouth went dry. Clearly, whatever proof Rainier had, he didn't want to share. That boded ill for her. It meant that whatever he found, it had involved her.

"Things make a little more sense now," she admitted. "My mother's personality is very different from mine. She's extremely quiet and lives to please my father. She's very devoted, nearly hero-worshiping him. My father keeps her wrapped in a loving cocoon. He loves my mother above all else. He would do anything to protect her, even getting word to an assassin to kill his own daughter to prevent his wife from suffering when he no longer believed his daughter could be rescued." It was a guess, but one she was certain was the truth.

Rainier remained silent.

"It's difficult for my mother to even look at me now, but when I'm away from their home, she becomes frantic over my safety. My father wants me to live on their estate in order to give her peace of mind. When anyone crosses him, he becomes very angry, and that's putting it mildly. He's used to getting his way. When it has anything to do with my mother, he rages until he fixes the problem."

Rainier brought her hand to his mouth again, pressed kisses to her fingers and then sighed. "I understand Jack, Shabina. I don't agree with the way he handles things, and I have no intention of allowing him to manipulate you into going back to his home just to please Yasemin, but I would do almost anything to protect you."

Everything in her froze. She sat up very straight. *Manipulate you.* The words echoed through her mind. Another puzzle her mind would want to solve but she wanted nothing to do with. She was fairly certain her father had hired an assassin to kill her when she was in Scorpion's camp to spare her mother more pain. To be fair, he had to believe he couldn't get her back. But would he manipulate her now in some vile way, such as deliberately triggering a PTSD episode in order to force her home?

She studied Rainier's profile. This was a man she trusted implicitly. She'd learned that trust in the worst of times. She knew she could count on him. He had her loyalty and her love. She knew he would protect her, but he wouldn't be like her father. He would never hire an assassin to kill one of their children because his wife was upset. He would move heaven and earth to find their child—and so would she. That was where the "almost" came in.

Rainier was the type of man to expect her to learn how to use weapons, and he would teach their children to do the same. He would make their world as safe as possible but at the same time prepare them for every contingency. He wanted a partner, not someone to dance to his tune. Others didn't see that in him, but she did. He was her safety net always, but he wanted her to be strong and free to do the things she loved most.

Rainier would shelter her in the worst of times if she needed him that way. She knew that was a large part of who he was. He was a leader. Decisive. He would be loyal and faithful. He would put his family first. He would expect her to be the same, although she knew if they had disagreements—and they would—he would listen to her arguments with an open mind, but ultimately, he would decide what course they would take if they still couldn't agree.

She wasn't going into their marriage blindly. Rainier didn't hide who he was from her. He had shown her every side of himself, the good and bad. He admitted his flaws, and when he made a mistake, he owned it. He had no trouble apologizing to her if he thought he was in the wrong.

"Blom could arrange a meeting with Lefebre," she suggested, wishing her voice didn't shake. She couldn't prevent that, but she had to make the offer even if it terrified her. "I'd know if it was him."

"Absolutely not. You're not to go anywhere near him. He has diplomatic immunity. He'd likely pull out a gun and shoot you just to spite your father."

"If you really think Lefebre is Scorpion, then we should do

everything we can to bring him to justice. He can't continue killing people."

"You don't have to do anything but be safe, Shabina." There was steel in his voice. "His government conducted an investigation when his two friends were found, but he acted shocked and horrified and appeared open with those investigating. There is still suspicion, but he's very popular. Taking him down legally would be nearly impossible. I don't want you anywhere near him."

"How are you going to catch him, Rainier? I could positively identify him if he's Scorpion."

"Shabina." Just her name—that was a bad sign.

She sighed. "Just tell me what you found that convinced you those two men were guilty and what you expect to find to prove he is."

"Babe, you aren't going to like it."

She knew that already. "Just tell me."

"They took video of the things they did to you." His voice had gone completely flat, without expression.

Her entire body froze. Her brain refused to work. Her stomach lurched. She opened her mouth to protest, but only a squawk came out. She hadn't expected that. Those men had violated her over and over and then watched themselves doing it on video. "Rainier." She whispered his name. "You think Scorpion has video as well?"

He tightened his hand around hers. "Yes. Both men admitted to me that he keeps video of all his assaults. He has a viewing room in his home to watch himself."

She bit down on her lip. Hard. "Do you think he sent copies to my father?"

"I don't know, *Qadri*."

The gentleness in his voice turned her heart over.

"I know this must feel like it isn't ever going to end, but I swear to you, Shabina, I will end it. It's taking longer than I thought, but I won't ever stop until it's over."

She believed him. Her rock. If he could stand to look at her scars, at the scorpion tattooed on her arm, feel love for her despite the terrible things Scorpion and his men had done, then she could deal with whatever came.

His fingers tightened around hers. "Are you still going to marry me? Knowing the things I've done, baby, are you still willing to bind your life to mine?"

What had he done but save her? Love her through the worst. "You aren't getting out of it," she said. Her voice was very firm.

A slow smile touched his mouth briefly. Rainier didn't smile often, and when he did, it always felt like a gift. "Let's get it done, then. I've looked forward to this day for a long time, *Qadri.*"

"That's why you always called me Destiny."

He nodded. "I knew that was exactly what you were to me. My destiny. You just had to catch up."

That made her laugh. "I caught up a long time ago. You need to be better at *communicating*. You have heard of that word, haven't you? Because you're going to need to learn to speak out. Not bossy stuff either."

"That rules out a lot of dialogue." He glanced at her, a mock frown on his face. "What is it I'm supposed to be speaking out about?"

"Sentiments. Showing affection."

"I show you affection all the time," he objected, a hint of amusement in his voice. "Over the last few years, I made certain you knew you were loved."

"You did? How was it that I missed those declarations?"

"I have no idea. When you and Vienna went after that killer and Zale and I caught up with you, what did I do?"

"I believe you grabbed me by my jacket and shook me. You weren't at all happy with me. There was no declaration of love."

"Yes, there was. I sang the bird love call to let you know it was me. I showed how much you scared me in front of two other people, something I've trained myself not to do. I never wanted to allow any enemies I have to know how important you are to me, and yet I couldn't help myself. Sometimes you terrify me with your courage."

He started off teasing her, but he didn't end that way. She heard the sincerity in his voice. The admiration and respect.

"Rainier." She whispered his name. He was her personal talisman. "I love you with every breath I take." She put her hand over her heart. "You have no idea how much you're loved."

"Good thing when it's clear my communication skills need improvement." He sent her another brief grin, this one a little mischievous.

Her heart reacted to his playfulness with a ridiculous flutter. She knew as long as she lived, she would react that way around him.

CHAPTER FOURTEEN

T he café is hopping this morning," Vaughn said. "I think everyone decided to get breakfast here today. Our poor new workers are learning what it's really like to work here on their first day."

Shabina bit her lower lip as she watched Tyrone seating Bale, Sean and two interns, Oliver Smythe and Maurice Vanderpool. "That looks like trouble right there. Tyrone sat them in Patsy's section, so that's helpful."

"He knows what pains they are. He wouldn't give them to the newbies," Vaughn assured. "In any case, Raine and Vienna are here, and neither of them put up with Bale's crap. Not to mention, you've got your man washing dishes out of sight. Anything goes wrong and my guess is, he'll be all over it."

"Maybe not in a good way. I don't want him in jail," Shabina said. "Bale's uncle, Rafferty, is here with Rob Howard and Len Jenkins, the two FBI agents. Unfortunately, having his uncle here will make Bale think he can get away with anything."

"The two women, twins—or I guess they would be triplets still, even if one passed," Vaughn said. "They seem really nice and determined to put down roots here."

"Felicity and Eve Garner." Shabina supplied the names. "They said they feel closer to their sister when they're here. More at peace. They seem to really love experiencing all the things their sister, Freda, enjoyed so much. Apparently, they hadn't done backpacking and climbing the way she did."

"Kind of strange when they were so close," Vaughn mused. "I can see why they'd find peace here though. All of us do."

"Unless Bale is around," Shabina corrected and sent Vaughn a small grin.

"Fortunately, I don't think they're really on his radar. But he is watching Edward. He isn't happy that Edward is sitting with that woman at the table tucked away in the back corner. Bale keeps scowling at them, but Edward seems so absorbed in the conversation with the woman that he hasn't even looked up."

Shabina followed his gaze to the back table. "That's Janine Hale. She's visiting from Washington with two of her best friends. They're sitting at the small table next to the window in front of Bale's table. Theresa Nelson and Val Johnson. They were on the bird-watching tour. Edward went as well and seemed to enjoy it. He's been painting. Janine is an avid bird-watcher and she also enjoys painting. The two of them really hit it off. I think Janine extended her vacation time so she could get to know Edward a little better."

"Did you warn her Edward isn't very nice to women?"

Shabina shook her head. "No, unless he does something else, I'm giving him a chance. He's cleaned out his house, which should have been done years ago. Hopefully, he's really breaking away from Bale."

"He's totally absorbed in the conversation with Janine," Vaughn pointed out. "The twins seemed to be chatting with Janine's friends. That's a good sign."

The two women had gotten up from their table and were

gossiping with Theresa and Val. All four women were laughing. That made Shabina uneasy. Their laughter drew Bale's attention—never a good thing in her mind. He pointed to the women several times and leaned into the other men, clearly making jokes. That was Bale's way. He started with stories about women, and then the jokes became progressively more demeaning. By the time he got to actually harassing a woman, the others were more than ready to go along with him.

"Those students from the university apparently only like to come here to eat," Vaughn said. "They order the same breakfast every morning and come in right before closing to order brunch. They think of it as their dinner, I guess." He indicated Jules Beaumont, Emil Salhi, Jamal Talbi and Deniz Kaplan. "It's really paid off with you making one or two meals from other countries. People that far from home enjoy eating the foods they're familiar with once in a while."

"Or every day." Shabina did her best to make a joke of it. She'd taken tons of cooking lessons and gone to a prestigious school to learn international dishes.

Having so many potential enemies in her café was disconcerting. She felt the beginnings of the headache that heralded a breakdown. Her thigh burned and throbbed, aching with pain. Her skin felt clammy. The symptoms got worse when the two men claiming to be Interpol agents limped in. One was using crutches. Knowing they were part of Scorpion's cabinet made her skin crawl. How was she expected to act normal with them in her café?

She glanced toward the kitchen, needing the reassurance that Rainier was close, as Tyrone seated them near the entrance, taking pity on them because of their obvious injuries. Under any other circumstances, Shabina might have felt their wounds served them right, but she was too cognizant of Rainier in the next room. He might be out of sight at the moment, but that didn't mean he'd stay that way. She wanted the assurance of his presence, but she didn't want the men to see or identify him. They might not realize he was Deadly Storms, but they would know he was lethal.

Theresa waved at her and indicated a table for four that had just been set up. She circled with her finger, including the twins, making it clear they wanted to sit together. Shabina nodded and forced herself to go to them. Two tables needed to be cleared to allow more customers in. If a party of four had been waiting a longer time, they could put the tables together. There would be less room for the servers to move around, but they'd made it work many times.

"Good morning," she greeted as the four women settled into the new seating arrangement. "Have you ordered?"

"Tyrone took our drink orders," Eve confirmed.

"And Patsy took our food orders," Felicity said. "We were just telling Theresa and Val about the natural hot springs and how so many climbers use them after bouldering. We've learned so much just from hiring Miguel Valdez. He's so knowledgeable about the area. He's introduced us to quite a few businesses and locals already."

"Do you go out to the hot springs, Shabina?" Theresa asked.

"I've been out to them," Shabina said, "but never *in* them. I stick to my regular routine because I have so little time. When I take days off, I head for Yosemite to study the birds. That's what makes me happy."

"You don't go alone, do you?" Val asked, concern in her voice. She cast a swift glance around the room and lowered her tone to a whisper. "These murders are very concerning."

The other three women nodded, each radiating apprehension for her. She found that strangely sweet. These women were virtual strangers, and yet they were worried about her safety. She didn't tell them some of the biggest threats to her safety were right there in her café.

"It was bad enough when the victims were strangers, but Lucca Delgotto was born and raised here. He comes from a lovely family. He's always taken care of his parents. He was a member of Search and Rescue as well and helped to save lives," she told them.

"I feel terrible for that family," Felicity said.

"We lost our sister, Freda, and our niece and brother-in-law, all three, to the Sierra," Eve explained to Theresa and Val. "It isn't the same as murder, but it felt like it."

"We're actually triplets," Felicity added. "It was always Freda, Felicity and Eve everywhere we went. We loved being together. What one did, the others did. Same schools, same interests."

"Then Freda fell in love," Eve added. "It was difficult sharing her with her husband at first. They would go off and do things on their own. That took getting used to."

"But then our niece was born, and we were so happy," Felicity continued. "We decided we could share Freda after all."

"That must be so difficult," Shabina said. "I can't imagine that you ever get over a loss like that, especially when you three were so close."

"It feels as if part of our souls was ripped away," Eve admitted, sorrow in her voice.

Shabina laid her hand on the woman's shoulder briefly, sympathy overcoming her natural reluctance to touch others. "I'm so sorry," she said. "I wish there were adequate words or something I could do to help."

"You've been kinder to us than anyone has," Felicity assured. "During that terrible time when they were investigating what happened to the three of them, you were the one advocating for us and making certain we ate. You let us pour out our grief to you, and never once, even if we stayed long after closing time, did you have us leave."

"I was more than happy to help in any way I could." Shabina gave the women a small smile. "I'd better get back to work before my staff decides to mutiny."

"I noticed you have a couple of new waiters today," Eve said. "Where's Chelsey?"

Shabina sighed. "We decided we weren't a good fit. She's taking a job at the hotel."

"That's too bad," Felicity said. "She seemed nice."

Shabina didn't comment. What was there to say? That she'd trusted her until she'd stolen spices and dates out of the kitchen with the possible motive of helping to implicate Shabina in the murders? Where was Chelsey's loyalty?

She turned away from the table and did her best to avoid Bale, who was talking louder and much more belligerently now that his uncle was in the café, as she made her way back to the counter, where Vaughn was handing out orders to the staff.

The restaurant was packed with tourists and locals. Bale loved an audience. She recognized the local veterinarian, Dr. Amelia Sanderson, having breakfast with Carl Montgomery, the local contractor. That surprised her. Amelia worked long hours, as did Carl. She pointed them out to Vaughn. He knew the gossip on everyone in Knightly.

"Dr. Sanderson had a couple of renovations made to the clinic," Vaughn said. "She talked Carl into adopting a dog. He told her only on the condition that she help him train the dog. He told her he didn't know the first thing about having a pet. From what her techs tell me, they've turned into a couple."

"I'm so behind the times," Shabina complained.

"Too busy eloping and not giving a single clue to your friends. I nearly had a heart attack when Rainier announced that you were married. I thought maybe an engagement party, certainly not an actual wedding reception."

She nudged Vaughn. "Great, the gang's all here. Jason Briggs just came in with Bruce Akins. Bale's getting loud. Even his uncle is glaring at him."

Vaughn turned pale. "Did Bale just make some homophobic slur at Jason and Bruce?"

"If he keeps it up, there's bound to be a brawl in my café," Shabina said. "Technically, I should go tell him to stop or leave. He's making the other customers uncomfortable."

"You've got to ban him for life, Shabina."

She knew Vaughn was right. It was just that Bale's outrageous behavior was escalating. His threats were getting worse. She believed he was capable of burning down her café and shooting her dogs. She hadn't at first. She wanted to believe he was all talk, a coward and bully who would just harass her. He hadn't seemed evil. She judged every threat by the evil she'd encountered growing up. By comparison, Bale hadn't seemed nearly as bad. She decided she was simply a bad judge of character.

Patsy began to thread her way through the packed café toward Bale's table. With a sigh, Shabina moved quickly to intercept her. "I'll deal with him, Patsy."

"They haven't paid." She pulled the bill from her pocket and handed it to Shabina. "Good luck. He's going to be a complete you-know-what. He's always so unpleasant, and for some reason, he's being extra unpleasant this morning."

Shabina straightened her shoulders, lifted her chin and walked straight to the table. Immediately, Oliver Smythe and Maurice Vanderpool whistled. Oliver wiggled his tongue around. Shabina ignored both and laid the check on the table. Sitting with Bale and Sean, the two men seemed to have regained their confidence.

"I think you're done here, Bale. Once you pay your bill, please leave and don't come back."

"You bitch. Do you think you can tell me I can't come back to any restaurant in this town? It's *my* town. For all we know you're a foreign spy. That's why you've got so many A-rabs coming in here. You're selling government secrets to them."

"Just go, Bale."

He stood up aggressively, forcing her to step back to avoid contact. "We're not paying for this crap. You're trying to poison us." He swept his arm across the table, sending dishes crashing to the floor.

Time slowed down. The plates shattered, pieces appearing like diamond teardrops falling to the floor in slow motion. Silverware skittered across the floor in brilliant silver flashes. Shabina found herself sitting in the middle of the broken plates with tears running down her face.

Instantly, angry voices berated Bale. Edward walked partway up the aisle. "I'll pay for the meals, Shabina. Don't be upset."

Several others called out that they'd pay. Others told Bale to leave. Abruptly, silence descended in the café. It was so quiet just the sound of breathing could be heard. No one so much as rattled the silverware. Instinctively, she knew who had walked onto the floor. It wasn't Rainier, her husband. This was Blom's Rainier. The "ghost" sent out to bring justice where his government dictated. This was Deadly Storms, the assassin rising out of the worst sandstorms and leaving behind nothing but bodies. She didn't have to look to know that only that man could command an entire room with his presence.

Rainier reached down and lifted her to her feet. Both palms framed her face. *"Qadri, la tamnahi li hada arrajol motaata roayati domoik, idhabi li almatbakh baynama aatani bi hada."* His thumb slid across her lips, his eyes staring down into hers, compelling obedience.

Shabina didn't look at Bale or anyone else. Rainier had said, "Do not give this man the satisfaction of seeing your tears. Go into the kitchen. I will handle this."

Shabina didn't look at Bale or anyone else. She nodded and walked back to the counter, where Vaughn, Patsy and Tyrone crowded close to her protectively.

"Gentlemen, here is what you're going to do. You'll pay the bill and leave the restaurant quietly. Landry, Raine has gathered evidence of your harassment and threats against Shabina, the café and her dogs. It's all recorded. You can't erase the evidence because Shabina's cameras were installed by the military. If you believe you can make the evidence disappear, you're mistaken. Shabina will be filing for a restraining order, but her complaint will not go through the present law enforcement officials. With the amount of evidence we have against you and zero chance of it being lost or destroyed, there is no question she will receive it."

"Who the hell are you?" Bale demanded, his face beet red. He looked to his uncle.

"I'm Rainier Ashcroft, Shabina's husband and partner in this café."

Rafferty came up on Rainier's left side. "What's the trouble? I'll need to see some ID."

"I'm shocked that a member of law enforcement doesn't understand the trouble," Rainier said.

His voice had dropped an octave, sending a shiver of apprehension down Shabina's spine.

"If I heard you correctly, you were implying that you believed evidence would disappear if Shabina turned it over to our office." Rafferty sounded as belligerent as his nephew.

Rainier didn't respond. He simply opened his wallet and showed something to the sheriff. Paling visibly, Rafferty stepped back and shook his head. Then he took a careful sweep of the long stretch of windows.

"Pay the bill, Bale, and get the hell out of here," he snapped and moved away. "Do it now. You're going to be very, very lucky if you walk out of here unscathed."

Cursing, Bale threw money at the table and stomped out, lifting his middle finger in a rude gesture toward Shabina as he left. The customers in the café broke into applause as he went out the door. Sean, Maurice and Oliver put cash on the table and, heads down, without looking at anyone, followed Bale out.

Patsy and Tyrone hurried to the table with a broom and dustpan to clean the floor. Rainier went straight to Shabina, wrapped his arm around her and led her into the kitchen out of sight of the customers in the café.

"You're shaking, baby. It's over. He's gone, and you're going to file a restraining order. Raine's been gathering evidence against him for some time. It's irrefutable. You'll have a lawyer representing you as well. Bale is going to find he won't be able to frequent all the places he's been able to in the past. If you're at the Grill, he won't be allowed in."

"He's only going to get angrier, Rainier." Shabina didn't

understand how a man as astute as Rainier wouldn't see that Bale was spiraling out of control. A restraining order preventing him from entering businesses he'd patronized for most of his life would only increase his behavior.

"I believe Landry will prove to be a reasonable man given the right incentive." His thumb brushed over her lips very gently. "Trust me to deal with this man, *Qadri*."

Shabina glanced around the kitchen to ensure they were alone. "You can't kill him, Rainier. Everyone saw you with him, including two members of the FBI, as well as Rafferty. If he died, even in an accident, they'd look at you."

He bent his head to feather kisses along her lips. When he lifted his head, his smile made him look more like a wolf than ever. "Bale will be given a clear choice. I can make him disappear in a not-so-easy way, or he will make certain there is never so much as a scratch on you, your dogs or the café. I'm very clear when I state my conditions. He'll understand."

She knew there was no way she could dissuade him from visiting Bale. Fortunately, Rainier was a "ghost" when he wanted to be. No one would see or hear him.

"Boucher and Cormier are in the café. They saw you, Rainier. And you passed your identification to Rafferty. It was plain to everyone that what he saw in your wallet scared him into backing off."

Rainier gave her his wolfish smile again. "I am aware of them. And just to point out the obvious, Deadly Storms wouldn't have an ID card."

Of course he'd noticed the two men in the café. He saw everything. That was his job, what kept him alive, and admittedly, he was extremely good at what he did.

"I would prefer that you didn't work the floor for the next half hour. Raine has information for you that you're going to be interested in. I'll have Patsy bring you tea with honey. You've had a shock, and you need to give yourself a break."

"I'm okay now. I can get the job done."

"I have no doubt that you can, Shabina. You have more courage in your little finger than I've seen in most people. I'm asking for me, for my peace of mind, that you take a break for at least half an hour. If necessary, I'll break down tables, although more of your beautiful dishes could get broken, and it would be excruciatingly painful to be out there among all those customers. One or two are bound to congratulate me."

Despite everything, Rainier made her laugh. He could be sent out alone in any environment, never flinching from the task of hunting a dangerous criminal, but a few customers wishing him well made him pretend to shiver. She wasn't buying it for a second. He didn't break things either. He could turn on the charm when he chose. He just didn't bother to do so very often.

"I don't think that will be necessary. Where would I get another dishwasher? You're fast and efficient and the dishes are very clean. You pay attention to detail. I appreciate that quality in you. I'll let Vaughn know he'll have to help with clearing tables for a short while. He's going to give me a hard time about being the manager now reduced to busboy, breaking down tables."

Rainier quirked an eyebrow. He looked less than amused.

"You need to find your sense of humor," she reprimanded. "My staff is very close. We've been working together for a long time, and we tease each other. Vaughn wouldn't be serious. If anything, he would have suggested that I take a break as well."

Rainier nodded. "Message understood. I'll work on my sense of humor."

Shabina knew he meant it when he told her he would work on

his sense of humor. "I love you." How could she not love him when he was willing to do so much for her?

His eyes softened from a glittery, piercing silver to a soft, tender gray. He placed his hand over his heart. *"Qadri."*

One word. Destiny. He'd always called her that. She should have known how he felt. She left the kitchen and immediately Vaughn stopped her at the counter.

"You need to take a little time, Shabina. The minute you start stopping by tables and greeting the customers, they'll ask you all kinds of questions," he cautioned.

"Rainier just said the same thing."

"Great minds and all that," Vaughn pointed out with a grin.

"That means you'll be clearing tables and bringing drinks." She kept a straight face.

Vaughn feigned shock and outrage. "You're demoting me."

Behind them, Rainier had stepped into the kitchen doorframe, his wide shoulders filling the space. He flashed Shabina a heart-stopping grin. It didn't last long, but it was beautiful. Real. The most amazing expression ever. There was nothing remotely boyish about Rainier, but in the brief couple of seconds, that grin gave him a mischievous look.

"What?" Vaughn demanded.

Rainier shook his head and retreated into the kitchen.

Vaughn fanned himself. "Good grief, girl. That man of yours is a heart-stopper. Scary, but that only adds to his appeal."

"I can't imagine why you think he's scary," she said, managing a straight face.

"I think the other customers were so shocked at Bale's behavior and upset on your behalf that they all want to do something to make up for the way he talked to you. And the broken crockery. They're leaving tremendous tips. Some paid double for their breakfast."

Her heart fluttered. Knightly. That was the town she'd chosen to live in. She had made friends despite her natural reticence. She had known she had Stella, Vienna, Harlow, Zahra and Raine as firm friends, but she had so many others. She'd gotten close to Vaughn, Tyrone and Patsy. Now she realized there were others in town who considered her their friend.

"Go sit with Raine and Vienna. I'll bring you tea and scones."

"Thanks, Vaughn. I appreciate you more than you could ever know."

"You tell me all the time and give me far too many bonuses. I think you're cutting into the profits." He waved her toward the back, where her friends were seated.

Shabina made her way quickly through the café. She lifted her hand and sent a small smile to the customers who called out a greeting to her. Most of them did.

Vienna and Raine looked her over carefully as she pulled out a chair to sit with them at their table.

"That man of yours handled that little tantrum of Bale's perfectly," Vienna stated, admiration coloring her voice. "With an entire café filled with people as well as two FBI agents, I thought he was magnificent. Quiet. Stern. Stated the facts. Made certain everyone knew there was evidence of Bale threatening you and that you intended to ask for a restraining order."

"I was worried when Rafferty decided to intervene," Shabina admitted.

"He was incredibly foolish," Raine said. "To attempt to stand up for Bale in front of two FBI agents? It did make him look corrupt and guilty of making evidence disappear."

"I would have given anything to see what was in Rainier's wallet or on his ID that made Rafferty back off the way he did." Vienna lowered her voice. "I know he works for the CIA, but the department he works for isn't well-known. They don't identify themselves as a rule. In fact, Zale told me that if they're sent out on a mission and they get caught, most likely they're on their own. The government doesn't admit they're part of the agency."

"Rafferty is the sheriff in this county, and he's been in the military," Raine pointed out. "Both Sam and Zale live here. He would have checked into them both. He may be foolish when it comes to his family, but he's an intelligent man. Did you notice the way he immediately stepped back away from Rainier and looked at the windows?"

Shabina had noted Rafferty's strange reaction to Rainier's ID. She nodded.

"He was smart enough to figure out Rainier wasn't alone in defending you. Rainier owns a security firm that operates worldwide. He employs ex-military men and women as well as retired agents. Each of his employees receives additional training, which he personally supervises. His firm is considered elite already, and he just started the company a few years back. His equipment is the best one can buy, and his intel is always accurate. Rafferty has connections in the military. He has to have heard of Rainier's company and the people he employs. They're no joke. Any one of them, or even half a dozen of them, could be outside with sniper rifles."

Raine nodded toward a table in the front. It was located directly across from the two men from Paris, the ones who had claimed to be Interpol agents. "Those four men sitting at that table work for Rainier's company. All of them have had distinguished careers, and when I say they're lethal, I mean it. Rainier's got a full security team here."

Shabina's breath hissed out between her teeth. "That man is going to hear from me about this. I should have known when he agreed to take all the dogs running with us. I thought he was being sweet. He wanted to leave three at home to protect the property. All along, that snake had a security team watching my home and the . . ." Her voice trailed off.

"And the?" Vienna prompted.

Shabina sighed. "Bale threatened to burn down the café. I believe he's serious about it, and I told Rainier I was afraid he might really do it. Rainier can't be in both places at once, and he's training the dogs to work together as a team, so we have them inside the house with us and outside on the property. I should have realized he'd bring in someone to watch the café and make sure Bale couldn't get to it. That was why, when we had visitors at the house and nosing around the café, he didn't seem very concerned."

"You can't fault him for ensuring the café was protected," Raine pointed out, always the reasonable one.

"I can fault his lack of communication skills," Shabina said. "We're supposed to be a partnership. He doesn't get to arbitrarily make decisions."

Raine laughed, the sound unexpected and very musical. "Seriously, Shabina? Rainier will always be the one making decisions when it comes to your safety. He's been doing it since you were sixteen years old. No one has ever been able to stop him, and believe me, your father tried. He went out of his way to try to ruin Rainier's career in the CIA."

"My father is going to lose his mind when he finds out I married Rainier. I haven't told him yet."

Vienna raised an eyebrow. "You haven't told your parents you got married?"

Shabina shook her head. "I have this terrible feeling my father is involved in some of the crap that's been going on."

"Such as?" Vienna prompted, casting a worried frown toward Raine.

Shabina noted Raine didn't look surprised. In fact, she wore an expressionless mask, conveying to Shabina she knew more than she was telling.

"I hate to even say this and feel guilty for thinking it, but if my mother's upset because I'm not living with them, I believe my father's capable of going to any lengths to bring me back home. That would include doing his best to trigger a PTSD episode. If he did that, he might put me in a hospital and try to get the doctors to state I need constant care. He isn't above paying doctors to get his way."

Vienna looked horrified. "Your own father? Do you really think he'd do that?"

It was Raine who answered. "Yes. He's paying two university students a great deal of money to do just that."

Shabina closed her eyes at the confirmation. She allowed her mind to absorb the blow. For a moment she considered walking back into the kitchen and putting her arms around Rainier, just having him hold her. She felt safe with him. Loved by him.

She took a deep breath. "I was so afraid that would be the case, but at the same time, at least I know I'm not being framed for murder."

"But he's taking the chance of driving you insane." Vienna was angry now. "And who are these students helping him? What are they doing?"

"Emar Salhi and Jamal Talbi both come from Algeria and are students attending the university," Raine said. "Jack Foster, Shabina's father, has been placing money in their accounts for weeks.

I traced the sale of two laughing doves, the toxic desert rose, a Qaisumah diamond, oud perfume, and miswak sticks to Shabina's father. He had the items sent directly to Salhi and Talbi at a rented Airbnb here. It's a small farmhouse they're sharing with two other students."

"Do the other students know what they're doing?" Shabina asked.

"I doubt it," Raine said. "There's no money going into their accounts."

Vienna looked furious. "We should talk to Harlow and see if her father can get their visas revoked. I'd like to see them deported. What jerks. I can't believe they would be a part of such a vile conspiracy."

"Rainier has already started the process of sending them back to their country," Raine said. "Your man doesn't tolerate attacks on you. That's the bottom line. Jack's only protection is that he's your father."

"I'm worried about what he might do to Bale," Shabina admitted. "Rainier is always calm and purposeful, but I know him well enough to realize Bale could be a target for him. No one should put themselves in his crosshairs, and Bale did that. Unfortunately, Rafferty and those FBI agents were right there. If Bale has an accident and someone gets suspicious, they'll look straight at Rainier."

Raine shook her head. "Even if they did, Rainier will have an ironclad alibi. I'm not above saying, I hope Bale gets a visit from Rainier."

BALE WOKE AT the first touch of the knife against his throat. He gasped and brought both hands up in an attempt to move what must have felt like a steel arm holding him immobile.

"What . . . who . . ." he spluttered.

"I thought we should have a quiet chat, just the two of us," Rainier said. "I want you to be very clear on who and what you're dealing with."

"Get out of my house. I'll have you arrested. You'll be thrown into prison," Bale blustered. His fingers dug into the arm holding him still, but the arm remained locked around him, preventing all movement.

Rainier ignored the posturing. "I do a certain job for the government. They send me in when they want someone to quietly disappear. You may have heard rumors about my friend Sam or even Zale. Just to be fair so you know exactly who you're dealing with, I'm far, far worse than either of them. No one wants me coming after them."

"You can't arrest me."

"I don't arrest people," Rainier corrected. "I end them. Sometimes I take my time. When anyone threatens my wife or makes her cry, I find it brings out my skills as an interrogator. It's always good to hone them. I've taken days to kill men, making sure they felt everything their victims felt before they died. In the end, they begged me for mercy. It didn't affect me in the least. I'm sure their victims begged and didn't get mercy."

Bale tried to shake his head, but the blade of the knife was still pressed against his neck and bit deeper with each movement. Blood trickled down to his shoulders in a steady stream.

"I don't like the threats you made to my wife. I don't like the way you spoke to her. I just want you to know that if anything happens to her, the dogs or the café, if there's so much as a scratch on her, you will get another visit from me, and I'll be the last face you ever see. You're damn lucky Shabina has compassion for you. I don't. You're a coward and a bully. I've met hundreds of men like you, and all of them ended up crying and begging for their lives."

Bale had gone very still, recognizing the merciless conviction in Rainier's voice.

"I want to know you understand. There won't be another warning. You go near her or hire someone else to do your dirty work for you, I'll be coming for you. You'd better make it your mission in life to ensure nothing happens to her."

"I get it," Bale choked out.

"I hope you do, Landry."

He was gone as silently as he'd entered the bedroom. Like an apparition. A ghost. Bale lay in his bed, his heart pounding wildly, one hand covering the cut on his neck while blood trickled through his fingers.

CHAPTER FIFTEEN

The café was packed, and the line outside was long. Shabina was thankful she'd hired two new waiters instead of just one. She'd gotten up early to run the dogs before they started their long day. Rainier was already gone, and the house seemed empty without him. Even the dogs seemed to miss him, crowding around her when she first got up as if seeking reassurance. They searched the entire house before returning to her to wait patiently while she fixed them food. When she sent Sharif, Morza and Malik out to patrol the grounds, she let Sonar, Bomber and Mick inside so she could lavish attention on them and give them their food.

When she took the dogs running, three of the men ran with her while one stayed at her home with the dog team left behind. The other kept guard over the café. Instead of feeling uncomfortable with the men as she normally would have, they made her feel safe because they worked for Rainier and he was the one giving them orders.

Quite a few locals were in the café, business owners showing their support of Shabina after hearing how Bale had treated her. She wasn't sure how to respond to so much kindness, so she worked hard to help her staff and made her rounds, greeting customers, locals and tourists alike. Morning turned into afternoon, and some of her favorite customers came in for lunch.

Edward and Janine were back, sitting closer than ever, laughing softly and whispering intimately to one another. Shabina wasn't sure how she felt about them, but Edward had immediately stood up for her during what she now dubbed "the incident." He'd even offered to pay for the breakfast Bale had initially refused to compensate the café for. She didn't know if his offer had been genuine or if Janine had been so offended, she had offered and shamed him into standing up for Shabina. It didn't really matter, since Edward had stood up to Bale, and she knew he would incur Bale's wrath.

The Garner sisters sat with Janine's two friends, the four women laughing together as they discussed Theresa, Janine and Val attempting to climb a boulder for the first time with Felicity and Eve. They had video, which they were watching on Felicity's laptop. Miguel had been with them and seemed to be shouting advice as he stood on the crash pad, arms up to guide Val when she fell—and she did fall, more than once.

They showed the videos to Shabina as she stopped by to greet them and ensure they had everything they wanted for their lunch. Felicity's laptop was top of the line. Shabina recognized the laptop of a professional after being around Raine so much. It occurred to her she'd never asked about either of the women's work, not even when they'd first come to Knightly after they'd lost their sister, niece and brother-in-law.

Felicity and Eve had recounted how their sister met her husband, Emilio, at work and the two had fallen in love. They'd talked about Freda's and Emilio's jobs and how proud they were of Freda for the work she did with youth. She even knew Emilio had coached both soccer and baseball when he didn't have children

playing either sport. Shabina was upset with herself for not asking Felicity and Eve what they did. Sometimes it felt as if she had
little experience when it came to connecting with new people.

The videos had been filmed by someone who knew what they
were doing. Each video was clear and taken from angles showing
the boulder and the climber in close-up shots as well as long shots
that allowed the viewer to see the entire rock and the difficulty of
attempting to ascend it. Shabina couldn't help but ask.

"Who took the videos? They look professional."

Eve lifted her hand. "Thanks. I've been shooting videos for a
number of years professionally for people. Weddings. Kids' sports
games and gymnastics. You name it, I've probably photographed
or shot video of it. It also helps to have a laptop like Felicity's. I
have one I use to Photoshop and clean up my pictures, but her
programs are so much better. The quality really comes across
when you play a vid on her laptop."

Felicity flashed her a grin. "I'll admit I'm a little in love with
my laptop. And prideful. At least until I saw Raine's. I've never
seen anyone with that powerful of a laptop." She glanced over to
Raine's table and waved. "I tried to hack her."

Shabina was shocked. The other women gasped aloud.

Eve laughed. "She really did. She thinks she's the best at what
she does."

"You're lucky you still have your laptop. Most of the time
when someone tries to hack Raine, they get viruses that destroy
their hard drive beyond repair," Shabina said.

Felicity nodded, her smile fading. "I knew I was hitting military safeguards and triggering alarms. I could see there was no
way in. I immediately contacted her and told her what I'd tried to
do. She was very gracious about it."

"No one from the military visited you?" Theresa asked.

"I'm sure Raine explained things to whoever would have arrested me. I told her to feel free to hack my computer if she could. I gave her my permission to take a look at it so she could see I wasn't after military secrets. I doubt she did, because she seemed to believe me and I didn't see any evidence of her taking over my laptop. I've never seen anyone better than she is, although she told me there is always someone better. She's so intelligent, she must be off the charts."

Theresa and Val both looked across the room at Raine. "She is so quiet," Val said. "I don't always notice her. Your other friends seem to be always laughing and talking to everyone, but she keeps to herself, stays more in the background."

Shabina smiled at Raine. "That's her way. She doesn't brag to anyone about how intelligent she is. She even stays quiet in a debate, unless you're disrespectful to someone, and then she has no problem setting things straight. Crossing Raine's sense of justice is a huge mistake."

Feeling eyes on her, she glanced up to see the four students from the university sitting across from the women. The two men from Algeria kept looking toward Raine as if seeing her for the first time. Shabina immediately felt protective. She knew Raine was quite capable of protecting herself, but she had been horribly injured, the bones in her leg shattered when she'd been shot. The bullet meant for Vienna had hit her instead. Vienna and Shabina had kept pressure on the wound to allow a helicopter to land and transport Raine to a waiting surgical team. Still, it had been touch-and-go whether they could save her leg.

The students had heard most of the conversation between the women. If Emar Salhi and Jamal Talbi wanted to blame anyone for their current problems, they would believe it was Raine who was having their student visas pulled. She didn't want attention on Raine.

"The other thing is this: Raine is totally protected at all times by a couple of different branches of the government. She's considered valuable. Someone shot her; that's why she limps and walks with the cane or crutches right now. The shooter was hunted relentlessly. He is no longer alive, and everyone involved in the plot is gone as well. It isn't a good thing to try to attack her. Felicity, it was a good thing you owned up to what you were doing immediately."

Shabina made the statement more for the benefit of the students than the women. She didn't feel Raine was threatened in any way by the women. If anything, they admired her. She wasn't so certain the conversation had that same effect on the male students.

"Enjoy your lunch," she told the women and turned toward the students, greeting them in Arabic. The moment she stepped close to the table, Larado and Zero, two of the security team, stood and walked through the café quite casually. Zero stopped, appearing to look at the view through the window while Larado took up a position close to her, draping himself coolly against the wall. "Is there anything else I can get for you?"

Jules Beaumont and Deniz Kaplan both shook their heads and thanked her for the wonderful meal.

Emar held up a hand. "Jamal and I would like to speak with you. And perhaps with your friend." He gestured toward Raine.

Shabina shook her head, trying to look regretful. "I'm sorry, there's nothing to say."

"It is of the utmost importance," Jamal said. "We wouldn't intrude otherwise."

"I won't be available until after six, and I won't be alone. My friends will be with me. Whatever you have to say to me will have to be said in front of them."

Emar and Jamal exchanged a long look, and then Emar nodded. "Where?"

"I think you're familiar with the address to my home. Don't try to enter the grounds without permission. The dogs will attack, or a member of the security team is likely to shoot you. You'll have to stop at the gate and wait for an escort inside the grounds." She figured if they were desperate enough to see her under those circumstances, she might as well ask the questions she wanted answers to.

Both men nodded and murmured their appreciation.

"I intend to ask you questions. Don't bother coming if you aren't prepared to answer me honestly."

There was a brief flurry of activity at the table nearest to where Zero stood. Zero was tall with dark skin and tight curls on his head. He wore his hair longer so that it fell around his forehead and ears, giving him an unruly appearance. He had wide shoulders and a lithe body, all muscle. He had inserted his body between the men at the table and Shabina. To her horror, she realized that Sean wasn't with them, but the two men who had been seated while she was talking with Theresa, Val, Felicity and Eve were the two interning with Sean.

She hadn't banned them from the café, so technically, they could come back and clearly had. She pressed the tips of her fingers to her lips and forced herself to breathe. She didn't want the students from Algeria, the ones reporting to her father, to see her go to pieces again. Rainier wasn't close and she couldn't reach out to him while he was in the field. She didn't want to call attention to the fact that he wasn't around. She hadn't seen Boucher and Cormier around, but if they were still searching for information, she didn't want it known that Rainier was out of the country while Scorpion's cabinet members were assassinated. That would put him under suspicion for sure.

"We're just asking to talk to her." Oliver Smythe's voice was belligerent, sounding oddly like Sean.

"If you'll excuse me," she said to the university students. As she started toward the table, Vaughn moved to intercept, but Larado got there first.

"What do you think you're doing?" Larado demanded, inserting his body between hers and the two men.

Zero pointed to the chairs. "Sit, gentlemen. I won't tell you twice. If you insist on causing a scene in this café again, you will be physically removed."

"I'm going to tell Mr. Smythe and Mr. Vanderpool exactly what Zero just told them," Shabina informed Larado. "I own this café, and my customers aren't here for the drama."

"I don't know, Shabina," Carl Montgomery called out. Once again, he was seated with the local veterinarian. "I think we're all just waiting to see what happens next. The drama is pretty interesting."

"Carl," Dr. Amelia Sanderson reprimanded with a little laugh.

"If it keeps happening and is that entertaining, I'm charging double for the show along with the food," Shabina threatened. The customers within hearing laughed, just the way she knew they would.

Larado stepped aside. "I think you've got this under control, ma'am."

"Shabina," she corrected and stepped closer to the table, pinning both men with as stern a gaze as she could manage. It wasn't her strong suit. The dogs didn't believe her when she threatened to give them away or cut off their food. "Say what you need to say, but there aren't going to be any more scenes in my café by Sean, Bale or either of you. I will press charges against anyone refusing to pay after they've eaten, or if they threaten me, the café or my staff. Am I making myself clear?"

Oliver flushed and Maurice looked annoyed, but both nodded, indicating they understood.

"We came in to apologize for what happened the other day," Oliver said. "None of us, including Sean, had any idea Bale would break your dishes and refuse to pay. The meal was fantastic, which is why everyone comes here. One minute we were all laughing and the next he was raging. I didn't know what to do and neither did Sean or Maurice."

"And then your husband came to the table," Maurice continued. "I've never met anyone like him before."

If there was a question in his statement, she wasn't going to answer it. "He's very protective." She made that her response. "I accept your apology. I have no problem with you coming to the café as long as you don't cause a scene, you treat my staff with respect and you pay your bill. Have a good day, gentlemen."

Abruptly, Shabina turned away from them, refusing to allow them to take up any more of her time. Raine, Zahra and Vienna waited for her at their usual table in the back.

"It's girls' night tonight," Shabina greeted as she sank into a chair beside Vienna. She didn't want to discuss any of the men she'd spoken with. She needed a little reprieve from thinking about the problems she faced. "Raine, I know it's your turn to have us over, but I've been thinking it might be better to hold our get-together at my house. Your leg is still hurting, and I know you had physical therapy today."

Raine shook her head. "I can still pull it together. I'll get the food from the Grill, so no one will starve. You've worked all day, Shabina. You deserve time off."

"You know I love to cook. In any case, I already have tons of food prepared from here. And, just so you know, Rainier insists I have a security team looking after me, and they love to eat—a *lot*."

Zahra rolled her eyes. "I've seen those men." She indicated a table near the door. "They ate breakfast, and now they're eating lunch."

"I don't think there has been a pause between breakfast and lunch," Vienna added. "They do like to eat."

"You know what's annoying?" Zahra said. "They can eat like that and never gain a pound."

Silence greeted her statement. The women stared at her in astonishment. Shabina cleared her throat. "Zahra, you eat anything you want and never gain a pound. We should know; we watch you do it."

Vienna nodded. "Don't say you don't. We all want to strangle you."

"That's Raine," Zahra objected. "She can put away an entire large pizza and not gain an ounce. I watch my diet very carefully." As always, she sounded a little haughty. One dark eyebrow raised as if to dare them to contradict her.

"That's you too." Vienna wasn't intimidated. "Stop denying it. You can even eat desserts with no problem. I look at whipped cream and have to go running for miles in order to get the pounds off my hips."

Shabina refrained from rolling her eyes. Vienna looked like a model, with her tall frame, gorgeous hair and figure. "In any case, I'd really feel more comfortable having our night at my home, Raine. The security team eats like locusts."

"If you're willing to do the cooking and host, then I'll say yes if I can pay for the food," Raine conceded.

"It's settled, then. I'll run the dogs after work and then get busy." She hesitated. "The two students from Algeria asked to come to the house to speak with me. With us," she corrected. "They may have the mistaken idea that you are doing something to have their student visas revoked. I think they want to plead for mercy."

Vienna and Zahra both looked confused. Shabina sighed. "It's a little bit of a story. I'll tell you tonight."

"I'll come early and help," Vienna said. "I've had too much time on my hands after the search. I need to keep busy, and they won't allow me to go back to work until the end of the week."

"Have you been talking to the counselor?" Zahra asked. "Maybe she can advocate for you. I know what it's like to have my mind running a hundred miles an hour."

"After we find bodies instead of live victims, it's mandatory to take time off," Vienna explained. "Because there were two bodies, one a friend, and both were murdered, the counselor is insistent I take time off work."

"Well, I'm coming early as well," Zahra said. "I can't cook, but I can help out with the dogs and the sideboard, getting everything out for us."

"You know how to cook," Shabina objected.

Zahra shrugged. "I don't *like* to cook. Not all the time, like you do. In any case, your food is always delicious. Mine can be hit or miss."

"Would you mind giving me a ride, Zahra," Raine said. "I may as well get there early too. I won't be much help in the kitchen, but we should put together a game plan when it comes to questioning those two."

"Harlow will make it just before dinner. She's working today.

And Stella is driving down from Sunrise Lake, so who knows when she's going to show," Vienna said.

"They'll come as early as possible once I text them you're going to give us the 411 on what is going on with those students," Zahra promised.

Shabina couldn't help but laugh. "Are you saying they'll come early for gossip?"

"*Exactly.*" Zahra was adamant. "We all like to be in the know. Besides, we need to figure this murder thing out fast. The cops don't seem to have a clue. We're smart. We can put the clues together and catch this person. He has to have slipped up more than once."

"I wish we could," Shabina said. "Losing three people already is three too many. And he seems to be escalating his behavior." Just uttering the statement made her think of Bale and his increased threats. She didn't voice her worry because there were too many ears in the café.

"It's hard enough when the victims are strangers," Vienna said, "but when we know them, like we all did Lucca Delgotto, it seems so much worse."

Shabina had to agree. She wasn't on the Search and Rescue teams. She cooked food and made certain the crews had everything they needed. Unless they wanted advice on the trails that were closed and she knew them from documenting nests, she stayed away from the teams looking for victims. She'd seen too much death, men, women and children, and those deaths haunted her.

Vienna nodded toward Miguel Valdez, who was sitting with Avita Delgotto. Twice, the personal trainer reached across the table and covered Avita's hand briefly. "Miguel and Lucca Delgotto were best friends growing up. Miguel sometimes tells the funniest stories of the trouble the two of them got into together when they were teenagers. By today's standards, the things they did were more like pranks than actual crimes."

Zahra followed her gaze and took in the trainer and his grieving companion. "I remember him telling stories about the two of them going into an old house that had 'no trespassing' written all over it. They broke out the windows or something idiotic like that, and then Lucca confessed to his mother when he was sleepwalking."

"You're kidding," Raine said. "He really did that? Walked and talked in his sleep?"

Vienna nodded, her face lighting up at the memories. "Shabina, do you remember Miguel telling us that Lucca always talked in his sleep and confessed everything they'd done to his mother? He wouldn't remember sleepwalking or -talking, so he just thought his mother was psychic and knew everything."

"Miguel had us laughing so hard when we were supposed to be doing planks," Shabina said. "It was impossible to stay in that position, and he called us all wimpy."

Zahra lifted an eyebrow. "He didn't call me wimpy."

"He wouldn't dare," Raine said. "No one would dare."

"His stories about his adventures with Lucca were always the best," Vienna said. "Although they were little hooligans. If my parents had either of them, they would have put them in military school."

Zahra dipped a zucchini stick into the special sauce Shabina was so famous for making. "Weren't they both arrested for something? I'm sure Miguel said one of Lucca's confessions led to their arrest."

"Yep," Vienna said. "He confessed to his mother in front of company that they broke into the local grocery store to get snacks and word got out that the two of them had been stealing from the grocer. They were arrested and convicted. I think they were fifteen or sixteen, but the judge had a list of their criminal activity, as petty as most things were. I suspect someone enlightened the judge so they would have to make reparations and not get off lightly."

"Miguel said they mostly straightened up after that," Shabina said. "They had to work off the debt they owed, so they both had jobs and not a lot of time to get into trouble."

"I like that he used the term *mostly*," Zahra said. "But he said it wasn't as fun because Lucca had grown out of his habit of sleepwalking and confessing all to his mother."

"Look at the way Miguel is with Avita." Shabina indicated the two with a barely perceptible nod of her head. "He's in love with her."

Vienna agreed. "I once asked him why he didn't date her, and he said it was a respect thing. Lucca is very protective of Avita." She cleared her throat. "*Was* protective. He said Lucca was like his brother, and the Delgottos had always treated him as if he were a part of their family, even after it came to light that the boys were up to no good together. Lucca's family still welcomed Miguel with open arms."

"The Delgottos are wonderful people," Shabina added. "And I doubt that they would have objections to Miguel dating their daughter."

"It looks to me as if she reciprocates his feelings," Zahra said. "Miguel's a good man and he would work hard for his family. Avita must see that in him."

"She's known him all of her life," Shabina agreed. "It would be nice if their families could find a little happiness in the middle of losing Lucca."

"It would," Vienna agreed.

SHABINA FOUND BAKING and cooking with a security team underfoot wasn't as easy as it was when Rainier was helping her. The men rotated: sometimes Dimitri would be in the kitchen with her, then Zero and Larado would exchange places with the two men, Altair and Torin, who often watched over the café.

Shabina knew Altair had been friends with Rainier for years. His name was Arabic and meant falcon. He had a tattoo of a falcon on his upper right shoulder. Torin was Irish American and had the reddish hair and freckles to prove it. She liked all of them but felt the most comfortable with Larado and Altair.

Each time one of the men entered the kitchen for the first time, they wanted to sample the food or baked goods. She ended up baking double the amount she normally would have. The alarm went off, and then a call came in from the gate that she had visitors.

"Ma'am, I can't let those men in here with you. It isn't a safe situation," Larado said.

He sounded as firm and calm as Rainier. Just as tyrannical. He might be polite, but he wasn't going to back off.

"It's necessary for me to hear what they have to say. I've got questions that need answers, Larado. I'm not trying to be defiant. My father is involved in this somehow, and I have the right to know what he asked of them. Some of the items on those altars with the murder victims were from Saudi Arabia. They were the ones in possession of the items, at least I believe they were."

He looked thoughtful but not wholly persuaded.

"All my friends are here. I'm armed. Raine is as well. I'll have three of the dogs inside with me. We were expecting them."

"You should have kept me informed."

Shabina nodded, conceding he was right. She didn't have to like it, but he was responsible for her safety.

"Rainier isn't just my employer, ma'am. He's my friend. You're the most important person in his world and he's trusted me with your safety. I can't take chances with your life, not that I would, even if Rainier hadn't pulled me out of some tight spots more than once."

"Would you feel more comfortable if you were in the room with us?" That was a hard concession for her to make, but she understood Larado's hesitation. If either of the two students pulled out a gun and started firing, someone might get hit before Raine or she was able to neutralize them. On the other hand, the men would be more likely to answer her questions if her personal protectors weren't standing around looking threatening.

"I'd feel more comfortable if they didn't enter this house, but I can see your point that you want to question them. I'll bring Altair inside as well. He speaks Arabic fluently, and if they converse in their language and I miss something they say, he'll get it."

"I speak Arabic," Shabina felt compelled to point out.

Larado ignored her. "I don't like this, but I'm going along with it because you need answers. Dimitri will be stationed just outside the front door. If it all goes sideways, he'll take them out."

There was a finality to his statement and his tone. She could take it or leave it. Shabina nodded her head. "Let them come in, and I'll do my best to get them out of here quickly."

Zahra immediately went into the kitchen and positioned herself behind the island. Raine stayed in her chair, but she had the gun in her hand out of sight. Stella and Harlow positioned their chairs a distance apart and partially in the shadows and toward the back of the room where there was cover they could dive behind. Vienna sat on the other side of the room away from Raine. She was also armed.

Once the women were in position, Shabina sent the dogs to their places. They separated and went to the corners of the room, making it impossible for the two men to kill all three dogs easily before one or more took them down.

"Not your first rodeo, I see," Larado commented. "Not a bad setup. Let them in, but make sure we always have a clear shot at them."

Shabina wasn't about to get caught in the cross fire. She knew how to position herself. Altair escorted the two men inside.

"I checked them for weapons," he reported to Larado. "Neither was carrying a gun, but both were armed with knives."

Rainier had drilled it into Shabina that in some instances, particularly at close range, a knife would be far faster and deadlier than a bullet. The fact that the two men were carrying knives into her home immediately aroused suspicion with her security team. She directed them to the chairs provided. Sitting would make them much more vulnerable. If Altair had missed any weapons—which she highly doubted—they would have more trouble throwing from that position.

"We came here to plead with you to keep the officials from revoking our student visas," Emar said. "Our families will be humiliated if we return home in disgrace."

"We need this education to help our tribe," Jamal added. "Not only with the newer practices for farming and growing crops but learning about the various irrigation systems that will work for our people during the droughts."

"Maybe you should have thought of that before you took that money," Vienna stated without the least hint of sympathy.

"We have a few questions that need answers," Raine said. "How is it those feathers and the flowers from Saudi Arabia, as well as other items, ended up on the altar with a murder victim?"

Shabina didn't take her gaze from Emar's face. He was uncomfortable answering questions, particularly when Raine asked them, but the two men hoped to get their visas restored before they were deported. If they wanted help, they would have to answer whatever questions were put to them, and both believed it was Raine who was instrumental in getting them revoked.

Jamal sighed, took a quick glance at the grim-faced security guards and then answered. "We had the items in a box. We were given the information that Shabina is the only one allowed to enter this one area that is closed to everyone else. We decided to scatter the items on the trail where we knew she would find them."

"Your purpose in doing that was to cause her to have a PTSD episode?" Raine pursued.

Again, there was hesitation, and then Emar nodded. "Yes."

"The two of you were paid by Jack Foster to bring about a PTSD event?" Raine's voice was mild, gentle even.

"Yes, he put large sums of money into our accounts and had the items delivered to the Airbnb where we are staying. He had precise instructions we were to follow. Feathers on the steps of her café, scatter items where she runs along the canal, find places where she works in Yosemite and make certain the items are there where she would see them," Emar said.

Harlow's scowl indicated complete disapproval. "You didn't think that what you were doing was wrong? Trying to drive a woman crazy enough that her father would force her into a hospital? You believe that's acceptable behavior?"

Jamal's features hardened. "My belief is that a woman obeys

her father. He ordered her numerous times to come home, but she refused."

"You don't believe a woman has the right to live her own life?" Vienna asked. "Especially if she's making her own living?"

Jamal shook his head. "She shows no respect for her father. He is head of the household, and she should do as she is ordered."

"Rainier is head of the household," Shabina corrected softly. "I follow his lead, not my father's."

"Your father did not tell us about your husband," Emar pointed out, as if that made what they had done acceptable.

"Let's get back to how those items ended up on the altar with a murder victim," Raine interrupted before the others could get into an argument about a woman's rights.

Shabina knew the men would never agree, no matter how logical an argument might be made. It was ingrained in them that women did as their fathers directed and if not their fathers, their husbands.

"We had the box open and were discussing what to put out on the trail she used when she checked on her birds. We heard voices, people coming toward us. We weren't supposed to be there and thought Shabina was coming up the trail with someone else, perhaps an official," Jamal said. "They seemed very close."

"Too close," Emar agreed. "We shoved the box under some brush because if we were found, we didn't want to have to explain what was in it. We figured we could come back in a couple of hours and get it. We took off into the forest, looking for another trail to get us out of there."

"Did you see the people on the trail?" Raine asked.

Emar shook his head. "We moved as quickly as possible to get off the trail and into cover so *we* wouldn't be seen. We didn't hide or stop to look back. I believed it was Shabina with an official there to document the nest."

"When we went back a few hours later, the box was gone. At first, we thought we just didn't remember the exact location," Jamal said. "But then the items turned up with a murder victim. We knew we had to keep quiet, or we would be suspects."

"You used the term *voices*," Raine persisted. "That indicates you believed more than one person was coming up the trail."

The two men exchanged a long look. "Definitely more than one person," Emar confirmed.

"And then when you took the bird-watching tour, you had a box of items you left on the hood of her vehicle," Vienna said. "Where did you get those things if the box was gone?"

"We had sorted out some of the items and left them at the Airbnb where we were staying. We didn't have a lot left but thought at least we could earn our money by leaving the things on her car," Jamal said. "We'd taken his money and owed him."

He sounded so righteous it was all Shabina could do not to laugh. They felt justified in helping her father because, in their minds, she was a rebellious daughter and needed disciplining. She glanced at Altair. Like Rainier, he had been raised in the Middle East. He'd had similar experiences to Rainier. He shook his head, indicating he didn't share the same beliefs and, like her, thought her father, an American, was totally in the wrong.

Jack Foster couldn't even claim his upbringing or customs would lead him to such a decision. Shabina knew it was entitlement and arrogance. No one defied Jack when he decreed something, least of all his insignificant daughter—the one she was certain he'd gotten word to the assassin Deadly Storms to kill all those years ago.

"We spoke with your father to ask for his aid in stopping the deportation and hopefully getting our visas back. He assured us it was no problem, but then he called and said he'd run into all kinds of roadblocks, that we have a powerful enemy who has enough clout to make it happen." Emar looked at Raine the entire time he spoke.

Jamal did his best not to glare at her.

"You're mistaken in believing Raine had anything to do with revoking your visas. That would be my husband," Shabina said. "He does make a powerful enemy when you do something such as try to take his wife from him or have her committed to a hospital."

Both men looked uncomfortable at the news.

"Is it possible to speak with him?" Emar ventured.

"I think it best if I speak on your behalf before he talks with you," Shabina said. "If you anger him by saying anything against me, you won't have a chance."

Altair approached the men and gestured toward the door. "Rainier will contact you," he assured. "Not that I believe you have much of a chance of dissuading him."

Shabina knew the men couldn't fail to hear the note of satisfaction in his voice.

CHAPTER SIXTEEN

Shabina rarely looked at her messages while she was working, but with Rainier gone, she couldn't help herself.

> Just got home, Qadri. Will come to
> the café after I rest.

She wanted to close the café immediately and rush home to him, but she knew if he said he needed rest, he did.

> So happy you're home. Can't wait to
> see you. Get sleep. ❤

Raine entered, waving at her, indicating she needed to talk to her immediately. She pointed to the corner table in the back. Shabina hurried to take Raine's laptop so she could concentrate on walking through the café and not worry about dropping the backpack she carried her laptop in. It was surprisingly heavy.

"You didn't drive yourself here, did you?" Shabina asked.

"Zahra and Harlow are working. Vienna had a meeting this

morning. I had to get here." Raine settled into the chair and reached for her case.

"You should have called me, Raine. I would have gone to get you myself. I thought you had strict instructions not to drive a car."

Raine shrugged. "This was important, and I didn't want it to wait. The information is for your eyes only, not even one of our friends can see this."

Shabina's heart jumped. Rainier had come home. The assassin, Deadly Storms, must have completed his assignment. She couldn't imagine what other information Raine would have that she couldn't show to their friends.

"Besides, I can't keep relying on everyone else for rides. I'm kind of losing my mind without my independence," Raine admitted.

Tyrone hurried up to the table. "Ladies? Do you know what you want this morning?"

"I'd like my usual order, tea included," Raine said.

"I'll have a cup of tea as well," Shabina added. "Thanks, Tyrone." She slid into the chair beside Raine's seat so she could easily see the screen on the laptop. It would be impossible for anyone else to see what Raine shared with her.

"This information came in late last night," Raine whispered. "I have alerts on anything to do with Lefebre or the men he works with. The government of Jordan announced that four Canadian men were found killed by the elusive assassin Deadly Storms."

"They're really dead?"

Raine nodded. "Proof was left behind that these men went on killing sprees with Scorpion. This is the second time that men working closely with Lefebre have been accused and condemned. If the governments of Jordan, Saudi Arabia and Syria, as well as several other countries Scorpion murdered in, all put out contracts on Scorpion and have sought proof of his identity, this will point the finger straight at Lefebre. He'll have alibis, but they will be looking closely at him now."

"How do you know they're dead? Just because an announcement is made doesn't mean it's true." Shabina's palm shaped her suddenly aching thigh muscle.

"The bodies were unmistakable proof. Each had died hard with the same wounds that covered your body. The brand of the assassin Deadly Storms was on each of their left arms. His work is distinctive, very unique. I believe that any government contracting with him to hunt down Scorpion and his men insisted he provide proof of their crimes. The US government won't admit it, but they have used him more than once, and I believe they also have put out a contract on Scorpion and his men."

Shabina knew her hands were shaking so she folded them together in her lap. "No wonder he has money. If he does a job like this one, he gets paid from several different sources." She just wanted to get home and ensure there wasn't a scratch on him.

"No doubt he has money," Raine confirmed. "You do realize only Lefebre and one other of the men Scorpion referred to as his cabinet are still alive."

"Do you have any idea where those men are at the moment?"

"We think Lefebre has been playing it safe, staying in the embassy in Jordan. If he is, Owen Pelletier is most likely with him."

"Where were these men killed?" Shabina pressed her fingertips deep into the muscle of her thigh. It ached. Throbbed painfully.

Raine hesitated before answering. "Two of them were guests of one of the prince's sons, and they were in the palace."

Shabina felt the color draining from her face. "He broke into the palace and killed two men, right under the noses of the guards? And won't the prince be just a little angry?"

"That's what I find the most interesting about Deadly Storms. He has better intel than even I can get. Where are his sources? Who are they? And you know he must have allies to get into a heavily guarded palace with the prince in residence. Is the prince his ally? Someone very high up is. Maybe more than one person. Deadly Storms couldn't possibly operate the way he does without having a ton of resources."

"He grew up in that country," Shabina murmured.

Rainier had gone into a palace with fully armed guards—guards renowned to be some of the best in the world. She knew he did dangerous work. She'd always known. He'd come to her at her worst hour in the middle of a violent sandstorm. Scorpion had left behind a small army of men, and Rainier had dispatched every single one of them.

"Was there evidence of the assassin being injured? Was there an incident reported?" It took every ounce of discipline she had not to text him. Not to rush home. This was going to be her life with Rainier. He would leave, and she wouldn't know if he was coming home in one piece—or at all.

"He was in and out without a trace," Raine assured. "That's why he's considered so extraordinary, and his services are sought after by several governments. He epitomizes the term *ghost.*" Raine slowly closed the laptop. "You need to take a deep breath. Everything is good."

"Were you able to look into my father's financials?" She uttered the question in a low whisper, guilt sliding over her like a familiar cloak.

"Yes. He transferred a great deal of money into the accounts of Emar Salhi and Jamal Talbi."

"They admitted that they were working for him. I'm talking about when I was sixteen. Were you able to find out if he had contracted with Deadly Storms to kill me?" She said it aloud. Rainier had stopped short of confirming it, but she knew she was right.

"I'm so sorry," Raine murmured. "I detest being the one to give you bad news."

Strangely, instead of feeling abandoned and hurt by her father's decision to terminate her life, she felt freer. That heavy cloak of constant guilt she wore lifted. "I would rather know the truth, Raine. I'm grateful I have two people in my life I can count on to give it to me when I ask for it."

"I know what it's like to have your family abandon you."

"This wasn't a decision my mother would make. I can guarantee you without a trace of doubt that my mother has no idea. He did it for her. Just the way he's trying to force me to come home. She's upset because she doesn't believe I'm safe. He'll do anything, including forcing me into a hospital to keep her from being upset. It doesn't make sense, but there is no room for anyone else in his world. Not even me. She loves me, so he will do whatever it takes to get me home with her. In his mind, that's perfectly logical."

"How is contracting with an assassin to kill his daughter logical?" Raine asked.

Shabina shrugged. The more she knew of her father and talked about him and what he'd done, the more the weight of guilt lifted.

"I had been held for six months, and the videos going to my parents had to have been brutal to see. You've seen photographs of what I looked like when I came home."

"I've seen the videos of the ransom demands." Raine's voice was tight. For the first time, she appeared emotional. "If anyone needs killing, it would be Scorpion. Your father should have put out a contract on him, not his own daughter."

"He obviously didn't believe I would ever be returned. If my mother was distressed, his logic would have been if I were dead, she could eventually accept that. If I were to guess, she probably wanted to give into Scorpion's demand for an exchange, her for me. Jack would never have allowed that. Viewing the videos, he probably convinced himself he was being merciful to me."

"I think that's bullshit, but that's my opinion," Raine said.

"I'm grateful you wouldn't hire a killer to come after me. I've got the FBI and Rafferty breathing down my neck, and I have a terrible feeling Deniz Kaplan wants to take me home to his mother. Then there's Bale. Who knows what he's going to do?"

Raine was silent as Tyrone delivered the food and drinks to the table. She smiled up at the man. "Thank you, Tyrone. I see you're wearing a new ring."

Shabina was shocked that she hadn't noticed. "Did you and Vaughn go to the courthouse? Did you? I'm going to strangle you both if you did and then didn't even let me throw you two a reception."

Tyrone's smile grew wider, his teeth flashing white with his boyish grin. "Vaughn said if you knew, you'd insist on throwing a party for us."

"Well, now I know. You tell that knothead husband of yours that he's in so much trouble. And I *am* going to throw a party. We need to celebrate every chance we get."

Raine nodded. "I agree totally with that. I'll help too."

The grin faded from Tyrone's face. For a moment he looked as if he might be choked up. He shook his head. "I have my brother, but Vaughn's family is totally against our marriage. They refuse to speak to Vaughn. No one will come."

"Vaughn and you have a family in us, Tyrone," Shabina corrected. "And I know Vaughn has a sister, who will be so happy for the two of you. His parents aren't there yet, but they'll come around."

Raine smiled up at him. "We have a bit of an odd family, Tyrone. We all come from different backgrounds and have had difficulties in our lives, but we're choosing to make our friends our family. You and Vaughn are part of that."

Tyrone nodded his head but didn't speak. He turned and made his way to the counter, where Vaughn leaned into him, gripping his shoulder. They spoke briefly, and then Vaughn looked up, his eyes meeting Shabina's. He blew her a kiss and put one hand over his heart.

"I love living here," Shabina said.

Dr. Martha Fendy, the medical examiner, walked in with Mary Shelton, a deputy sheriff. Martha looked tired. After a brief discussion with Patsy, they were shown to the table in the back beside the one Raine and Shabina occupied.

"Is everything all right?" Shabina asked. "I can make something special for you, Martha."

"Do I look that bad?" the medical examiner asked.

"Just tired. Both of you look tired," Shabina admitted. "I don't mind making your special breakfast." Martha had a love for food from Saudi Arabia.

"Thank you, but I'll order your special this morning. I have been up all night. There was another murder, but this time the body was found near the hot springs, not up in Yosemite. This one hit too close to home. Just like Lucca."

Shabina's heart sank. "Another local? At the hot springs?"

"He wasn't local," the deputy said. "A runaway. He arrived in a stolen van and was living in it out by the springs. He has a history of arrests for petty crimes."

Martha shook her head. "It's so sad. He was seventeen years old. A kid with his entire life ahead of him."

Mary Shelton sighed. "His name was Craig Barker, and he looked twelve to me."

"He must have been experienced in stealing cars to get away with a van like the one he was driving," Martha said.

Mary shook her head. "I checked him out, and he certainly wasn't a hardened criminal. His parents are drug addicts and from the reports I read, there was physical abuse in the home. His father was incarcerated on two occasions for theft. Both parents were brought up on child abuse charges several times when he was younger, but the courts continued to give him back to them. In my opinion, this is another failure of our system for these kinds of kids."

Shabina rubbed her temples. She had seen so many children in loving families in Saudi Arabia when she was with Salman Ahmad's tribe. Even then, before she knew the truth about her father, she had felt more loved in that environment than she had in her home with her parents.

"Is it a copycat?" Raine asked.

"Not in my opinion," Martha said. "I don't know what the FBI is going to conclude."

Theresa, Janine and Val entered with Felicity and Eve. Tyrone escorted them to one of the larger tables near the windows. Felicity spotted Shabina and hurried toward her, ignoring the chair Tyrone had pulled out for her.

"Did you hear?" Felicity appeared very distressed. "We recommended the hot springs to Theresa, Val and Janine. They went out there yesterday with Edward. He showed them all around, and they even saw that boy's van."

"How did you hear so quickly?" Raine asked.

"Theresa and Val heard it from Tom and Judy early this morning. They walk together in the mornings. Tom and Judy know everyone in Knightly, or at least it feels that way."

Martha and Mary both gave a low, humorless laugh. "That's the way it is in a small town. News spreads like wildfire," Martha said. "Tom and Judy saw we were working late, and they stopped to ask if we needed anything. Tom offered to get us food from the Grill."

"The FBI agents were there as well," Mary volunteered.

"What's your impression of them?" Raine asked.

"Very professional. Good at their jobs and very thorough. They don't miss anything," Martha said.

"Yet they let Rafferty throw suspicion on Shabina," Raine said.

Mary shook her head as did Martha. It was Martha who answered. "They may have had to follow up if there was a reason to suspect you, although everyone knows you work here in Knightly at the café. You can't be in two places at one time. They do their job to rule out any suspects."

"I can't believe anyone would think you were involved in murder, Shabina," Felicity said, indignation in her voice. "Why would they even consider you a suspect?"

Shabina shrugged, not able to answer adequately. She knew law enforcement hadn't disclosed information to the public about the items on the altar.

Raine answered for her, sounding casual as she explained. "All the victims were here in the café at one time. As far as I know, that's the only tie between them. They don't look at all alike. I don't see a common denominator yet. If the agents were looking for something, anything at all, to tie them together, it would be this café."

"I see," Felicity said, a bit mollified.

Theresa, Val and Eve waved frantically at Felicity. Patsy stood next to their table.

"Felicity, you should order your food. It gets packed in here, and once we're slammed, getting your breakfast to you takes more time," Shabina pointed out.

"You shouldn't feel bad about recommending the hot springs," Mary added. "You're just trying to share the various places you enjoyed seeing with your friends."

Felicity sighed as she turned to walk back to her table. "I still don't like that Theresa, Val and Janine were out there while a murder was taking place." She looked back over her shoulder. "They ran into Miguel and Avita. They weren't using the hot springs, but they'd gone climbing, and a small group of their friends were gathered around a firepit. I think they met out there because Avita's brother went there a lot with Miguel when they were kids."

Raine stared after her for a minute. "It's always amazing to me when someone new moves to Knightly and they're so friendly that within a matter of weeks they know as many people here as I've met after years of living here."

Martha shook her head. "You know everyone, Raine. You're just quiet about it. I'm glad those two women are settling in and finding a semblance of peace after what happened to them. It was so terrible for them losing their entire family last year. These murders must be difficult for them. They know what it's like to feel overwhelming grief."

"They've been supportive of Avita," Mary said. "Pablo, one of her brothers, told me that many people had reached out to their family. Miguel introduced those women to Avita. She needs friends right now."

"How do they know Miguel?" Mary asked.

"He's not only their personal trainer, but he's helping them learn to boulder," Shabina said.

"I heard a rumor that you're married, Shabina," Martha said, clearly wanting to change the subject. "Is that the truth?"

Shabina nodded, reluctantly showing the ring on her finger. She didn't want her hand to tremble, and she was still unsteady every time she thought about Rainier and any possible harm that could come to him.

"That looks so perfect for you. I think it matches your eyes," Mary gushed. "I also heard your man is a hottie, and when Bale threw his hissy fit, he just calmly walked out of the kitchen and informed him he expected Bale to pay and that you were taking out a restraining order against him."

"I am. It's already in the works. Rainier was in the kitchen doing dishes. No one was aware he was in there. He doesn't like the spotlight on him."

"He's the dishwasher?" Martha was amused.

Shabina laughed. "It's true. He hides in the kitchen, preferring to do dishes and not have to talk to anyone."

Mary glanced at the table where the two FBI agents were eating breakfast and lowered her voice even more even though the two men were a distance away. "Rafferty was furious that there was an implication that if you turned in evidence against Bale, it would disappear. He didn't like it stated in front of the feds."

Martha made a disparaging sound in her throat. "I don't know why he would get upset when it's the truth. He makes a good political sheriff, and he's intelligent when it comes to running his department, but when his family is involved, his brains go out the window."

"He had to realize that sooner or later, someone was going to call him out on it," Mary added in a whisper. "Do you really have evidence proving Bale was harassing you, Shabina?"

Raine answered. "He wasn't simply harassing her, he threatened to burn down the café with her in it, shoot her dogs and her. He started with harassment, but his behavior has escalated in the last few months. He believed he could blackmail Lawyer into destroying the evidence before I could get to it. He had no idea we had installed military cameras and they're always monitored and backed up. There is no way, even if the evidence was removed, that we couldn't reproduce it."

"Good," Martha said firmly. "It's about time someone let Bale know that he isn't running Knightly, and neither is his family."

"Lawyer told me Bale was attempting to blackmail him," Mary said. "He knew if he swore out a complaint, Rafferty would ignore it. Things like that make the entire department look bad. We have good men and women working for us. It sucks that Rafferty was elected and doesn't represent everyone, only his family."

"Have you seen Bale since the incident in the café?" Martha asked.

Shabina shook her head. "I haven't, but then my security team is with me in force everywhere I go. Someone is always watching the café. Bale is probably aware of that."

"Tom and Judy said he was out at the hot springs with Sean and the two new ones interning under Sean."

"What in the world would Bale and Sean be doing at the hot springs?" Shabina asked.

"They were part of the group sitting around the fire and telling stories about Lucca," Mary said.

"Bale didn't like the Delgotto family," Shabina said. "Why would he be there? That makes zero sense."

"I think when you go out on a rescue and discover a body,

especially one from your hometown, and they worked together on Search and Rescue, it can change your perspective," Martha said.

Shabina had to admit that was probably true. Had she known about the get-together, she still wouldn't have gone. She knew Larado would insist she take a protection team as well as her dogs. That was something she would have to discuss with Rainier. She didn't want to make decisions about where she could go based on worry that she would cause a scene with too large of a protection detail.

And what about the times the women all went hiking together? She couldn't very well bring along her protection detail. More than once she'd gotten in trouble for leaving her dogs behind when they rented an Airbnb that didn't allow pets. She knew she could get around that or ask the women to find a different house, but she always did her best to be as normal as possible.

Hopefully, once the danger to her from Scorpion passed, Rainier wouldn't worry so much about her safety. That was another conversation they would have to have.

"Raymond Decker called. He presented the evidence against Bale to the judge and a restraining order has been granted. It is temporary, giving Bale the opportunity to fight it. I doubt that he would be that ridiculous, but you just never know with him."

"Isn't Mr. Decker a lawyer with the CIA? Why would he continue to work for me? I haven't even seen a bill."

"You won't see a bill," Raine guessed. "I asked him to come to the meeting with the FBI agents as a special favor to me and he did. He refused to take payment. I believe he knows Rainier. I know for a fact that he knows Sam and Zale. Apparently, one or more of them have done him favors in the past. The men in the Special Activities Division of the CIA often work for one another by trading favors."

"And he presented the evidence to a judge on my behalf? I didn't have to be there?"

"Not in this case, but if Bale were to fight it, you would have to go to court with Decker and present your evidence. Decker would do that for you as your representative."

She hoped she wouldn't have to go to court. No doubt Rainier would insist on going. There was no getting around the fact that Rainier could dominate a room.

Her phone vibrated, and she glanced down at the screen. The text was from her father demanding to know if the rumor of her marriage was true. She had no desire to speak with him. None. Where before just getting a demanding text from him left her shaky, now she didn't feel anything at all. Had her mother called her, she would have answered and spoken to her, but she truly had no desire to interact with her father.

The thought of never having to deal with him again brought her peace, but it hurt to think she would never have interactions with her mother. Jack didn't allow Yasemin to go anywhere without him, at least Shabina had never seen her mother venture anywhere away from him. If he forbade her to see Shabina, no matter how much Yasemin wanted to, she would never defy Jack.

"Why are you looking so sad, Shabina?" Raine asked.

"I was just thinking about my mother. I miss her and wish we were closer." She shrugged. "I'd better hurry up and get out on the floor. I had hoped the two FBI agents would eat fast and leave, but it looks as though I might have to interact with them."

"I shouldn't even ask you, but you do remember their names, right?" Raine said.

"Yes."

"Don't answer any questions. I believe you've been ruled out as a suspect, but that doesn't mean they won't keep prying. And now that they know Rainier's in the picture, they might think he's involved."

"We do have knowledge of evidence and how it came to be on those altars," Shabina pointed out. "Technically, we should relay that information to them."

"I think it's a good idea, especially since I doubt Rainier's going to reverse his decision to send those two students back to their country. He isn't like you, Shabina. I can see you're already worried about them."

"It's just that it's possible they were telling the truth about bringing disgrace to their families. I could see, from their point of view, why they thought they should help Jack."

She couldn't quite bring herself to call Jack Foster her father any longer. Shouldn't fathers protect their daughters? He couldn't claim a religious belief. He wasn't a believer in any kind of worship. Yasemin was, but not Jack. He was raised by his parents and grandparents with a different value system—one Shabina didn't understand.

Shabina had embraced Salman Ahmad's love of his family. The way he treated his wife and children. The way he valued every member of his tribe from oldest to youngest, male or female. That was the type of person she wanted to be. The type of man she wanted for a partner. The kind of family she'd dreamt of having someday.

"You have a great deal of compassion and kindness in you, Shabina," Raine said. "It's easy to see why Rainier fell so deeply in love with you. You must have been like the sun rising, such a bright light that he could see for the first time when he rescued you. He was in such a dark place."

Shabina shook her head. "You've got it wrong. I was the one in the dark place, Raine. He not only saved my life but my sanity.

He's my bright light. Without him, I don't feel safe or truly happy. I feel alone until he's back with me. I know not everyone sees him the way I do, but I know him, the heart of him. What's inside him. He shares that with me. He doesn't get upset when I cling to him. He never gets impatient with me."

Raine rubbed her forehead, frowning. "Rainier isn't a saint, Shabina. I don't want you to look at him through rose-colored glasses. You'll end up disappointed. Things between you will fall apart fast."

Shabina gave a short laugh, feeling lighter just thinking about Rainier. "I doubt I could ever make the mistake of viewing that man as a saint. He doesn't even try to pretend he's not a bit of a dictator."

"Are you able to stand up to him?" Raine sought reassurance.

Shabina thought about the question before she answered. Did she stand up to Rainier? She nodded slowly. "Unless what he's saying is very logical or it matters to him more than it matters to me. When I want something or feel I need it, I have no problem letting him know."

Raine sighed with relief. "I think Rainier is a good man, Shabina, but he's also as tough as nails, if you'll excuse the analogy. He's going to walk all over someone who can't stand up to him. You need to stay strong when you're fighting for what you want."

"I survived what most others couldn't," Shabina pointed out, realizing it was the truth. Her time with Scorpion had been horrific. Most others, men or women, would have broken. She had been sixteen. The longer she was held prisoner, and the worse the tortures and rapes, only made her more determined not to break.

For the first time, she realized how strong she really was. She had managed to stand up to a man others feared for good reason. Rainier kept reiterating that to her, telling her no one else had ever done what she had, but all that time she considered herself weak. Mostly because she had PTSD from the trauma of what she'd seen, heard and experienced. When she felt weak and vulnerable, it colored how she viewed herself.

Scorpion had taken every opportunity to make her feel weak and useless. His men followed his example. Eventually, no matter how often she told herself the things he said weren't true, a part of her believed them. That had also colored her belief that she was weak. Rainier often asked her who she wanted to believe—Scorpion, a man who lied and murdered, or Rainier, the man who loved her. Of course, in the beginning, he'd never used the word *love*. He just had said "the man who's always honest with you."

"Yes, you did, Shabina," Raine said. "You think he's your light, but I *know* you're his. The jobs he's taken on were some of the worst. The most dangerous. He goes places no one else dares to go. And most of the time he volunteers. What does that say to you?"

"I used to believe the same thing, Raine, that he didn't care whether he lived or died, but I don't think that's the truth. I think Rainier takes those jobs on because he believes he has a better chance of surviving than anyone else. He's off-the-chart protective, and it's not just me he looks out for."

"You'll always be his number one," Raine said. "After the fiasco of that horrible casino owner trying to kill Vienna, I became very interested in Rainier. For one thing, he made you cry. You were obviously in love with him."

"You couldn't tell that."

"I could. It was the way you looked at him. More important, to me, was the way he looked at you. Once I began looking into him, I realized very quickly that he's built his entire life around you. It was obvious to me that he was determined to keep you safe. Not only that, but that he wanted you happy."

Shabina frowned, trying to comprehend the things Raine was telling her. "I didn't see him very often. I wanted him to have a life. I worried that as long as I kept him coming back to me, he wouldn't find anyone to share his life with. I wanted him happy."

"He didn't realize you had feelings for him. He thought he lost you by showing you who he is. That didn't stop him from setting up a home base close to you, one where he could take a small plane and get to you very quickly. He made it known to those he employed in his security company that you are always the first priority. He acquired planes, helicopters, boats and more weapons than you can imagine. His employees are men and women who were always the best in their field. Even his dogs were trained with the idea that they would look after you. Rainier was obsessed with watching over you."

Rainier had declared she was his world and she believed him. Raine had used the word *obsessed*. That was a red flag to her. Her father was obsessed with her mother. She didn't want to have a relationship like her father had with her mother. She nearly voiced her concerns, but then she forced her brain away from panic to think logically.

Rainier wasn't anything like her father. He might appear to be on the surface, but she knew him. She could see into the heart of him. He would protect their children and expect her to do the same. Rainier would never do the things to his daughter—or son—that Jack had done to her.

"I love Rainier," Shabina said, fingers stroking her aching thigh. Rainier had healed the open lacerations there. He'd healed so many wounds, both body and soul.

Raine smiled at her. "Fortunately, Rainier is very much in love with you. There's one more thing before you talk with the FBI agents, and I'll warn you again not to give them information until we have a chance to talk with Decker. Those two men from Paris claiming to be Interpol agents? They took a flight to Jordan. When they landed in Jordan, they were met by a car sent from the palace. They never made it to the palace. The two men were found dead in the back seat, and evidence of their participation with Scorpion was prominently displayed."

Shabina closed her eyes briefly, inhaling to take air into her lungs. She would have to get used to Rainier taking chances. He might forever deny that he had anything to do with the deaths of the double agents, but she knew he had. He probably was working for the prince and receiving his information directly from the palace. She told herself that at least he had powerful allies.

CHAPTER SEVENTEEN

M y client has information pertinent to your case," Raymond Decker informed Rob Howard and Len Jenkins, the two FBI agents working on the murders in Yosemite.

The two men exchanged a long look, and then both sat in the chairs at the table Rainier indicated. Raine was already seated there. Rather than meet at the house, Decker had suggested they meet in the café. He was very clear that Shabina wasn't to answer any question without his permission.

Rainier sat beside her, his hand firmly circling hers. Just having him there gave her more confidence. Shabina was surprised that the revelations about her father had given her more confidence and strength—not less. Without the heavy guilt weighing her down, guilt that she'd caused her parents such pain. Guilt that she wasn't doing as they wanted. Guilt that she wanted her own life and not theirs. So much. Realizing that her father had gone to such lengths to be rid of her or force her into compliance had not only lifted the guilt from her shoulders but left her feeling much more confident.

Rainier had asked her what she wanted to do about her father. He sat across from her in one of the comfortable chairs her friends loved sitting in. A fire blazed in the fireplace, and her dogs crowded around her. Rainier had looked at her not only with love but with compassion. And he'd asked what *she* wanted to do with the revelations about her father.

Just remembering how he gave her the choice to make the decisions—that he cared how she felt—made her love him more. She knew what his preference was. He told her without hesitation that if it were up to him, he would kill her father and free Yasemin and Shabina from his tyranny. He went on to say the decision was ultimately hers.

Although the subject had been serious, Shabina had wanted to laugh at Rainier's simplicity of solving the problem. "You can't use killing as a solution every time someone is a bully or mean."

He'd raised an eyebrow. "Actually, *Qadri*, I can. Enemies tend to disappear when I'm around. It is that simple."

"You're going to have to turn over a new leaf. Once we have children, what is that going to teach them?"

"Survival."

She did laugh then. "Fortunately, I think good came out of the newest revelations about my father. I don't feel guilt anymore. I'm happy to never talk to him again. I don't want him in my life. I feel sad that by cutting him out of my life, I won't be able to see my mother, but I know there is a price to be paid when you do something so drastic."

"You could have your mother if you let me do what needs to be done."

Shabina had shaken her head while she stroked her fingers through Malik's fur. "No, my mother loves my father. She isn't like me. She's very fragile. She needs him. I'm good with my decision to cut him out of my life. I do feel it is necessary to give the information about the items from Saudi Arabia to the FBI. They can decide if they want to question Jack or just leave it be. I'm sure if they try to question him, he'll threaten their careers."

"That isn't your problem."

"No, it's not. Raine wants Decker—he's a lawyer for the CIA—to arrange the meeting. I'd like you to be there for moral support, but I'll understand if you prefer not to go."

"My preference is always to be with you."

Now they sat side by side at the table facing the agents. Her dogs lay in their beds in the room off the kitchen where they stayed when she was working. Outside the café, she was certain Larado and Dimitri were close.

Decker nodded at her, indicating she should give the agents the information they needed.

"It's recently come to my attention how the items from Saudi Arabia ended up on the altars of the murder victims. At least, what most likely led up to the murderer using them."

Howard and Jenkins had placed recorders on the table with her permission. Now they exchanged an alert look. Jenkins indicated for her to continue.

"As you are aware, I was kidnapped at the age of fifteen and spent a year and a half in captivity, held for ransom. The last six months I was held by a man known as Scorpion and his men. Those months were horrific. I suffer from PTSD, and a couple of times I've nearly landed in the hospital."

Rainier's fingers tightened around hers, and he brought her palm to his chest, over his heart. "When I'm with her, we can combat the episodes together, but if I'm away on business, she has a much more difficult time."

"I don't know if you've had dealings with my father before, but if you haven't, he's a man who wants his way in all things, and he goes to any length to get it."

Decker held up his hand and leaned in close. "Be careful what you say here. Clarify exactly what you mean."

Shabina nodded. She was being truthful about her father, but she could understand the lawyer's worry that if Jack was played the recording, he might sue her for defamation of character. That would be like him. It would never occur to him that she would speak the truth in a court of law and deliver evidence against him, not only for hiring the two university students but his attempt at contacting a known assassin to murder her.

"I would describe my father as ruthless if he wants something. Determined. He wanted me to come home. He claims he wanted me home for my own good, but the reality is my mother is upset and worried for my safety. Jack insisted I give up the café and living here in Knightly and return to Houston. When I didn't, he decided to act to force me to comply."

Raine placed two photographs on the table in front of the FBI agents.

"Jack hired these two university students to do whatever was necessary to bring on a PTSD episode. He believed he could bring me home, hospitalize me and get power of attorney so I had no say in my life. That way he could keep me home."

Shabina thought she would feel an enormous amount of guilt relaying to the FBI what her father had done, but she felt nothing. She truly had cut off her emotions toward him.

"The students have been officially identified as Emil Salhi and Jamal Talbi, both from Algeria," Raine said. "I will turn over the correspondence and proof that Jack Foster hired them. Both men confessed to Shabina in my presence. Stella Harrison-Rossi, Harlow Frye, Zahra Metcalf and Vienna Mortenson were also present."

"State your name for the record, please," Len Jenkins said.

"I'm Raine O'Mallory."

"Jack sent several items from Saudi Arabia to Salhi and Talbi. Specifically, flowers, two live birds and a number of other items," Shabina continued.

Decker broke in. "We've prepared a list of the items."

"The men sacrificed the birds to get feathers to leave at my workplace and home. They had taken a box with some of the items on a secluded trail where I go to film the nest of a mated pair of California condors. That trail is closed to all park visitors, but Jack told them it would be a good place to put some of these items. According to the two men, they heard voices coming toward them, and, thinking it was me bringing someone with me, they hastily shoved the box of items in the brush and took off. When they went back, they couldn't find the box. They thought they just didn't remember where they'd put it until the items showed up on an altar at a murder scene."

Shabina fell silent. The agents didn't have to believe a word she said, but she didn't see how they could spin it and make her a suspect again. In any case, she felt protected with Decker, Raine and Rainier right there.

"As you can imagine, I am very upset that these men took part in a scheme to essentially push my wife into a PTSD episode," Rainier said. "They are here on student visas. I asked my boss to pull some strings and have their visas revoked. There is plenty of reason to do so."

"Are you telling us these men may be leaving the country soon?" Rob Howard asked.

"I've attempted to explain to my husband that these men come from a different culture. It is ingrained in them that women obey their fathers, brothers, and husbands. I wasn't doing as my father requested, so in their eyes, I am a disrespectful daughter. My father, according to the way those men were raised, had every right to do whatever it took to get his errant daughter to comply with his demands. Jack, however, was not raised in that culture, and he knows better."

Len Jenkins regarded her with shrewd eyes. At another time in her life, he might have intimidated her with his direct stare, but she was married to Rainier Ashcroft. No one could give a more penetrating, unsettling look than Rainier. His stare was laser sharp and seemed to lay bare one's deepest secrets.

"You don't want these men to be deported," Jenkins guessed.

Shabina shrugged. "Being deported could very well bring disgrace to their families. They need the education to help their tribe. I didn't give you the information to exact revenge. I believe you need it to help solve the murders. Whoever is committing these crimes must be stopped."

Jenkins looked over the list of items carefully and then handed it to his partner. "That kid at the hot springs doesn't fit with the others. The ME doesn't believe it's a copycat. I don't either, but he doesn't fit."

"Yeah, it put the entire murder spree out of focus," Howard added.

"Age isn't the same with any of the victims," Raine said. "They don't look alike. They aren't in the same profession. A couple of them had girlfriends. They came from various backgrounds." There was speculation in her voice.

She looked up at the two agents when silence met her conjecture. "I'm sorry. I have a fancy title, but essentially, I'm an analyst. I can't help myself. When there's a puzzle, my brain won't rest until it's solved."

"She has a reputation at the CIA and with the military," Decker said. "I wouldn't dismiss any ideas she has."

Jenkins arched an eyebrow. "Do you have ideas?"

"Not yet," Raine admitted. "But one or two hypotheses are forming."

"Are we finished, gentlemen?" Decker asked.

"Just one or two more questions," Howard said.

The one or two questions turned into an additional forty minutes. In that time, Shabina realized the two men didn't altogether trust Rafferty. Just because they had breakfast or lunch with him, didn't mean the three men were friends. She managed to put in a question or two of her own, and their answers led her to believe they thought Rafferty was deliberately steering them in a wrong direction—namely, trying to implicate her. After witnessing Bale, Rafferty's nephew, and the sheriff's reaction to the encounter, they were less than satisfied with having to work with him. Naturally, they didn't voice their opinions aloud, but a few things they said led her to believe they weren't sharing their findings with Rafferty. Twice Jenkins apologized to her for not intervening when Bale had been so rude.

"My husband handled the situation," Shabina assured them. "I don't know why I fell apart. I'm used to the way Bale makes scenes. I'm sorry you were uncomfortable in the café. We do strive to give our customers the best experience to start off their day. Hearing Bale spew his toxic opinion of me and the food I serve doesn't make for a great start."

Both men looked to Rainier. "Rafferty wanted us to see where you were during the times of each of the murders."

Shabina tried to stay relaxed, realizing the agents had introduced casual, informal conversation that had nothing to do with the murders to make them believe they were no longer interested in them as suspects.

"I'm aware," Rainier replied easily. "The minute you ran me, red flags went up everywhere, and I was informed. No doubt you talked to the head of my department."

His fingers tightened around her hand when Shabina made a move to rub her thigh. She blinked up at him. Rainier hadn't changed expression, but when he looked down at her, his shrewd eyes softened momentarily.

"Everything you do seems to be classified. Blom assured us you were nowhere near Yosemite at the time of the murders."

"There you have it, gentlemen," Decker said, closing his brief-case. "We're done here. If you need to speak with either of my clients again, contact me, and I'll set up an appointment." He sent Rainier a look that told him not to say another word.

Shabina pressed her fingers against her lips in an effort to keep from laughing. Decker was a powerhouse in his own right. Rainier might be a dangerous, scary man, but Decker was utterly confident in his own abilities to protect his clients lawfully. That included Rainier.

"Don't think I didn't notice the amusement," Rainier said as Decker walked out with the two agents.

"It's pretty funny to me that he thinks he can tell you what to do."

Rainier shrugged. "He's good at his job. I'd be a fool not to listen, and he knows it. He only throws his weight around when necessary to protect his clients."

Shabina leaned into Rainier, rubbing her head against his arm affectionately. Her man was intelligent and confident enough that he acknowledged others' expertise. That was another reason she loved him. Her father didn't do that. Scorpion hadn't. Salman Ahmad had been like Rainier. He had listened to the members of his tribe and recognized their abilities. She hadn't realized what a profound influence Ahmad had been on her. She always thought his wife had inspired and guided her to be a better person, but she recognized that Ahmad had shown her what traits she wanted in a partner.

Rainier glanced down at his phone. "Larado is texting that Chelsey Sarten just parked her car and is coming this way."

The café was closed. They'd met with the agents after hours, but their vehicles were outside and the lights were on, a clear indication that Shabina was in the café. She sighed. The last thing she wanted to do was to have a disagreement with Chelsey. She'd managed to avoid talking to her because Rainier had been the one to confront her over stealing. He hadn't accused her of trying to help implicate Shabina in the murders, but they were certain that was what the spices and dates from her kitchen had been taken for.

"I can send her away," Rainier said. He made the offer casually, the way he did each time he was willing to stand in front of her. He gave her the choice, and there wasn't judgment. She knew he would be perfectly fine with speaking to Chelsey on her behalf.

Shabina shook her head. "No, if she has the guts to come straight to me, then I can listen to her. She worked for me and was always a good employee. Not only did she work her shift, but she was always willing to help when the hours ran over or we were shorthanded. More than once she came in on her days off when we were preparing food for Search and Rescue or the elderly during winter months."

"You always give generous bonuses aside from paying overtime," Raine pointed out. She held up her hands. "Just saying."

Raine had a bit of a temper and could hold a grudge if anyone trifled with her friends. She had a protective streak in her, just the way Rainier had. Shabina flashed her a grateful smile. She felt lucky to have the friendships she'd acquired in the time she'd been in Knightly.

Rainier opened the door for Chelsey and indicated for her to enter. Chelsey hesitated, looking up at him, clearly finding him intimidating. He didn't soften his expression. Apparently, Rainier could hold a grudge too. Shabina idly played with the idea that there was something about their names that gave them shared characteristics.

Chelsey squared her shoulders and came inside, marching up to Shabina with determination. "Thanks for seeing me, Shabina."

"No problem. Would you care to sit down?" She made it clear there wasn't going to be a private conversation. Trust had been broken, and she wasn't taking chances Chelsey might be recording everything they said. What she would use it for, Shabina had no idea, but she wasn't going to speak with her alone.

Chelsey hesitated a second time and then lifted her chin and sank into the chair opposite Shabina. "I should have come to you immediately and told you what happened. I understand completely why you wouldn't trust me to work for you after what I did, but I had no idea that there was any kind of a vendetta."

Shabina raised an eyebrow. "If you had wanted the spices and dates, even a small amount, you could have asked me."

"I know," Chelsey said. "I know," she repeated. "Bale asked me to get the spices and dates for Sean. I really liked Sean. Bale said it was a big surprise for him. I asked him why he didn't go directly to you. Bale said you didn't like Sean or him."

"That didn't raise a red flag?" Shabina asked. "You've been in the café when Bale and Sean have accused me of trying to poison them. Once they even called the sheriff. Fortunately, the detective they sent wasn't a member of Bale's family."

Chelsey pushed stray strands of hair behind her ear. Shabina noted that her hand trembled. "Yes, I was aware you had a problem with Bale, but Sean didn't act the same way. He stayed silent, and that did bother me, but he wasn't nearly as bad as Bale."

Shabina sighed. "I don't understand why you didn't just come to me, Chesley. We always had a good relationship. At least, I thought so."

"We did. We do. I was so into Sean that I listened to Bale. He came to me with this idea of getting Sean something special for his birthday. He told me you despised them both and wouldn't likely give either of us the spices and dates if you knew they were for Sean. He told me the ingredients were ordered from somewhere only you knew of."

"And you believed him?"

Chelsey nodded. "I had no reason not to believe him. He's always with Sean and they seem to be close friends. I understood you're having a problem with Bale. He's not a very nice man when it comes to women."

"And that wasn't another huge red flag for you?" Raine asked. "That Sean is Bale's best friend, and he sits silently when Bale is degrading women? Or worse, he participates and encourages other young men to behave in the same way? You didn't look at that and worry that he'd treat you as less than you are?"

Chelsey ducked her head. "I didn't like some of the comments they made about me being 'only a waitress.' Implying I don't have brains. They weren't frequent comments but were said casually offhand and made me feel bad about myself. I made excuses for Sean when I shouldn't have." She looked directly at Shabina. "I get lonely, and there aren't a lot of men with decent jobs who live here year-round. Sean is good-looking and smart. He's funny.

And he has a job that will last. I want a family and I'm getting older. I suppose that makes me look desperate, and I think I was feeling desperate."

Shabina understood loneliness. She had felt isolated from her friends because she knew the experiences she'd had set her apart. But she'd let that happen. Her friends had reached out to her over and over, proving that they would be there for her. She also understood the desire to have a family.

"I'm sorry, Chelsey, I had no idea you were feeling so alone."

"I didn't talk to you about it. Vaughn even asked me several times if there was something wrong, but I felt silly telling him I wanted a family when he's estranged from his. In any case, I decided to do what Bale asked, and I took the spices and dates. I did leave money and an explanation for you under the notepad in the second drawer below where the keys are. I thought you or Vaughn used that notepad to make lists of what you had to order, and you'd find it right away."

Rainier immediately went into the kitchen to ensure the note and money were there. "Why didn't you tell me this when I confronted you, Chelsey?" he asked as he returned and placed both items on the table.

"There had been a terrible fight between Sean and Bale when I gave the items to Sean. Bale was with him, and I expected Sean would be really happy, but he wasn't. He was furious. He was angry with me and called me not-very-nice names. But he was worse with Bale. Much worse. He accused him of trying to embroil you in the murders and said he wasn't going to plant evidence that would lead the cops to you."

"Bale threatened me many times, and I knew he was trying to implicate me in the murders," Shabina said. "I'm surprised they talked in front of you."

"I've never seen either of them so angry. They scared me. Especially Bale. Sean also said Bale would blackmail me, and the moment it came out that the dates and spices were at a murder scene, I would go to the cops and say I took the items and gave them to Sean. That he would then be implicated."

"At least he was smart enough to know if he did what Bale wanted him to do, he would ultimately take the fall when it came out that evidence had been planted," Raine said.

"Sean kept yelling at me, asking if I would go to the cops if I realized he'd used the spices and dates to plant evidence against you at a murder scene. He was yelling. Bale was yelling. I was so scared, but I realized Sean wasn't worried about you, or even me. He was worried about himself. I shouted back at him that I would go to the police, and they'd better not use the things I gave them to implicate you. Bale slapped me." Chelsey cupped her left cheek as if remembering the way Bale had struck her. "He threatened me if I dared tell you or anyone else and kept saying his uncle would keep him out of trouble."

"Bale hit you?" Rainier asked. "He slapped you in front of Sean, and Sean didn't react? Weren't you two dating?"

Chelsey nodded, and for the first time tears glittered in her eyes. "I knew I had to get out of there or things were going to get worse. But then Sean took the little jars I'd given him and threw them at Bale. They got into a terrible fistfight. I took off while they were on the ground."

"You should have told me all this when I confronted you," Rainier said.

Shabina was thankful he had gentled his voice. "I would have listened to you as well, Chelsey. I was so hurt when I believed you were part of a conspiracy to implicate me in the murders."

Chelsey paled visibly, and she shook her head, her hair swinging around her face. "Absolutely not. I would never have done that. I only wanted to give Sean a surprise for his birthday. I should have known Bale wasn't telling the truth."

"I can't imagine it occurring to you that Bale would try to implicate Shabina in the murders," Raine said. "But, Chelsey, I hope you realize Sean isn't a good man in all of this. He was angry on his own behalf, not on yours or Shabina's."

Chelsey sighed. "I faced that fact right then. If I hadn't been reeling, I might have talked to you about the entire mess, Mr. Ashcroft, but I didn't know Shabina was married, and quite frankly, you're very intimidating."

"Call me Rainier."

Shabina noticed he didn't try to look less intimidating. She doubted he could.

"I didn't come here to try to get my job back, even though it honestly felt like I was working with family. I'm grateful to the hotel for hiring me. It's just that I couldn't live with you thinking so badly of me, and I felt it was important to let you know Bale's intentions."

"I appreciate you setting the record straight," Shabina said. "I know it must have taken a great deal of courage for you to come here this evening."

Chelsey stood up. "If you do ever need me back, reach out. I'll give my notice at the hotel and join you. Thanks for listening to me."

Rainier locked the door after her and then helped Raine to her car. Larado was in the driver's seat. Rainier forestalled her protests by shaking his head. "I spoke with your doctor. He said driving right now is detrimental to your progress."

"You spoke to Rush, didn't you?" Raine glared at him.

Shabina could have told her glaring didn't work on Rainier. He merely shrugged casually. "Rush is your doctor, and he was adamant. He said if you don't comply, we're to let him know, and he'll make time to come and stay with you. And just for your information, Sam wasn't happy with any of you for not letting him know the extent of the problems facing Shabina. I'm sure Zale feels the same way, although he can't get here. Sam, however, is offended and will have a few things to say about all of you keeping secrets from him."

That meant Sam would be upset with Stella. Shabina hadn't meant to get her friends in trouble with Sam. Sam had been a part of their circle nearly from the moment he'd arrived in Knightly. Now, married to Stella, and the fact that he had at one time worked for Blom in the same capacity as Zale and Rainier, more than ever he would feel the need to protect Shabina.

"I felt it was important that I tried to handle my own problems." It was a lame excuse, and Rainier's look told her he wasn't buying the explanation, but he swept his arm around her waist, nodded to Larado and walked Shabina to her four-wheel-drive RAV4. The dogs loaded up when he opened the back and waved them inside.

"What you really meant was you didn't want Sam to know how bad things were because you knew he would contact me."

She tried not to smile. "You know me very well."

"See that it doesn't happen again, Shabina."

She just stopped herself from rolling her eyes, but she nodded to show him she would comply with his not-so-unreasonable command.

Once they were headed home, Rainier spoke. "I would like to leave again this evening, *Qadri*. I've received information on the location of Scorpion and his friend Owen Pelletier. If the information is correct and I can get to them before they move again, you'll be free of that threat."

Shabina found her heart pounding. Her mouth went dry. She sat in silence, twisting her fingers together until Rainier took one hand off the steering wheel and covered her restless hands.

"You said you needed proof before you went after Lefebre. He's too big, Rainier. If you get caught . . ." She trailed off. "He'll be surrounded by guards. Possibly mercenaries."

"I have all the proof I need."

"What does that mean?"

"One of my friends, Hawkin Wilder, found the videos in Lefebre's home theater."

Her stomach lurched again. Videos of her torture. Of rape. This friend of Rainer's had seen them, or he wouldn't have green-lighted taking Lefebre out.

"Babe, don't. Lefebre made numerous videos, not just of you, but other young women he'd taken throughout the last few years. I believe we were able to acquire every video made with you in it. Before your kind and very compassionate heart worries for the other girls if their videos come to light, remember, he succeeded in murdering them. If we need to use the videos as proof of Lefebre's double life, they aren't going to care."

"Their families might."

"*Qadri*, the videos aren't for the public."

She hoped not. She pressed her lips together to keep from protesting. She didn't want him to leave. She didn't like the idea of him being in danger.

"I won't go if it's too soon. You're still very fragile right now, and there's a lot going on. I have a five-man security team here, and you'll have all six dogs. Sam is alert now as well. I'm not worried about your safety so much as your peace of mind, Shabina. You need to be honest with me. If you need me with you, I'll stay."

"I can handle the pressure, Rainier. It's not that. I am feeling fragile, but I'm gaining strength and confidence. I know I can rely on my friends, and I've made peace with the fact that Larado is going to get all bossy." She took a deep breath and admitted the truth. "When you're gone, I'm so afraid something will happen to you, and you won't come back."

"I understand, Shabina. When I'm away from you, I will admit, I become anxious about your safety and well-being. If I didn't have to go silent, I'd be blowing up Larado's phone seeking assurance and giving him orders."

She loved the fact that Rainier didn't chide her, but instead admitted he was anxious as well. "I worry if my father finds out you're gone he'll try to see me or force me to talk to him."

"Larado and the others have strict instructions not to allow him to get near you. You did block him from calling you, didn't you? Both phones?"

"Yes. It was difficult because I know my mother can't call either. That hurts," she admitted.

"I'll send you a text when I believe it's okay to unblock your mother's number, so she'll be able to stay in touch with you."

"What are you going to do?" she asked suspiciously.

"Sort it out."

JACK FOSTER WOKE with a start. Beside him, Yasemin lay sleeping peacefully. It hadn't been her that disturbed his sleep. Without lifting his head, he scanned the room while one hand found the drawer in the nightstand beside the bed. Carefully, he slid it open to retrieve the fully loaded gun he kept there. He moved his hand all around the drawer, only to find it empty. The gun wasn't there.

A shadow moved across from the bed. It was impossible to

make out who was there in the room with them, but he knew they weren't alone. He sat up slowly, angling his body slightly to protect Yasemin.

"It took a minute for you to wake up, Jack."

The voice came out of the darkness. Low. Amused. Arrogant. Jack winced inwardly. He knew that voice. He should have expected a visit.

"What do you want, Rainier?"

"I thought it was time we had a talk, so you clearly understand the rules regarding your daughter."

"You can't . . ." Jack began.

"I think it best you listen to what I have to say. I'm not asking, Jack. I'm telling you how it's going to be. Shabina wants nothing more to do with you. You forgot, or didn't notice, that your daughter is highly intelligent. You can't hide the truth from her. She was always suspicious when it came out that I rescued her in the nick of time, that the sandstorm hit right after we got away and an assassin struck the camp. She wondered if you had contacted that assassin and taken a hit out on her. Unfortunately for you, she has a friend who can gather information from various sources, and it turns out, there was a connection. A transfer of money from you to an account known to be used by that assassin. She was also able to access your email, the one you use for encoded emails. Her friend can decode the emails. The correspondence between you and the intermediary was right there with your orders."

Jack's mind raced with the possibilities of putting a spin on what he'd done. The last thing he wanted was for Yasemin to know that he'd tried to have their daughter killed. He glanced down at her. Even though Rainier spoke in low tones, she should have wakened.

"You drugged my wife." He made it an accusation, hoping to deflect.

"This is your one chance to hear me out before I take action. I am giving you this one chance to keep the truth from your wife and for you to stay alive. I don't agree with that decision, but Shabina loves her mother and would like to prevent more heartache than she's already experienced. The truth coming out or you dying would certainly cause Yasemin grief."

Jack breathed a sigh of relief. His daughter was intelligent, but she lacked a killer's instinct. She felt far too much compassion, just like her mother.

"Shabina is also aware you orchestrated an attempt to get her locked away in a mental hospital. She's spoken with the two men you paid to frighten her into believing Scorpion was stalking her again. This had to be one of your more despicable schemes to force compliance and get your way."

"I can explain to her—"

Rainier cut him off. "You aren't listening, Jack. If you want to keep your marriage and, ultimately, your life, you should listen closely."

A chill went down Jack's spine and for the first time, real fear crept in. He tasted bile. Rainier was capable of carrying out his threat—and that was a direct threat to Jack's life. Rainier came and went from his heavily guarded home at will, showing his ability to end Jack's life easily.

"I'm listening." He choked out the words. His voice sounded strangled even to his own ears. Rainier's calm demeanor was getting to him. In truth, he'd always been a little afraid of the man, which was one of the many reasons he had for despising him.

Men were afraid of Jack, not the other way around. He gave orders and everyone listened, but not Rainier. Rainier gave the orders, and no matter how Jack tried to get around the man, he never came out on top in an argument between them. He'd tried to use his considerable clout to get Rainier fired from his job with the idea he would lose government protection as well as his information sources. Jack discovered very quickly that Rainier had much more power and influence than he had. He hadn't found a way to remove the "ghost" from their lives.

It wasn't just Jack's marriage Rainier had threatened. He warned Jack his life might be forfeit. If he knew anything about Rainier, it was to take everything he said seriously.

"Shabina doesn't want to see you or talk to you, and you're going to respect her wishes. She does want to be able to talk with her mother and see her. You're going to allow that to happen. You're going to encourage Yasemin to call her daughter and suggest a visit because you must go out of town and Yasemin can't go with you. Tell her you'd feel better if she was with her daughter and under my protection."

Jack found himself shaking his head, his heart pumping wildly. "No, I can't do that. Yasemin stays with me, where I can look after her. We don't separate for any reason."

"That's too bad, Jack. I'm sorry you see it that way." Rainier stood up. He was no more than a faint shadow of gray in the unrelenting darkness. "Make sure your affairs are in order. You have two weeks to get that done. Make the most of your time with your wife. Teach her anything she might need to know about running your business in those two weeks. Prepare her."

Rainier spoke so casually that it took a minute to sink in, to realize what he was saying.

"You're going to kill me." Jack made it a statement. He was so scared that he feared he might disgrace himself by vomiting, or worse, his bladder letting loose.

"What did you think I'd do when you tried to lock my wife in a mental institution? When you put a hit out on her? I gave you my terms, and you refused them. I'm not going to argue with you. For me, I find it much easier just to kill you and get you out of the way. Yasemin will grieve for a while. Shabina probably will too, but they'll both get over your death. Life goes on." He sounded pragmatic. "Believe me, Jack, after what you did to Shabina, I will find great satisfaction in ending you."

Jack swore under his breath. Rainier was the man the government sent to carry out dark deeds. A "ghost." One of the best, if not *the* best. He had walked into Jack's home dozens of times, right past the guards. He had come into Jack's home tonight despite the number of security personnel scattered through the house and on the grounds. No alarm had gone off. Jack could almost believe Rainier was an apparition. He did believe he would carry out his threat and never look back. There would be no way to stop him.

"I agree to your terms," he capitulated.

Rainier sighed. "If you think you can renege on our agreement, Jack, even if I miss somehow, if you manage to find a way to kill me, my men will lock on you so fast you won't know what hit you. You climbed to the top of our hit list the moment word of what you'd done got out. We all stick together and look after one another's families. You're already considered a dead man walking. Don't be stupid enough to make it real."

"I understand," Jack said. "I agreed to your terms, and I'll stick with them. That doesn't mean eventually I won't try to get back in my daughter's life. Hopefully, she'll be able to forgive me."

"I'm sure she will, given time," Rainier said. "But I won't."

CHAPTER EIGHTEEN

I screamed," Theresa admitted. "We were there to have fun. We'd been talking so much about how Felicity and Eve were helping us. Miguel sometimes too. I had pointed out this one boulder and said it looked epic and I wanted to climb it, but Eve said no, that was a 'highball' and I wasn't ready for a climb like that. Janine loved the name and wanted to see it, so Edward offered to take us out early in the morning."

Shabina sank into the empty chair at their table. Raine, Zahra and Harlow leaned closer to hear.

Three days into Rainier's absence, a fifth victim was discovered. The fact that he was discovered alive, but in a coma, shocked everyone. Lawyer Collins, a man well-liked and respected in the community, had been out climbing the Buttermilks. Usually, there were numerous people around this time of year, and that was probably what saved his life.

"Edward said he knew a good boulder for Janine to start. We'd already put our crash pads down and were discussing who would climb first, but he didn't think the boulder was right for Janine. He was going to check out another one to see if any climbers had beat us to it."

Val took up the story. "I was going to climb the boulder where we had our gear when Miguel showed up with Avita and her brother, Pablo. They had the same idea as Edward—to get there really early before too many climbers were out. Edward did have a flying gig later in the afternoon, so he wanted us to have fun and all of us get our climb in before he had to go."

"We heard moaning. But it sounded awful like someone was really injured and in pain. We decided to investigate," Theresa said. "There was a spot just where the next boulder was, and there was blood all over the ground. I'm not going to lie, I was scared."

"Terrified," Janine corrected. "I started yelling at the top of my lungs for Edward. We followed the blood trail and drag marks in the grass. His body had been dragged away from the boulder into the brush."

"Miguel got ahead of us, and he was the one to find the body on the ground," Val said.

"I screamed," Theresa reiterated. "I'm surprised everyone in Knightly didn't hear me. The man's skull looked as if it had been bashed in."

"It looked like a scene from a horror movie," Val said. "Edward and Miguel said they knew him. They kept calling his name, Lawyer, and told him to hang on, help was coming. We called the emergency number, and they sent the paramedics and the sheriff."

Shabina gasped. Lawyer. She knew and liked him. Why would the murderer choose Lawyer?

"Edward said it looked like his skull had been smashed with a rock, not once but twice," Theresa said. She brought a shaky hand to her eyes as if she could blot out the image.

"A flat rock had been set very close to where his body lay, but only a few items were on what appeared to be a makeshift altar," Janine added. "Some were scattered on the ground."

"By that time, with all the screaming we were doing, or I was," Theresa said, "more climbers showed up. Felicity and Eve arrived. They were meeting Miguel and Avita. They became very distraught or looked like it to me. Eve especially. I felt sorry for her and Avita. Miguel asked Felicity and Eve to take Avita away from the scene while we waited for the paramedics to arrive. I wasn't any help with my screaming, so I volunteered to do it."

Val continued their story. "The sheriff came to the conclusion that we must have scared off the murderer before he could finish off Lawyer and build his altar the way he wanted."

Shabina dropped her head into her hands. "We need to figure out who's doing this." Her eyes met Raine's. Raine nodded and immediately sent out a text to their friends to come to Shabina's house if possible after work. She told them why.

Vienna and Harlow already knew about the attack on Lawyer because they were surgical nurses and had been called to the hospital to help try to save their friend.

"He was struck from behind," Raine said, reading the text from Vienna. "He most likely didn't even see his attacker. The sheriff believes he was actually on the boulder, back to the assailant, when the first rock smashed into his head. He was dragged into the heavy brush when he was unconscious. It was the murderer's bad luck that, even unconscious, Lawyer made noise, and the other climbers heard him."

"I was so scared once I realized we were right there, in the same place with whoever is killing people," Janine said. "Poor Edward was so distraught. So was Miguel. Edward told me later that Lawyer Collins is a good friend and a really good man. I felt terrible that I couldn't console him."

"This killer has to be stopped," Shabina reiterated.

THE WOMEN GATHERED at Shabina's home once again. As usual they brought their dogs with them, and Shabina had made more food than they could possibly eat. They were there for one real purpose—it was time to figure out who was doing the killing. They were all intelligent, and they had the same facts and clues the FBI had. They also had the advantage of knowing the two locals who had been victimized.

"This person is a serial killer," Stella declared. "I haven't touched them, or I would be having nightmares. That's the way it's always happened. I can't imagine that I would suddenly lose the ability to envision the details before the murders happen."

Stella's father had been a serial killer, and more than once, she had helped the police track down killers.

"That doesn't mean you haven't seen the murderer or even spoken to him," Raine reminded. "It just means you haven't had physical contact with him. That's the way it works, right?"

Stella nodded. "It always has in the past."

"I'm glad you don't have to go through the nightmares, Stella," Zahra said. "It's so hard on you, even with Sam there now."

"Sam is *very* upset with me for not telling him you were in trouble, Shabina," Stella informed her. "And I think he's slightly hurt as well. He considers himself part of our group and doesn't understand why you didn't include him when you told us everything."

"He would have gone straight to Rainier. You know he would have. It's the same with Zale. Had he been told about the severity of my PTSD and what was triggering the episodes, he would have let Rainier know immediately," Shabina explained. "I lucked out that Zale is in the field and can't be reached."

"I'm sure Sam reached him," Stella said. "Rainier made it clear to Sam that you're to be watched over."

Shabina wasn't surprised that Rainier had included his friends in her protection detail. "I'll talk to Sam, Stella. I knew he would feel it was necessary to talk to Rainier, and I didn't want to put him in that position. Not when I was asking for confidentiality."

"I tried explaining," Stella said. "Rainier apparently found you with a gun, Shabina." Her voice was very quiet, and the other women instantly fell silent, exchanging looks.

Shabina sighed. "I was in a bad way, trying to figure out how best to give Rainier his life back, and yes, I did have suicidal thoughts. I was grateful that all of you kept coming to my house and even up to the campsite. I needed you, and you came through. I couldn't ask for better friends."

"That was too close, Shabina," Stella said. "If Rainier isn't here and you're triggered, someone needs to stay with you."

Vienna agreed. "We can't lose you because you have a momentary lapse in judgment. That's what PTSD can do to you—make you feel as if the world would be a better place without you."

"We'd like you to agree to have one of us stay with you when Rainier is away," Raine said. "Especially if you're having a difficult time."

Shabina swallowed her pride and nodded. She didn't want to lose her life in a moment of despair. She had everything she wanted right there, and yet she was intelligent enough to know another event would happen at some point. She had to be prepared with a plan.

"I can do that. Thank you for caring so much."

"You won't be thanking us after Sam and Zale get with Larado and his crew to boss you around," Vienna said. "They'll probably sleep on the floor of your bedroom."

Shabina groaned. "Don't say it out loud. I wouldn't put it past them to have listening devices in here."

"I checked." Raine sounded smug. "They don't. Moving on. I've been thinking about these murders and trying to put it all together. They must have a common denominator."

"The Sunrise Café," Harlow said. "All the victims ate in her café at one time or another."

Shabina shook her head. "The young kid, Craig Barker, living out of his van, had never been to my café. He's the only one that hadn't."

"It wasn't his van," Vienna pointed out. "It was stolen."

"Could you be mistaken?" Raine asked Shabina. "Maybe he came for takeout. He would only have been there a few minutes. You might not have spoken to him."

"I have this weird gift," Shabina admitted. "I don't forget faces or names. It's a thing with me. The boy had never been in my café."

"You often give food away to the dirt baggers when they're staying near the hot springs," Zahra reminded. "I've helped you. Maybe you took food to him."

"I haven't been out to the springs for weeks. Months, even. I've been too busy, and once the two university students began leaving the various items from Saudi Arabia, my mind was all over the place. I didn't even think about taking food to anyone other than my usual customers."

Harlow rolled her eyes. "I like how you call them customers when they don't pay for the food you bring them."

"I think of them as customers," Shabina defended. "But the tie-in with the victims can't be my café if the boy, Craig Barker, has never been there."

"They don't look alike. They aren't the same age. They don't have the same occupations," Zahra mused. "Maybe they were chosen randomly. The opportunity presented itself, and the murderer took advantage."

"That's possible," Raine said. "But not probable."

"We know both Lucca and Lawyer," Vienna pointed out. "What do they have in common?"

"They were friends," Harlow volunteered. "Both were great with the elderly. Lucca really took good care of his parents and a couple of other families in town. Lawyer fishes, hunts and grows food. He gives most of it away, especially in the winter."

"Bale despised them both," Stella added.

Raine agreed. "He couldn't control either of them. He tried to blackmail them into doing what he wanted them to do."

"What did he have on Lawyer?" Stella asked.

"Lawyer told us he'd been present when Bale and his friends robbed and beat up their football coach," Raine answered. "He was a young teen then. Lawyer confessed to him when he was a kid and ended up paying back the money. They became friends, and he looks after the family now that they're older and can't get around so well, especially in the winter. It was just a week or so ago that he was interviewed, and he told the interviewer about it. When he did, he praised his former coach. At the same time, he pulled the rug out from under Bale's attempt to blackmail him."

"Why was Bale going to blackmail him?" Stella asked.

"Lawyer initially installed the security system at the café for me," Shabina said. "Rainier just had the cameras replaced with others of his choosing. The same as at my home."

"Bale thought he could force Lawyer to erase all the evidence showing Bale had graffitied the café and threatened Shabina multiple times," Raine said. "Lawyer installed the security cameras in most of the businesses in Knightly. Bale wanted everything from the Grill destroyed because the incidents showed a pattern of harassment."

"That skunk," Stella hissed. "I take it Lawyer refused."

"Lawyer came to me," Raine said. "He told me the story of his high school coach and that he wanted me to get the information off the security feed immediately, just in case Bale found another way to remove it."

"We know for certain Bale didn't like either man," Harlow said.

"What about the other victims?" Zahra ventured. "The first was Deacon Mulberry. He was interning with Sean for Fish and Wildlife. Would Bale have a grudge against him?"

"The truth is, Bale could have a grudge against anyone," Stella said. "He's been that way for as long as I've lived here. Do you really think the killer is Bale?"

"He's capable," Raine said. "Especially now that he's lost his hold on Edward and Jason. Sean seems to be sticking with him, but the other two have distanced themselves from him. Once he realized he was no longer protected by his uncle, it's possible he stepped up the killings because he needs to control something."

Shabina shook her head. "There might be a tie-in between Bale and the other victims, but unless he has a partner, he can't be the killer. He wasn't in Yosemite at the time of the first murder. And he's being watched by my personal protection team. They know where he is at all times. He was prowling around my café in the early morning hours while I was doing the prep for breakfast and lunch. Unfortunately, my men are his alibi."

"I wanted it to be him," Zahra said. "He's the nastiest man in Knightly. I imagined him in prison and, I have to tell you, the vision was highly satisfying."

The women laughed. "Sadly," Harlow said, "you'll have to let go of that particular dream."

"I think all of us have that dream," Vienna said with a sigh. "Moving on from Bale. Who else is a suspect?"

"What about Edward?" Zahra said. "Are all of you really buying that he's turned over a new leaf and is Mr. Wonderful? Because I find it very difficult to believe. And if you notice, he was in the café, at the hot springs, with the Search and Rescue crew and at the boulders. There was a block of time that he was out of sight. He easily could have bashed Lawyer over the head and then rushed around acting the hero."

"I can't see Edward as a suspect," Vienna protested. "Maybe I don't want it to be him. I see a man finally standing up and taking charge of his life."

"He would have to have a partner. Bale? Sean?" Harlow mused.

"Sean is a viable suspect," Stella said. "He was with the first victim. Even if he thought that would cast suspicion on him, it would be a brilliant move. We've seen a serial killer hide right in our midst, and we didn't suspect him. Sean was around for that. He might have learned a few tricks of the serial killing trade."

"He was with Search and Rescue when Lucca went missing," Raine said. "But where was he when Charlie Gainer was killed? Charlie worked on the rehabilitation crew. Sean certainly would have had the opportunity to interact with him."

"I just don't see that he has a motive," Vienna said. "I don't like the man, but I don't see him killing men. I don't think he has that kind of confidence in himself."

Shabina agreed. "He's a follower, not a leader." She told the others what Chelsey had told her about the incident involving the dates and spices. "He was concerned that he might be blamed. He wasn't upset that Bale struck Chelsey or that I would be implicated in the murders. It was all about him. He did get into a physical altercation with Bale, but from what Chelsey said, Bale attacked him first. I agree with Vienna. I don't think he has the nerve to be a serial killer. He isn't a narcissist like Bale."

"We keep coming back to Bale," Zahra said. "Let's get food to refuel the brain cells. I can't think clearly when I'm starving."

Shabina waved them to the sideboard, where the warmers were waiting. Before she could follow them, Raine indicated for her to look at her computer screen.

"I just received this alert." She spoke in a low tone and pointed to words scrolling across her screen.

Shabina's breath caught in her throat. The assassin Deadly Storms had struck again. This time he'd brought down one man. Owen Pelletier. He wore the mark of the assassin just above his left wrist, and he appeared to have been subjected to torture. Again, those wounds mimicked the scars Shabina had on her body. Evidence had been provided showing Owen Pelletier had been a part of the mass murders and torture Scorpion perpetuated.

Nothing in the report mentioned Lefebre.

Shabina stroked her fingers over her aching thigh. "Do you think he'll get away with it?"

Raine shook her head. "You know Rainier won't let this go until Scorpion is dead."

Shabina took a deep breath. "There's no mention that the assassin was caught or wounded."

Raine smiled at her. "I don't think Deadly Storms is anything but smoke. A ghost. He comes out of the darkness—or a sandstorm—and then he's gone. How he can keep from having his skin peeled off in a violent sandstorm, I don't know. Most people can't move. They can't see or breathe. They cover every inch of skin and hunker down until the storm has passed."

"Hopefully, he's on his way home to me," Shabina said. "Let me get you your food."

"I've been trying to do more things for myself," Raine protested. "Although not only did the keys to my car disappear, Rainier said if I found another set of keys and tried driving, he would remove the car and let Rush know I'm not cooperating with my physical therapy plan."

Shabina burst out laughing. "I'm so happy he has someone else to boss around. Maybe that will take the pressure off me."

"Don't count on it. I'll start telling tales about your escapades. Trying to sneak off by yourself without your personal protection team."

Shabina gasped. "You wouldn't dare. It isn't even true . . . yet. I'll admit I've had thoughts of total rebellion, but I gave Rainier my word to stay close to the protection detail."

"You seem to be so much stronger, Shabina."

"I think finally realizing my father was responsible for so many things I took the blame for helped to free me from all the guilt. To finally know where I stand with him has been a good thing. You'd think it wouldn't be, that it would make me feel worse about myself because it is very apparent I mean nothing to him. Instead, the knowledge empowered me. I feel much stronger. I also made up my mind to cut him out of my life. I came to the Sierra for peace. I don't want toxic people in my life anymore."

Vienna's laughter bubbled over as she sank down into one of the cuddle chairs and placed the plate of food on the end table. "Can I just remind you that someone is murdering people we know, and this isn't the first time? I think our peaceful hometown and the surrounding mountains have been invaded by killers. If that isn't toxic, I don't know what is."

Shabina made her way across the room to the warmers to make herself a plate. Raine followed her much more slowly.

"I think the only one who wants to strangle me on occasion is Rainier. My enemies are across an ocean, and I'm grateful for that."

She helped Raine put the various food items on her plate. Trying to balance on one leg and lean over the sideboard when she was on the shorter side didn't make for success when getting her favorite foods. It was easy enough for Shabina to help her and then carry her plate back to Raine's favorite spot.

Once they were settled with their food, Shabina asked the question that had been weighing on her for a while. "What could possibly tie these victims together? I think if we can figure that out, we'll be able to see a clearer picture of the murderer."

"Random? Opportunity?" Zahra ventured.

Raine shook her head. "I've studied the crime scenes. This was premeditated, and the murderer chose each victim, waiting for the opportunity to be alone with them. It's probable he drew the victim to him. Even set up a meeting."

"I question the fact that none of them fought back," Shabina said. "How were they so distracted that they were smashed in the head with a rock? Twice. Didn't you say that was in the ME's report, Raine? I can see the second time because they would be disoriented, but not a single victim heard a noise behind him? Especially after the first murder took place, I would think they would be doubly vigilant, especially the ones killed in Yosemite."

"Shabina has a point," Raine said. "We have five victims and not a single one was on alert? Why? Even the kid should have been aware of his surroundings. He was a criminal. He stole vehicles. He must have kept his eyes open."

Shabina snapped her fingers. "You just named Craig Barker a criminal. He was seventeen. Lawyer was sixteen or seventeen when he robbed his high school coach. What age was Lucca when he confessed to the grocery store theft? He had to have been underage. I don't know how the murderer would know if the others had juvenile records, but Miguel told stories about Lucca and himself getting into trouble all the time. We laughed at the fact that Lucca sleepwalked and confessed everything to his mother."

Raine's fingers hovered above her keyboard. "And Lawyer felt pressured to give an interview to a reporter since he wouldn't cooperate with Bale. Not that anyone paid attention. But maybe the murderer did." She began searching for a tie.

"Charlie Gainer had a juvenile record," Raine said. "He didn't have it sealed when he was old enough. He and two friends stole a car and went joyriding. They crashed into a guardrail and Charlie suffered a broken arm. No one died as a result, but the car was totaled."

"That's four of our five victims with juvenile records," Stella said. "Who's left?"

"The first victim, Deacon Mulberry," Shabina said.

"I'm not getting a hit, but I'm looking into his hometown and news around the time he would have been sixteen or seventeen. Once I establish where he was living, I can hack into the juvenile records. It's possible he had one and petitioned the court to seal the record," Raine said.

"If he's got one, and it was sealed, either the murderer knew him or they're good with a computer," Vienna said.

"This is interesting," Raine said. "I recognize the name of this town. Deacon Mulberry is originally from Galaxy, Maine."

Shabina looked up quickly. "That's the same place Emilio, Freda and their little girl, Crystal, lived."

"Are you certain?" Harlow asked. "That's too big to be a coincidence."

"I agree," Raine said, her voice taking on that note that told Shabina her brain was already analyzing data and possibilities.

"Let's say this Deacon had a juvenile record," Vienna ventured. "How would that tie him to Felicity and Eve's family?"

"They said they didn't like Emilio initially, remember? It was only after Crystal came along that they accepted him," Shabina pointed out. "Emilio and Freda met through their jobs. What did they do? I don't think either of the sisters told me."

"There was a write-up in their hometown newspaper when the family died," Raine said, frowning at her screen. "Emilio worked as a juvenile correction officer. He was upfront about his concerns for youth. He'd been in the system when he was fifteen and again when he was sixteen. According to the write-up about him, he devoted his time to helping juvenile offenders turn their lives around. Apparently, he gives credit to a corrections officer for his turnaround."

"What did Freda do?" Harlow asked.

"She was a juvenile probation officer," Raine replied. "It seems that the two worked closely together for a year before they began dating."

Zahra drummed her fingers on the coffee table. Her dog pushed her nose into Zahra's other hand. Automatically, she slipped down to the floor so Misty could climb into her lap. "Emilio had a juvenile record when he was fifteen and sixteen."

"What are we saying here?" Vienna asked. "That we suspect Eve and Felicity of these murders? That would be insane. What possible motive could they have? And how could they pull it off? They're just learning to hike and boulder."

Shabina stood up to pace. She thought better when she was moving. "Maybe not. Looking back over things they've said to me, I think it's entirely possible they aren't amateurs when it comes to hiking and bouldering."

Harlow slid to the floor beside Zahra. She rested her head against the seat cushion as she watched Shabina pace the length of the room. "Like what? I just can't picture either of them bashing in someone's head with a rock."

"Felicity told me the triplets did everything together," Shabina explained. "She didn't just imply they were inseparable, she stated it. They went to the same schools, and they had the same hobbies. They were always together until Emilio came along."

"That doesn't mean they know how to hike or climb," Stella said. "Those are specific hobbies. I thought maybe Emilio got Freda into hiking and climbing, and that was part of the reason Felicity and Eve felt left out."

"They hired Miguel to help them learn to climb," Vienna pointed out.

"True," Shabina conceded, "but that doesn't mean they don't know what they're doing. It only means they're clever. They used the term *highball* when talking to Theresa and the others about a certain boulder. Most people would think in terms of drinks, not climbing, when someone drops the word *highball*. Theresa sounded as if Felicity and Eve explained what a highball is and did so thoroughly enough that the women were aware they couldn't boulder that rock."

"The two women could have had Miguel explain it to them," Vienna said. "I just can't see them doing this. It makes no sense. They'd *both* have to be a little insane."

"Let's, just for the sake of argument," Raine said, "put them as our number one suspects. What motive could they have? Why would they go on a killing spree a year after their sister died?"

"Preparation. Thinking of a plan from every aspect," Harlow said. "If we're going there, the two of them are intelligent and personable. They get people to talk to them."

"We know Felicity is a hacker. She tried hacking Raine's computer," Shabina said.

Raine nodded. "She tried, and then she apologized and made the whole thing into a prank. One hacker to another to see who could come out on top."

Zahra rolled her eyes. "Are you kidding? She just came out and admitted she tried to hack you?"

"She realized her computer was being fed viruses as well as being tracked. It was in her best interests to confess," Raine said. "You don't get to attempt to break into classified documents without repercussions. Felicity knew as soon as she triggered the alarm that she would have to do something to get herself out of trouble."

"So you think they're that methodical?" Stella asked. "That these murders were premeditated, and they chose each of their victims ahead of time?"

"I think it's a possibility," Shabina said. "No one would suspect them. They could have met Deacon on the trail, one in front of him, holding his attention, pretending to be lost, while the other one bashed him in the head with a rock. It wouldn't have been difficult to lure Lucca off trail when he was searching for bodies. Like I said, they're personable. They seem to know everyone and make it their business to do just that. If one of them came off of a trail and told Lucca they were lost, he would believe them. They presented themselves to the community as newcomers to the hiking and climbing world. Lucca had a reputation for taking care of others. He was conducting a search and rescue mission. He would listen to the tale of woe and not hear the other one coming up behind him swinging the rock at his head."

"What about the ritual?" Zahra asked. "The strange altar with feathers and rocks and sticks on it? Flowers from here and Saudi Arabia. What would that represent to them?"

"That's the question, isn't it?" Raine asked. "I've acquired several photographs of the altar. The FBI asked if I would help analyze the data, so no, I didn't hack my way into the case. We want the chain of evidence to be as pure as it can be."

"What is your take on the items on the altar, Shabina? You've seen quite a few rituals. Does this feel like a familiar one?"

Shabina shook her head as she studied the photographs. "No two altars are exactly the same. The murderer chose items they found nearby, or in the case of the things from Saudi Arabia, I doubt they even knew they were from a different country. They found a box and used the items discovered inside."

"The two men from Algeria said they thought Shabina was coming up the trail," Raine reminded them. "That would mean they heard a female voice."

"If it is Felicity and Eve, what's with this ritual and the altar?" Harlow asked. "Is it real? Did you look up rituals to see if they match anything, Raine?"

"I did. I put the various items on the altar into a search engine with as many details as possible. There are a few similar but no exact matches. I searched religions, cults, countries. The computer is still searching, but I believe the murderer or murderers came up with their own ritual."

Shabina had been studying the photographs of the crime scenes, the ones Raine had on her computer. "What would be the point of a fake ritual?"

There was a short silence while they all tried to come up with ideas that might answer the question.

"To throw everyone off? Make the investigators believe there is a cult or religious reason. It isn't voodoo. It isn't witchcraft. Or satanic." Shabina frowned as she drummed her fingers on her thigh. "They literally used random items they found. They didn't bring them to the murder scene. The petals were from flowers in the meadows, easily gotten. They used sticks and rocks they found close to the murder scene. They used items they found in an abandoned box."

Raine nodded in agreement. "The murders were carefully planned out, yet this ritual wasn't."

"So," Harlow ventured, "you're saying you don't believe the ritual is real."

"I don't," Raine said. "I'm with Shabina on this one. I think they studied various serial killers and wanted to have a signature. They just didn't want whatever they used to point to them."

"They would have done better to copy a voodoo ritual," Vienna said. "Any kind of real ritual."

"Maybe," Raine said, "but in any case, there is no proof of guilt. Not one single piece of evidence. If it is Felicity and Eve doing these murders, they planned them out carefully. I'm going to do my best to put them in the vicinity of each murder scene before I turn the evidence over to the two agents."

CHAPTER NINETEEN

Shabina loved having Rainier home. Even the dogs seemed happier. Her protection detail wasn't quite as happy. They claimed they weren't getting as much good food as they had before. Rainier told them to go running and work off the weight they'd gained in his absence. Since not a single one of the men looked as if they carried an ounce of fat on them, Shabina just laughed and told them to come to the café every morning and at lunch and she'd make them whatever they wanted.

Everything seemed different without the heavy weight of guilt hanging over her. She ran with Rainier twice a day. Practiced with a gun every day. Did hand-to-hand combat with him. He was so fast that he forced her to increase her speed just to stay on her feet.

She filled him in on the speculation that Felicity and Eve Garner were the number one suspects in the murders, although they hadn't been confronted.

Rainier nodded toward the two women seated at the smaller table near a window. "They're coming to the café every day."

"Practically every day," Shabina admitted. "If not for breakfast, they come in the afternoon for lunch. We take turns inviting them places or going with them to anything they're doing, so if our theory is correct, the two won't have an opportunity to find another victim. Since we're trading off, it doesn't appear as if we're watching them, just that we're extending the hand of friendship." She sighed. "I'm going to feel awful if we're wrong about them."

Rainier stood behind the counter watching the two women as they waved to other customers and engaged in a lively conversation. "If they're the killers, Shabina, they're very good at what they do."

"I think they're brilliant," she admitted. "We're particularly worried about Miguel. He had a juvenile record, and he frequently goes climbing with them. We all made him promise to call anytime the women want to go to the boulders or anywhere else for that matter. He didn't ask questions, but he's been our friend for so long, he'll do it."

"I take it Raine turned over any evidence to the FBI."

"Sadly, there is no evidence, only a trail, and it's a thin one. I told you how we came to the conclusions we did."

"Too big of a coincidence," Rainier agreed. He glanced at his watch. "Babe, I've got to sort out the supplies. I'm heading into the shed. Vaughn mentioned he's worried there's a glitch in the refrigerator. I'll take a look at it when I've inventoried the supplies. If you get overwhelmed and need a dishwasher, send someone for me."

Shabina nodded and blew him a kiss as he turned back to the kitchen. He preferred using the back door so he didn't run into customers. Rainier was never going to be the friendliest of men, but she didn't care. She could handle the customers, and he could run his business. She just hoped he'd be home most of the time.

The Sunrise Café was popular, and this day was no exception. Quite a few locals were present, including Felicity and Eve.

Edward and Janine were having an intimate lunch together. Tom and Judy Rosewood had come in for lunch, and with them were Mary Shelton, the deputy sheriff, and the ME, Martha Fendy. Dr. Amelia Sanderson once again was having lunch with Carl Montgomery, the local contractor. With them were John Mc-Allister, one of the vet techs, and Greg Daily, Patsy's husband. The two FBI agents had asked for the table across from Felicity and Eve. The two women engaged them in conversation often. Laughing and flirting, talking about the sights in the Sierra and how they had a new love of bouldering and the two men should try it while they were so close to the famous boulders. It was interesting to see how easily the men seemed to flirt and banter with the two women. In no way did the men act as if they considered the women suspects.

Fortunately, Bale heeded the restraining order, choosing not to fight it. Sean didn't come back, and neither did his two interns, Oliver Smythe and Maurice Vanderpool. Shabina was grateful that they hadn't. She really didn't want her café to be known for drama, and she feared it was fast gaining that reputation.

They were halfway through the lunch hour when Harlow rushed in, her face pale. She went straight to the kitchen, gesturing for Shabina to join her. It occurred to Shabina she had thought too soon that the drama was over. The moment the door swung closed behind her, Harlow caught Shabina by her upper arms.

"My father brought a group of diplomats to Knightly. They claim they want to see the Sierra and eat at your wonderful café. My father bragged about how great the food is."

Shabina had never seen Harlow so upset. "To my knowledge, your father has never been here."

"He hasn't. He always has to play the big man. There are reporters traveling with them. Shabina, one of the diplomats is the ambassador for Canada." Harlow's voice trembled. "I have this very bad feeling. I texted my father and asked him who he was bringing here. He told me Darian Lefebre and that he was practically a celebrity. He implied Lefebre was so popular with the people that he was being considered by the Liberal Party to run for prime minister."

She dropped the bombshell fast, gripping Shabina's arms hard. "He's actually bringing that horrible man here. Lefebre has diplomatic immunity. If you or Rainier were to kill him, even in self-defense, there is a federal law that was passed, protecting diplomats and their families. If you were to kill him, you could even face the death penalty. Rainier can't go near him. You should leave. Leave right now and take Rainier with you."

Shabina pulled out her phone and texted Rainier, giving him the information Harlow had given her.

No fear, Qadri. He won't see me. No one will. Tell me your intentions.

I refuse to allow him in my café.

Stay back away from him when you confront him. I'm sending in the team. Put them close to the door, dividing them so Lefebre will be boxed in. If he makes a move, he's a dead man. There will be a sniper rifle on him.

Promise me you won't confront Lefebre.

Scorpion has multiple contracts out
on him. He belongs to Deadly
Storms, not me.

Shabina sent Rainier a heart and slipped her phone into her pocket. "Grab one of the back tables, Harlow. I don't want your father to blame you for anything that happens. He's going to be very embarrassed by my refusal to allow them to eat here."

"You'll risk that in front of reporters?"

Shabina lifted her chin. "Absolutely. Lefebre does not get to come into my café. I love this place, and he is not going to set foot inside. It was bad enough that Boucher and Cormier managed to get inside. It's best you stay out of sight or leave through the back."

"I'm staying with you," Harlow declared. "Don't you know by now that I despise my father? He takes advantage of young women all the time. He has a sense of entitlement you wouldn't believe. My mother won't leave him even though she knows. She's had to do damage control on more than one occasion. But then there's all the perks of being a senator's wife she'd have to give up."

Shabina studied her friend's expression of complete determination, and then she nodded. "I didn't want to talk to my father after I found out the things he'd done. I didn't bother to confront him because he wasn't worth my time anymore. I understand better than most, Harlow. Just remember, Lefebre is dangerous. He might try to kill me, knowing he has diplomatic immunity. That's his style."

She led the way to the door. Larado and Zero sat at the small table just inside the door. Tyrone had moved a couple to a window table. Altair stood just inside the doorway, lounging against the wall, while Dimitri and Torin were seated at the table on the opposite side of the door. Shabina nodded to them and moved to stand in the doorway. Most of her customers would think she was there to greet clients as they came in. A few who knew her well were aware something was up, especially when Harlow moved to stand beside her.

"Keep out of the line of fire, Shabina," Altair cautioned in a low voice.

"None of you can kill him," she responded without turning around. "I'll be careful, but you can't touch him. He insisted on coming here to taunt me. He thinks he'll force me to serve him food. And he most likely believes he can cut my throat and get away with it. He's wrong."

"Shabina."

Larado just said her name. Nothing else, but she knew he was giving her an order. She didn't care what any of them said. This confrontation was important to her. Darian Lefebre had terrorized her for too long. She wasn't going to let fear rule her, not one minute longer. She lifted her chin at the approaching small party of men surrounded by bodyguards, the senator and several reporters with cameras.

"Shabina. It's wonderful to see you," Senator Frye greeted jovially. "I've brought these gentlemen to your wonderful café." He gestured toward the men dressed in impeccable suits.

"I'm sorry, Senator, but those men are not allowed in my café."

The smile faded from Frye's face. "You don't understand, Shabina. These are important guests of our country."

Lefebre looked her up and down, his dark eyes filled with malice. She didn't so much as flinch. She shot him back a look of utter contempt. The cameraman with them began to take video while the reporters held microphones out.

"The man you are attempting to bring into my café is not

welcome. He isn't an important diplomat, or at least he wouldn't be if his country knew his real identity."

Lefebre stepped closer to her, moving out of the circle of his bodyguards. "Be very careful what you accuse me of."

"He goes by the name of Scorpion. He kidnapped me and held me for months. He raped and tortured me. I have scars to prove it. In fact, there are many photographs the government has of what I looked like at sixteen before I was rescued. That's the man you're so eager to do business with, Senator."

The cameraman had centered his attention on Lefebre. Lefebre shook his head. "She is mistaken. It is true that the men I traveled with were proven to be Scorpion and his accomplices. I feel terrible that these men were allowed into countries because they worked for me. If what she says is true, she would have been traumatized to such an extent that it is no wonder she is confused." He sounded forgiving, sorrowful and benevolent at the same time.

"It would be impossible to be raped repeatedly by the same man and mistake him for someone else," Shabina said. "I personally witnessed you murder men, women and children. Even infants. I have the right to refuse service to anyone, and I'm refusing service to you."

Lefebre stepped even closer, and she caught the flash of a gleaming blade as the sun struck the curved knife he pulled from his sleeve and tried to conceal along his wrist as he glided straight at her.

Shabina turned slightly and stayed on the balls of her feet. As Lefebre suddenly burst toward her in a show of speed, she slammed her fist against his arm, blocking the upward stab at her abdomen. She swept his legs out from under him, catching his wrist and snapping his arm behind his body, forcing him to drop the knife.

"She attacked me," Lefebre said. "I want her arrested."

His bodyguards surged forward, but Larado and his team became a solid wall in front of her, preventing them from getting to her. She kicked the knife away and bent down to whisper in Lefebre's ear.

"Deadly Storms knows you're here. You made a big mistake, and now he's locked on to you. You won't escape death this time." Stepping back quickly, she avoided Senator Frye and the reporters, backing up until she was once again in the doorway of her café.

Furious, Lefebre shouted to his men to come to his aid. Her protection team stepped aside, moving to block the entrance and any access to Shabina. Frye and his people hastily got Lefebre back into a vehicle, but not without Frye stating he would have her investigated. That she was a disgrace for treating an important man from another country the way she had.

Shabina turned and fully entered the café. At first there was total silence, and then applause broke out.

She sent her customers a wry smile. "I'm really going to start charging extra for the show. It seems this is the place to come if you want to see drama." She did her best to make light of the situation.

Her customers applauded again. She had the best customers, locals and tourists alike. Well—as long as Bale or Sean didn't show up.

Her phone vibrated, and she pulled it out to look at the screen.

Proud of you, Qadri. That takedown
was classic.

He ended the sentence with three heart emojis.

Will see you after I finish the job.

She knew he wasn't talking about inventory. She sent him several hearts.

LEFEBRE WOKE SWEATING. He was surrounded by bodyguards. Two were on alert in the bedroom. One was over by the window, the other lying across the doorway, making it impossible for an intruder to enter. Three others were outside his room. He was three stories up, and he'd made certain the room he was in was difficult to access.

Still, he woke sweating. Afraid. He was supposed to be the one to strike fear into every man or woman who came across him, yet he'd been humiliated in front of the world. Those traveling with him looked at him differently now. Even the ridiculous senator wanted to distance himself from him when he'd been fawning on him earlier, eager to do business.

Lefebre had taken a private plane to Washington, DC, and entered the Canadian embassy. No one would be able to get to him, not even Deadly Storms. There was no sandstorm for the assassin to hide in.

He admitted to himself he was in trouble. With members of his cabinet exposed as aiding Scorpion, many people would believe Shabina. The video images had been playing in the news for the last two days. He had been commanded to get home. If the prime minister did believe Shabina, he was in deep trouble, yet he was certain there was no proof that he was the notorious Scorpion. He could recover from this.

Lefebre knew several governments had contracts out on Scorpion. He had secretly laughed at the various governments. He'd been right out in the open, the charming, benevolent ambassador who everyone loved. Every single country he'd gone to, he'd managed to kill entire communities. He kept track of those killed, wanting his numbers to be higher than Vlad the Impaler, his idol. He especially found it delicious to choose a girl around the age of fifteen or sixteen that reminded him of Yasemin to hold for weeks. He encouraged his men to be as brutal as possible with her. She deserved everything done to her.

He believed he was very clever blaming the men he worked with, naming Owen Pelletier the Scorpion. He had learned acting at an early age and was able to convince those around him that he had the best interests of the smaller farm communities at heart.

A slight breeze washed over him, chilling the sweat on his body. The hairs on the back of his neck stood up as fingers of fear walked down his spine. He threw back the covers and glared at his bodyguard, the one who had opened the window. The man sat on the floor, back to the wall, clearly asleep. Lefebre swore and stalked across the room.

"You're useless to me," he snapped. "I should slit your throat right here." He held up his knife, his favorite, the one with the wicked curved blade that he showed to the men and women and even children before he sliced them into pieces.

His bodyguard moved fast, his hand slamming so hard into Lefebre's elbow that he heard the bone snap. Before he could shriek in pain, the knife was torn from his numb fist, the curved blade sinking into his left thigh muscle over and over. He'd tortured Shabina with this exact move. He opened his mouth to scream in protest, but a fist punched into his throat hard enough to break everything in its path and take away his voice.

The man was lightning fast and incredibly strong. This was no guard. The guard had to be dead. Both guards had to be dead.

There was no fighting that knife or those strong hands. There was only pain. More pain. He pried his eyes open to see the hard, merciless features of Deadly Storms.

"You'll go to your grave with my brand covering yours," Deadly Storms informed him, never once flinching from inflicting cruel knife wounds. Each deep cut followed a precise pattern, and the assassin reminded him of where he had placed those wounds on Shabina. "The world will know you for the murderer you are."

THE NEWS OF Scorpion's death was on every news channel. He'd been killed on the premises of the Canadian embassy. No one in the United States could be blamed, nor did the prime minister demand explanations. The evidence of Scorpion's guilt was left on his body for all to see with a message for the prime minister. The note simply read, **GUILTY OF UNSPEAKABLE CRIMES**. Deadly Storms left his calling card, the artwork he left behind on the body of Scorpion was reproduced as a signature on the note.

There was speculation that someone had aided the assassin in entering the Canadian embassy, or perhaps that he was a high-ranking diplomat that had accompanied Lefebre on his journey to the United States. In the meantime, Rainier simply took his private jet home, and his people removed all evidence of his flight.

SHABINA UNLOCKED THE door to the café to allow Felicity and Eve entrance. The sun had set, and the cleaners had gone home, leaving the building empty. Deliberately, she looked around carefully before she stepped back inside and locked the door, still staring out into the gathering darkness.

"Thanks for coming." She pitched her voice low—a conspirator's whisper. "I need to talk to you about important information I found out about the murders but didn't want to take a chance on anyone overhearing us."

Felicity glanced around the café and then her gaze settled on Raine. She flashed a smile. "Oh, you're here as well."

Raine nodded, her expression solemn.

"The thing is, this is the best place I could think of where no one will be lurking around." Shabina bit her lower lip. "I do have security cameras in here, quite a few of them. Lawyer installed cameras for me when I started getting harassed by Bale, Sean and their friends."

Eve scowled. "Those men are so obnoxious to you. I was really happy when your fiancé threw Bale out."

"I was too." Once more, Shabina glanced up at one of the cameras. "I don't know, maybe we shouldn't talk in here either. There's audio. The cameras aren't manned, meaning no one looks at the feed unless we have an incident." More lip biting and indecision.

"What's this about, Shabina?" Eve asked. "You're very nervous."

"I know. You both are observant. You had to have seen the various men coming to the café from the Middle East. The students." Again, she hesitated then lowered her voice another octave. "This is about the murders."

"The cameras aren't a big deal," Felicity said. "I'd like to hear what information you have."

"Me too," Eve said.

Raine interrupted. "I'm starving, Shabina. It smells so good in here."

"I fixed something for us to eat," Shabina said. "I knew I was interrupting your dinner and you'd all be hungry. Give me just a second and I'll get us plates."

She didn't wait for the sisters to agree but hurried through the café to the kitchen. Felicity and Eve sat at the table with Raine.

"These last few weeks have been hell for Shabina," Raine disclosed, keeping her voice low. "You know she was kidnapped when she was only fifteen and held for a year and a half in the Middle East."

"That was so brave of her to tell that man and the senator they couldn't come into her café," Eve said. "The things she went through sounded horrific. I was so glad she stood up to him."

"Me too. It's been a long road for her recovery," Raine said. "And then these last few weeks made things come crashing back." She leaned closer to them, her gaze on the kitchen. "It appeared as if someone was trying to frame her for the murders."

Felicity gasped and pulled back, one hand covering her mouth while she exchanged a horrified look with Eve. "You said that before, but I didn't really think it could be true. Who would do that? And who would believe that Shabina could possibly be involved in murder?" Eve demanded.

"That's ludicrous," Felicity agreed. "Absolutely ludicrous. Shabina is the kindest person I know. Seriously, if that had been me Bale Landry said those things to, refusing to pay, breaking my dishes, I probably would have stuck a fork in his heart."

"When Shabina started to cry, I got up with my plate in my hand," Eve said. "I was prepared to bash him right over the head."

"Someone needs to knock some sense into him," Raine agreed. "If it weren't for my leg . . ." She broke off as Shabina came out of the kitchen, carrying all four plates, two resting on each arm. "Wow, girl." Raine raised her voice. "You're such a pro. I would drop all that food."

A reluctant smile took some of the tension from Shabina's

face. "Patsy is amazing at handling multiple dishes. I'm not up to her expertise."

"I couldn't do what you're doing," Eve defended her staunchly. She looked a little militant as she rose to help. "I'll get the drinks you put on the counter for us."

"Thank you, Eve." Shabina gave her an even bigger, more genuine smile. "I hope you both enjoy this vegetarian lasagna. I know you like lasagna and thought it would be fine to serve a vegetarian dish so Raine could eat it too."

"It smells wonderful," Felicity said.

Eve set a basket of bread in the middle of the table after she placed drinks in front of each person. Shabina had remembered they preferred iced tea in the evening.

"There's plenty of garlic bread, so we'll all have to eat some in case it gives us garlic breath," Eve said, laughing.

They each began eating before Felicity brought up the reason they were there. "Shabina, I know you're distressed over whatever information you have on the murders. If you want to share it, we're listening."

"It's not so much that I want to share it as I need to." Shabina put down her fork and sank back in her chair as if the weight of her knowledge was too much of a burden to bear. "I'm going to have to give you a little background on what's been going on."

"I told them a little bit," Raine volunteered. "But you'll need to fill them in completely."

"Two of the university students were being paid to trigger my PTSD. I think you know I was kidnapped when I was fifteen and held for a year and a half. I do suffer terrible episodes at times. To make a long story short, these men were sent items from the region where I was held by the man who paid them. They had taken several of the items to leave on a trail that they were told only I use."

Shabina paused and shook her head, stroking trembling fingers down her throat revealing nerves. She'd learned to be a good actress in Saudi Arabia, and she called on those skills now.

"Go on," Eve encouraged.

"They were on the trail with a box of the items when they heard you coming." She had dropped her voice to a whisper. "They hid the box in the brush. You took the box containing the items and those items ended up on the altar beside Deacon Mulberry's body."

There was silence as the twins stared at one another and then turned their full attention back to Shabina.

"I had to tell you," Shabina confessed. "I don't know what he did, but it had to be something for you two to decide to kill him." She ducked her head and stroked her throat nervously again. "If I'd had the ability to kill Scorpion and every single one of his men, I would have done so."

Raine took over before either denied it. "I researched Deacon Mulberry because he seemed such an unlikely candidate for murder. He's from Galaxy, Maine."

Shabina nodded and pressed her forehead into her palm. "Galaxy is an unusual name for a town, and I remembered you said you were from Galaxy. It was obvious you knew him. I began to think about things you'd said about your sister and you two always doing the same things together. You knew what a highball was when referencing bouldering."

"You gave me permission to look into your computer," Raine added. "I did. You have the most beautiful photographs and videos of your hike on the Appalachian Trail. The Pacific Rim. You three hiked the John Muir Trail. This wasn't your first or even second visit to Yosemite. You summited Whitney more than once, and you went up Half Dome. The three of you hiked the Alps together. You have so many climbing photographs and videos stored of the three of you. It must be so terrible not to have your sister with you. You clearly were very close."

Raine paused and then sighed. "My father was murdered. I ended up being blamed for his death by my family. Not one member acknowledges I'm even alive. The loss of the people I love is with me every day. I can't imagine what it would be like if I were a triplet, and I lost my sisters."

Tears appeared in Felicity's eyes. "I'm so sorry, Raine. Losing Freda feels as if part of our souls is gone. Maybe the best part."

"Did Deacon have something to do with her death?" Shabina asked.

"He was Emilio's little pet project," Eve said. "Emilio made him out to be such an example of what social programs and help could do to turn disadvantaged youth around. Deacon didn't come from a poor, needy family. He was a kid with all kinds of privileges. He had the means to hike all over and live like a bum, never contributing to society."

"Emilio was like that. He had a record as well. He liked to get in front of the cameras and explain how these programs helped him," Felicity added. "He lived in the spotlight with his great deeds. Everything was always about him. He didn't want Freda to ever have any attention. Everything had to be his way."

Eve carefully drank the last of her iced tea, set down the glass and gripped the fork so hard her knuckles turned white. "Emilio and Deacon practically controlled the articles coming out in our hometown about how great they were and all they accomplished.

It was really Freda who did the most work with those troubled kids, but Emilio and Deacon just had to have all the credit and attention."

"Freda knew far more than Emilio when it came to hiking. She'd been all over the world, but he never listened to her," Felicity added. "Deacon told him all about Yosemite. Freda tried to tell him about trails that needed to be rehabilitated, but he refused to hear anything she said. I was right there. I heard him snapping at her, telling her he'd gotten maps from Deacon, that Deacon was going to eventually be a park ranger and that he knew what he was talking about."

"The altar?" Raine interjected. "I saw on your computer where you had researched several different kinds of rituals that involved murders."

Eve shrugged. "We decided to just make up our own based on three different rituals Felicity found. There was no real rhyme or reason, and we used whatever we found. I'm truly sorry you were dragged into this, Shabina. We had no idea the items in that box would throw suspicion on you."

"We wouldn't want to hurt you for the world," Felicity affirmed. "We had no idea when we were bringing justice to Deacon that you would ever be accused."

"What about the others?" Shabina murmured. "How were they connected?"

"All of them were criminals, just like Emilio and Deacon," Felicity said firmly. "Every single one of them. They hurt people and got away with it."

"Lucca Delgotto turned his life around. So had Lawyer," Raine pointed out.

Eve and Felicity both bristled, shaking heads with identical expressions of hostility. It was Eve who spoke, her voice shaking with anger. "Once a criminal, always one. They got away with it, and they'll continue to think they can. Just like Emilio."

Shabina stood up to clear the table, making certain to collect the silverware. "I might understand about Deacon, but I don't agree with your assessment of Lucca and Lawyer." She carried the dishes to the counter and returned for the glasses. "I'm very sorry for the loss of your sister and niece. Their deaths were such a tragedy."

"And preventable if Emilio had just listened to Freda," Felicity said, anger boiling over in her tone and into the expression she wore.

Shabina didn't point out that Freda shouldn't have followed her husband if she knew where they were going was dangerous. She had choices. She had taken her daughter into a bad situation whether Freda's sisters wanted to blame her or not. She was every bit as responsible as Emilio was for their deaths, maybe more so since she knew much more about hiking.

After she was certain the table was clean, Shabina walked to the door and unlocked it. "I'm very sorry for both of you," she said as two women followed her to the door. "Those other men were good men, at least I'm certain Lawyer is and Lucca was. I can't condone their murders. I just can't."

Felicity and Eve stepped out the door onto the wide patio outside that held numerous tables and chairs beneath a canopy.

With the sun already set, grayish shadows were cast all around the patio and into the surrounding beds of flowers and shrubs. The women went down two of the three stairs leading to the street. In that instant, they realized they weren't alone.

Rob Howard and Len Jenkins closed in from either side. With the two FBI agents were several members of the Sheriff's Office SWAT Team.

"Felicity Garner, Eve Garner, you're under arrest," Rob stated.

Felicity didn't wait for him to get close to her. She leapt off the stairs and took off running toward the street, Eve right behind her, matching her steps. Sheriff Rafferty and deputies Griffen Cauldrey and Mary Shelton blocked the street, weapons drawn.

Without hesitation, Felicity turned toward Rob Howard, a gun in her hand. It was already blazing fire at the agent. Eve had also pulled a weapon, but she fired at the wall of law enforcement personnel in front of them. Len Jenkins shot Felicity as she continued to fire toward Rob. The agent went down just as Felicity crumpled to the ground. Eve followed her, landing over the top of her as those in the sheriff's department returned fire.

Shabina had been yanked back into the café by Rainier and Larado the moment guns appeared. The two men instantly placed their bodies in front of hers. She couldn't even see around them at first. Neither man fired a weapon, although both had them out.

Jenkins pronounced Rob alive and well, that the vest he wore had stopped the bullet from hitting his heart. He looked up from the twins' bodies and shook his head.

Shabina closed her eyes and pressed her forehead against Rainier's back.

"I didn't want them to die, Rainier," she whispered. "I guess I should have expected that they would have a plan if they were caught."

"They wanted to be with their sister," he reminded, turning around to draw her into his arms. "You and Raine had them dead to rights. They confessed with a security camera going. You even informed them about the camera. They also gave Raine permission to search Felicity's computer even though she knew there was damning evidence on it."

"Her computer indicated she'd recently put them in," Raine

supplied. "Most likely she'd removed them, putting the videos and photographs on an external, and then when she was certain I wasn't going to take her up on her offer, she put them back."

"They trusted us," Shabina murmured softly.

"They should have known you well enough to realize you both have a sense of justice," Rainier pointed out. "Go sit down, *Qadri*. It's going to be a very long night."

CHAPTER TWENTY

Shabina held out her left arm to show the scorpion that was tattooed two inches above her wrist. The tattoo artist was considered one of the best. Rainier knew him. He had once worked in the same occupation as Rainier.

"I want this tattoo covered, and I brought in the artwork I would like to replace it with. I believe it will cover it nicely."

Across from her, Rainier held out his hand to her. Shabina immediately put her hand in his. There was a special intimacy in going together to get two tattoos each. One on the arm and the other on the thigh.

"Why didn't you have this done years ago, *Qadri?* You should have rid yourself of him completely."

Shabina thought about her answer. She knew the reason, but explaining it to someone else was difficult. She'd always worn long sleeves and kept the tattoo covered. Even when she swam with her friends, she wore a shirt over her bathing suit.

"It was important to me to know I belonged wholly to myself. I wanted to know I was strong, and that he could never take that strength and belief in myself away from me again."

"He never took your strength, Shabina," Rainier pointed out, his voice gentle. His gaze softened to tenderness. "He tried, but you refused to give in to him no matter what he did."

His obvious pride in her touched her. She wasn't used to compliments or having anyone look at her with such love the way he did.

"Rainier, I know you love me, and I appreciate you thinking I'm a strong person, but you know I suffer from PTSD and the episodes are horrific at times."

The tattoo artist's head jerked up, his dark gaze moved over her face and then settled on Rainier's.

Rainier didn't seem to be in the least bothered by the fact that the man heard everything. "*Qadri*, I suffer from PTSD. Most of my men do. We've all seen and had to do things that stick with us. PTSD isn't a sign of weakness. Our brains and bodies are on overload at times and we need a little help. Everyone does. That isn't a weakness."

She found herself frowning. Rainier was the strongest man she knew. "Do you go to a counselor?"

The tattoo artist once more bent over her arm. He would place her own tattoo there, the one that said *eye of the storm* in Arabic. Rainier helped design the artwork with a friend of his.

"It isn't like we can just talk to anyone. Most of what we did and do is classified. Finding a counselor is not always easy for men like us, but it's necessary. It's also necessary to reach out to one another when we're in crisis."

She hadn't considered that Rainier suffered from PTSD, but it made sense. Just his childhood alone was enough to have given him psychological issues, let alone the many missions he'd been sent on by Blom as well as his role as the assassin in the Middle East. It hadn't occurred to her that Larado or any of the other men on her protection detail had moments like she did. She considered herself weak because she couldn't overcome the episodes when she was triggered. She would never consider Rainier or his men weak. Not ever. Why hadn't she thought of herself like them?

Being with Rainier made her feel safe, but it was the way he empowered and believed in her that made her love him so much. More every day when she hadn't thought she could love him more.

"Where are you putting the second tattoo? I'd like to see the artwork," the tattoo artist broke into their conversation.

She'd almost forgotten why she was there. "My second tattoo will go on my left thigh. You'll see the scars. I'd like it put there." She showed him a second version of the Deadly Storms tattoo. She wanted Rainier's identity over that mass of scars. She pulled up her skirt to show her leg. "Can you do it?" She couldn't keep the anxiety out of her voice.

"No problem. The way the tattoo was designed, it will fit the scars you have nicely."

"My tattoo will be placed on my left arm two inches above my wrist," Rainier said. "A different version of her tattoo will be on my left thigh. It also says *eye of the storm* in Arabic, just like hers, but is a little different." He showed the man the drawing of the tattoo. "You've seen the scars I have."

"It won't be a problem, Rainier," the man assured. "Let's get to work. Doing four tattoos is going to take some time, particularly when they're so intricate. I take it you want as close to a gold color as possible?" He indicated the coloring on the art.

"Yes, as close as you can get."

"There isn't a metallic gold yet, but by mixing yellow and orange I can achieve the look you want. It just takes some time. I've done a few very gold-looking tattoos. I'll show you the color before I tattoo it on."

They sat side by side while the artist began work on Shabina's wrist. Finally, she would remove Lefebre permanently and replace Scorpion and his claim on her with a symbol of her own strength. She was the eye of the storm. The calm in the middle of chaos. She had her own strength, the ability to withstand the storm.

The second tattoo would cover the ruin of her thigh muscle with Rainier. She would wear the symbol of him rising out of a sandstorm to bring justice no one else could have. He would wear her on his thigh, symbolizing she was his calm when everything else was out of control. It was perfection.

THE PARTY FOR Vaughn and Tyrone appeared to be an overwhelming success, which made Shabina very happy. The two deserved everything wonderful they could possibly have. Vaughn's family seemed to have abandoned him completely, but his sister arrived halfway through the festivities. Tyrone cried when she flung her arms around him and told him how much she approved the match and how grateful she was to him for making her brother so happy. She hugged Vaughn and whispered she was sorry about the rest of their family not accepting them.

Vaughn was Vaughn, hugging her tightly and assuring her that she made their day by coming. Stella and Sam had come, of course. Raine, Harlow and Zahra were there. Patsy and her husband, Greg, came, as did one of the waitresses Nellie Frost. She was accompanied by Sonny Leven. The vet and Carl Montgomery attended. Edward and Janine arrived together. Chelsey Sarten had come as well, and Shabina was happy to see her. Judy and Tom Rosewood attended, and so many more locals that Shabina's large house seemed small.

The party was in full swing when Shabina's cell phone vibrated. She nearly ignored it, because everyone was toasting the couple, but something compelled her to see who was calling. With trembling fingers, she took the call, hurrying out into the garden away from the noise.

"Mom? Is everything all right?" Her mother never called on her own.

"Yes, little mama. Everything is perfect. I'd like to come see you next week. Your father is going to be out of town on business. I can't go with him, and he said he would feel better if I was with you and your protection team. I'm so excited. Will you be able to have me?"

It was the last thing she expected her mother to say, and it was all she could do not to burst into tears. "Of course, I'll have you. I can't wait to see you. And you'll get to see Rainier with me and know he really loves me. I know you were upset that there was no big wedding, but it was better for me to marry him quietly. He always does what I ask him."

She hesitated. She was talking too much, but she couldn't help it. "Well, except when it comes to safety. He's a bit of a tyrant then, but I don't mind."

"I've always liked Rainier," Yasemin admitted. "I have no idea why your father took such a dislike to him. I thought perhaps jealousy. You relied on Rainier when you didn't on either of us. I told Jack that was natural after all you'd been through, but he didn't listen to me."

"I felt I was hurting you just by my presence," Shabina admitted. "I needed to stand on my own two feet and get strong. To know I could withstand any storm."

"Have you done that?"

"I believe I have," Shabina said with conviction. "I love you,

Mamma. I can't wait to see you. Will you send me all the details, when you're arriving and how long you get to stay?"

"Yes. I'm working that out now. I love you, Shabina. I'll be there soon."

Shabina hurried back into the house, looking for one person. It didn't matter if dance music was playing, and champagne and sparkling grape juice were being served so more people could toast the couple. What mattered to her was that one person, the only person. Their eyes locked across the room and she didn't wait. Couldn't wait. So much happiness was almost too much to bear.

"You did this." She flung her arms around Rainier's neck right in front of everyone. "I know you did." Tears brimmed over, but they were tears of sheer joy. "You made it happen. That was my mother. She said Jack was going out of town and she couldn't go with him. He suggested she come visit me. He was concerned for her safety and told her that you and my protection detail would alleviate his worries for her. Jack would *never* allow her to visit on her own. Not ever. I know him. You did this."

She caught his face between her palms and brought his head down to hers so she could kiss him. There was no other way to express her happiness. Her joy. How thankful she was. It didn't matter that she was kissing him in front of everyone.

She didn't normally show affection in front of others, but she was blaming her lack of restraint on him. He put his arm around her all the time in front of others accustoming her to shows of affection. And he did the most extraordinary, wonderful things for her. Miracles. She had no idea how he persuaded Jack to allow her mother to visit her—even going so far as to suggest it—but she knew Rainier had brought it about.

"You are the most remarkable, extraordinary man. The love of my life. I can never repay you for making this happen." She kissed him again because she had to.

Rainier caught her close, fitting her body against his. No matter how many times she was in his arms, it always felt perfect. Right. She knew absolutely that he was the man she was destined to be with. She had no regrets. Not a single one.